Kiss Me Better

A Novel

मुझे बेहतर चूमो

Dr. Stephen Kaladeen

Jean Kaladeen

Table of Contents

Dedication

This book is dedicated to my parents Harry and Ruby.

Luck begins before you are ever born.

Thank you both for your faith, love and enouragment.

Acknowledgments

I would like to acknowledge the many friends, family members and colleagues that assisted in reading, editing and helping make this book a reality.

Thank you Beverley Slopen for your encouragement and help.

This story is about the many doctors and nurses who have shown kindness, professionalism and real concern for humanity.

Inspiration doesn't come from a textbook. It comes from the other people around you who take on the job of helping others.

सर्वं द्रष्टव्यम् स्वप्नानां साकारीकरणात् सर्वं द्रष्टव्यम् स्वप्नानां साकारीकरणात् सर्वं द्रष्टव्यम् स्वप्नानां साकारीकरणात्

About The Authors

Stephen Kaladeen was born in Georgetown Guyana in 1962. He emigrated to Canada with his brother and parents in 1964. They first lived in London Ontario and then moved to Toronto. Stephen grew up in a small house in East York. He was an early member of the great Indian diaspora that arrived in Canada over the past many decades. His parents never regretted moving to Canada and encouraged many of their family members to eventually join them.

Stephen has been practicing front line medicine in Trenton Ontario since 1992. He is a long serving member of the staff at Trenton Memorial Hospital in the Departments of Anaesthesia and Family Practice. Dr Kaladeen has been published in a variety of magazines including the Medical Post and Maclean's Magazine where he wrote a seminal article on the doctor shortage in Canada.

His first book 'The Secret Life of Doctor's' was welcomed by the health care community as an influential and authoritative treatise on Burnout and how to treat it. Dr Steve has been committed to providing front line medical care to his community that includes a large number of Canadian military families and veterans.

Jean, the daughter of an Italian immigrant father and a Scottish mother, met Steve at Mount Sinai Hospital where she was working as a cancer researcher. They met and fell in love over Chinese noodles and BBQ duck. Jean and Steve have three children and one grandchild. Jean is a trained Cordon Bleu chef and healthcare manager who runs a 9-doctor family practice group in Trenton.

Jean has had a life-long commitment to animal welfare and supports a local animal shelter and a number of other charities including Habitat for Humanity and the Quinte Humane Society.

Jean's first book, the immensely popular story - 'Larry the little Orphan dog' is a children's book that was designed for young children to develop empathy towards animals and other people.

'Kiss me Better' is their first collaboration.

Prologue

July 1st, 2010

The morning air was a bit cooler when Anjali woke up in her little bed. It was a pleasant relief from the summer heat. Her bed was very old and a little bigger than a cot. The early morning was quiet except for a rooster crowing out in the street. There were only a few cars and motorcyclists outside. She looked around at the bare concrete walls, peeling paint, and the old, corrugated tin roof. Outside, the Mumbai slums were getting busier. She had a little radio that she turned on while pouring out some water to wash her face. Outside, women in their colorful saris were walking about doing chores and hanging laundry.

Anjali washed her face, put on a clean dress, and pulled her hair back. She was sixty-six years old; however, few could ever really guess her age. She looked at her little mirror, and her eyes drifted past the many Hindu gods and deities on the wall of her tiny home. There was her bed, a small couch, and a few plastic chairs. She also had a tiny oven that burned charcoal and cooking oil. There was a small plastic table filled with various spices and incense.

Today was a pivotal day. Something important was going to happen, but she was unsure what. She recalled something from her previous night's sleep. It was something from a radio address she had heard by a politician a few years ago.

Anjali prepared her meager breakfast of tea and porridge. She smiled to herself. *'I could have had it so much easier,'* she thought. She could have gotten married. A husband and children would have been nice, but it would never have happened. She was the seventh child. The seventh child *and* a daughter. She had the *'gift'*, and people sought her help. She was glad to help and often took no money if they were poor.

Anjali had dreamed of a strange leaf that turned red, but in her dream, there was also happiness and joy – the kind that comes when someone beautiful sings. She hummed a little bit as she cleaned up her little home. Outside there were little streamers and a sign advertising her skill.

While Anjali watched the local ladies bustling about and little boys playing street cricket, she wondered about what life was like in the far away world of America. She rarely thought about a world outside of her own little community. Something was about to happen far away from her, but she had a role in it. She just knew it. Then she remembered the message:

'You have to dream before your dreams can come true.'

Chapter One

On the morning of his last day at home in his parents' house in Toronto, Raj retreated to the basement, ostensibly to pack books. Instead, he sat on the old couch and ate a Samosa, wiping his hands frequently, as he was a fastidious eater. Not one to feel nostalgic about leaving home, he was staring intently at the large-screen television. *Bollywood Music Countdown* was playing, and a young woman was singing and swaying in front of a group of dancers. Raj didn't like the song but thought the singer was a study of human perfection. Her glittery top was pulled tight across her full round breasts, which jiggled ever so slightly as she moved. She sashayed into the group of female dancers, their brightly colored saris swirling. Raj was just imagining what it would be like to plant his face right between those perfect breasts when the sudden entrance of his younger sister, Chandra, startled him.

"Are you into Hindi film music now, or are you just checking out the eye candy?" she asked.

"I kind of like the music, actually," Raj said.

"Sure…mental masturbation."

"Mental masturbation isn't a sexual term, Chan. It's about how people keep thinking too much. Who is this girl, anyway?" Raj gestured at the singer and tried to sound casual.

"I think her name is Yana. She's really pretty, isn't she?"

For a moment, Chandra watched with him; then, she smiled knowingly. Raj could never keep a secret from her. She had a way of reading people – especially him – that he found uncanny. She had figured out that behind his façade of "doctorly" success, he was desperately lonely. He hadn't gone to his graduation formal, and Chandra rightly guessed it was because he didn't have a date. She hadn't said anything to their parents.

She broke the silence. "I can't believe you're leaving."

"It feels kind of weird," Raj said, "but I'm really excited. The apartment is close to the hospital and not that expensive. And I'm going to buy a car."

"You're going to turn into a regular playboy," she teased.

"Right! A playboy with a ninety-hour work week. I'll probably be lucky to see daylight some weeks."

"Listen, maybe when you get a weekend off, you can come down and visit my housemates and me. I mentioned that you're a doctor, and they all want to meet you."

Raj liked the idea. His sister's friends were usually attractive. "Maybe, if I can get some time off, Chan," he said. "But I have to impress the head doctors. They might let me do some extra training in emergency medicine after my internship."

Chandra brought them back to the moment. "Mom and Dad want to get going, so you'd better pack up your books and things.

There's still some room in the trailer."

They heard their mother call from upstairs. "Raj, Chandra. Come up here and help your father lift these boxes. He's too fat to lift them himself. He'll put his back out."

"I'm coming, Mom," Chandra hollered as she raced upstairs. "Raj still has to pack his books."

Raj rummaged about the basement looking for the textbooks he wanted to take with him. He preferred to read real books rather than ebooks. The basement bookshelf was crammed with his books, and Raj already had a couple of cardboard boxes half-filled. As he was tossing in some anatomy and pharmacology books, he spied a couple of smaller books that had fallen behind the shelf. The first book was The Erotic Traveler; the other was Kama Sutra: Lessons of Love. It was older, and its pages had yellowed. On the cover was a painting of an Indian woman kneeling and playing flute, a subtle smile on her lips. Curious, Raj opened the book and found an old black-and-white photograph stuck inside. It showed his father and a woman sitting in a restaurant, holding hands. They looked to be in their twenties, and the woman was exquisitely beautiful. On the inside cover was a brief, handwritten note in Hindi. Raj didn't know what it said, but he was intrigued, as the woman in the photo was not his mother.

"Raj, are you coming or what?" Radhu called from downstairs. All morning, he had seemed almost anxious to get rid of his son now that he had a paying job. The car and the trailer were loaded, and it was time to go.

Raj snapped the book shut and threw it into the box with his textbooks. He wasn't quite sure why he did this; it just seemed the right thing to do.

* * *

In Mumbai, the Sun was beating down on the throngs of people scurrying about in the early morning. Diana watched them from the balcony of her friend's apartment, amazed by the sheer volume of humanity traveling to work in the city. Her friend, Kalpita, had invited her to visit Mumbai after they graduated, and Diana had jumped at the chance for an adventure. She had spent the last three weeks sightseeing across India with Kal and her mother. The holiday had come to an end in Mumbai, in Kal's parents' small apartment that perpetually smelled of greasy Indian spices, a scent Diana had grown used to and enjoyed.

Kal's mother, Nalini, came out onto the little balcony where Diana was sitting and offered her a glass of thick mango juice with ice, water already condensing on the glass. Diana wished it were coffee, but it seemed no one in Mumbai drank it.

A few minutes later, Kal appeared, sipping chai (tea). She asked Diana if she had slept well.

"Just fine," replied Diana. "The air conditioning is really good."

"Mom wants us to go see the crazy lady," said Kal.

"What do you mean?"

"There's this crazy lady who's a psychic. Everyone goes to see her, and Mom thinks we should see her, too."

Nalini was both a loving and bossy mother. She and Kalpita would get into arguments, and Diana had already learned it was best to do what Nalini wanted. Besides, there was nothing else to do in the Mumbai heat. *Maybe it would be interesting?*

"Sure, Kal, one last adventure."

* * *

Like the Beverley Hillbillies, the Mehta family drove out of town with the trunk full and towing a small trailer loaded to the limit. Raj sat in the front passenger seat of the little Honda sedan, and as his mother prattled on about the family, he daydreamed about living on his own for the first time. He wanted a car – a Honda hatchback. He wanted his own place and maybe even a girlfriend. In the backseat, Chan had earpieces in and was listening to music on her phone. This was a reflex she had developed over the years whenever she was forced to be with her family.

Mena had already taken to referring to her son as "Dr. Raj". Her many brothers and sisters were also proud of him, but they found Mena's constant reference to "Dr. Raj" annoying. Shamila, her sister, had been keen to let her know how well her own son, Roger, was doing. Now Mena leaned forward, so her son and husband could hear her better.

"Shamila says Roger has been posted to London by the bank," she said. "They're putting him up in a fancy house with a maid – all for free."

"Why must your sister always boast about Roger, the Banker?" Radhu said.

"He's not just a banker; he's an investment banker and a financier!"

"So what?"

"I just think the hospital should give the interns an apartment for free, like the bank," replied Mena.

"The banks have lots of money, but the hospital is being run by the government."

"So?"

"The banks have a lot more money. Don't you see how they're lending it out to everybody?"

The family rode on in silence for a while.

Mena was wearing the same old frumpy dress she nearly always wore, the one she had purchased in the Indian Bazaar on Gerrard Street. It embarrassed Raj to think that some of the other interns would see her. Then, with a rush of guilt, he remembered how his parents had scrimped and saved every nickel they had in order to put him and his sister through school without any student debt. They had never once mentioned how hard it had been, but Raj and Chandra both knew.

Mena broke the silence with a statement that seemed to come out of nowhere. "I see that a few of your classmates have already married, Raj."

"Yes, Mom," Raj sighed. "I'd say ten or fifteen of them."

"You need to find a nice girl and get married too."

The subject of marriage had first sprung out of his parents' mouths the day after Raj's graduation, but he had stubbornly declined to discuss it with either of them. His father had quickly backed off, accepting his son's refusal, but his mother constantly brought it up. She believed that she could find someone 'nice' for Raj – nice meant Indian, educated, and from a good family. Her friend's son had recently married a Jewish girl, all because he had insisted on choosing by himself. Jews were to be respected, but they weren't for getting married to. And didn't Jews also frown upon mixed marriages? Mena now referred to the young man as 'the goy'.

Chandra stopped moving her head to her music, gave her brother a look, and spoke up. "Mother! Why do you keep bugging Raj about getting married? He's only just finished school!"

"Raj has devoted his life to studying, and he should have the help of his parents in choosing a wife," Mena spoke with an air of finality. "Have you never read Jane Austen?"

"What on earth are you talking about?" Chandra said.

"Jane Austen. Have you not been going to college, Miss Smarty Pants? *'Every young man of a good fortune must be in want of a wife.'*"

"Mom, that story was written hundreds of years ago." Chandra rolled her eyes.

"Have you actually been studying literature or just trying to be a Starbucks employee of the month? You know, it's not too late to become a dental hygienist like your cousin."

Chandra was about to get into an argument with her mother when Radhu spoke up. "The apartment is a good deal, son. Did you remember to pack the new pants and shirts I bought you?"

"Yes, Dad."

"What about the shoes?"

"Got 'em."

Raj's father had splurged on new clothes for him – sensible dark pants, light-colored shirts, and unobtrusive ties – and had told Raj the docs liked to see everyone dressed a certain way. Raj doubted he would wear any of the clothes but had packed them anyway. He really wished that his dad had set the money aside for a car.

An hour and a half later, the family arrived at Raj's little apartment building behind a grey, older-looking hospital. The weather was sunny and not too hot – a perfect day. They stood in front of the six-story red brick building that was to be Raj's home.

Radhu turned to him and spoke quietly. "Raj, you will never be as free as you are right now. You have no debts, and your only responsibility is to yourself and those people you will help. Enjoy this time, Raj. True freedom doesn't last forever."

Chapter Two

Later that day, Kal and Diana jumped into a three-wheeled taxi and rode for about twenty minutes through the maze of modern Mumbai. They found themselves in a slum neighborhood where kids milled about everywhere, and there were even a few cows on the streets. The day was hot and humid, and the air smelled of greasy cooking and sewage. Diana was feeling a bit faint. The driver pointed to where the crazy lady lived, and Kal paid him to wait for them. The place was a little more than a shack made of corrugated steel, and, like so many homes in India, it had little tinsel decorations on the corners.

"I don't know, Kal. It looks scary…" Diana said hesitantly.

"Don't worry," said Kal. "The cab is going to wait for us. It will be one last adventure for your last day in India."

Both women walked carefully up the dirt path to the rickety door and knocked. A short, older woman with dull brown eyes, dressed in very simple clothes and a threadbare shawl, answered and motioned for them to come in. The room was dim, cool, and adorned with pictures of various Hindu deities. "Namaste," the woman whispered, directing them to a low couch in front of a small central fire pit. A small plastic table held brass bowls, plates, and what looked like spices or incense. The scent reminded Diana of something familiar – like cinnamon.

Kal spoke with the woman in Hindi for a few moments, and

Diana heard her name. The woman stared at Diana for quite a long time, almost as if she had been expecting her, then she took her hands. She spoke in Hindi, barely whispering while staring into Diana's eyes and swaying back and forth. She mumbled in a singsong fashion for several minutes, and Diana felt a brief sensation of vertigo. Suddenly, several things happened at once. The old woman squeezed her hands, and Diana let out a yelp.

"What's wrong?" Kalpita grabbed hold of Diana.

The old woman let her hands go and turned to put a small kettle on the fire to boil.

Diana turned to Kal. "Well, that was different." She smiled, seeing the worried expression on Kalpita's face, and added quickly. "I'm fine."

"Good, yeah, it was," Kalpita replied, looking relieved. "I wasn't expecting that." She looked at the old woman who turned to her.

The woman spoke to Kalpita in Hindi. "Your friend is tiresome, filled with thoughts all over the place. I have seen her future. I will tell you all about it. Do you want some tea?"

Kal nodded yes for tea and asked, "Auntie, what is in her future? She wants to know."

"Tell her that we have met before, and somehow, we will meet again. Her life will bring joy to others. There is so much to tell. I can feel the great wheel turning… I know what I must do."

Kal turned to Diana. "She's really laying it on thick. Says she's met you before. Something about you bringing joy to people. Maybe she means you'll land an acting job!"

Diana brightened at this prospect and thanked the woman.

The woman passed them brass cups filled with strong tea. For a few moments, they sat quietly, sipping their drinks, and Diana felt herself calming down.

The woman turned to her table and began mixing various colored pastes in small pots. Satisfied with the colors she had created, she gestured to Diana to stand up. To Kal, she said, "Make her take her dress off."

"Why, Auntie?"

"I need to see where to place the words… the dream mantra…"

Kal was mystified. "Words… mantra…?"

"Yes. If she has the dream mantra, the right things will happen. She will lose the words or forget them if they're written in jewelry. I must tattoo them on her."

Diana was surprised but did as she was told, slipping out of her light cotton sundress.

"Your friend is pretty but skinny. Ah… her legs are nice. We'll put it on her thigh," said the old woman.

Kal asked, "Will it hurt?"

"Tell her it will hurt a bit, but not much. It is not even for her, but for someone else to notice."

Diana had been listening and was a bit worried. "Okay, Kal, what's going on?"

"She wants to tattoo something on you. A mantra of some kind. She calls it a dream mantra."

"A tattoo? That's cool. I've always wanted one. But what's a dream mantra?"

"It's like a message – something about making your dreams come true."

Diana looked at Kal suspiciously and said, "Okay, but remember, you got me into this."

The woman gestured for Diana to lie on her side, then carefully inked a few Sanskrit words on Diana's leg in the swirling pattern of a helix. It didn't hurt too much, and Diana thought it looked pretty. No one else would have a tattoo like this, that was for sure.

The woman told them to wait while the ink dried, then they bade her goodbye. She graciously accepted more money than she had ever seen from the two young women. To Kal, she said, "Shanti, tell your friend that good fortune is waiting for her back at home."

"I will, Auntie."

Chapter Three

Raj's family left shortly after setting up a twenty-year-old television, assembling an IKEA table and couch, and arranging the bedroom furniture. His mother, apparently convinced that the previous tenant had leprosy, Ebola, or some hospital superbug, had wiped everything down with Lysol and offered to wrap the toilet seat in Saran Wrap.

She had brought some twenty containers of food: an assortment of curries, vegetables, and rice, and had ordered Raj to avoid *'greasy white people food'* and bring back the Tupperware containers to be refilled. As a final touch, she had placed a small potted sunflower on the little kitchen table.

Before she left, Chandra surprised him with a new iPhone, which she had loaded with several new diagnostic medical apps. Raj reckoned the phone had easily cost $500 and was impressed that she had spent so much on him.

"Thanks, Chan. The apps are really good," he said.

"Now I can Facetime you." She was grinning.

"You'd better not call me much, if at all."

"What's with that?"

"A guy in my study group was caught texting while we were doing rounds and got sent home. They told him it was unprofessional."

"You doctors – always acting like it's life or death."

"It was a life or death thing, actually. Anyway, I don't want to piss off the senior docs – I've got to impress them."

Chandra rolled her eyes but hugged him anyway. "Okay, bro. No Facetime unless I'm at a really good restaurant, and I know you're eating Mr. Noodle."

"Thanks, Chan. Just send me a picture so I can be jealous."

Then everyone hugged, and the family drove off, leaving him alone in his new apartment.

The apartment was small and dusty and needed an air conditioner, but Raj could not have been happier. The rent was only $560 a month, and from the living room window, he could see the hospital, a short walk away – St. Jerome Hospital: a monument to the Canadian belief that no man, woman, or child should be made destitute because of ill health. Looking at the sixty-year-old building, Raj wondered how many thousands of lives had begun within those walls. In a way, his own life would begin there too. He would no longer be just Raj Mehta; he would be Dr. Mehta, an intern, one of four newly minted doctors training there and destined to serve the people of Canada. For a brief moment, Raj was proud of himself, and the long years of hard work and study seemed to melt away. He was a twenty-six-year-old 'stem cell', capable of becoming almost anything.

The only real luxury Raj possessed was an iPod and stand that he had bought with a small scholarship. It was his prized possession, and he set it up now, next to the television. When he switched it on, the television produced only a fuzzy orange-and-brown picture of the local news. He unpacked his meager belongings, throwing his father's book on the bed. Then he went into the minuscule bathroom to shower and spent a couple of minutes regarding himself in the mirror. His black hair was a bit long, he thought, and his goatee needed a trim. Lean and about six feet tall, he wanted to be bigger and stronger. Did he look like a doctor? Too young? Maybe people would see his lack of confidence. His teeth were white and straight, and his eyes a clear, dark brown. He hoped that he had the kind of masculine face and quiet air of competence that someone would find attractive. He took a pair of scissors and trimmed them here and there, removing tiny hairs that threatened to give him a *'unibrow'*.

What Raj didn't know was that his stare was so penetrating that it could make people uncomfortable. He had a habit of rarely ever smiling for fear of looking stupid in the eyes of his instructors. This did him no favors.

Raj returned to the bedroom feeling a sense of anticlimax. He had dreamed for years of leaving his parents' home. He wanted his own life. Most of all, he wanted a girlfriend! He had thought about signing up on a dating website by the name of Dr. McDreamy, but that would have to wait until the Internet was hooked up. In the meantime, he couldn't even get on the Internet. There was nothing to do, and he was stuck in the restless, bored, and horny state he had been in since his graduation.

He went to bed and opened the only non-medical text that he possessed – his father's book, Kama Sutra. He flipped through it, surprised by how beautiful the illustrations were. The women had breasts like ripe melons. Their hips curved as they sat and played cards or music. There were many pictures of couples having intercourse. Raj tried to ignore his erection. The book began…

* * *

Diana left Mumbai the next day for the long trip back to Toronto, and she had already forgotten about the tattoo by the time she arrived at her parent's house in St. Jerome. The journey was exhausting, and Diana needed a full twenty-four hours to adjust to the Canadian time zone and cooler weather.

On Sunday morning, as she was lounging on her bed reading People Magazine, her father walked in. Never a man to make small talk, he said, "I know you mean to start looking for a job. Marg, my secretary, fell last week and broke her hip. So, I'm hiring you. You're my new secretary."

Taken by surprise, Diana burst out, "What? But, Dad, I'm going to look for acting jobs in Toronto. How can I do that if I'm working as a medical secretary in St. Jerome?"

"I don't know, and I don't really care," he said. "You're going to work in my office until I find a suitable replacement. Your mother has refused the job. She said something about your education being so expensive, it was the least you could do for me."

"Dad, you know I was planning to stay home for just a few weeks," Diana reminded him.

Irony evident on his face, Dad replied, "That's what everyone's kids say."

"Can I at least borrow the car and check out apartments?"

Her father replied, "Apartments cost money, and you don't have any. Maybe I can get you an apartment near the hospital – they're supposed to be cheap. I expect you at the office tomorrow morning at eight. Don't be late." He turned to leave.

"Dad, you're a real killjoy."

"Welcome to my world, sweetie – the real world." He left her room, looking quite pleased with himself.

Chapter Four

"If you're a patient, you'd better wash your hands."

"Uh…pardon? Excuse me. I'm Raj Mehta…"

"If you're a patient, wash your hands!"

A rather large, lemony-looking lady at the reception desk in the lobby was glaring at him through horn-rimmed glasses. Raj quickly washed his hands at the nearby sink.

"Hi. I'm Dr. Raj Mehta, one of the new interns."

Her manner changed abruptly. "A doctor! Well, I guess I'll have to show you where to go." She smiled sweetly, but only for a moment, as she spied on an older man walking into the hospital. "You! There! Wash your hands! And please be aware of the hospital's reduced-scent policy!"

She sniffed loudly and turned back to Raj. "I'll take you to the coordinator's office." She did not say, "Welcome to St. Jerome's," nor did she make any further pretense of being polite. Raj was glad he had not worn aftershave. Perhaps she would have taken him to the basement and scrubbed him like a potato if he had.

He followed her down one corridor and then another, the click of her heels on the terrazzo floor echoing off the walls. As they went deeper into the bowels of the hospital, the corridor seemed to age: the air began to feel damp; the paint on the walls was peeling. They were in the basement of the hospital, and there was a faint but nauseating smell of formaldehyde.

"Are we in the morgue?" Raj asked his guide, who replied, "Actually, we're right beside it. The postgraduate office is right here." She pointed to a dusty old office door that showed a light around the edges. "This is Dr. Sinclair's office. He's in charge of the internship program. Have a seat, and he'll be in to see you shortly."

Raj had hoped for a more grand welcome. The least they could have done was set up a reception with the hospital CEO and perhaps a fancy breakfast. He had heard that law school graduates were fêted at parties or taken to swanky restaurants before signing on with a firm. Evidently, this kind of generosity was lost in the medical profession.

The waiting room was tidy but dingy. There was no natural light, yet cacti and ferns created a little jungle in the room. The furniture was old and worn; the chairs must have been at least forty years old. The green linoleum floor was cracked in places, but it was scrubbed clean. Impressionist posters crowded the walls. Behind the secretary's desk was a print of Van Gogh's famous painting of sunflowers in a vase. People and US Weekly and other trashy magazines littered the secretary's desk. It looked as if she didn't work much.

Raj was surprised to see a potted sunflower among the plants. The only person he knew who grew sunflowers was his mother, who grew them in the backyard and the kitchen – it was her "thing". She said they reminded her of Bangalore, India, where fields of sunflowers surrounded the village where she grew up.

So preoccupied was Raj that he failed to notice another person in the office. He was sitting in the corner on an old red leather chair with his feet up on a coffee table. He looked to be about Raj's age, with dark hair styled to look as if he had just got out of bed. Later, Raj would realize that it wasn't a style – the guy routinely walked around with a bedhead. Blue jeans and a scruffy beard completed his cool, anti-establishment look.

Raj introduced himself, and the bedhead lowered his feet.

"I'm Dan Freedman," he said.

"Are you an intern?"

"Yeah, I am. You too?"

"Yes," said Raj.

They eyed each other, then smiled and shook hands.

"I hope you washed your hands," Raj joked.

"She actually wanted to shave me. I won't say where." Dan replied. "Why so dressed up? Did you think they weren't going to hire you?"

"First day on the job. Thought I'd work it a bit," Raj said.

"Did you get an apartment?"

"Yeah, and not at a bad price."

"Who else lives in the building?"

"I don't know, man. Maybe nursing students."

The two men grinned like a pair of schoolboys up to no good.

Raj was about to sit down when a lanky, silver-haired man wearing a lab coat walked in, trailing two young women in his wake.

"Hello, I'm Dr. Sinclair," he said, "Intern Coordinator and Chief of Staff." His lab coat was stiff with starch and monogrammed with his name in blue above the breast pocket. He had the handsome, clean-shaven face and neutral expression of a J. Crew model. His pants were grey flannel with cuffs that sat perfectly on highly polished loafers. Dr. Sinclair looked to be the kind of successful, conservative man for whom Lexus automobiles were designed.

He introduced the two women as their fellow interns, then cleared his throat loudly and led them beyond the waiting room into his private office, which contained a desk and several chairs. Everyone sat down in the cramped office.

"Welcome to St. Jerome's Hospital," he said. "This is the first year of our internship program, and we're all excited about it. I thought we'd get to know one another today." He passed around paper stickers and instructed the interns to print their names on them and place them on their shirts. "If you don't mind, I think each of you should stand up and introduce yourself and tell us a bit about your personal background."

The young woman who stood up first was wearing lipstick, which was rare for female doctors – at least the ones Raj knew. Her long hair was swept back in a stylish ponytail, and she was dressed in a blouse, pants, and high heels. "Hello. My name is Kelly Davis. I'm from Montreal, and I went to McGill. I have a boyfriend who's a musician, and I'm looking forward to this internship in Ontario."

Dan stood up next. "Hello. My name is Dan Freedman. I don't have a girlfriend who's a musician, and I'm not married or anything like that. I went to Western, and I hope to gain some knowledge from this year."

It was Raj's turn to introduce himself. "I'm Raj Mehta. I went to the University of Toronto. Before medical school, I was in computer science, and my thesis was on artificial intelligence and how computer algorithms can be simulated using game theory."

Sinclair smiled. "Ah … a University of Toronto grad, like me. Are you married, engaged?"

"Uh ... no, sir."

Everyone turned to the fourth intern, who said her name was Paula Johnson. She wore glasses and had straight brown hair done in a little bob that made her look professional. She smiled a lot.

"I went to the University of Calgary," she said, "and I'm really happy to be in Ontario. I grew up out west – I'm a farm girl. I always tell people that I was a member of 4H but also a vegetarian. By the way, vegetarians are different from vegans."

Raj was grateful that she had not shared much personal information. He liked to pretend he was a private person when, in reality, he simply had no personal life worth talking about.

Dr. Sinclair began to tell them about the hospital. "In the first year of your internship, you will be exposed to a wide variety of clinical experiences, including two months in internal medicine, two months in surgery, and two months in the ER. The year will conclude with two months of family practice and some elective time. Next year, you'll do the other specialties, including psychiatry and obstetrics, if you haven't completed them this year." He paused for a moment as if expecting some sort of complaint or comment. There were none. "We're going to make seasoned veterans of you. When you work at St. Jerome's, you'll be working as full-fledged doctors. We have a shortage of doctors here, and you interns will find yourselves on the front line very quickly."

Kelly spoke up. "Dr. Sinclair, when do we get our rotational schedule?"

"I'll have it ready later today or tomorrow. You'll have to excuse my tardiness. My secretary fell and broke her hip last week. I have a new secretary, but she's just getting used to the work."

"What about holidays?" asked Paula.

"Holidays?" repeated Dr. Sinclair. "I hadn't thought about

holidays. Let me know what your preferences are, and my secretary will deal with it. Oh, we also have to meet the CEO of the hospital. As you know, you're the first interns at St. Jerome's in over thirty years. The CEO has very important information for you."

* * *

The CEO's office was a complete contrast to Sinclair's office. It was on the top floor of the old building, and the waiting area looked as though it had recently been repainted and refurnished with comfortable leather chairs. Her secretary was on the phone but cupped it with her hand as she spoke to Dr. Sinclair. "You have the students with you, I see."

"Actually, they aren't students," he replied. "They're doctors, here for their internships."

The secretary ignored his remark. "Ms. Fletcher will see you shortly," she said and returned to her phone conversation.

The five of them sat, and Dr. Sinclair checked his watch, clearly irritated by having to wait. He was about to say something to the secretary when the CEO came out of her office. She was an attractive middle-aged woman in a dark grey power suit, wearing an unctuous smile. "Hello, John. I see you've brought the new students."

"They aren't students, Wendy. They're doctors completing their final training," stressed Dr. Sinclair.

"Yes, as you say," the CEO replied vaguely and turned to the interns. "Hello and welcome to St. Jerome's Hospital. I'm Wendy Fletcher, the new CEO, and I was appointed about four months ago by the Minister of Health. The decision to take on interns was made by the previous CEO, who has moved on to other challenges. I've instituted some changes at this hospital to run it more efficiently, and I have some valuable information for you that will help things run more smoothly."

The CEO gestured them into an adjoining meeting room where a large video monitor was turned on. The interns sat down around a large gleaming table and, for the next ten minutes, listened to Ms. Fletcher as she clicked through several PowerPoint graphs and bar charts that seemed a bit dire. She talked ominously and repeatedly of "cost per weighted case" and "budgetary overruns".

"As you can see," she said, "St. Jerome's faces several challenges in order to fall in line with the Ministry of Health's overall plan."

Raj glanced at Dr. Sinclair, whose deep frown suggested he did not like what he was hearing.

Ms. Fletcher concluded by showing them an organizational chart on which doctors and nurses were at the bottom of the pyramid, along with the orderlies, cooks, and cleaners. Above them were two layers of department managers and division leaders, and at the apex of the pyramid was the CEO, all alone. "Now, if there are any problems during the next month, don't hesitate to speak to your department manager, who is directly above you on this chart."

Paula spoke up. "Out west, we were always supervised by a staff doctor or a medical department head."

The CEO replied, "Well, here at St. Jerome's, we run a very tight ship. Any problems or concerns are to be taken up with the department manager – or with me."

Dr. Sinclair's frown deepened at this, but he ignored her remark and addressed the interns. "Okay, people, now that we're done here, let's get back to my office and talk about your rotations."

"Excuse me, John, but I'm not done yet." Ms. Fletcher interjected. "We have to get a picture for the local newspaper." She gestured to them to gather around her, then moved in close to Dan and put her arm around him. Raj turned his head to straighten the collar of his new lab coat and saw the CEO's hand settle on Dan's buttock, which she gave a little squeeze.

The secretary brought in an older man with a large camera. Wendy spoke. "Okay, everyone! Smile and say money."

They obeyed, although Raj silently said "cheese," and the cameraman took a few shots.

"Now, run along, you all!" Fletcher said. "I'm sure John has lots of work for you. I'll be speaking to each of you individually over the next few weeks."

The interns filed out of the office, eager, excited, and confused. As Raj left, he thought he saw the CEO give Dan a little conspiratorial wink.

Chapter Five

"Fuckity, fuck, fuck!" Diana was exasperated by her inability to find anything in her father's office. He kept asking her for files that weren't related to patients, and he insisted that she address him as Dr. Sinclair. He seemed to have no idea how his own office ran. She silently cursed Marg for breaking her hip but then had a twinge of guilt and quickly hoped that Marg got better – and returned to work – soon!

Diana had no idea where to find the intern schedule. She did not want to meet any of them until she had found their schedule. There would be questions, and they'd probably treat her like an idiot. They would have to take it up with her father, who would then have to make excuses like, "My daughter is an unemployed actress who just graduated from school," implying that she was a loser with a flighty artistic personality disorder. They would chortle over their coffee while celebrating their doctorliness and superior intellect. Diana knew that medical secretaries typically get blamed for everything that goes wrong; she had worked for her father while Marg went on vacation for several summers and had seen how things worked at St. Jerome's.

She found what looked like a rough schedule for the interns on her father's desk. But she still didn't want to see any of them this morning and came up with the idea that would even give her enough time to get a coffee, a low-fat muffin, and her favorite read, People Magazine. She placed sticky notes on the outside of the office door:

- Dr. Raj Mehta: Report to Emergency Room

- Dr. Paula Johnson: Report to Internal Medicine (3rd Floor)
- Dr. Dan Freedman: Report to Orthopedic Surgery
- Dr. Kelly Davis: Report to Labour and Delivery (5th Floor)

* * *

The next day, bright and early, Raj made his way to Sinclair's office. The secretary wasn't there, but he found the note stuck on the door. Raj liked the idea of ER work but was deathly afraid that he would screw up. He had learned some of the emergency protocols, but his book smarts were matched by a complete lack of practical knowledge. He tried to summon up some optimism and checked his look twice in the mirror of the ER bathroom.

Raj had abandoned his father's shirts and adopted what he thought was an 'urban hip look' with a mock turtleneck and Dockers. He rolled up the sleeves of his lab coat and put his new iPhone in the upper pocket. It weighed down that side of the coat so much that he had to put a reflex hammer and a flashlight in a side pocket to balance things out. He draped a stethoscope around his neck and rubbed his "Dr. Mehta" nameplate to a shine.

He made his way to the ER, where he was pleased to see that there were quite a few nursing students around, women in their early twenties wearing uniforms in shades that matched their lip gloss. Raj smiled at each of them, glad that his little plastic nameplate was visible. A nurse introduced Raj to his boss, a staff doctor named Rick Marley, who looked about forty and sounded like he was from somewhere in the West Indies, Jamaica, perhaps. Marley had barely said "welcome" when he was called away by a frantic voice on the intercom.

Raj wandered over to the nursing station. Not yet having done any work, he actually thought he might like emergency medicine. He was trying to catch the eye of one of the nurses while a middle-aged, heavyset nurse, whose tag said "Nursing Team Leader," spied on him. She should have been named 'The Drill Sargent'

"Dr. Mehta, would you come over here and have a look at this gentleman? He seems to be having some difficulty breathing." She said this with a toothy smile as she grabbed his arm and led him behind a curtained-off cubicle

In front of him sat a portly, unshaven man whose tongue was lolling out. He had an oxygen mask on and was connected to various monitors. Raj noticed he was sweating profusely.

"Hello, sir. I'm Dr. Mehta. What seems to be the problem?" Raj made himself sound confident to reassure the patient. He didn't feel confident at all.

The man, gasping for air, could wheeze out only a few words. "Can't talk… can't breathe."

An alarm on one of the monitors went off, and the man grabbed Raj's arm and pulled him to his knees – like a drowning man pulling him under. *Holy shit,* Raj thought, the guy was going to die! Another alarm started pinging, while the other one was bleeping.

Raj looked around for the nurse, but she was gone. He felt desperate. He might have to give the man mouth-to-mouth resuscitation, but through the clear plastic oxygen mask, he could see brownish, rotting teeth and yellowy saliva dribbling out.

Raj was immobilized with fear when Sandra reappeared carrying a mask attached to a tiny plastic cylinder. She looked at Raj quizzically, the patient now resting his jowly face on Raj's shoulder.

"I, uh, was just examining the patient," Raj stammered.

"Did you listen to his lungs?" asked Sandra.

"Uh, not yet," mumbled Raj.

Sandra rolled her eyes as Raj freed himself from the man's grasp. He jumped up, grabbed his stethoscope, and placed it on the man's slippery and rather hairy back. The patient was wheezing loudly.

"Here, we'll try Ventolin and Atrovent – it usually works for him," Sandra said.

The patient grabbed the mask from her and began inhaling slowly. She clicked off the oxygen monitor alarm and then pushed Raj aside to shut off the other alarm – a silent reminder that he was completely useless.

"Doctor, just sign the order sheet on his chart that I gave him the nebulizer treatment, okay?"

"Okay," Raj muttered.

He scurried away to a bathroom to look up asthma medication doses on his new iPhone. He also wanted to change his lab coat, which was sticky with sweat. The iPhone didn't seem to have the right information, and as Raj pecked away with his finger, the medical program kept giving him words that began like asthma... as, ass, asshole. What if the man was getting worse while he hid in the bathroom? Raj's hands were sweaty. As he pecked away in the bathroom stall, the toilet flushed, its automatic sensor triggered somehow. The sound startled him, and he dropped his iPhone in the toilet.

"Shit! Stupid and inept ... and stupid!" Momentary panic seized him. He bent to retrieve the iPhone, which triggered the auto-flush sensor again, and the phone was nearly sucked into the Great Beyond. Raj caught the phone before the current carried it away but was sprayed in the face by the violent flush as he did. He dried the phone as best he could with toilet paper. Then, after listening for a moment to make sure no one else was in the bathroom, he opened the door to the stall. After wiping his face with hand sanitizer, he was finally able to leave the bathroom.

One of the other interns had arrived in the ER – Paula, the girl from out west. The note on Dr. Sinclair's door had said she would be covering Cardiology. Paula had that wholesome look that spoke of a childhood in the country and a quiet air of doctoral competence that Raj knew he didn't have.

Raj caught Paula's eye, and she smiled. "Hi. It's Raj, isn't it?"

"Hi, Paula. What are you up to?"

"I'm down here seeing a consult for Dr. Froeder – he's a cardiologist."

Raj said, "I'm working in the ER. I just saw an asthmatic guy. Man – he's pretty sick!"

"Did you give him Ventolin and Atrovent?"

"Yes - and some oxygen." Raj hesitated a second, then asked, "Paula, when you dose Ventolin, how much do you give?"

"I forget. Let me check my book." She pulled out a small, thick book from her pocket and quickly leafed through it. Raj recognized it as Pocket Medicine, the book he'd hoped his iPhone app would replace. Now he knew it was better than his iPhone app, and his iPhone was soaked and likely not working anyway.

If he were seen talking to Paula, Raj thought it would look as though he was working. He didn't mind working, but he was deathly afraid of screwing up. Besides, it would be smart to be nice to a fellow intern – perhaps they could get a party organized. Paula was far from home and likely had no friends around.

"Have you been downtown yet?" Raj asked her. "Maybe we could all go out for dinner some time."

Paula brightened at this proposal. "Sure, Raj. That would be great. Let's get together and do something." She showed him the dose of Ventolin, then slipped the book back into her pocket and strode off.

Raj was thinking of what to do next when Sandra reappeared and informed him that there were six people in the ER waiting to be seen. "I've made a list of your very own patients to see," she said. "You'll be working in exam rooms four to seven." Sandra pointed at the chalkboard for his patients.

Raj's heart sank when he saw what she had lined up for him:

- Room 4: Adult male. Sweating too much/smells like cheese.
- Room 5: Elderly female with a rash on her buttock (shaped like a toilet seat).
- Room 6: Child complaining of an earache.
- Room 7: Male with dementia. Thinks he's in a restaurant (wants lunch).

He picked what looked like the easiest case and made his way to Room 6, where he almost collided with a boy, aged about six and holding a red Popsicle, who was running away from his brother. The boy swerved too abruptly, and both he and the Popsicle fell to the floor. Raj was about to tell him to leave it when the boy picked it up, now coated with hospital-issue germs, and put it in his mouth. Waiting inside the room were several other dirty-faced youngsters and their mother. Raj winced at the sight of her bare belly protruding beneath a crop top that was too short and at the Coke she was drinking at 9:30 in the morning.

"Mrs. … Morrison. What can I do for you?"

"It's Dakota. She's got an earache." She gestured at a blonde girl, perhaps four years old. She was trying to get past Raj and out of the examining room and the clutches of her older brother.

"Dodge, stop bothering your sister!" the mother yelled.

On the chair beside her was a baby asleep in a car seat. *Probably named Chevy or Ford,* Raj thought.

"Let's have a look at your ear, Dakota," he said, lifting the girl up and sitting her on the examining bench. She had a mesmerizing smile and wide blue eyes.

"Hi," she said. "My dad says I was conceived in a pickup truck."

Raj stopped for a moment, wondering what to say – and said nothing. He peered in her ear. Dakota had a very red eardrum and would need antibiotics.

"Mrs. Morrison, does Dakota have any allergies?"

"No, doc. She can take anything," the mother replied, "but make damn sure that anything you prescribe is covered by my drug card."

The demand took Raj completely aback. How would he know which pills were covered?

Later in the day, Raj asked Rick Marley about this.

"Raj, folks around here don't have a lot of money, so make sure you prescribe only medication that's covered on the provincial plan. I've seen patients come back to the ER when someone forgot, and they raise one hell of a ruckus – even if the pills cost less than twenty bucks."

By mid-afternoon, Raj had figured out that there was a rhythm to how the ER operated. The trick was to make an assessment and then order the necessary tests. While the tests were being done, he had to see another patient right away, or the waiting room would fill up with people getting angrier and angrier. The place relied on speed, but accuracy and ruling out potentially serious problems were of utmost importance. Raj's day flew by in a blur of sick people and the results of blood tests and X-rays, which he was constantly looking up on the hospital computer system.

As five o'clock approached, Rick came over for his final review of the cases Raj had seen. Every case had to be checked with the ER staff doctor before the patient could be discharged.

"Well, how was your first day?" Rick asked. "Do you like working in the ER?"

"Yeah, I do. It was busy though, Dr. Marley," said Raj.

"Did you sort out the old gal with the rash on her bum?"

"It was just a contact dermatitis from her bathroom cleaner.

Actually, her main concern was that it might be herpes."

Rick laughed. "Raj, we get everything and anything through those doors. Listen, you're going to do just fine here. Remember to listen to the nurses. If they have a hunch about a patient, give them a careful listen."

"Thanks, Dr. Marley," Raj said. "That sounds like good advice."

"Some of the older nurses have worked here for ages. They know practically everyone from around here. They'll save your bacon, my man." Rick clapped Raj on the shoulder, then added, "One other thing. We have to be good, but try not to spend too much money. CAT scans cost money. We aren't a fancy teaching hospital, and we're on a tight budget."

"I got that impression from the CEO."

"She makes it clear to everyone."

They walked out of the hospital together, and as Rick got into his BMW coupe in the parking lot, he said, "Tomorrow, bring in coffee and doughnuts for the nurses. They'll think you're the greatest intern ever."

Raj gave him the thumbs up as Rick sped away.

* * *

Diana's first day at the office went by in a panicked rush.

People came in regularly, and they were, by and large, quite elderly. She had to pull their files and escort them to the examining room and, at the same time, field phone calls and faxes. Most of them were elderly farmers who, when they entered, viewed her with frank astonishment, and this slowed things down even further.

One of them asked, "Who are you? Where's Marg?"

"Marg is on sick leave," Diana explained.

"Well, that's no good! Marg always used to call me the day before to remind me of my appointment. You didn't do that this time."

"Well, sir, I just started today. I'm sorry, but I didn't know she does that for you regularly," Diana explained.

"Well, you're a lot prettier than Marg anyways. 'He hasn't run off with you or anything like that, has he?' The old man was smirking now.

"No. Marg will be back fairly soon. She has to recover." Diana said for the umpteenth time that day, her patience wearing thin.

"Well, thank God for that!"

Sometimes, after her father went in to see patients, Diana would overhear them making the same complaint to him, including the wild surmise that he was having it off with a younger secretary.

At the end of her first day, she was glad that she had moved to an apartment close to the hospital and did not have to go back to her parents' house. Their endless questions about her career had been exhausting her. She had spent the last four years studying drama at the University of Toronto. Just one day of secretarial work had made her more determined than ever to find something – anything – that would help her become what she most wanted to be – a stage actress.

Chapter Six

Sandra had used her chalkboard to assign all sorts of oddball patients to Raj, people who had strange symptoms like "feeling yeasty" or "getting a bloated sensation" when they ate bread. Raj was tired of treating them. He looked at the main board above the nursing station and realized that Rick Marley was getting all the difficult patients, those in heart failure or with some other dire condition. Those were the patients he wanted to have. He wandered down the row of examining rooms looking in each one for an elderly man who he knew had been waiting a long time. When he spotted him, the old fellow was sitting on the examination table, looking uncomfortable.

Raj grabbed the chart from the slot beside the door, quickly glanced at it, and entered the room. "Hello, Mr. Martin," he said. "I'm Dr. Mehta. What can I do for you?"

"Hey, doc," the old man replied. "I can't piss. It's drivin' me crazy. Feels like I'm goin' to explode."

Raj was hoping for a heart problem or something similar, but people came to the ER with all sorts of serious complaints.

"Okay, let's have a look at you," he said, and he examined the patient carefully, including his prostate, by way of a rectal exam. The prostate was as big and bulbous as a ripe plum. "Sir, I think you've got some trouble with the prostate."

"That's what they tell me," said Mr. Martin. "I'm on pills, but they ain't workin'.""

"Usually, in situations like this, we have to do surgery to open up the passage." Raj tried to break the news gently, but the old man roared anyway.

"Surgery! I don't want any surgery down there. Just give me some more pills."

"If your pills have stopped working, there aren't any others that will work. I think you have to have a resection of your prostate."

"What in hell is that?" cried the old man.

"The surgeon will tell you about it. But, basically, he goes up the penis and scrapes out the blockage using a laser."

The old man was speechless, and Raj took the opportunity to step into the corridor and call the staff urologist, Dr. Ventner, who answered the phone, saying, "I'm in the OR right now. Whatever it is, I can't be there for another hour or two."

Raj explained the situation, and Ventner said he'd deal with Mr. Martin later that night. "If he hasn't got a catheter in yet, admit him to my service and get a Foley in him. He's probably quite uncomfortable."

Raj was about to tell Dr. Ventner that he had never put a catheter in anyone. Instead, what came out of his mouth was, "No problem, sir. I'll get a Foley in him shortly."

"Thanks, Raj. I'll see him after my OR."

Raj cursed his lack of experience. Why had he volunteered to take this patient? How does one stick a catheter up a penis? Would it hurt? Obviously, it would! Just the thought of it made him squirm. He didn't want to ask a nurse, especially not Sandra.

He was still wondering what to do when he spotted Paula. He greeted her, trying to sound carefree.

"Hi, Raj. How's it going?" Paula said.

"Good. They're keeping me quite busy here."

"Me, too," said Paula. "My staff is Dr. Froeder. He's a nice guy, but there are a lot of consults in ER."

Raj screwed up his courage. "Paula, do you know how to put in a Foley? I haven't done one yet."

"I did one in the operating room once. The guy was asleep, though, so it's not like he could complain."

"Well, you know more than I do. Can you give me a hand?"

"Sure," Paula said with a smile, and Raj felt a modicum of hope that he would be able to get through this man's problems without injuring his penis – or anything else.

* * *

Diana arrived at work early. She had no Internet at her

apartment and wanted to use the office computer to check out talent agencies in Toronto. It took only a few minutes for her to realize that nothing had changed since she last checked. Although Toronto was a hub for film and television productions, the agencies represented only established actors who already had lots of exposure. This was particularly true for stage actors. No one was willing to take on someone who had only done a handful of stage productions at the University of Toronto.

Diana smiled wryly. Was this any worse than waiting tables in Toronto? Maybe…

After her father's patients started arriving, she juggled charts, telephone calls, and her search for a job – any job that would get her going in the right direction.

Frequent interruptions by her father's patients tested her nerves. All of them seemed to have something wrong with them. Obviously, they did have something wrong, or they wouldn't be there, but everyone who came in also sneezed, coughed, belched, or did something that wasn't normal. One old gentleman coughed so loudly and frequently that Diana was sure he had the bubonic plague and shuddered when he managed a noisy fart during a coughing spell. She wished there was a plastic wall around her desk to protect her from their germs. There were no windows and no natural light in the office, and it was stifling. She made a mental note to get an air purifier.

"Excuse me, miss. I don't have an appointment. I just need a refill on my pills." The old fellow looked hopefully at Diana.

"What are the pills for?" asked Diana. "Did Dr. Sinclair prescribe them for you? I need their name before we can call them in."

"I don't know the name, but they're pink and oblong. The doctor will know which ones they are."

Diana reviewed the man's chart. She'd have her father see him and figure out what was going on.

She was already planning her coffee break when Dr. Sinclair (Dad insisted she call him "Doctor") came out and told her to get the interns to sign a couple of forms affirming they had insurance coverage and a work contract. They were supposed to have signed them before starting work at the hospital. She pulled their files and looked at the first one:

Raj Mehta: University of Toronto, School of Medicine Class of 2010.

Undergraduate degree: Computer Science and Applied Mathematics.

There was also a note from his medical school advisor saying that he had great promise as a doctor but needed much more clinical experience.

Mehta had graduated that year, just as Diana had. There was no picture in the file. She wondered if she had ever seen him on campus.

Diana picked up the phone and called the ER. "Is Dr. Mehta in the department? Can you get him to call Dr. Sinclair's office when he gets a chance? Or maybe have him just come by. Thanks."

* * *

Raj and Paula were attempting to place the thin silicone tube up their patient's penis. They had frozen the passage with jelly, but they couldn't get the catheter past the prostate.

"What the fuck are you guys doing to me?" Mr. Martin hollered. "Feels like you're stabbing me!"

The penis was already slippery with the freezing gel. Raj had tried, and then Paula had a turn, trying to get the man to relax. "Just take a couple of deep breaths, sir."

"Yeah – just a couple of deep breaths while you jab me with a hot poker. This is worse than the Army!"

Raj remembered a catheter with a different type of tip that might make it easier. Cursing and sweating, he grabbed the new, stiffer catheter and pushed – hard.

"Jesus! Holy Mother of God!" bellowed the patient.

Success! The catheter slipped past the overgrown prostate and into the bladder. Out flowed liquid gold – and it kept flowing and flowing, at least 2 liters. Once his bladder was drained, Mr. Martin felt fine but was persuaded to stay and see the specialist. Paula and Raj pulled off their gloves, grinning as if they had performed a medical miracle.

"That was tough!" Raj said. "Thanks for your help, Paula."

"I don't know how you managed it."

"I couldn't have done it without you."

They sat outside the ER for a moment, discussing their weekend plans. Raj wanted the group of interns to go out for dinner. Dan was around, but they hadn't seen Kelly, who was in Labour and Delivery. They were about to call her when a young nursing student approached them. She had a ponytail and was wearing magenta scrubs with matching shoes and lipstick. Raj noted that she was tall and leggy with a sexy bounce to her stride. Paula rolled her eyes as she walked up to Raj.

"Excuse me, Dr. Mehta. Can you have a look at the boy in Trauma 1? He was hit by a car. The staff doctor is running an emergency code, and Sandra said I was to get you."

"Do you want to come with me?" Raj asked Paula.

"Sure. I'm not too busy right now."

Happy that he had made a friend, Raj did not think at all about what he might be faced with.

Chapter Seven

The student nurse accompanied Paula and Raj into the room where a boy of about twelve lay on a gurney, writhing, and moaning. He was connected to ECG monitors and a finger probe that registered his oxygen level, and this alarm was bleeping frantically. The machine showed an oxygen level of 95 percent. Raj noticed right away that there was some bruising on his right lower chest.

A nurse was trying to get a blood pressure cuff on the boy. She glanced at Raj as he came in and said, "Doctor, I haven't been able to get an IV in him – he keeps moving too much."

Raj grabbed the boy's chart and checked his name.

"What happened, Andy?"

The boy stopped writhing for a moment. "I dunno, doc. I was skateboarding, and this guy hit me with his truck."

"Well, Andy, it looks like you got hit pretty bad."

"Oh man, my dad's going to kill me." The boy looked about to cry.

Paula moved up to the head of the stretcher and put an oxygen mask on Andy. In a low voice, she said, "Raj, I don't know about this. He just doesn't look right. His oxygen level is a bit low, and I've put him on six liters of oxygen by mask. "

The nurse finally got the boy's blood pressure. "It's 83/46," she said. "I'm going to get Rick in here." She rushed out.

Raj decided he'd better do something – anything. "Okay, let's start an IV and run Ringers Lactate," he said.

He held the boy's arm still while the student nurse swabbed it and tried to insert the IV catheter. A voice over the overhead intercom intoned: "Code Blue, ER Room 3. Code Blue, ER Room 3."

The nurse reappeared and told them that Rick couldn't come. He was in Room 3, treating a middle-aged man with a heart attack and cardiogenic shock. Paula and Raj could hear the commotion down the hall. Raj told the student nurse to find another doctor and to be quick.

Andy was still squirming. "Doc, I need to sit up. I need to catch my breath or something."

Paula tried to sit him up, and Raj could see that he was not doing well. His oxygen level had slipped to 92 percent. Then the alarm on the pulse monitor began to beep louder and in a lower tone. The boy's oxygen level was dropping despite the additional oxygen. Raj felt anguished. There was danger here - real danger.

Paula quietly said, "I don't like this. He's struggling, and he can't breathe." She ran to the supplies cupboard and flung the door open.

Andy was still squirming and even tried to talk, but he was weakening and was holding his chest. Paula ran back and put a full resuscitation oxygen mask on him.

"Raj, I think he's going to arrest on us! We have to do something!"

The student nurse ran back in. "No one can come. They're doing CPR on the guy two beds down, and they've shocked him twice."

Raj absorbed what the student had said and felt time compress – a sucking feeling as if he were going under. The boy's oxygen level was still sliding:

89 percent.

84 percent.

Paula was frantically trying to stick a breathing tube down Andy's throat, but he struggled against her.

78 percent.

Raj knew that when blood flow to the brain ceases, brain death comes quickly. If he didn't do something now, Andy would be nothing more than an organ donor.

His mind screamed, *Solve the problem. SOLVE THE PROBLEM... Electromechanical dissociation... pulmonary embolus... cardiac tamponade...* Subroutines flitted through Raj's mind as he tried to remember... Multiple voices were now yelling: Paula's, the nurse's, the voice in his head.

"Raj, we've got to do something! Let's get my staff doc in here!" Paula shouted.

72 percent.

68 percent.

Andy had turned blue and pale – the look of death!

Raj stared helplessly at Andy, sure that he was witnessing his death. There was something wrong with the appearance of Andy's chest – the right side was too large, and the veins in his neck were bulging. He had stopped moving.

Barely aware of what he was doing, Raj grabbed a large intravenous needle, pulled the safety cap off, and plunged it into the side of Andy's chest. Blood and air under high pressure shot out the back of the needle and sprayed Raj in the face.

"Paula," Raj said, "don't try and intubate him. He's got a tension pneumothorax. We have to get a chest tube in."

Andy started to make slow, strained attempts at breathing. Slowly... ever so slowly... the oxygen level came up to 74%... 82%... 87%... 92%... 94%... and then held steady. The alarm stopped at last.

Sweating profusely, Raj tried to sound as if he knew what he was doing.

"Okay, let's put a chest tube in."

An older, white-haired doctor in green surgical scrubs came in with a serious look on his face. "What the hell is going on in here? This nurse came running down the hall into the OR, screaming that a boy was about to die."

Raj stared at him blankly. He had never met this man, who was obviously one of St. Jerome's surgeons.

The nurse spoke up. "Dr. Williamson. Thank you for coming, sir. Dr. Mehta has just run an arrest on this boy,"

Raj summoned the nerve to speak. "The patient was involved in a motor vehicle accident. I believe he sustained blunt trauma to his right thorax. He was deteriorating rapidly, and we were called in to assist. We tried to get the staff doc, but he was running a code."

Paula backed up Raj's story. "Sir, the patient's status deteriorated so quickly; there just wasn't time to get someone else. It looked like a tension pneumo."

The older doctor surveyed the mess in the room and then focused on the large needle in Andy's chest, which was audibly hissing as air passed in and out. "So you went ahead and treated him?"

"It was the only course of action, sir. The boy was dying," said Paula.

Rick and Sandra both burst into the room. "Raj! What the hell happened?"

The older doctor looked at Rick and then at the patient. "These two interns just saved this kid's life."

"Is he okay?" asked Rick.

"He's okay, Rick. I'll take over," Williamson said. "He's going to be admitted under my service," He nodded at Raj and Paula. "You two stay here."

The nurse was getting surgical equipment ready, speaking to the older doctor with a great deal of respect. Obviously, he was important.

"Dr. Williamson, will you need a chest tube tray?" she asked.

"Actually, no," he replied. "Dr. Mehta will place the chest tube, and I'll be assisting. Get him a 16-French chest tube with trocar in, 10 CC of lidocaine 2 percent, and some 3-0 Prolene. And we'll need a stat portable chest X-ray."

Andy was starting to come around. Paula noticed him moving and quickly started an intravenous line so that she could administer medication quickly.

"Holy crap!" said Andy. "Did I just die?"

"No, Andy, but you'll be in the hospital for a while," said Raj.

"It doesn't matter. My dad's going to kill me anyway."

Raj asked him, "What does your dad do?"

Andy replied, "He's an officer at the military base. He's away on a mission in Afghanistan, and my grandma's looking after me right now. Jeez! My chest hurts all the way to my arm."

Raj checked Andy's chest. It wasn't quite so overinflated now.

The nurse handed Raj a syringe loaded with a local anesthetic, and he moved closer to the puncture site, which was now covered with antiseptic. His hand was shaking, and Dr. Williamson grabbed it and directed it to exactly where he wanted to freeze, saying to Paula, "Let's give our young friend 1 mg Versed and 25 micrograms fentanyl to help him relax."

Paula gave Andy the drugs via intravenous, and Williamson said to Raj, "Now, Doctor, I want you to make a small incision deep into the chest wall."

Williamson leaned over the boy. "Don't worry. You won't feel a thing. I promise."

Raj did as he was told and gradually probed the incision.

"Good," Dr. Williamson said. "Now feel inside the chest – you'll feel a space. The lining of the lung is quite sensitive, so you may have to put in some more freezing."

As they cut deeper and probed around, Raj felt the lung tissue at his fingertip. The surgeon invited Paula to don a glove and feel the lung moving within the chest.

"So, you didn't bother to get a chest X-ray, and you didn't bother to intubate him. I'm curious. Obviously, you must have been considering a diagnosis of tension pneumo. What finally tipped the scales and made you act?" Dr. Williamson asked.

"I'd run out of other diagnoses," Raj said. "When I saw the neck vessels bulging, I surmised that they were kinking."

"So you eliminated everything else," the surgeon said. "Even then, you probably didn't believe what you were seeing, did you? I suspect one of the lower ribs impaled the lung and acted like a flap valve to create the pneumo."

"I didn't believe it until it was staring me in the face," Raj said.

"That's the thing, isn't it? Trusting your instincts at a moment when you have imperfect information is always the hardest thing. You two did a fine job."

They finished the procedure by inserting a chest tube hooked up to suction. Williamson leaned over Andy again. "You got really lucky there, son. These two docs saved your bacon. We'll call your grandmother."

Dr. Williamson turned to Raj. "This boy is your patient now. I don't care if you're working in the ER. I expect you to round on him daily until he's ready to go home. You saved his life – that means he's yours for the duration."

With that, he left the room. Sandra said she would call the

grandmother and also arrange for Andy to be transferred upstairs to a ward, and she left too.

Raj had forgotten the blood spatter on his face, and now Paula wiped it off with a green OR towel, a very gentle touch, and a smile. Their adventure had cemented their friendship.

Chapter Eight

Diana was sitting in the dreary little office, sipping coffee and nibbling a muffin. It was 8:00 a.m., and she was already annoyed. Yesterday, she left a message for Dr. Mehta, but he had not come in to sign his contract and insurance forms, although the other interns had. It was stupid of him to put off signing them. If something bad were to happen, there would be no record that he was employed at the hospital, and he wouldn't be covered for medical malpractice. She shrugged. There wasn't much she could do about it.

A few minutes later, a young man in a lab coat came in. Diana looked up and saw a guy with straight black hair and a penetrating gaze that made her a bit uncomfortable. He looked serious as if he were in a hurry to rush off and do something important.

"Hi, I got a call to come in and sign some forms," he said.

"It's Dr. Mehta, isn't it? I was expecting you yesterday," she said.

"Sorry. I was really busy yesterday."

"You need to fill in your employment and insurance forms, and I have to get some other information."

"What other information?"

"We need to know that your immunizations are up to date and you have no communicable diseases – and, of course, where to deposit
58

your pay. We should also get your next of kin. Are you married?" she asked.

"No…" Raj seemed flustered by the question.

"Who do you want to be listed as next of kin?" Diana asked.

He paused for a moment. "I guess my next of kin would be my sister, Chandra. I'll give you her number."

Diana fetched the forms, attached them to a clipboard, and handed them to him. She was wearing a short, light sundress as it was a warm day. She suddenly felt uncomfortable under his gaze. She quickly sat back down. He surveyed the forms and finally offered her a smile, which gave his face an open, honest look.

"I forgot to bring a pen. May I borrow one?" he asked.

"Sure. So, how do you like St. Jerome?" asked Diana, handing him her pen.

"It's been great so far. It's nice to be in a community hospital rather than a big hospital in Toronto." He took a seat and started to read the forms.

"Save any lives yet?" Diana joked.

It looked as if he was going to say something, but then he didn't. Instead, he looked around at the prints hung in the office and said, "I like the one with the vase of sunflowers. It's by Van Gogh, isn't it?"

"Yes," said Diana. "I chose that one myself."

The intern nodded. "One of my professors theorized that Van Gogh was schizophrenic. Something about his ear and his choice of colors."

Diana had heard doctors trivialize the accomplishments of other people by associating them with a disease, and she snapped. "I'm quite sure your professor never met Van Gogh – so really, what would he know about him?" she said.

Raj stared at her for a moment; he didn't know what to say.

"Sorry… of course… You're absolutely right. Here are your forms. Hope you have a nice day." He said stiffly as he hurried out of the office.

Diana slouched in her chair. The intern hadn't looked back at her. He was just another arrogant know-it-all.

It would be an hour before any patients arrived, so she used the computer to hunt for an acting job in Toronto and soon found something interesting: a job at a dinner theater for a play called Tony and Tina's Wedding. There was supposed to be a lot of audience participation. She emailed the production company asking for an audition. Then she emailed her friend Kal, who was still in India working for a large multinational manufacturer. Her parents had been nagging her to get married. Diana told Kal that if she were a guy, she was sure that they wouldn't bug her so much.

Diana was writing another email when her father arrived. "You look busy!" he said. "How are things going?"

"Well," Diana replied. "I have been busy. I've got all the interns' forms signed."

"Thank God! This intern business has been quite exhausting. I'll be in my office reviewing some test results. Let me know when the first patient is here."

Diana turned back to the computer and continued to look for acting jobs. She was debating whether to run away to Hollywood when the first patients arrived, which did nothing to persuade her to stay in St. Jerome.

The day drifted on slowly, and Diana was about to fall into a midafternoon stupor when her email blipped. There were two new messages. One invited her to audition for Tony and Tina's Wedding. The other email was from her old boyfriend, Star Yanofsky, and she opened it, filled with trepidation. She had not expected to hear from him ever again after their breakup several years ago when Star had moved away. He had been a hockey player with the local St. Jerome Vikings – a hometown Viking hero, as he put it.

Hey, baby. It's Star! Guess what? I've been drafted by the Toronto Maple Leafs, and I'm coming back to play for them! I'm also doing a little modeling gig for Rococo. They're calling the ad campaign Star and Stripes – get it? Miss you, baby. Let's get together. Will be in TO in a few weeks. XXX /// The forward slashes are my signature stripe on the underwear. So cool! See you soon.

Star xxx (***)

Diana gritted her teeth. Rococo was an international fashion house – how on earth did he get a job like that?

Star had a way of intruding on her life like no one else. He had been her first boyfriend when they were in high school. Young, handsome, and a hockey player – everyone loved him. Her friends would ask her about intimate details of their relationship, and when they weren't questioning her and making nice, they were hitting on him. They broke up just after she left for university. She could never be a 'puck bunny'. It seemed now that his dreams had come true. But how on earth did he also wind up being a fashion model?

St. Jerome was a hockey town. Her father had gone to the local games and had even volunteered to be the team doctor. Diana, who was an only child, often suspected that her father wanted a boy. Star's father was a local attorney, and his family was Ukrainian and quite wealthy. Everyone seemed to think the two of them would get married after graduation, but it never happened. Hearing from him did make her a bit nostalgic.

Her mind drifted back to their visit to the family cottage after high school graduation, when her parents had allowed all the grads to go. Diana had thought they were each other's first. Now that she thought about it, she probably wasn't his first, but it was still special. They had smoked a joint and got a little drunk. It had been easy because they could hear everyone else in the cottage doing it. Everyone there hit a home run!

Diana was shaken out of her reverie, a little out of breath, by the beeping of the hospital's internal phone line. She picked up the phone, and a voice said, "Please hold for the CEO."

"This is Wendy Fletcher, the CEO. Can you put Dr. Sinclair on the line?"

Diana knew this was probably important. She opened the door to her father's office and mouthed that the CEO was on the line. He picked up his receiver immediately. "Wendy, what can I do for you?"

Diana went back to her desk and was about to put the phone on the cradle when she heard them talking. She had forgotten to put the line on hold. Someone sounded angry. She put her hand over the speaker and listened.

"John, I heard your interns got into some trouble yesterday," said Wendy.

"What do you mean?"

"They weren't adequately supervised. John, they could have killed someone! I'm devastated. Think about this young boy's family. I'm afraid I'm going to have to report this to the chairman of the board."

"What are you talking about? As I understand it, Dr. Mehta

63

and Dr. Johnson saved that young boy's life!"

"They should never have been put in a position where they had to make those decisions. They should have spoken to their manager, and she would have allocated the necessary manpower to deal with the situation."

"Do you have any idea what you're talking about?" Sinclair was exasperated. "If they'd done that, we'd be facing a coroner's inquest. The press would be all over us as the hospital that failed a young boy!"

"John, I agreed to take on your gang of junior MDs only because the previous CEO had agreed. But things are going to be different here. The minister put me in charge to make this hospital run more efficiently, or else it will be closed."

"Listen, Wendy. I know you don't want this hospital closed. Think about the community it was built for."

"John, you don't run this hospital; I do," Fletcher barked. "I have an MBA, and I know the Minister of health personally. We are trying to transform healthcare. If that means this hospital has to close, then so be it. I'm trying to be part of a solution. And you and your little intern squad had better make sure that you follow the rules, or I'll personally make sure that their hospital privileges are cut off."

"Wendy – can't you see that these guys are heroes? That boy would have died. And you don't call a manager when someone's about to die. You tell the chairman that!" Dad sounded furious.

"John, you should be aware that you and any other doctor at this hospital can be replaced. If anything happens with those interns – and I mean anything – I will hold you responsible."

"That's just fine –"

Click. The CEO hung up.

Diana heard her father slam the phone down and quickly replaced her receiver. He came out holding his briefcase, his jaw clenched and his face flushed. "If anyone calls, tell them I'm in the ER."

"Yes, Doctor," she replied. She had never seen her father this upset before.

When she left the office later that day, her mind was filled with questions. Would she get a job in Toronto? Would she get together with Star? What did the hospital CEO mean about closing the hospital? Were Dr. Mehta and Dr. Johnson in trouble? It didn't sound like trouble – they had saved someone, and her father had tried to defend them. She had always thought of her dad as invincible, but he was under terrible strain, she realized. He'd been more tired than usual lately, and Diana realized that even the strongest of men couldn't last forever.

***

Raj, Raj, Raj! Why do you do these things to yourself? You're a total spaz! The only thing you could have done worse would have been to start talking about how your mother makes frozen dinners for you!

Raj was replaying in his head the brief interaction with Dr. Sinclair's secretary. He had managed to look stupid – or worse, arrogant. And she had called him out on it. Why did he always wind up sounding extra wrong and stupid when a good-looking girl was around? Kryptonite! The girl's sundress had made her look like a fashion model. And what was with those markings on her leg? They looked vaguely familiar. Were they Sanskrit letters?

Raj was sitting at his kitchen table eating a microwaved dinner his mother had made. He was pondering the nature of sex as if it were an equation that could be solved. The paradox was that a young man wanting sex wasn't get any because of his off-putting desperation, and the only way around the problem was to not want sex. Raj was sure that if he didn't really want sex, somehow women would recognize this and would want to sleep with him. Wasn't that what happened to Mr. Spock on Star Trek?

Raj finished his meal and started searching online for answers. He learned that in the nineteenth century, a substance called saltpeter had been given to prisoners to reduce the incidence of masturbation. He also learned that a drug used in the treatment of prostate cancer would be effective as it induced "male menopause". Unfortunately, these treatments had side effects, and Raj rejected them.

No wiser for all this research, Raj went to bed with the Kama

Sutra, which had become his companion at night. He studied the fine illustrations of ancient people holding each other in semi-nude poses. Were these people any different from his own generation? Did humans ever really change? No, he decided. Despite the Internet and telephones and cars, we were all still the same. People still needed one another.

Chapter Nine

Three weeks later, on a rare day off work, Raj got ready to visit his family in Toronto. Before he headed out, he ran through his mental list:

- Nice shoes – Rockport's. Check.
- New GAP ensemble – copied from a mannequin in a store window. Check.
- Teeth – brushed and flossed. Check.
- Shaved – he had even trimmed his eyebrows. Check.
- New car – purchased very recently. Check.

Raj had bought a second-hand Honda Civic from Leonard Chang, an old computer-science classmate. He would have to return the license plate – CHANGSTER – when he got a replacement. Len was making a fortune programming for a company that specialized in violent and often pornographic video games in Toronto. He had practically given Raj the little Honda free in exchange for the promise that, one day, Raj would prescribe him erectile dysfunction medication.

He was hoping the car would make him look cool, which was his new goal. The clothes he'd brought from home made him look as though he was going to a funeral and doctors no longer wore grey flannel, white shirts, and brogues. So he had bought a leather jacket and Terminator-style sunglasses to go with his black Honda.

Raj enjoyed the ninety-minute drive back home. He was looking forward to seeing his sister, Chandra, who was studying media and communications at Ryerson University. It was a pseudo-high-tech kind, of course, that was supposed to lead to a job, but lately, it had involved film studies. His father said this sounded suspicious, like watching movies and eating popcorn.

The most important reason to go home, however, was to eat, and as he neared Toronto, his mouth began to water. Raj's mother was overweight and had high blood pressure and diabetes, but she was the finest cook Raj knew. He realized that the delectable, spicy smells emanating from her kitchen would stay in his clothes for days, but he didn't care.

The Mehta house was a nondescript East York bungalow near Danforth Avenue's Greektown. It was largely an immigrant neighborhood, but lately, it had become pricey, like the rest of Toronto, even though the houses were tiny. Theirs was the kind of practical, functional home where immigrant dreams are made. A cloak of familiarity, like a long-dormant memory, enveloped Raj as he entered and saw his parents' smiling faces.

"Where's Chandra?" he asked.

"With her boyfriend!" Radhu did not sound happy. He looked Raj up and down and remarked that his clothes looked unprofessional. "I shall have to take you to Eugene again."

"No, Dad. The clothes are fine. I keep them for work only so

I don't wear them out."

"That is good thinking, son."

Raj asked about Chandra and learned that her current boyfriend, trying to emulate Quentin Tarantino, worked at a "high-end" video store that specialized in foreign films. Radhu was not impressed. Raj had not yet met the latest man in Chan's life. Raj had always been a little envious of Chan, whom he thought had been endowed with much better looks than he had. He also thought she was at least as smart as he was, but during college, most of her nights were taken up with partying, not studying. Her tales of clubbing, rarely mentioned in front of their parents, usually left Raj feeling sorry for himself.

He made straight for the kitchen, where Mena had covered the table with food cooked especially for him. Radhu served him a Carlsberg beer, and he tucked into the dishes of curried meats, lightly cooked vegetables, pickles, and roti. After the bland food he had been eating, he was struck by all the intense colors and aromas: dark green peppers, red chili, the brightest mangoes, and the summery smell of cilantro. Even the rice had been subtly flavored, and its color changed by a pinch or two of turmeric.

As Raj ate, he talked about his experiences in the hospital Emergency Department. His parents seemed impressed, but Radhu wanted to know whether he was keeping up with his studies. He lied and said that he was studying hard, thankful that it was hard to talk between mouthfuls of food.

70

His parents began telling him the family news. Aunt Shamila, Mena's sister, had been particularly annoying of late. She was an 'alpha female,' or so Radhu called her. Shamila was now a successful real estate agent. Her husband, Gustad, a restaurateur, had expanded his business into making what he called "the Finest Frozen Indian Entrées West of Bombay" and was selling them in retail. Mena and Shamila had a long-running rivalry, and the latest development involved Raj becoming a doctor. Shamila had wanted to top that. Roger, her own son, had become an investment banker, she'd reported, and was now vastly wealthy and living in the Chelsea area of London.

Mena had fresh news about Roger. "Apparently, he is going out with the daughter of an industrialist named Khan. The family came from India to London – they live on Grosvenor Crescent – where the billionaire set live."

Radhu added that this industrialist was a fellow from India who owned a steel conglomerate that had just purchased several factories in the UK. His daughter had gone to an English boarding school and then Cambridge University. She enjoyed riding and playing Polo.

Raj asked the girl's name.

"Her name is Uma Khan," Mena said. "The family has only one daughter and no other children." She showed Raj a photo of Roger and Uma mid-jump astride their horses, with "Winning - at the Royal Berkshire Club" written underneath. "Apparently, this Polo and riding

Club is quite close to Windsor Castle and an amusement park called Lego Land." Royalty always impressed Raj's parents.

Raj was struck by the paucity of words, but the picture said it all. Roger was rich and cool, and he was not. Roger had slimmed down a bit, and Uma had the look of Indian nobility, her hair perfect under her riding helmet.

Radhu spoke up. "I wonder how he met her."

"I think Roger met her at work, and they both have an interest in horses," Mena said.

Raj knew that Roger's only interest in horses was how to make money on them and was surprised he had suddenly taken an interest in riding them.

"You know, Raj, we have to go to Aunt Shamila's house tomorrow. It's Gustad's sixty-first birthday," his mother said.

Raj cringed. He hated family functions but had to go because his grandmother would be there, and the only time she ever saw him was at family events.

"Can't you tell them I'm not in town?" Raj begged.

"No, Raj," chided Mom. "That would be lying, and Grandma wants to talk to you about her arthritis."

He was thinking about how to weasel out of going when Chandra came in, dressed in blue jeans, a stylish leather jacket, and high heels – her Beyoncé outfit. She sat down beside Raj. "I see you're in your usual place doing your usual thing – eating. So, have you saved anyone yet, Doctor Boy?"

"Maybe," Raj said. "How's Quentin Tarantino?"

Chandra made a face and said that Quentin – his name actually was Quentin – was trying to get a screenplay picked up by a movie studio.

"Right! So many careers have been launched while working at video stores." Chan punched him hard on the arm.

Chan helped herself to a plate of food and asked about Uncle Gustad's party. "I hope Sir Roger, Lord of Mississauga, isn't there." Chan found Roger and his family's pretensions of grandeur annoying.

Raj showed her the picture of Roger and his girlfriend.

"Wow, Raj, he looks positively Firthian."

"Firthian?"

"Colin Firthian, Pride and Prejudice mini-series worthy. Does he now have a manservant taking pictures of him?" Chan asked.

"I think it was his butler or the butler's butler."

* * *

The next day, they piled into Radhu's Honda sedan and drove to an upscale suburb of Mississauga. Shamila and Gustad's house was enormous and had a large circular driveway.

"Here it is... the Taj Mahal," Radhu said, as he always did whenever they arrived. He didn't like visiting his in-laws because of their wealth and pretense. Shamila was particularly fond of telling everyone that her Mercedes was vastly superior to other vehicles. Radhu was known to get into heated arguments with her about his car, which he insisted was more reliable.

Aunt Shamila was outside greeting people. "My dears, you have arrived!" she cooed in a newly acquired faux English accent. "Come in, come in. We're serving tea and scones in the backyard."

Chandra looked at Raj with the silent message: no samosas. He half expected Shamila to break into "God Save the Queen".

The house was decorated in gaudy splendor and featured several large statues of elephants, lots of gilded ornaments, and splashes of jade and Italian marble. The statue of a multi-armed Hindu god, with rubies for eyes, dominated the foyer. Raj stared at it until his father nudged him and said, "Don't stare too much at it, Raj, lest it brings you an evil omen." A large family portrait looked down on them from the wall.

Shamila's husband, the stout, elderly Gustad, came forward to greet them. He was balding and had a fringe of hair that made him look like an overweight Franciscan monk. Radhu and Mena wished him a happy birthday.

Gustad spotted Raj. "Oh, the doctor! I shall have to watch my cholesterol lest you put me on a diet!" His jowls and absent chin reminded Raj of Jabba the Hut. Gustad ignored Chandra, which was both typical and rude of him.

Raj spent the afternoon mostly listening to his grandma, aunts, uncles, and cousins. Shamila and Gustad made sure they told everyone about their son, Roger.

"You know, we were so worried when he moved to England because the weather is so damp. We really had no idea just how fabulously successful he would become. He couldn't come to Toronto for his dad's birthday because he's far too important to the bank and they simply could not give him time off." Then, Shamila announced that Roger and Uma were engaged, and the family was now obliged to attend "a grand wedding in England next spring." Almost everyone was excited at the prospect, especially the old ladies, who loved a good wedding.

"You know, really, it was I who got Roger and his girlfriend together." Shamila was bursting to tell everyone. "You see, Roger has terrible allergies, and they were acting up in London. I suggested that he see an herbalist – you know, the Royal Family uses them. Roger met Uma at the herbalist's, and they realized that they both worked at the same bank. They both have allergies and can only eat non-GMO gluten-free diets."

Raj was feeling sick, not because of Shamila's story, but because he was having a major allergic reaction to all the flowers in the living room. His nose was running, and his left eye was swelling shut.

"Raj, you don't look so good. You should see a doctor!" Gustad laughed at his own joke and brought in some tissues. "You know, Raj, what you need is a good woman to look after you." Only Gustad could turn an allergic reaction into a sign that Raj needed to get married.

Mena whipped out a Ventolin puffer. Raj didn't need it, but she still puffed it around his face like perfume.

The Mehta family left the party early with a box of tissues and the address of Shamila's herbalist. An antihistamine that Mena had in the car was the only thing that helped.

On the ride home, Raj's parents expressed their annoyance with the various relatives they had met. His mother was especially peeved. "She put all those flowers in the living room so that Raj would have an allergy attack, I'm sure of it!"

"Is Shamila happy that Roger is marrying this girl?" Radhu asked her. "They can't know that much about the family."

Mena snickered. "She is only unhappy that she can't take all the credit for it – you know what a social climber she is." She fell silent for a moment, then said, "Shamila spoke to me before we left. She knows of several girls from nice families and she had them all lined up for Roger. Now that Roger won't be meeting them, she thinks Raj should."

"What is it with that woman? She should mind her own business!" Radhu said, glancing at Raj to see his reaction.

The whole wedding thing seemed to have sprung out of nowhere. A few weeks ago, his parents would talk only about how happy they were that he had graduated. Now, at the point in his life when his sole intention was to join the legions of young men who spend their twenties drinking and carousing, his parents were talking marriage!

They drove on in silence until Chandra spoke up. "You know, Mom, Raj might not want any help meeting girls, especially ones that are 'all lined up'."

Mena turned to her and spoke sternly. "Unlike you, always going out to clubs and dancing with every Tom, Dick, and whatever his name is, Raj has devoted himself to his studies. He should have some help from us."

Raj wanted to mount some sort of feeble protest, but he realized his mother was right. It's hard to argue about your dating potential when you have a runny nose.

Chan, who always spoke her mind, retorted, "I'm not going to spend my holiday going to England so that I can hang around at a wedding!"

The thought of traveling to England for the wedding did strike the family as rather pricey and just the sort of expensive and pompous thing the family liked to burden each other with. Raj anticipated having to go and was already worrying whether he would have a date for the wedding. Everyone brings a date to a wedding – but all the way to England?

Chapter Ten

Diana was excited. She had just received an email telling her she had the part in "Tony and Tina's Wedding". It would be her very first acting job. She had auditioned on the weekend, and it had gone well. The part as a bridesmaid was neither big nor important, but there were some dance moves she would have to learn, which looked like fun. The pay didn't impress her – a little more than minimum wage and not enough to allow her to quit her job and move to Toronto. Instead, she planned to stay in St. Jerome and drive to Toronto for performances, which were only Friday and Saturday evenings and Sunday matinées. She could still work as her father's secretary and keep her little apartment. It wasn't much, but it was a start.

Diana was about to text all her friends the news when she noticed that Star had emailed her again. She hadn't replied to his first email yet. She wasn't sure why; perhaps it was pride. But she had a job now, and she considered seeing Star when she was next in Toronto. Her new job wasn't as prestigious as modeling for Rococo and playing in the NHL, but it was better than just working for her father as his secretary.

The phone rang, interrupting her reverie. It was Wendy Fletcher, the CEO, looking for Dan Freedman.

"You mean Doctor Freedman?" Diana asked.

" Yes, Doctor Freedman – the intern. Aren't you supposed to

know where he is?" The CEO sounded testy.

"He's on his surgery rotation," Diana said. "He'll be either on the surgical ward or in the operating room assisting with orthopedic surg—"

The CEO cut her off. "Just find him and see to it that he presents himself to my office at four o'clock."

"He might have emergency surgery at that time—" Diana tried to answer, but the CEO interrupted.

"Advise Doctor Freedman that he works for me and that he'd better be here at four p.m."

"Should I let the Chief of Staff know?"

"No. This is a private meeting." The phone went dead.

Diana made a few calls before she reached Dan, who asked what the CEO wanted. Diana was unable to help him out. She remembered that Raj and Paula had got in trouble with the CEO the week before and wanted to warn Dan, but she wasn't sure what to warn him about. She considered telling her father, but then she thought that would be unprofessional, and so she didn't. She didn't know what was going on, but she knew that her dad and the CEO were at odds.

* * *

Raj's triumph with Andy had secured his position in the ER.

Sandra no longer assigned him the strange patients and treated him more like a staff doctor. The nursing staff frequently asked him how they should handle a certain patient. It all came as a surprise to him.

Raj continued to check in on Andy even though he was not attached to the surgical service in the hospital. When the Chief of Surgery tells you to look after someone, you do. He had reviewed Andy's x–rays with Dr. Williamson, who peppered Raj with questions about the lung. Raj had held his own when asked about the anatomical landmarks of the middle lobe of the right lung and what to do with serious blunt trauma to the thorax. Perversely, the more answers he got right, the harder the questions got. Williamson was testing him, and Raj was relieved when he was finally told to 'read up on a device called a Pluero-Vac'.

In the short time, he'd been on the surgical ward, Andy had endeared himself to the staff. He rarely complained and ate whatever was given to him with a ravenous appetite. Raj liked him, and they usually ended up chatting about baseball and hockey. Andy's grandma was supposed to be looking after him while his father was overseas, but Andy admitted that she was a little mixed up, and he managed by himself most of the time.

While Raj was visiting Andy at the start of the week, a middle-aged woman peered in the door.

"Excuse me. Is this Andrew Fournier's room?" she asked.

"Yes, it is. I'm Dr. Mehta. Are you a relative?"

"No, I'm from the Children's Aid Society." The woman sounded haughty. "Are you aware that Andrew's grandmother has advanced dementia and is being admitted to a nursing home?"

"No," said Raj. "I was not aware of that."

"When he's ready for discharge, his father has to be home or else he will be placed in foster care."

"What?"

"Andrew is a minor."

"I'm sure Andy's father will be available, Miss?" said Raj.

"My name is Ruth Krendell. I'm in charge of Andrew's case file."

"Okay," said Raj. "Andy will be here for several more days. In the interim, we'll see what we can put together."

The woman stared at Andy for a moment and took her leave.

Andy had started to cry. "Whatever you do, doc, don't call my dad," he pleaded.

"Why not, Andy? Your father would want to know you had an accident. He has to look after you for a while."

"No! Doc, you don't know my father. All kinds of people depend on him. He's all the way in Afghanistan, and he's in charge of a team. They depend on him. He told me I was supposed to stay out of trouble and that if he left Afghanistan, other people in his unit could get hurt. I'll do the foster thing, doc. It doesn't matter. My dad says I'm supposed to be tough – like him."

Raj didn't know what to do. He didn't want to involve Dr. Williamson; it was his job to handle the problem.

He returned to the ER and continued his day. He knew he was out of his depth with this issue and spoke with Sandra. She listened carefully and said she would make some calls on Andy's behalf.

Working in the ER kept Raj busy dealing with all kinds of people and their many problems. Like the other interns, he was under considerable work stress, and he and Paula had talked about getting together with the other two to let off steam and talk about how they were coping. Dan was working in the surgical department, and he and Paula were frequently in the ER. They had not seen much of Kelly as she was in Labor and Delivery, and pregnant patients were sent directly up to the fifth floor.

As Raj walked past the cast room, he spotted Dan placing a splint on a young woman's arm and decided he'd get things moving. He caught Dan's eye and beckoned him into the hallway.

"Hey, Dan. Want to get together with us this Friday night?" he said

"Sure, Raj. I've got a date on Saturday, but Friday works."

"You've got a date?" Raj was impressed.

"Yeah, this super hot dietician. She works up on the medical floor."

"Nice!" Raj was more than a little envious. "I'll set it up with Paula and Kelly."

"Sure thing, bro. Hey, nice job with that kid! You're making us all look good. By the way, did you get called to the CEO's office?" asked Dan.

"No, I didn't." Raj was puzzled. Why would the CEO want to see an intern?

"Do you know if anyone else did?"

"I'm pretty sure Paula didn't. I haven't seen Kelly, though."

Dan looked uncomfortable. "I got a call from the CEO's office telling me to meet her at four this afternoon. Why would she want to see me, Raj?"

"I don't really know, Dan," said Raj. "Maybe she likes you?"

* * *

"Raj, I've called the base," Sandra said. "Andy Fournier's father is a bomb-disposal expert, and he can't be brought back for another month." She had been on the telephone for several hours, dealing with various people, and had finally been put through to the base commander, who was reluctant to tell Andy's father that his son had been injured. The military officer's work was "sensitive," though he didn't explain exactly what that meant.

"I don't know what to do, Sandra. They don't tell you about this stuff in medical school," said Raj.

"I know, Raj. I'm stuck – and I've been working here for almost twenty years." Sandra sounded frustrated.

"What happens to a kid who goes into foster care?" Raj asked.

"Well, it's supposed to be good – three meals a day and regular school. He'll probably get moved out of town."

"Why?"

"He'd be a crisis placement, which means he'll have to go anywhere they found a family able to take him."

"This isn't good, Sandra. Andy's dad is going to come home and find his house uninhabited, his mother in a nursing home, and his son in foster care!"

"Raj, I'm trying my best. Let me see if I can figure something out."

"I can keep him for another day or so," offered Raj.

"Okay, Raj," said Sandra. "It's a start."

* * *

Just before four p.m., Dan wandered up to the CEO's office on the top level of the hospital. The office turned out to be an executive suite, with several small meeting rooms and a teleconference room with a large table and a large monitor at the far end.

The receptionist in the outer office looked up from her desk as he approached but continued typing, making Dan wait a few minutes before she finally looked up and asked what he wanted.

"I'm Dan Freedman. The CEO asked to see me."

"I wasn't told she was having any meetings this afternoon." The young woman pressed a button and a slightly older woman came out. Both of them were dressed in pant suits, and both had dark, straight hair. Neither one of them smiled. The older woman introduced herself as the CEO's executive assistant, Jennifer.

"I wasn't told about this meeting," she said. "You are…?"

"Dan Freedman, one of the interns. I got a message to come up here."

"Why wasn't I notified of this meeting?" Jennifer asked the receptionist

"I didn't know about it, either." The receptionist looked intimidated.

"Maybe I can come back another time. I don't want to interrupt anything important," said Dan.

At that moment, Wendy Fletcher came out of her office.

Seeing the three women together, Dan realized that the other two were dressed to match their boss – dark suits and black leather pumps. Even their expressions looked similar.

Wendy ushered Jennifer and Dan into the inner meeting room, where a large TV was on. The Minister of Health was on screen, talking with Wendy, who now turned and addressed him.

"Jim, I know that next year is an election year. Whatever you do, do not visit any hospitals – especially the ones dealing with an outbreak of influenza or even head lice. No one likes to see a politician in a hairnet or an antiviral mask."

"Thanks, Wendy," the minister replied. "I appreciate your help on the political front."

"No problem, Jim. I'll be getting back to you regarding this particular institution over the next few months."

Wendy clicked the remote and the screen went blank. She sat down at the large table and picked up a tray with several small turd-like lumps on it.

"Would anyone like to try one of my muffins? They're fat-free and gluten-free and lactose-free."

Dan saw Jennifer cringe ever so subtly, but she took one. Dan did too. The muffins were heavy, denser than any other baked thing he had ever had.

Holding her muffin, Jennifer asked, "Will you need anything else, Wendy?"

"No, Jen. Leave Dan and me for a while and see that no one interrupts."

Dan sat down and nibbled at the muffin. It tasted like Play-Doh, with a slightly meaty aftertaste. He stuck it in his pocket and mumbled something about eating it later.

Wendy got up and moved to the chair beside him. "Dan, as you know, I was appointed to this hospital a short while ago. You and your fellow interns were matched here, and I'm sure it was a surprise."

"I think most of us wanted to go to a smaller hospital," Dan said. "I wanted a small hospital because I thought I'd get more responsibility."

"Of course, Dan, but here's the thing – if this hospital closes, I'm prepared to get you an internship at Toronto General Hospital." Wendy leaned back in her chair.

"Why would St. Jerome's close?" Dan asked. "It's in an underserviced area. Heck, we're so busy in the surgical ward that there are times we have to park people waiting for surgery in the ER hallway."

"Dan, it's a lot more complicated. The government wants to restructure the health care system, and I'm not sure St. Jerome's fits the plan."

Dan was puzzled. "What does this have to do with me? I'm just an intern."

"Dan, I might need you to discuss this with the public. Perhaps you can help the community understand the changes. Like an intern spokesman…"

Wendy crossed her shapely legs and leaned toward Dan. He could smell her perfume. She touched the back of his hand with her finely manicured nails.

Dan swallowed. He was totally unprepared for this. "So … so you're saying that, if the hospital closes, the internship program closes," he stammered.

"That's right, Dan," purred Wendy. "But I don't want to see you and your little friends stuck, so I'll make sure everyone gets into another hospital."

"You mean the other interns?"

"Yes, Dan – but I'm reserving a special spot at Toronto General just for you."

Wendy smiled slyly. "The others will get in somewhere. There are lots of little hospitals like this one looking for people."

"I'll have to think about this." Dan stared at her hand as it gently touched his.

He stood, but Wendy held onto his hand. "Be careful, Danny

boy, the Wendy Fletcher train moves out of this little backwater soon, and you'll want to hitch a ride."

"I'll get back to you soon, Mrs. Fletcher," said Dan, eager to escape.

"Dan, Dan, Danny boy, it's Wendy to you," she cooed, giving his hand a squeeze and flashing her white teeth.

Dan left the executive suite feeling horny but also a bit dirty. What the hell had just happened?

Chapter Eleven

Diana was sipping a Diet Coke on the sidewalk patio of Café Nervosa in Yorkville, an area of downtown Toronto frequented by an eclectic mix of money and hipsters. The day was warm, and a large lunchtime crowd was strolling along the narrow street. A brand new Porsche Boxster convertible pulled up outside the café, and Star jumped out. He was wearing a black leather jacket and aviator sunglasses. Star's face was classically handsome, and he sported a star-shaped birthmark on his left cheek, for which his parents had named him. Seeing Diana, he smiled, jumped over the little iron fence, and sat opposite her.

"Hey, baby. Like my new wheels?" he said.

"Very nice, Star. How are you?"

"I'm so good it's unbelievable!"

The waiter approached and asked Star if he wanted a drink.

"Yeah. Do you have protein smoothies?"

"No. We don't make smoothies here." The waiter sounded disapproving.

"I need a high protein shake," said Star. "Can you do that?"

"I can ask the bartender," the waiter sniffed.

Star smiled at Diana but left his sunglasses on. "I've got this great recipe for a high-protein shake. I think it's the same one that David Beckham uses. It's got cacao nips in it – some sort of pure antioxidant."

"Star, they're cacao nibs – it's a raw form of chocolate," said Diana.

"Nah… I think it's nips. Actually, I just wanted to make you say 'nip'. Anyway, it's an amazing shake. Look what it's done for me – I'm totally pumped. Check this out." Star held out his right arm and placed Diana's hand on his biceps; it was rippling hard, and he made it jump up and down.

Despite herself, Diana had to smile. If nothing else, Star was entertaining.

They ordered lunch and chatted while they waited. Diana asked about his parents and his new job as a forward for the Toronto Maple Leafs. He said he would get some ice time when the season started, and in the meantime, he was modeling clothes for an agency in Toronto, and this had led to the deal with Rococo. His agent had told him that people liked his look, especially in a swim thong. Diana had never seen a male thong and wondered what men who wore them did when they had an erection on the beach.

Star looked very, very good – like a young Brad Pitt.

After they had eaten, Diana was telling him about her trip to India when he interrupted. "You know, babe, I've been thinking a lot about you."

"Something nice, I hope?"

"Yeah, baby! I was thinking we should get back together, like old times. You, me, and my little buddy – Big Head Eric. Think about, it, Di? Big Head misses you. Actually, I think he's missing you right now." Diana blushed. Big head Eric was the name he had given to his penis. "C'mon, Di. I know you miss him just a little bit."

"Star, I've got a lot on my plate right now. I'm working for my dad and doing this dinner theater."

"That's okay, babe. We'll figure it out. Now I've gotta' go and meet my personal trainer and dietician. You know they say you are what you eat, but I don't remember eating a sexy beast today, ha, ha! Anyway, I'll call you soon. Maybe you can come to one of my photo shoots. I've got everyone drinking my new smoothie."

Star reached over and took her hand. He gave it a little squeeze and placed it on his thigh. As Diana pulled her hand away, she noticed his watch. It looked very expensive – perhaps a Rolex. Star paid the tab with a hundred-dollar bill, vaulted over the fence, jumped into his car, and sped off.

Diana sat for a few moments, wondering at all the twists and turns life took. There was no man in her life at the moment, and she wasn't the kind of woman who desperately needed one. But Star was exciting and fun. Maybe she'd give him another try.

* * *

Raj and Dan entered the Chinese restaurant where they were to meet Paula and Kelly. It was Friday night, and Raj hoped that getting together with the other interns would become a regular thing.

The two young men took a booth and ordered soft drinks. Dan was happy to have a chance to talk to Raj by himself – he had a lot on his mind.

"Raj, something's come up..." Dan began but faltered. He couldn't think how to put it.

"What's up, man? Is that dietician taking too much of your attention?" Raj teased.

"No... she's perfect, but.."

At that moment, Paula and Kelly came in and joined them in the booth. The four chatted as the waiter took their orders. Unlike Toronto Chinese restaurants, this one offered traditional dishes. The waiter asked each of them, "You want wonton or chicken ball?"

Dan screwed up his nerve to tell the others about his latest encounter with Wendy Fletcher. "Guys, you won't believe this. The CEO called me up to her office and implied that she was going to close the hospital."

"What?" The others were astounded.

Dan went on. "She implied the government wants to close the hospital and that we'd all get moved to different intern positions elsewhere."

"What the hell?" Paula was especially angry.

"There's more, guys. This sounds weird, but the CEO made a pass at me. I think she has a thing for me."

"I knew there was something I didn't like about her!" Kelly looked annoyed.

"I don't know about you guys, but I'm not going to allow that woman to ruin my first year as a doctor!"

Raj agreed. "You know, I really like it here. I don't want to go back to Toronto."

The three of them looked at Dan, who was eating a chicken ball speared on a chopstick. He paused a moment, then nodded his agreement. "Well, what do we do now?" he asked.

Raj replied, "I don't think the CEO can close a hospital all that easily. St. Jerome's is fairly large, and besides, Sinclair would know something about it."

Kelly narrowed her eyes as if she were formulating a plan. "Dan, you have to investigate this."

Paula spoke up. "Yes! You have to be our undercover agent. We want you deep, deep undercover. An undercover lover!"

"Yes... deep under the covers. Leave nothing unexplored,"

Kelly laughed.

They spent most of the rest of the evening talking about the cases they had dealt with. Raj had learned that a large part of the top floor of the hospital had been converted to Geriatrics, and Dr. Antonin Lazar was the supervising physician. Rumor had it that he had been conducting secret research. The four of them decided this was probably boring, and none of them wanted to volunteer to work for him.

Kelly told them that her boyfriend from Montreal was going to visit soon. Paula mentioned her significant other, an Alberta cattle rancher. She wasn't sure she wanted to keep the relationship going. "I don't know… He wants kids, and he's a nice guy. I just don't know if I want to be stuck on a ranch for the rest of my life."

As the others talked, Raj listened and nodded, grateful that no one asked him about his love life. He steered the conversation toward Dan. "What about you and the dietician?"

Dan smiled. "Yeah. I'm going out with her tomorrow."

Kelly and Paula teased that he must be some sort of male slut or man whore.

Dan shrugged. "I can't help it if women find me indescribably attractive."

As they were about to leave, Dan grabbed Raj's arm. "Hey man, why don't you come out with me sometime?"

"What do you mean?"

"We should go out sometime – you and me. I need a wing man."

"I don't get it."

"You will, Raj. We'll go cougar hunting sometime."

Raj finally understood and smiled. This was something that he had only dreamed about. He had few friends in medical school and no social life to speak of. He admired Dan and wondered if his own life was changing.

Back at home, Raj checked his email. A message from his father caught his eye, as usually only his mother and sister emailed him.

Raj, I tried to call you on your cell phone, but you didn't pick up. My friend Ramesh Ramsaran from the old country gave me a call the other day. He has a daughter who is twenty-six. She is an accountant and works at some big international firm called KPMG. She has grown up in Toronto, like you. Maybe you would like to meet her. He sent me a picture of Raj and I have to tell you that you must see her. It would be insulting to Ramesh if you didn't. Let me know when you have a weekend off.

Raj looked at the attachment. It was a LinkedIn profile picture of a beautiful young woman.

He pondered for a moment. What did he have to lose? He chafed at the idea of his parents fixing him up, but at the same time, he knew he could use some help. Reluctantly, he emailed his father that they could meet her family soon on any upcoming weekend.

He finally drifted off to sleep after reading a few chapters of the Kama Sutra. The many pictures and descriptions of sexual encounters had set him adrift on a salty sea – and he was dying of thirst.

Raj dreamed that he was in a castle courtyard, the scent of jasmine drifting in the warm, summery air. He stepped into a room darkened by beaded curtains covering the windows. Persian rugs, low cushions, and chairs were scattered about on the tiled mosaic floor. In the background, a sitar played vaguely familiar music, and Raj heard women's voices, their laughter soft and light, interspersed with the music and a bubbling fountain. He saw a woman reclining on a low upholstered bench dressed in a dark blue sari with an intricate pattern wrought in metallic thread and a slit that bared her midriff and her left leg. She was wearing delicate sandals that accentuated the perfection of her legs and feet. Her face was covered by a silk veil revealing only her warm chestnut-brown eyes. He could tell that, under the veil, she was smiling at him.

"Who are you, and why have you invaded my dream?" he asked.

The woman stared at Raj, and as she stretched her long legs, he saw on her left thigh a strange pattern of Sanskrit symbols. She
98

stood up slowly, took his hand in hers, and whispered, "It is you who has invaded my dream. Come with me. The great wheel is turning."

Chapter Twelve

Raj awoke with a start to the sound of his alarm. He had slept in despite his deeply ingrained habit of getting up at six a.m. He was surprised at this – and surprised at the large erection he was sporting. He knew he'd had a sexy dream, but it was vague now, and he put it out of his mind. He needed to get going. He was, after all, a man of action, and people depended on him. He showered (a cold one), got dressed, and arrived at the ER a full hour before his eight a.m. shift started. It was a rainy morning, and the department wasn't busy. He was in the cafeteria buying coffee when an ER nurse in line behind him reminded him that he was supposed to see a patient on the surgical floor. Raj remembered Andy and took the elevator up to see him. He also remembered that Williamson was in the OR that morning and so was unlikely to be on the ward.

Raj was surprised to see Ruth Krendell from the Children's Aid Society in Andy's room. He had forgotten about her, and his heart sank.

"Good morning, Dr. Mehta." She wasted no time getting to the point. "I understand Andrew is ready for discharge."

"Well, I'd like to review his X–rays before he's finally discharged."

"That's fine," she replied. "I'll wait for him here."

Andy looked unhappy and near to tears. His chest tube had

been removed the previous day. Raj went to the nursing station to check the chest X-ray and make sure that Andy's condition hadn't worsened. *Being part of a military family must be really tough,* he thought. *What had happened to Andy's mom?*

The X-ray showed no signs of air around the lung, and Raj was sure that Andy would be fine medically. However, he didn't like the CAS worker's rigid and condescending attitude, as though she thought he and the hospital staff were naïve or stupid or both. He wanted to find someone who could help the boy and save him from foster care. It was ridiculous that a military family could find themselves in this situation.

Raj was on his way back to Andy's room, wondering what he should do, when he heard a voice calling his name. Raj turned to see Sandra running towards him, carrying a thick file.

"Is something going down in Emerg, Sandra?"

"No, Raj. It's about Andy. I'm taking him home with me."

"What are you talking about? He has to stay with someone in his family, or else CAS will take him."

"That's what I'm trying to tell you."

Raj was confused. "I have no idea what you're talking about."

"Just wait a second. You'll see!"

Andy brightened up as soon as Sandra and Raj entered his

room. The CAS worker looked from Raj to Sandra and back again. Then Sandra stepped forward.

"I'm Sandra Burnside, Andy's next of kin."

"Excuse me, but we have no recorded next of kin for Andrew Fournier other than his father." Ruth stared at Sandra suspiciously.

"Well, I am Andy's next of kin," Sandra said.

"I don't know what you're trying to pull here, but we've done our due diligence, and Andrew has no other next of kin." Krendell was getting angry.

"Well, your records aren't correct, and I can prove it," Sandra said.

"Oh, really? What's this proof you're talking about?"

Sandra placed the thick folder on Andy's bed and began to flip through the numerous pages. "Here it is. This is a copy of Andy's birth record," she said, showing the CAS worker the chart.

"And how is this relevant?"

"Do you need glasses?" asked Sandra. "Look right here under next of kin for Andy's mother. That's my name – Sandra Burnside."

The CAS worker looked carefully at the old document. Raj also looked and, indeed, Sandra's name appeared as next of kin and as a witness to the birth.

"This is highly unusual," Ruth Krendell sniffed. "Why didn't you come forward and contact us?"

"I thought you people knew about me already. I've been visiting my nephew every day. We've already talked about him coming to stay with me, haven't we, Andy?"

The boy looked confused for just a moment, and then his eyes brightened. "Yes, Aunt Sandra! We've got it all planned. You keep talking about getting me to like spinach."

"Right, Andy," said Sandra. "I put it in a pie, and it's really good."

Andy was beaming. "Please, Mrs. Ruth… Aunt Sandra can look after me, and I can stay at my school until Dad gets back. Pleease!"

"Well, this is highly irregular." Krendell glared at Sandra. "You should have contacted CAS. Why aren't you listed as next of kin anywhere else?"

"I didn't know I had to be. Look, honey, I'm the team leader of Emergency Services and head of the Emergency Improvement Program at this hospital. I also have two adult children; one's a cop in Ottawa, and the other is a teacher. There is absolutely nothing you can do that I can't do better."

There was a long pause as the two women stared each other down.

At last, Krendell turned to Raj. "Dr. Mehta, I was expecting to take custody of this boy upon his discharge. Did you know anything about this? Who's the official attending doctor?"

Raj had no idea how in the world Sandra had got her own name on the hospital record and hesitated for a moment. Then he saw Sandra's face. She was pleading with her eyes. Raj decided to do what he thought Dr. Williamson would do, and hoped he wouldn't get in trouble. He tried to make his face a mask of professionalism.

"Dr. Williamson is the attending doctor," Raj replied. "But he's in the operating room performing cancer surgery and can't be disturbed. I was aware that Sandra Burnside is next of kin – she showed me the document yesterday."

"Why wasn't the Children's Aid Society notified?" Krendell demanded.

"My job is to make sure this boy is as healthy as I can make him. I wasn't even sure I was going to discharge him today. It is my very clear opinion that Sandra is the most qualified person to care for this boy. He'll require ongoing surgical care for the next four weeks. Were you aware of this?" said Raj.

"No. The nursing staff never mentioned it."

"Well, Sandra was aware. She's been visiting Andy daily, as any family member would," said Raj.

"Well, Dr. Mehta, it's very unusual that someone comes out

of the woodwork and claims to be a relative of a youngster when we have no record of it."

"Our record shows that Sandra Burnside is the next of kin, and I will release this patient to her custody. If you want to argue this, you'll have to take it up with the Director of Medical Records and the Chief of Surgery," said Raj.

Krendell was clearly annoyed, and Raj worried she was going to escalate the confrontation. To break the tension, he pulled his stethoscope from around his neck and listened to Andy's chest. His heart was pumping hard with anxiety.

Krendell pulled out her cell phone and marched into the hall to make a call. While she was out of the room, Sandra checked Andy's chest wound and changed the bandages. None of them said a word, in case Krendell was eavesdropping on them. After several minutes, Krendell marched back in and said, "This is highly unusual, but my boss is going to allow this. We're going to close the file."

"Well, that wasn't such a problem, was it?" Raj said.

Ruth eyed all three of them suspiciously. "If anything happens to that boy, Dr. Mehta, it's on your head."

Raj stared at the woman for a minute then said, "I'll make sure he doesn't get into any trouble." He winked at Andy. Ruth Krendell marched off after recording Sandra's address and telephone number.

On his way back to ER, Raj realized that he had been sweating under his lab coat. When he started, he had been afraid of Sandra, but over the past weeks, they had dealt with all sorts of problems together, and she had even covered for him when he needed help. Sandra was now a friend, someone he trusted. Whatever she'd done to make herself Andy's next of kin, he would sort it out later.

* * *

Diana finished work that day craving her favorite fix – Asian eggplant – and walked over to the Lucky Star grocery just five minutes away from the hospital. Diana knew the store well as it was not far from where she grew up, and she liked its informality. Its shelves were stuffed with all sorts of products, and it had surprisingly good vegetables and fruit as well as spices that were hard to get anywhere else. It smelled like an Asian market because it was one.

Mr. and Mrs. Hong, the owners, were fond of Diana, who would pick up comic books and salty Chinese snacks there when she was a kid. Later, she bought flowers for her parents and mangoes and pineapples, which she could always find here even when they were unavailable everywhere else.

When she got to the store, she decided that she was also craving mangoes. She picked up a basket and waved hello to Mrs. Hong, whose smile revealed gaping teeth. Mrs. Hong's English was just good enough for her to get by. "How you, Mama?" she asked.

"She's very well, Mrs. Hong," Diana said.

"Tha' good. I got a special on radish. See, looks good."

"No thanks, Mrs. Hong. I need mangoes."

"You look at back. I got good ones in back," said Mrs. Hong.

Diana wandered around for a few moments, simply enjoying the scent of the fruits and spices, then quickly filled her basket with a large melon, some eggplants and tomatoes, a small package of frozen shrimp, and a tin of bamboo shoots. Last to go in were four mangoes, which tipped the precarious balance of the basket. One fell out and landed … in someone's hand. Diana turned to find the intern standing beside her. He had caught the fruit in his hand.

"Oh!" Diana said. "You scared me!"

"Sorry. I didn't mean to sneak up on you. I saw you were going to lose your mango," he said.

"Thanks. It's Raj, isn't it?"

"That's right. And you're Diana at Dr. Sinclair's office." Raj smiled and handed her the mango, saying, "You know, I just can't stand a mushy mango."

"Me, too. I like them a little firm. If you let them get overripe, they lose their tang," Diana said.

Raj wanted to keep the conversation going. "Do you shop here much?" he asked. "This is the first time I've been here."

"Yes, I'm from St. Jerome," Diana said. "Are you shopping or just going around saving fruit?"

"Yup, that's me – quick on the draw when it comes to fruit emergencies. I've already saved a Kiwi today."

"Really?" said Diana, laughing now.

"I guess people from New Zealand refer to themselves as Kiwis. A guy was visiting the area and came in with a green fuzzy rash. He's better now…and oddly crisp and refreshing."

Diana noticed that Raj's basket was filled with many packages of one item – Mr. Noodle. "Are you training for a marathon?" she asked. "It looks like you're carb-loading."

"No, I'm not much of a cook. These are great. You just add water," Raj said.

"I would think a doctor would try to eat a little better."

"True, but there are so many different Mr. Noodle flavors. All I need now is a breakfast-cereal flavor."

"You should try some fruit. An apple a day keeps the doctor away."

"That's a common misconception. Almost any fruit will keep the doctor away. You just have to throw it hard enough!"

Diana realized that Raj was trying to be charming, and he didn't look quite so officious and "doctorish" in his leather jacket and blue jeans.

"Do you live near here?" she asked.

"Yes. I've got one of those apartments by the hospital. Pretty good rent."

"I live there, too. It's OK, but the hot water doesn't work sometimes."

"How long have you been working for our fearless leader, Dr. Sinclair?"

"I'm only a substitute because his regular secretary fell and broke her hip."

"I hope you hang around for a while. There's so much going on," said Raj.

"I know. My –" Diana caught herself. She didn't want Raj to know that his boss was her father. "Actually, I was thinking about moving to Toronto," replied Diana.

"Really? I'm from Toronto and I like St. Jerome – it's really friendly."

"Yeah, it is. But I'm trying to get work as an actress and I have to go where the work is."

"So the secretary thing is just a temp job?"

"Yes. I have to pay the bills somehow. I'm in a play in Toronto – Tony and Tina's Wedding. It's on Fridays and Saturdays at a dinner theater," Diana explained.

"Wow! That's really cool!" Raj was impressed. "You know, I figured there was something special about you. You'll probably become famous, and I can say I knew that girl when she was a secretary."

"I doubt that, but the play is fun." Diana smiled.

At the checkout counter, Diana put the mango in his basket. "You rescued this. It's yours now."

"I'll cherish it always. Maybe I'll see you around?"

"I hope so." Diana smiled again and turned to pay for her shopping.

Mrs. Hong leaned over the counter and pointed at the rack of newspapers. "Look! Look! Boyfriend in newspaper! Very nice! He so handsome. Big Star!" A photo of Star Yanofsky was on the front of a Toronto newspaper. He looked heroic in his hockey jersey and his blond hair was done up in a ponytail. The headline read: "STAR YANOFSKY TO PLAY FOR THE MAPLE LEAFS! COULD THIS BE THE YEAR THE LEAFS FINALLY MAKE IT TO THE CUP?" Diana didn't know what to say. It was so like her old boyfriend to be everywhere. She grabbed her bags and said goodbye.

Raj bought the paper and went outside to read about the good-looking hockey player. Diana had a rich and famous boyfriend. He was crestfallen. He drove home thinking that she was cool and beautiful and totally out of his league.

Chapter Thirteen

Raj headed back to Toronto to spend the weekend with his family. Although he appreciated his parents' counsel and encouragement, he had begun to realize that their suggestions for his life were disconnected from reality. He had reached that point when he arrived on Saturday morning, and his mother wasted no time telling him she wanted him to be more like Dr. Sanjay Gupta.

"Who's Sanjay Gupta?" Raj had never heard the name.

"What do you mean, 'Who is Sanjay Gupta'?" Mena exclaimed. She said that Dr. Gupta was an extraordinarily handsome man who was both a neurosurgeon and a medical correspondent for CNN. "He went to Iraq and even helped some of the people there in one of those mobile military hospitals."

Raj realized in a half-hearted way that his becoming a doctor allowed her to celebrate being the mother of someone successful. Perhaps her own ambitions had been thwarted, and his life had become hers. She was a Momaholic. No matter how painful it would be, the many thousands of dollars his parents had spent on his tuition, lodgings and yes, new clothing would have to be paid back. And the only way to do that was to listen earnestly, nod his head and make his parents feel that his accomplishments were as much theirs as his.

"Why don't you go down to California and study under Dr. Deepak Chopra? He has a center for learning, you know," Mena said.

"I don't think his program is specifically for doctors, but I'll check it out online," Raj said.

"Tennis – Dr. Chopra plays tennis, Raj. That's what you should play," Radhu suggested.

"I'll think about it, Dad."

Raj went to the fridge, which was always stocked with Carlsberg because it was one of the few beers one could get in India, Europe and Africa – all places Radhu had traveled to when he was in the British Navy. Although he now worked in the electricians' union, Dad prided himself on his military service with the Royal Navy, and Raj was proud of it, too.

"So, what's going on tomorrow?" Raj asked. He knew they were scheduled to meet the family of a friend of a friend – of sorts. He may have been a friend of a cousin of a friend's business partner. The details were sketchy.

Radhu refused to elaborate other than to say that the family was from southern India and had two children – a twenty-six-year-old daughter and a teenaged son. The daughter was an accountant with an international firm and, he said, was "making quite a lot of money." Raj's parents were impressed that she earned an income, but Raj was interested in her only because of the picture his father had emailed him. Chan wouldn't be at the gathering, which disappointed him. She had called and carefully advised him on his clothing choices claiming to have studied this sort of stuff at her college. She was studying and couldn't come along. Raj guessed this was a lie and that she would probably be just hanging out with Quentin at the video store.

Raj was nervous about meeting the young woman, and the fact his family had set it up made him feel like a loser. He had agreed only because Chandra thought it might be a good idea. She knew all about Raj's ineptitude with women and had persuaded him by saying, "Hey, try not lurking about and most likely, she won't like you, and that'll be the end of it."

On their way over to the house of Radhu's "old friend", Raj asked, "Who are these people, Dad, and do they have any inherited diseases I should know about?"

Mena spoke up: "I don't think your dad knows, son. The truth is that a lot of these young girls don't have a big interest in getting married. Most of them want to focus on their careers."

"Yes, son. My friend says she is very successful," Radhu added.

The Ramsarans lived in a posh area of Mississauga, what Radhu called "the Land of the Big Houses." He was very loyal to his own neighborhood of East York.

They drove into the circular drive in front of a large, white-brick, colonial-style house. The lawn was immaculate, and perfectly spherical bushes lined the stone driveway.

Raj felt less confident than he usually did even though he was working and not just a student. He had dressed carefully but casually in new slim-fit jeans, a Ralph Lauren shirt under a blue blazer, and aviator sunglasses. He stood up straight and told himself not to try too hard, not to look desperate, even though he always was.

They were greeted at the door by a couple, both about five feet tall and well dressed in business attire. Hellos, big smiles and double handshakes were exchanged. Raj moved slowly and shook everyone's hand with an almost painful grip. The son looked about sixteen and was dressed like a wannabe rap star – baseball hat on sideways, untied basketball shoes and with an iPhone plugged into his ears. Raj shook his limp hand, and the boy avoided looking at him. Raj immediately disliked him, thinking he was a gangster wannabe in his father's Lexus, straight out of Londonstani.

The hosts gave the Mehtas a take-off-your-shoes look and escorted them to the living room, which was ostentatiously appointed with lots of gold fabric and Indian paintings everywhere. Tea and biscuits were served, and finally, Shari Ramsaran descended the large curved staircase.

She knew how to make an entrance. She had a casual grace and hesitated slightly as she approached Raj. He assumed she was used to meeting people and was treating this situation much like work. She wore a long, floral-patterned white dress with a low neckline, a long side slit and matching high heels. Raj thought her dress was adventuresome.

Shari approached Raj with a smile, tossing back her hair. "Hi,

Raj. My parents have been talking about you for days. It's a pleasure to meet you," As they shook hands, Raj found it hard not to stare at her breasts.

She had beautiful skin and almond-shaped brown eyes. Her hair was cut in a short bob, had red highlights and framed her small oval face and nice teeth. Raj found himself mentally undressing her. A brief image of her wearing only Indian jewelry and nothing else came to mind, like one of the illustrations in the Kama Sutra. Shari looked as if she could handle any one of the unusual positions shown in the book.

Raj was pulled back to earth when he noticed that her mother was sizing him up as if he were a horse. Raj quickly unglued his eyes from Shari and attempted a proper smile. Then Mr. Ramsaran joined his daughter and started talking earnestly about "the pancreas" his diabetes and his vow to "beat diabetes by exercising the pancreas". Raj knew that diabetes was quite common among Indians.

Shari winked at Raj. "Would you like a drink?"

He asked for a Coke, and watched her as she went to the kitchen. Her mother caught Raj eyeing her swaying hips and gave him a severe look.

Shari returned with the drink in a tall glass with a slice of lime. "When I was in Mexico, they always put lime in Coke. Have you been to Mexico?"

"No, but I'd like to go," Raj said

As Shari talked, Raj got the impression that he was being handled – in a pleasant way. She led Raj into the den to show him her father's collection of Indian art – and his latest blood sugar tests, which she said he had made his doctor photocopy for him. Her father belonged to an Internet diabetes support group, which she thought was funded by a multinational pharmaceutical company.

Raj looked at the lab tests, pretending to be interested, to stop himself from staring at her breasts.

She touched his jacket – just a flick of her well-manicured hand – and said, "Raj, my parents mentioned that you've never had a girlfriend. You aren't gay, are you? You know, it's okay with me if you're gay,"

Raj's stunned look betrayed his reaction.

"But my parents said you've never had a girlfriend or even a date, so I thought you had to be gay."

Raj couldn't breathe. The world was closing in. What the fuck was going on here? "What makes you think I'm gay?" He had to ask – maybe it was the slim-fit jeans Chandra had insisted he wear.

Shari said that he had to be the only man she'd ever met who was twenty-six and had never had a girlfriend. "Statistics show that any guy well into his twenties who hasn't had a girlfriend or dated is most likely gay. Also, you're kind of handsome and even dress a little metro."

"You mean the jeans?" Raj was still not over his shock.

"I read it in a magazine," said Shari. "Men in your situation may be unaware or unable to accept that they are homosexual." She went on to explain that she believed that the whole idea of their arranged marriage was something that Raj's family wanted in order to hide the fact that their son was gay – or just somehow suppressed.

Raj was perspiring under his fancy shirt. "Do you mean to tell me that you and your family believe I'm looking for a marriage of convenience, like Prince Charles and Lady Di?"

"Well, sort of," Shari said. "I guess that's what we thought."

Willing his heart rate to slow down, Raj got up, saying nothing, and walked out of the room. Should he be angry or upset? He wasn't sure. Perhaps his parents had inadvertently conveyed some information to this family that was misunderstood. A traditional Indian family trying desperately to understand the modern world might have come up with something absurd like this.

Raj longed to go back to St. Jerome and just be a doctor. The entire family made him a bit angry. Even if he were gay, why would they want to marry off their daughter to a gay man? Was he somehow putting out a gay vibe? This was somehow Chandra's fault! Raj started to leave, determined to at least introduce Mr. Ramsaran to something useful for his diabetes before he left.

Mr. Ramsaran cornered Raj in the front hall and, speaking loudly, showed Raj his "pancreatic exercise" which involved pushing

118

his right hand into his belly while using his left hand to squeeze his back, karate chop style. Then he would alternate his hands "as using only the right hand on the belly might upset the chi forces". Raj didn't understand what the "chi forces" were, but he had heard the term used in a karate movie. He told Shari's father that the most important thing was to continue to do light exercise every day for an hour or so. Years ago, one of his instructors suggested every diabetic should get a treadmill. Mr. Ramsaran nodded vigorously at this suggestion.

Raj edged closer to the door. "I have to get going now. I have a long trip back to the hospital," to which Mr. Ramsaran replied, "You doctors are so busy, aren't you?" Raj nodded and gave him his serious doctor's look.

"What kind of patients do you deal with, Raj?" Mr. Ramsaran asked.

"You know, we deal with every single kind of ailment under the sun and it's all free for any Canadian." Raj replied. He realized afterward that this made him enormously proud.

The Mehtas left hastily, and Shari looked upset as Raj waved goodbye from the car. He tried to convey nothing when he looked at her, but he made sure not to suggest another meeting. He thought that his generation had moved beyond arranged marriages, believing them to be an anachronism that did little for anybody other than reassuring parents that their children would marry someone of the right color and religion – but not necessarily the right sexual orientation.

* * *

Kelly, Paula and Dan chose the healthiest food the hospital cafeteria offered – carrot muffins and yogurt. Raj looked for bacon and eggs, but there were none. He reluctantly grabbed a Danish and joined them. Happy to be at work after his disastrous meeting with Shari Ramsaran, Raj wondered if the others were having problems with their love lives.

"Hey, Raj, what's with the Danish?" said Paula.

"I'm celebrating," he replied.

"Celebrating what – your carbohydrate addiction?" Kelly was spooning granola into her yogurt.

"I'm celebrating being in my twenties and almost free of family obligations," Raj said. "Are you guys doing anything Friday night?"

Kelly spoke up. "My boyfriend is coming from Montreal and we need something to do."

"I'm free, Raj. What do you have in mind?" asked Paula.

"I thought we could go out somewhere – like a club."

Dan spoke between mouthfuls of his low-fat muffin. "Well, Raj, I think I can spare a night off from Jenny. She's been keeping me a bit busy lately and I could do with a break."

Paula and Kelly rolled their eyes, and Paula asked Dan, "Has the CEO asked you out on a date yet?"

"She's been away with the new provincial commission, looking at hospitals across the province. She called me and insisted that I follow her Twitter feed. Her last tweet was from Belgravia. She says the place is nice, but the hospital's too old and she wouldn't feed her cat in the cafeteria."

"That's pretty harsh," Kelly said. "Are they actually going to close hospitals?"

"I don't know," Dan said, "but I think some will be closed."

"Well, Dan," Raj said. "We want you to sacrifice yourself – for the good of the community and for us, too."

"Thanks, guys," said Dan, "but I think she has bigger fish to fry right now. I'll let you know if I have to sacrifice my body. What I need right now is some time off. I'm so damn busy."

Dan was grateful that Wendy was away. Jenny, the dietician, was very nice, but she was demanding and made him feel guilty about eating meat. He liked chicken and burgers. She would stare at him while he ate, making remarks like, "Have you ever seen a baby chicken?" But the more meat he ate, the more she demanded sex. Dan wondered if she was somehow offering sex as a substitute for meat.

Paula had not heard from her boyfriend in days and was worried that he had run off with a Mormon. Kelly was worried about her boyfriend because he smoked too much. He had cut back on cigarettes but this, paradoxically, made him smoke more marijuana.

Raj wanted to tell his friends about his parents setting him up, but it was just too embarrassing.

One thing was clear: it wasn't easy to have a relationship as an intern.

Chapter Fourteen

"I used to work in Obstetrics, Raj."

"How is that relevant, Sandra?" Raj wanted to know.

"Well, when a mother comes in ready to deliver, we need information about her. Andy's mother was a local girl. I vaguely knew her family – they lived a few streets over. Anyway, Andy's mother was okay, but I knew she wouldn't hang around St. Jerome. The last time I saw her, she was working in the entertainment industry."

"Entertainment industry?"

"She was a stripper, Raj. Her parents weren't around, and I knew she had no other family."

"I still don't get it, Sandra."

"Everyone who registers at the hospital has to state who their next of kin is. When she came in, she didn't have anyone, and that's why I'm registered as Andy's next of kin."

"Okay," Raj said. "You registered yourself as Lisa Fournier's next of kin when she came in to deliver. Then you were automatically registered as Andy's next of kin. Years later, you used this to take him home."

"Stranger things have happened, Raj."

"You must know Andy's father, then?"

"Yeah, I remember him. He was a fresh recruit back then. He was a really nice guy."

"So when does he get back home?"

"I think in a month or so," Sandra said. "The truth is Andy's better company than my cat. He's eating me out of house and home, though. Last night, he ate two giant pork chops, an entire box of Kraft Dinner and carrots and peas. But I don't mind. There's no rush. I'm getting their house back in order – you know, getting the hydro turned back on."

"I just don't understand why you're going to all the trouble," Raj said.

"Andy is so happy, and it's so nice to have someone around who's happy. Anyway, things will get straightened out soon."

It was the last day of Raj's rotation in the ER. He had never asked Sandra why she had temporarily adopted Andy, and Sandra had never really thanked him for helping her. After the incident, however, she had started to direct patients with the most dire problems to him. She had also taken to addressing him as Dr. Mehta and treating him like a staff doctor.

"I'm off to Internal Medicine on the third floor," Raj said by way of goodbye.

"You'll like it there. Everyone loves Dr. Cooper," Sandra said.

"So I hear. I'll come back and visit."

"You'd better! And bring coffee."

* * *

Diana was in the office, typing up her father's dictation. After she finished, she sat for a moment in the quiet, pondering things. Star had been hounding her to go out with him, and she wasn't sure why. Unbelievably, Star's father had called Diana's parents to let them know that Star was back in Toronto. Diana surmised that this was a way of letting her know that Star was available. And Diana's mother had hinted that she should consider getting married. Her own mother – a feminist who had spent most of her life telling Diana that it was important to have a career – thought she should get married because she wanted grandchildren someday, and Diana was her only child. Mom had learned that older men have a lower sperm count, and so it wasn't a good plan to marry late. Diana was grateful her father had kept quiet.

She had asked him casually about each of the interns, and her father had said that he liked Dr. Mehta. "We need more guys like him around, Di. Smart enough to figure out how we can modernize without shortchanging patients."

"Is there a chance the hospital will be closed?" Diana asked.

"I don't think so, but the provincial commission is a big thing, and our CEO is running it."

"Maybe she'll help keep the hospital open."

"I don't know, Di. I think she wants to make an example of St. Jerome's."

"This is serious, isn't it, Dad?"

"It is, but they've tried to close hospitals many times before. We'll figure it out."

Diana changed the conversation. "Dad, I'm taking Friday afternoon off and going to see Star."

"That's nice. Tell him we're expecting the Stanley Cup in Toronto next year."

* * *

"Now bite his nipple. Yes... Yesss ... harder now! Both of them. Don't smile!"

Diana could hear the rapid fire of the camera's shutter as the photographer circled his subjects.

"Show your teeth, tigress. Make me believe you're a wild animal. Okay, that's got it! Now straddle him and ride him a little bit. Someone get that fan to blow a little softer!"

Someone did, and the camera started clicking again. "Yes ... that's nice and sexy. Now get a little closer like you're about to kiss him– don't smile. Now bite his lower lip… Excellent! Okay, people, that's a wrap. Well done!"

Diana was seated behind the photographer in a little lounge area with comfortable chairs, coffee, low-calorie snacks, and bottles of mineral water on ice. Star was sitting on a leather chair before a white backdrop, oiled up and wearing only his new Star and Stripes underwear. The model who'd been biting his left nipple was named Mischa, from Russia, and she disengaged from Star almost reluctantly. She was strikingly beautiful, with very light blonde-flecked hair and crystalline blue eyes. She had a slim, athletic body and she was also lubed and shiny for the photo shoot. She was in a string bikini and knew how to handle the strappy high-heeled shoes she was wearing – she didn't walk, she strutted.

Star came over to where Diana was sitting. "Hey, babes! So what do you think of the photo shoot?"

"Nice, Star! Look at you, all oiled up."

"Let me clean up. I think I might have to shave. They want you to have a little stubble like David Beckham."

As Diana waited for Star to return, Mischa joined her in the lounge area, now wearing a short terrycloth robe that covered her body except for her legs and high heels. Diana was rarely ever envious, but Mischa's shoes were elegant and sexy, and Diana was acutely conscious of the old, forty-dollar flats she was wearing. Mischa lit a cigarette and inhaled deeply, with a challenging, almost insolent expression. She eyed Diana, attempting to stare her down, and in a thick European accent, asked, "So, you are girlfriend?"

"Actually, Star and I are just good friends. We used to go out." Diana said.

"So he is not a boyfriend?"

"No, he's just an old friend."

Mischa eyed Diana like a feral cat about to hunt or start hissing. She took a bottle of water and drank slowly. "You are… passingly pretty," she said.

Diana didn't have a good feeling about this girl. It was as if Mischa were trying to start an argument. "What do you mean?" she asked.

"You are passingly pretty, like the girl next door."

"What are you saying? I don't understand," said Diana.

This seemed to exasperate Mischa. "You look like the girl next door. Go home and make cookies. Leave Star to me. He's mine."

"Are you with Star now?" Diana was confused and angry.

At that moment, Star came out of the changing room dressed in blue jeans, a shirt, and a leather jacket. He looked like a million dollars. "Okay, Di, let's go! I'm so hungry I could eat a horse."

Before he took Diana's hand to help her up from the chair, he turned to Mischa, who stood up and made a point of kissing him twice, once on each cheek. She spoke to him in a low, quiet voice while fingering the buttons on his jacket. "Don't forget next Friday. We are going to drink vodka at Moscow Bar. It will be fun. We meet some of my friends. You will love them."

"Sure, Mischa," said Star. "We'll get together."

Diana grabbed his arm and led him away before the shameless hussy wrapped her legs around him and started humping him. Once they were outside, she exploded. "That girl is a real bitch!"

"She's just like that – overly touchy. It's because she's Russian."

"Russian, my ass," Diana retorted. "She's very aggressive – a she-wolf. You'd better be careful!"

"Hey baby, it's not Mischa I'm having dinner with. It's you."

"I know, Star, but she's like a wolf moving in for the kill!"

Star chortled. "You're jealous."

"I am not jealous, Star! But, oh, that girl really, really annoyed me!"

As they drove to the Lula Lounge, a club in Toronto, Diana decided to be the sexiest version of herself to get him to forget Mischa. The club played Mexican and South American music, and she tugged Star onto the floor to dance. She put her arms around him and flitted her hips at him. All evening long, she danced and flirted with him.

Many drinks later, they arrived at Star's condo, a beautiful penthouse on the waterfront. Diana was drunk, and being around Star reminded her how long it had been since she had been with anyone. He smelled nice, and he wanted her badly. He tossed her onto the bed, smiled at her, and showed off his muscles and a new tattoo. She couldn't resist him. She loved the way his body felt – hard and smooth. He was handsome and fun, and it was like old times. She was too drunk to remember that the hard part of being with him was all the other times when they weren't in bed.

The next morning, Diana awoke with a splitting tequila-fueled headache. Star was snoring behind her. She slowly opened her eyes and noticed something moving rhythmically by the bedside. What was it? The Sun was so bright. She rubbed her eyes and finally focused on what she had seen on the bedside table. It was a bobble-head doll with Star's face and a blue Toronto Maple Leaf jersey. She looked around the bedroom. There were dozens of Star bobble heads, all of them staring at her and nodding gently in the breeze from the window.

Creepy.

Chapter Fifteen

Raj found his days quite different in his new placement in the Internal Medical ward, where all the patients with heart and lung problems went. It was drab, cramped, and sterile-looking, without any natural sunlight, and patients stayed there for days, even weeks. Raj had started on the ward two days earlier, joining Paula, who was there for another few weeks, supervised by Dr. Froeder.

The ward could hold up to thirty-two patients, and it was always full – a clearinghouse for anyone who wasn't crazy, pregnant, or needing surgery. Raj learned quickly that the patients here were probably the sickest. No one had just one problem; they usually had several, like high blood pressure, bad lungs, and diabetes. Many of them were languishing in their beds, waiting to be moved to a nursing home. Paula told him on his first day that there were never enough nursing-home beds to satisfy the seemingly inexhaustible demand. In the past, Raj had often heard people say, "Just shoot me before I get packed off to a nursing home." Raj wondered if this fate was in store for him someday.

Raj arrived at the nursing station, carefully dressed in his cool new doctor clothes – suede loafers and an expensive Tommy Hilfiger shirt with a tie. He was feeling more comfortable in his doctor role. A number of nurses were chatting, and one attractive blonde with a fancy hairdo introduced herself as Candy and welcomed Raj to the Internal Medicine floor. After some small talk, she asked him if he was seeing anyone. Raj was stunned. No one had ever asked him such a direct question about his personal life – except Shari. He learned later that Candy, engaged to a local police officer, had taken it upon herself to be a match maker, and her questioning was a public service of sorts.

The attending staff doctor, Dr. Cooper, arrived at eight forty-five. He was a short Jewish fellow in his mid-fifties with stooped shoulders that made his shortness even more pronounced. He was wearing a lab coat and the same kind of dress shoes Radhu insisted Raj wear. It made him think of 'Sy Sperling, president of Hair Club for Men', whose advertisements were all over TV when he was a kid.

Dr. Cooper greeted Raj, saying, "Welcome to real medicine, Raj. Let's do rounds." It wasn't a suggestion; he wanted to see his patients quickly and told Raj to push the cart filled with charts. The head nurse accompanied them, a tall black woman with a thick West Indian accent. Dr. Cooper called her "the brown sugar of the nursing world." Her name was Stella, short for Estelle.

Dr. Cooper asked Stella, "How many admits overnight, honey?"

"Well, doc, we got Mr. Robarts wit' a bad case of de 'can't breed', and Mrs. Edna Johnson was admitted because she couldn't find her way home."

As they slowly made their way around the ward, Dr. Cooper updated Raj on the various patients. "Rosenplot: stable post MI.

Scarfina: pancreatitis, improving. Van Hubert: undergoing workup for lung cancer." Dr. Cooper spent time with each patient, checking what drugs they'd taken or procedures they'd undergone since he last saw them and chatting about how they were feeling, and introducing Raj as the intern. It took them until ten forty-five to see a total of sixteen patients.

At last, they were done and returned to the nursing station to sit down. Raj was tired and wondered why until he realized that he was exhausted from thinking so much about all the different diseases.

"Okay, Raj," Dr. Cooper said. "Spend the day familiarizing yourself with the patients. I'll expect you to present any new admits on morning rounds and make sure that you get some people out of here. We need beds!"

Paula was making rounds with her staff man, Dr. Froeder, with whom she had started her internship in the ICU. They were still only halfway through their hallway of patients. Raj felt sorry for her as Froeder seemed to take a long time with each patient.

Raj sat down with a tall stack of patients' charts. Incredibly, some were a good two or three inches thick, and it took him an hour to review just two charts. About half the patients had been in hospital so long that the reason for admission was long forgotten. They had developed other problems that kept them in hospital. After a month or so, most of them were so confused and weakened that they had little hope of ever returning home. They would have to go to a nursing home as soon as a space opened up. One man, Charlie Rosenplot, had been on the ward for almost eleven months. He had a heart attack, smoked like a chimney, and also had diabetes. He used to run a clothing business and live on his own. Now he was stuck in the hospital.

Raj went to see him. He was a thin, grey, wheezy old duffer wearing nasal prongs for extra oxygen, and he had to work hard just to keep breathing.

Raj introduced himself.

"What happened to Cooper – is he on holiday again?" wheezed the patient.

"Actually, sir, I'm an intern," replied Raj.

"Now listen, every one of you guys comes in and does a rectal on me. Gimme a break already."

"No problem, sir. Could I have a listen to your heart and lungs?" Raj said. Rosenplot's chest sounded like a small animal was living in there. He grabbed Raj's arm and hauled himself forward, almost leaning against Raj for support.

"God, I could go for a smoke and a nice glass of bourbon," he said. Raj thought he looked unhappy, perhaps depressed, and gently set him back on his pillows. "Jeez," Rosenplot complained, "my ass is sore from sitting in this bed."

Later that day, Raj spoke to Dr. Cooper and Stella about

Rosenplot and was surprised by the doctor's recommendation that Mr. Rosenplot should get married. "To a nurse," Stella added, "so she can cook and feed him and clean his bum!"

Cooper said he wanted to clear some beds on the ward and had been trying to get a few patients discharged. He had hit upon the idea that, if he could just get a couple of them married off to nurses, they could be discharged home in the care of their wives. There was a certain logic to this: getting married would be cheaper than going to a nursing home, and when the old man died, his new wife would collect his life insurance. Thus far, he hadn't found an "Anna Nicole in a nursing uniform" to rescue Mr. Rosenplot.

The following day, Raj presented a new case to Dr. Cooper. He decided he liked "the Coop"; the man was a virtual storehouse of medical knowledge. He never made Raj feel like an idiot and often passed on his insights about patients in such a way that made Raj feel like a colleague – even though they both realized that Raj knew almost nothing.

Dr. Cooper took a look at the patient Raj presented. He was a man in his seventies who had been admitted the previous afternoon, complaining of shortness of breath. "Okay, Raj," he said. "How about we get some blood cultures on this guy and, just to be on the safe side, let's get an arterial blood gas since he's huffin' and puffin'."

Raj had taken to bringing a few textbooks in his knapsack to look up information while he ate lunch, and he and Paula would then discuss their cases. This helped Raj stay on top of things. The work of keeping track of the numerous patients was becoming onerous.

Raj had become quite close to Paula. Despite what her scholarly glasses, Birkenstocks, and plain appearance suggested, she had an easygoing way that relaxed those around her. She was the kind of person whose few complaints and largely positive attitude inspired people. Rather than buying lunch, Paula always brought hers from home: a salad, yogurt, and other nutritious stuff, and she finished off with an apple and a Snapple. Addicted to French fries and hamburgers, Raj kept up his usual diet until Paula mentioned trans-fatty acids and a patient, only thirty-five years old, who'd recently had a heart attack.

Dan had moved to the ICU and Kelly to Surgery. Raj had seen her in her OR scrubs, which were quite tight around her hips. "You're looking very surgical," he remarked.

"I'm working with Doc Miller," Kelly said. "They call him the 'The Surfer Doc'. It's fun. How's it going for you?"

"Not bad," Raj replied, "but how good could Internal Medicine really be?"

"Are you around this weekend? My boyfriend is coming up from Montreal and bringing his kid sister. You'd like her. I think she has a nose ring."

Raj said he had already promised his parents a visit home on the weekend.

"You don't know what you're missing, Raj!" Kelly said, and

she winked at him.

At home that evening, Raj silently cursed that he had agreed to see his parents in Toronto. He had to confide in someone, and so he called Dan.

"Raj, listen, buddy," Dan said. "Do you actually want to get married?"

"No!" said Raj

"Then we gotta fix you up. I'm still going out with Jenny, but – tell you what – let's, you and I, go out Thursday night."

Raj perked up. "Okay. Where will we go?"

"You'll see," Dan replied. "I gotta go. Jenny's making me some sort of tofu thing, but I told her I'm on the new Atkins diet, and the only thing I can eat is animal protein. The very least I'll settle for is eating an animal that's been fed tofu."

Raj told Dan that tofu was best eaten raw, à la sushi and that it had a natural hormone in it and was, thus, an aphrodisiac. He didn't mention that the natural hormone was estrogen.

That night, Raj stared at the computer screen, mesmerized by a photo of a smiling woman with extra-bright teeth, apparently advising him to log on to "Toronto's best dating service." He wasn't quite sure how he had arrived at an internet dating service, but he did have time on his hands, and he was feeling lonely. Besides, he rationalized, one can look at the Kama Sutra for only so long before realizing that you have to do something – anything.

He began filling out the site's membership application form, debating whether to reveal that he was a doctor. He could just say that he was self-employed or that he worked at a hospital. Were people ever entirely honest with dating services, he wondered? He decided to register with the Toronto site, not with the local one, feeling he should stay as anonymous as possible by pretending to live there rather than in the much smaller town of St. Jerome. He sent off the form, hoping to meet someone through the site and eventually get together for some sort of fun date.

He told no one about his Internet adventure; it was far too embarrassing. Next day, he eagerly checked his email. Nothing! He was about to kill himself with a quart of tequila when a "you have a message" notice came up. "Yes!" he said to himself.

He quickly opened up the email. It was from his mother.

Hello, Raj. You are always on my mind, Raj. When are you coming back home? Your father has contacted several nice families, and it looks like a whole bunch of them want to meet you! Also, that girl Shari has called, wondering if you would like to get together. Rather forward of her to call us directly. She wanted your telephone number. I didn't give it to her, but I told her that you would call her.

Raj already knew that his parents liked Shari. His father told him on the way home from the Ramsarans' house that he thought she was very pretty. Raj had kept quiet about their little conversation. Both his parents had gushed about how nice Shari's family was.

Mena must have sensed that Raj was feeling lonely. Her mission to get him married had taken on a new level of urgency. Could she tell that he was sexually repressed to the point of mild depravity? Probably yes. Raj cursed his transparency and wished he could camouflage himself like a chameleon or actor. For all he knew, his mother was wondering at this very moment if he was using an online dating site. *There's no escape from one's parents,* he thought. *It's like running away from one's own shadow.*

Raj emailed his mother back, telling her he'd be there for the weekend and asking if Chandra was also coming. He didn't want to have both parents focused exclusively on him.

* * *

A few days later, Raj found himself in Whiskey Jack's nightclub. The seats were overstuffed but comfortable, and Dan and Raj were drinking beer. The club was filling up and loud music from the seventies and eighties was playing, currently Linda Ronstadt was singing, "You're no good." Dan didn't seem to notice. His attention was focused on surveying the other tables.

"You see, Raj," he said without looking at him, "the deal is that you have to make eye contact and then see if they look back."

This was an art, and Dan, the master, was educating him. "It's like fishing, Raj. You're trawling for a bite."

Raj tried to smile, mainly to hide his nervousness and discomfort. He felt quite out of place. Some of the men and women in the place looked old enough to be his parents. They were dressed up, drinking, and chatting up with each other. There was something almost sad and desperate about the whole thing.

Raj was wearing an expensive blazer of dark green cashmere that had cost him a good part of his monthly salary. If he owned sunglasses, he would have put them on in order to stay incognito. This was stupid, he knew, but the whole thing was stressful. You only "rent" beer for an hour or so. The bathroom beckoned.

A slow, circuitous walk there afforded Raj a better look at the people in the large bar. He perused them and subconsciously thought about them less as people and more as potential patients. One woman who was smoking had a largish chest – emphysema; the chubby middle-aged man was probably diabetic. The list grew as he got closer to the bathroom.

His gaze strayed to a table where a couple of well-dressed women were drinking Manhattans, and he caught the eye of one of them. Her blonde hair was swept back stylishly. She looked to be around forty and was wearing a tight dress and high heels. Raj wasn't thinking about anything other than what might land her in hospital – possibly an injury from her hot yoga class, like a nasty rug burn. She looked straight into his eyes, and he felt that she was reading his mind.

He looked away, feeling that he had invaded her space. He looked back after he had passed her. She was still watching him with an odd look – perhaps she thought he was a serial killer and was getting her pepper spray ready. Raj thought he'd better leave before they called the police and accused him of being a stalker. This evening was turning into a stressful bore.

On his way back from the bathroom, Raj took a different route to avoid the table where the blonde woman was sitting with her friend. He told Dan what had happened, and Dan, looking surprised, said, "You got a look, and you didn't go and talk to them? What are you – gay?"

"No! Why do people keep asking me that?" Raj said a little too loudly.

"Jeez, Raj," said Dan. "Take it easy, man. Let me have a look at them."

Dan headed for the washroom so that he could have a surreptitious look at the two women. On his return, he said, "Nice, Raj. The brunette is working a bit of a Sandra Bullock thing. We have to get moving before every greasy bastard in the room starts hitting on them. Both of them are totally hot. Okay, let's send them some drinks and then go over and introduce ourselves."

"But Dan, we don't even know them," Raj protested.

"Don't worry about it, Raj. They'll just have to learn how spectacular we are." Dan winked at him.

Raj had not admitted to Dan that he was a virgin, more or less. The whole situation was more nerve-racking than facing a patient in congestive heart failure.

Dan moved in quickly to sit beside the two women. The drinks he ordered arrived, and he went into what Raj assumed was a well-practiced routine. "Evening, ladies. We're trying to decide if you'd like to join our club."

"What club is that?" the brunette asked. "It's not what I'm thinking, is it?

"Raj and I are planning to start a … Cuddle Club because we like to cuddle, and we're really good at it! Do you like to cuddle?" Dan said this with a completely straight face.

The women couldn't help but laugh. The ice was broken, and they made their introductions.

The blonde with whom Raj had made eye contact was Judy. He wanted to address her as Mrs. and had to catch himself. Judy and her friend Lisa were out enjoying the music. Judy was a hairstylist, and Lisa was a bookkeeper. Both looked northern European, with bright blue eyes. Raj noticed they looked strikingly healthy, as if they exercised regularly.

Dan mentioned that he and Raj were doctors working at St. Jerome Hospital. The women seemed interested, but Raj wondered if they really believed Dan. Not wanting to give the impression they were wealthy, Raj spoke up and made it clear that, although they were indeed doctors, they were only interns – "you know, trainees." This didn't seem to affect their interest at all. Judy stared at him as he spoke as if he were a genius.

"How do you like St. Jerome?" she asked him.

He told her that it was great so far. It seemed to be a friendly town, much nicer than Toronto.

Dan ordered another round, and Raj wondered if he were trying to maliciously get the women drunk. It would be easy, as they were drinking Manhattans. Dan kept the women talking about themselves, and Raj learned that, indeed, they were fans of hot yoga and Pilates. Both were much more relaxed than any other women Raj had been around. The more tipsy Judy got, the more she smiled.

After a few more drinks, Judy and Lisa left together for the bathroom. Raj and Dan stared at their rear ends as they walked away. Judy's low-cut dress fit her like spandex, and she wore glossy high heels. Lisa's dress was just as tight, and her heels just as high. Raj surmised that they were probably out doing exactly what he and Dan were doing, and he was momentarily surprised that two women would want exactly the same thing he did.

"Dan, I don't know if I can handle that woman. She's so good-looking, and it looks as though she works out every day."

Dan agreed. "Yeah, they're both super hot. Man, we've hit the jackpot! Have you ever noticed, Raj, that really good-looking chicks have good-looking friends?"

"No," Raj said. "I've never noticed."

"It's something I've studied since my lowly undergraduate days."

"Dan, Judy is way too hot for me. I'm going to blow it." Raj was worried.

"Raj, you can handle her. She'll crush you between her beautiful thighs, and you'll love it. She's a total fox, isn't she?"

"She's totally hot. I can't figure out what she wants with me, though."

"It's obvious, Raj. Just go with the flow and let things happen. She's already made up her mind that she's going to sleep with you. All you have to do is not screw things up." Dan thought for a moment. "Maybe we should take them to your place since Jenny might call."

"My place?" said Raj. "Are you kidding? My parents might call."

"Better your place than mine because Jenny might call me. I borrowed her car, you know."

Raj did a double take. Borrowing a girlfriend's car to go out and pick up some woman in a bar? Raj found this completely amoral. Dumbfounded, he just stared at Dan.

"Well, my car needed a new muffler, and Jenny offered to lend me hers. Anyway," said Dan, "it's not about me. Tonight is about

144

you."

"I can't believe you borrowed your girlfriend's car. Whatever you do, don't make her think that I had anything to do with this."

As Judy and Lisa returned, Raj couldn't help staring at Judy's glorious breasts bouncing slightly in the skintight dress, and suddenly he didn't care whose car Dan had borrowed.

"Have you girls ever seen how a real doc lives?" Dan asked.

The four of them piled into the two cars and drove off. It was a cool late-summer night, Raj's favorite time of year. He wound down the window and let some air into the little Honda. Judy said she felt chilly, so Raj stopped the car and wrapped his jacket around her. He was very nervous and wanted to keep her talking.

"My place isn't much to look at, but I like it because it's so close to the hospital," he said.

"I guess you guys are kept fairly busy."

"Yes, they don't let us out very much. Unattached junior doctors released on an unsuspecting city are dangerous, you know."

"So you have to make the best of it, then – I guess?"

"Absolutely! This is the most fun I've had so far."

Dan parked his girlfriend's car beside Raj's, and almost immediately, he and Lisa were all over each other. Raj could hear them, and their passion encouraged him to be more assertive with Judy. He turned to wrap his arm around her, but she had already gotten out of the car. Minutes later, they were all at Raj's front door.

Raj stopped for a moment before letting them in, wondering if there was anything in there that could be embarrassing. Dirty underwear, dirty dishes, empty beer bottles? "Sorry, my place is a bit messy," he said.

"Don't worry about it, Raj," Judy said.

Lisa, hanging off Dan, giggled. "Yeah, I gotta pee!"

Raj opened the front door but didn't put the lights on, thinking it would be best to keep the place in semidarkness, to hide the dirty clothes and empty Chinese takeout boxes that were strewn about.

The only make-out music Raj could find was some old Bee Gees on his iPod. As "More than a Woman" floated from the speakers, Raj opened a bottle of wine that he had bought just that day. Dan had told him that wine was essential to seduction. Raj poured the wine into water glasses. They were all he had. Dan was already moving in on Lisa.

Raj looked at the beautiful woman sitting on his little IKEA couch, uncertain what to do next. He panicked briefly before he sat down beside her and said, "You're really beautiful, you know. It's like you stepped out of a dream. I think you're kind of magical."

Judy set down her glass of wine and came in close. "You're

handsome, Raj. You know I like younger men don't you?"

They began to kiss, slowly and tentatively, as Raj held her close, feeling the warmth of her body and breath. Her perfume invaded his senses, like pure glucose to his primitive brain. Raj was lost in the moment, but tried not to get too excited when Judy began panting about "Tantric sex" and "energy flows" He wanted Judy to think he knew what he was doing and wasn't just a young guy with a boner that was ready to go off.

"Come with me now," he whispered.

"Okay, Dr. Raj. Take me away," she whispered back.

They went into the bedroom.

Judy, not at all shy, quickly stepped out of her dress and high heels. She was tall with beautiful, large breasts and full hips. Her tanned skin was gleaming and a tiny diamond pendant swung from her pierced navel. In another time, he thought, she would have been a Viking queen. Her lovely body presented a buffet of carnal pleasure right down to her pedicure. She smiled at him with a completely open smile, and it seemed to him that all the secrets of the world were hidden behind that beautiful smile and her laughing blue eyes. She was enjoying his reaction.

Raj nearly lost control and began to tremble. He bit his lower lip so that he wouldn't come in his boxers.

Judy pushed him onto the bed, saying, "Let me show you the

right way, Raj." She straddled him and, leaning down low, dangled her perfumed breasts in his face.

Raj managed to unhook her bra and took her breasts in his hands. She slowed him down and gently guided his erection. She seemed hungry for his dark, lean body. Her hands stroked his chest, and then her nails dug into his shoulders as she became more excited.

Fast at first, and then slowly, rhythmically – again and again. Judy was a skilled lover. She continued the slow kissing and teasing until Raj was so excited that he was at last able to perform the way she needed him to, climaxing in a way that felt almost painful. He shouted as if some dark spirit had finally been released from within him. He lay on his back for a few minutes, a big smile on his face, while she stroked his chest and thigh. Then he became excited again, and they repeated it all – and this time, Raj performed with more determination. He used his pent-up energy until he was sweating and exhausted. At last, he was… comfortable. Before he drifted off, Raj felt something, just for a moment. Was it a shame? Guilt? But the sight of Judy's splendid body, like a goddess of love, swept these feelings away. Was she some sort of avatar? She rested her head on his shoulder, and both of them surrendered to blissful sleep.

Raj's awareness melted, and his mind took him to ancient India, where sunflowers bloomed, and exotic women danced. Once again, the dream ended with the woman with the spiral markings on her leg, her veil hiding everything but her laughing eyes. She whispered to Raj once again, "The great wheel is turning."

Chapter Sixteen

Diana spent her coffee break in the hospital cafeteria because it had windows and her father's office did not. She was texting some of the other cast members. They were partying after the show that night and wanted Diana to come along. She wrote, "I'll tag along, but you bitches better not have nicer shoes than mine." She was tired of people having better shoes than hers and had resolved to spend her next paycheque just on shoes. Maybe she would borrow some of her mother's for tonight; they wore the same size. As she sent the text to her mother, the intern walked in.

Dressed like her father, Raj looked more confident, even though he wasn't much older than Diana. She thought that he must have got advice about what to wear. He seemed to have a little more swagger today as though he belonged in his lab coat – the determined young MD. She was sure he wouldn't notice her in the big cafeteria and stared at him as he bypassed a Danish for yogurt and a low-fat muffin. Her phone chimed, and Diana saw that her mother had responded that she had several high heels that would work for Diana.

"Hey there! How's the soon-to-be-famous actress?"

Diana was startled; she had missed seeing him approach. He sat across from her and smiled.

"Just wanted to thank you," he said.

"For what?"

"Rekindling my love affair with fruit." He laughed. "It's been a while, but we're back together. You better watch out because that little market stocks enough mangoes for only one of us, and I've bought their entire stock."

"You're kidding!"

"I know you're their favourite, but my stock is rising with the Hongs."

Diana smiled. He was trying to be friendly.

"How's the acting business?" he asked her. "Are you working tonight?"

"Actually, I am."

"I'd love to see your show some day."

"Really?" Diana was flattered.

"Yeah. I think it would be fun."

Paula joined them at the table. "Hi, Raj," she said. "Hi ... Diana, isn't it?"

"Yes," Diana said. "I work for Dr. Sinclair down in the dungeon."

"Diana's in a dinner play in Toronto," Raj said.

"Really!" Paula said. "That's cool, Diana. So you're working for Dr. Sinclair part-time?"

"Yes. You know – the underemployed actress thing. Anyway, it's better than waiting tables."

"Paula, I told Diana I wanted to see her play."

"I'd love to go too – it'd be fun." Paula was enthusiastic.

"It's not a really big play, guys. It's just dinner theatre, but it's fun," Diana said.

"Why don't we get Dan and Kelly and the four of us to go?" Paula said.

"Okay," Raj said. "Diana, we can be your St. Jerome booster club. Are we allowed to cheer?"

Diana appreciated that Raj was trying to be nice to her, and she was warming up to him. She liked him, even his little beard and moustache. He was just a nerdy guy trying to be dashing. Perhaps he was looking better, or maybe it was just that he seemed genuinely interested in what she was doing. It was refreshing, and she decided to give him a chance.

"I'm hanging out with some of the cast members after the show tonight," she said. "We can all have a drink afterwards if you'd like."

"I'd like that," Raj said.

"The theatre is just off College Street in the west end, and the play is called *Tony and Tina's Wedding*."

"Okay." Raj was eager. "We'll be there tonight."

"See you there then, and hang around afterward so I can introduce you to the cast. Now I'd better get going – you know, my boss. See you tonight."

Diana left, wondering whether Raj and Paula were dating. Maybe Paula had a thing for Raj, and he wasn't aware of it. Diana had heard from a couple of nurses that he was turning in to an item of interest around the hospital. She would find out more tonight if the two of them kept their promise to come and hoped they would. She was curious to see what he and his friends were like outside the hospital.

* * *

There was singing and several funny monologues by actors playing Italian New Yorkers. The four interns were having a great time, drinking sparkling wine, and singing along with the cast. Diana was playing the part of a pregnant bridesmaid. Despite the fake pregnant tummy, she looked good and was a surprisingly good dancer. When the show was over, she came to their table to say hello. Everyone wanted to feel her belly, which was made of memory foam. She said she liked to bump into people with it and occasionally even rested drinks on it. She asked them what they thought of the show.

"That was the coolest play I've ever seen." Raj was being honest – he had not seen many plays.

"I thought you sang really well, Diana," Paula said.

As they were talking and joking around, a tall, muscular young man came into the little dinner theatre. The guy had a presence about him, and the little theatre seemed to get quieter as he came in – people noticed him. It was Star, his hair in his signature ponytail, wearing a leather jacket, blue jeans, and cowboy boots. Paula was the first to notice him. "Who is that *Adonis* coming this way?" she gushed.

"Adonis? Who calls someone Adonis?" Raj said.

"That guy coming over is a Hottie, Raj," Paula said.

Star winked at them as he came up behind Diana and gave her a little slap on the ass. "Hey, baby. Thought I'd see where you're working."

"Star! Why are you here?" Diana wasn't expecting him.

"I was in town and needed to see you," he said. "You know, that dress makes you look a little… fat."

"It's my costume, Star. I'm supposed to be a *pregnant* bridesmaid," Diana said.

"Oh! I thought you were eating too many carbs. Why don't you get out of that dress and into my car? Let's go out."

"Star, I promised my friends here that I'd go out with them tonight. They're all doctors at St Jerome's," Diana said.

"Hi, people!" Star pulled a chair up to the table between Paula and Kelly, who couldn't take their eyes off him. Diana said something about getting changed and slipped away,

"Are you the billboard guy in the racing-stripe underwear?" Paula wanted to know.

"Yes, that's me. You're obviously very observant. Many people don't recognize me because I have to wear a helmet when I play," said Star.

"I recognize the ponytail, Star. I love the highlights. Wasn't your hair pink for a while?" Kelly, too, was gushing.

"Thanks," Star replied. "It's a bit metro, but I use a lot of conditioners, especially after a game. I went pink for breast-cancer support week."

Dan steered the conversation to the subject of the Maple Leafs, and all of them, except Raj, chatted about the team's prospects for the season. Raj had never followed hockey that much and stayed quiet.

Diana returned wearing tight-fitting jeans and sat down next to Raj.

"Hey babe, your friends are a lot of fun," Star said.

Kelly and Paula were now more than a bit drunk and giggling and basking in Star's attention. He told them about his new smoothie with cocoa "nips," as he called them. "It's so healthy, you could call it a super food," he boasted.

"Really, Star? And you came up with the recipe yourself?" asked Kelly.

"Actually, it was developed by an ancient Mayan shaman I met in Belize. It's sweetened with agave cactus syrup, so it's okay for low-carb diets."

"You have so many talents!" Paula gushed.

"Well, if I hadn't become a hockey player, I'm sure I'd have been a scientist."

"One of those super-hot scientists with glasses, hunched over a microscope!" Kelly thought this was terribly funny and couldn't stop laughing. She grabbed Star's arm, looking like she was fondling his muscles.

By this time, the other cast members had appeared from back stage. One of them, a totally proud queer named Fred, set up a karaoke machine and started singing the Whitey Houston classic "I Wanna Dance with Somebody." The others cheered and hooted, and a couple of them got up to dance.

Diana watched her ex-boyfriend in action, unsure if she should be jealous or simply amused. Star wasn't even trying, and yet Paula and Kelly, two highly educated women, were acting like squealing teenagers who'd just met Justin Bieber.

Dan had left the table to talk to a couple of older women sitting at the next table.

The wine Raj had been drinking had loosened him up enough that he could speak freely. He leaned closer to Diana and said, "Your boyfriend is pretty cool."

"Yeah, I know – and he's got a Porsche convertible. Did you know he's from St. Jerome?"

"Really!" said Raj. "Home town, boy. He's pretty fly for a white guy."

"Girls do seem to love him."

"Does he always do that?"

"Do what?"

"Spend the entire evening talking about himself?"

"Yes, he does most of the time. You noticed?"

"It's hard not to. I feel like chopped liver here." Raj watched Star for a moment. He was now dancing with both Kelly and Paula and a couple of women from the cast, bumping his hips against theirs in turn.

"Do you think I should get some *Star and Stripes* underwear?" Raj said.

"I'm told that they're really tight in the crotch. Supposed to make your thing look big." Diana laughed, and Raj realized she was just teasing him.

"Narcissus and the sunflower," he mused.

"What's that?"

"Narcissus and the sunflower. That's what you two are."

Diana understood. "We're both flowers, but one bends toward the sun and the other just…..loves itself. You remembered that I like sunflowers! That's really nice of you,"

"You know our sun isn't just a sun, it's also a –"

"Star," said Diana. "You know, Raj, Hippocrates actually studied the stars to help people."

"How would you know about Hippocrates Diana? You know he's considered the father of medicine."

"I studied some ancient history at school. It was kind of cool, actually." Diana said and paused for a moment. Star was now on stage, about to sing karaoke.

Fred dashed up to the little stage and said with a flourish, "Ladies and gentlemen! We have a special treat for you tonight, straight from the National Hockey League, a very special guest. He does it all – he plays hockey, he models underwear, and he's the coolest guy that ever wore a ponytail. Ladies and gentlemen, I present STAR YANOFSKY".

Star grabbed the microphone and started singing "I'm Too Sexy." A couple of the cast members began dancing behind Star. He made some dance moves, took off his jacket, swung it around, and tossed it towards Kelly. The crowed went crazy.

Hours later, Kelly and Paula, now quite drunk, had to be driven home in Dan's car. Star finally left with Diana after they sang the duet, "I Got You, Babe." Raj had sobered up and was feeling a little dejected. He didn't want to drive all the way back to St Jerome and decided to spend the night at his parents' house in East York as it was a lot closer.

It was 1:00 a.m. when he pulled into the driveway. His parents, happy to see him, offered him food, but Raj, exhausted and just a little tipsy, went straight to bed, thinking about Diana. Did she like him? Maybe, but probably just as a friend. How could he compete with someone like Star anyway? He drifted off to sleep and once again dreamed of sunflowers, a softly lit palace, and a woman with smiling eyes.

Chapter Seventeen

The video monitor displayed a rapid spike pattern, indicating a heart rate of 200 beats per minute. Then the spikes began to fuse into a sawtooth pattern. Raj could feel his own chest tightening. Somewhere in the back of his mind, a voice was saying, "What are you going to do, Dr. Mehta? What are you going to do?" Fuck ... I'm going to lose him... I'm going to lose him...

Raj jolted awake from the nightmare, disoriented and sweating. It took him a minute to realize that he was at his parent's house, and his father was staring at him, looking concerned.

"Raj? Are you okay? I think you had a bad dream. It's time to get up. We are going to the temple today. Your mother has made you breakfast."

Raj sat up. It *was* a bad dream – one in which he needed to act quickly but was paralyzed by fear. He had talked about dreams with the other interns and learned that they all had nightmares about exams or really sick people in their care. He shook his head to clear those thoughts and got out of bed, happy to be back home in his parents' house, although he'd never admit it. The small story-and-a-half house with his little bedroom on the second floor reminded him of how close his family was. He smelled coffee and idli – soft, savoury little pancakes served with stewed onions, a typical weekend breakfast – wafting up from the kitchen. The whole house always smelled of food.

Raj's mother turned and smiled as he entered the kitchen, "Ahh, look at this! The chicks have returned to the nest to see the mother hen!" Chandra was already at the table, eating and reading a magazine. His father poured coffee for him. "Come, Raj," he said. "Sit down and eat, and we will talk a bit."

"You know, Raj, they're making us go to the temple today," Chandra said.

Raj took a long drink of the very strong coffee. "I'm surprised you're home. How's it going at Ryerson?"

"It's good, but I had to get away from my housemates. The kitchen's dirty, and Mom makes the best breakfast in Toronto."

Raj started shoving idli into his mouth. The mild flavour was the perfect antidote to a hangover. In the background, the television showed a stream of ads for saris, jewellery, and wedding halls. There were also ads for Gustad's frozen Indian entrees, which Raj knew was a constant source of irritation for his father.

After some cajoling, Raj's parents persuaded him and Chandra to come with them to the temple to celebrate the festival of Diwali. Radhu had never been particularly religious, and Raj and Chandra wondered if their parents had a religious epiphany in their old age. More likely, they were lonely and bored now that their children weren't living with them, except when they came home to eat.

As they entered the temple parking lot, Raj was surprised by how enormous the temple was. Inside the ornately carved marble
160

building, families sat together on the richly carpeted floor. The huge main hall quickly filled with people, the women in brightly coloured saris and dazzling jewellery. The Mehtas joined them, and the ceremony proceeded with priests, incense, chanting, and, incredibly, an elephant. The animal was beautifully painted and wore a silk cloth on its back. It looked at the large crowd with intelligence and curiosity, like a queen benignly observing her subjects with grace and mild interest.

Raj and Chandra understood nothing of the ceremony, and Raj wondered if his parents understood it, suspecting they knew nothing at all but attended merely for the spectacle. Raj was about to sit down and relax into a torpor brought on by breakfast and his hangover.

"Raj? I thought it was you!"

Shit! It was Shari Ramsaran, she of the malfunctioning 'gaydar'. What the hell was she doing here? Somehow she had appeared beside him.

"Raj, I didn't know you came to the temple. It's nice to see you again."

"Nice to see you, too," Raj said. "Are you here with your parents?"

"Yes. They're farther back because we just got here. Beautiful, isn't she?" Shari was looking at the elephant.

"She's quite regal," Raj said. "You have to wonder what secrets she has."

"Yes, there's so much more behind those eyes.

"What do you suppose she's thinking about right now?"

"Maybe she's wondering if everyone around her is who they say they are."

Raj laughed. "Maybe she's thinking she'd like some peanuts."

He wondered if going to the temple had been a plan his parents concocted for him to bump into Shari. But it couldn't have been because he had gone home on the spur of the moment.

Shari turned to his parents and Chandra. She chatted with them, and Raj was vaguely annoyed that they were so polite and paid so much attention to her. They quickly invited Shari to join them, and she finally sat down with Raj. He said nothing and kept staring at the elephant, its peaceful eyes and tinkling ornaments, wondering if it understood its place in the scheme of things. He remembered reading that female elephants maintain continuous relationships with their mothers for their entire lives. It dawned on him that his mother wanted another daughter, a daughter-in-law. Chandra was close to Mom, but their lives seemed worlds apart.

The temple ceremony lasted another hour, and it took a long time to get out of the giant hall to the parking lot. Before Shari rejoined her family, she squeezed something into Raj's hand and said in a serious tone, "For you." Then she flitted away like a fairy in a forest of dazzling, metallic, and pastel-coloured saris. Raj noted that Shari was wearing traditional sandals and a light purple sari, the kind one would expect to see on someone older. But on Shari, it looked good, especially how it clung to her breasts. She moved with sensual grace. He felt guilty thinking such impure thoughts in a house of worship.

The Mehta family slowly made their way to the large entrance hall, where food was served. The place was packed, and everyone seemed to know one another. Even Chandra knew a few people and was chatting with them.

A local politician was handing out little Canada flags. His father made sure to get one. His father was fiercely loyal to Canada as if his adopted country were the embodiment of all the hopes and dreams of his ancestors. He had often told Raj, "This is Canada, boy. Work hard and fit in, and you will be a success. We are here because of you and will never return." Radhu even wanted his ashes to stay on Canadian soil. In Canada, Radhu was sure his family would find all the good things they dreamed of. He was not the only one. Hundreds of thousands of Indians had come to Canada for the same reason –here for their children's sake.

Once they were outside, Raj remarked to no one in particular, "Rather surprising that we ran into Shari Ramsaran at the temple, wouldn't you say?"

Mena spoke up. "Not at all, Raj. She is probably a very spiritual girl and likes to meditate." Raj wanted to meditate on her breasts.

On their way home, trying to change the subject, Radhu mentioned that Shamila had again been boasting about Roger, who was making a fortune in London and had become a skilled polo player. In fact, he had become so good with horses that he and Uma had gone to South Africa to tour the wilderness on horseback. "Apparently, you can see all manner of wildlife – lions, elephants, and zebras."

Mena added, "You know, Raj, these tours are quite dangerous! An Englishman was eaten by lions just a few weeks ago."

Chandra had to point out that the most dangerous place in South Africa was not the savannah but the city slums, where groups of AIDS-infected street toughs roamed, indiscriminately robbing and killing.

When they arrived at the little house in East York, Raj wanted to head back to St. Jerome immediately, but his parents persuaded him to stay. The enticement was stir-fried cauliflower, eggplant, and tomatoes served with chapattis, which neither Raj nor Chandra could resist.

Radhu gave Raj a Carlsberg and sat beside him at the kitchen table. He cleared his throat as if he had something important to say. "Shamila and Gustad are very excited. Roger and Uma are coming for the Christmas holidays, and they're hosting a big New Year's Eve party."

Chan spoke up. "Oh, great, another family party where we hang around eating that disgusting food Gustad sells. I was planning to go out with my roommates."

"You will *not* be going out with your roommates," Mena said. "We are *all* going to Shamila's party. I have already promised her. Do you want to embarrass your father and me?" Chandra looked unhappy.

Raj's mother and father often spoke about Shamila and Gustad, and Raj wondered if they were jealous of their wealth. When Shamila and her husband first arrived in Canada, they had lived in his parents' house for a short while. Raj's impression as a child was that Gustad was a very hard-working but rather boastful man. Their son, Roger, seemed to have learned this from his dad.

Roger considered himself a winner and everyone else, including Raj and his sister, losers. His favourite television show had been "The Apprentice" – he loved Donald Trump. His upcoming wedding to a wealthy young Englishwoman reflected his belief in his superiority

"Raj, why don't you invite Shari to the New Year's Eve party?" Mena said.

"I've met Shari just a couple of times, Mom," Raj said, "and we don't really know each other. Besides, I'm on call at the hospital over Christmas."

"But you mentioned that you'll be off after Christmas so you can be home for New Year's. So think about it, son," Mena said.

Chandra chimed in. "If Raj is going to bring a date, then I'm bringing Quentin."

Radhu, who disliked Quentin largely because he was white and worked at a video store, told Chandra to ensure that Quentin washed beforehand not to embarrass the family. Raj was surprised he didn't object more and thought perhaps his father was anticipating – even hoping – that Quentin would get food poisoning at the party. Gustad and Shamila's parties always featured a large buffet of the entrées he sold at Indian supermarkets.

On the way back to St. Jerome, Raj remembered the piece of paper Shari had given him. He pulled it out of his pocket and read: *First, let me apologize to you for my behaviour when you and your parents visited my family. Obviously, I was trying too hard to be sophisticated and wound up sounding like a jerk. I think you're a nice person, and my parents think the world of you. Maybe we can get together sometime and start over again. I will leave this up to you. Call me on my cell sometime. Shari*

She'd written down her cellphone number. Raj reread the note and was struck by how she could admit that she had made a mistake. He could stay angry with her, but that would make him a small man, not the person he wanted to be. Thoughts of her plagued him all the way home until late that night. He recalled how elegant she looked in her sari, her hips gently swaying in what seemed to be an invitation.

166

Chapter Eighteen

On Thursday night, Star had taken Diana from the dinner club back to his apartment, even though she wanted to stay with the interns and perhaps dance with them. Raj had surprised her with his insight about Star. She almost felt a bit childish around the doctor. But Star had insisted she leave with him.

He had wanted sex as soon as they got in, but Diana was not in the mood, making him sulky and unhappy. When they finally got around to it, Diana heard Star's grunting and felt his thrusting, but she went through the motions, and only after fantasizing was she able to climax. She had never had to fantasize before, but this time someone came to mind – Raj.

The next day at work, she was still thinking about him – his lean body, his dark eyes staring into hers. It bugged her that he rarely talked about himself; it gave him an air of mystery. He wasn't as muscular as Star, but he had a lean, athletic physique and a handsome face. Diana began thinking about his body. Was he…circumcised?

"Hey! Are you working or daydreaming?" Diana's father had come up behind her in the office. She had forgotten about the patients in the waiting room.

"Sorry, Doctor. Just a moment." Diana pulled herself back into the real world and ushered the next patient into the consultation room.

She was mixed up and unsure what to do about her relationship with Star. He was trying to be nice, even attentive, but he seemed to take it for granted that she wanted to be with him. She had learned that her parents had met with Star's parents a few weekends ago and had talked about starting up a supper club. Star's parents had always liked her, and her mother was particularly charmed by Star. Mischa, however, irritated her. Diana knew that she had been texting Star on the weekend. Diana hoped the Russian she-wolf would trip over her high heels and break an ankle.

More patients entered the office, and the morning slipped by with little interruption. Then, just before lunch, a call from the CEO's office and Wendy Fletcher came on the line. "This is the CEO. I'm looking for Dr. Freedman. Can you locate him and have him call me?"

"May I tell him the reason for your call?" said Diana.

"No, you may not," came the brusque reply. "Just find him, please, and tell him to come to my office at 4 p.m."

Diana was puzzled why the CEO always wanted to see Dan. She tracked him down during the lunch hour in the cafeteria with the other interns. She joined them and told Dan that the CEO wanted to see him at 4 p.m.

The other interns grinned at him. It was clear to Diana that something was going on, but she didn't know what the inside joke was.

Paula said, "Shall we tell her?"

"Please don't," Dan said. "I'm embarrassed enough." He was blushing.

"It's okay, Dan. It's not like you're sleeping with her... yet," Paula snickered.

Totally confused, Diana asked, "What in the world is going on?"

Raj spoke on behalf of his friend. "The CEO has the hots for Danny Boy."

"Raj, you have to help me out of this. She's very aggressive!" Dan said.

"Sorry, man. It's obvious she has eyes only for you, and I'm not into threesomes!"

"Geez, I'd better clean up a bit. I've been in the OR all day," said Dan in resignation.

In a sexy voice, Kelly said, "Don't worry, Danny. She likes you dirty!"

"Nice and dirty, Dan," Paula echoed, and both laughed.

As the interns kept teasing Dan, Diana was looking at Raj. In his starched lab coat and expensive tie, he looked a bit like her dad. He smiled, showing his perfect teeth, and his eyes lingered on her for a long moment. Diana wanted to see him again – he was fun and easy to talk to. She slipped away and returned to her father's office.

Back at her desk, she opened her email to get her mind off Raj. There was a message from Fred of the dinner theatre cast: *Hey, Girlfriend! You're going to thank me when you hear this. I got you an audition! Mama Mia is coming back to Toronto, and they're looking for new people. I told the director (a pal from school) that you'd be perfect as one of the girls. It's a great gig and pays really well! You'll have to come in for an audition, but he's seen your head shot and likes your look. He wants you to come by next week. This is Big Time, baby. Don't screw up – my reputation is on the line. Hugs and kisses, Freddie*

Diana sat back in her chair. She loved ABBA's songs and had seen the musical with her parents on its first run in Toronto. Fred's news was stunning. It was the kind of job she dreamed about. She couldn't have been happier.

* * *

Raj's morning was as hectic as ever, with several new patients to see. Before heading in to see the next one, Raj stopped by the nursing station on the medical floor to read the patient's chart. It was hard to make out the hieroglyphics that Dr. Cooper had written. He had just realized it read "Transesophageal echocardiogram" when he felt a hand touch his shoulder and massage it. It felt nice. Was it Paula? Raj had wondered if Paula liked him. He turned around to say hello to her and found himself face to face with a smiling older man with a gap between his two front teeth and an orangish tan.

"Dr. Mehta, I presume?"

Raj's first thought was, *where did this guy get off touching me?* His second thought was that the man was a senior staff doctor. Raj clenched his jaw. What did he want?

"Hello, Dr. Froeder," he said

"I always try to get to know the interns – especially you, since you'll be looking after my patients this weekend, and a couple of them will need close observation."

"No problem, sir. I was just doing rounds on Dr. Cooper's patients," said Raj.

Dr. Froeder said that, after Raj was done with Cooper's patients, he'd introduce him to a few of his more interesting patients – those he wanted Raj to keep an eye on. Raj groaned inwardly.

Paula walked by, and Raj nodded at her. She gave him a smile, saying, "He touched you, didn't he? I told you so."

Raj spent the next hour visiting the rest of Dr. Cooper's patients, including Charlie Rosenplot, who had been in the hospital so long he'd become an institution. Charlie wanted bourbon and smokes, even though the hospital banned them and he had no family to smuggle them in.

Charlie had a new roommate, a man named Royal Finch, whom Charlie said he knew as a customer. Royal had been admitted after his chemotherapy treatment resulted in a drop in his white blood cells and, in turn, a bloodstream infection.

Royal was lying in bed, sweating, his wife at his side. Raj examined him carefully, noting the perspiration and looking for the cause of the infection. There was nothing obvious, so he started Royal on a broad spectrum of antibiotics and ordered a CAT scan.

"Is he going to be okay, Doctor?" Royal's wife looked to be near tears.

"It's hard to say, Mrs. Finch. I think so," Raj said.

"Royal didn't want chemo, but I talked him into it. I don't want to lose him."

"Mrs. Finch, we'll do everything we can to ensure he's okay. We'll know better in a couple of days."

By the time Raj finished his rounds, he was tired and headed to the cafeteria for a coffee. Paula found him there a few minutes later, slumped in his chair.

"I'm so happy you met Dr. Froeder," she said.

"Why's that?"

"I wasn't sure whether he likes feeling up only women and is basically a perv."

"So him massaging me means he's not really a perv, just a lecher?"

"Right, Raj. Now I don't think he's a lecher or even a perv – or maybe he is, but just a bit. The important thing is that he's an equal opportunity kind of guy, and I respect that."

"Maybe he's European. They like touching people," Raj said.

"So do I." Paula smiled.

The conversation didn't comfort Raj at all, and later that morning, Raj found himself in the hospital bathroom, wondering whether he gave off a gay vibe. Dr. Froeder not only massaged Raj's neck, but he also stood uncomfortably close. Was he gay and letting Raj know?

Raj stared at himself in the mirror, noticing his hair was getting longish, but his beard still looked carefully trimmed. As Raj was combing his hair, a hospital porter, who looked West Indian, came in. He smiled at Raj, revealing a gold front tooth. "Hey, Doc! Lookin' good, mon!" Raj hurried out of the bathroom, afraid that yet another person thought he was gay.

As much as he wanted to avoid it, an hour later, he joined Paula and Dr. Froeder to visit a few patients "for interest's sake," as Froeder put it. Raj, who was normally curious about new patients, was too distracted by his worries of coming across as gay to concentrate. But Froeder evidently was keen to make Raj pay attention.

"Have a listen to this man's heart, Raj," he said as they approached the first patient's bed.

Raj sensed a trap. He knew that when a senior staff doctor asks an intern to do something, it is usually to demonstrate that the intern is an incompetent boob. Raj had provided this kind of entertainment for teaching docs hundreds of times.

But now, Raj had no choice but to look carefully at the patient, an older man with oxygen on and wires stuck on his chest. Raj was immediately struck by the presence of a fourth wire because, usually, there were only three. This man had an extra one on his right side.

Raj listened but heard nothing: no heart beats, only the tiny whisper of air moving about in the lungs. For a second, he was puzzled, but then it came to him: the man had dextrocardia – a reversal of the internal organs.

"Very good, Dr. Mehta," said Dr. Froeder. "Dr. Johnson took a little longer to figure it out." Paula, standing behind Dr. Froeder, reddened. "Dr. Mehta," he continued, "perhaps you can tell me about this man's condition."

Raj couldn't remember much about the condition. In fact, he thought it was always fatal.

"Uh... I think it is an embryonic malformation occurring sometime around the twentieth week after conception," he said. "Are his abdominal organs reversed, too?"

"Yes, as you can see from his appendectomy scar. It's on the left side rather than the right." Dr. Froeder appeared satisfied with Raj's answer, and they moved on to his next patient.

Raj thought Paula was coping well, given that she had already done rounds on these patients with Dr. Froeder and had already gone through this teaching session with him.

The other patients Dr. Froeder wanted Raj to see were a man with tuberculosis and another who was swollen up like a balloon, desperately sick with pancreatitis. Froeder laid his hands on each patient, concentrating as if he were trying to do a Vulcan mind meld. "Yes," Froeder said, "I think I can hear inflammatory changes in this man's chest " after he listened carefully to the Tuberculosis patient.

Once the rounds were over, Raj and Paula both let out a huge sigh of relief.

"Phew, I'm glad that's over. I don't know how you manage it daily," Raj said.

Paula said, "At least you know something about dextrocardia."

"That was a lucky guess."

"I think Froeder likes you."

"What do you mean? He likes me, or he *likes* me?" Raj said coyly, giving Paula his cool, suave look.

"He doesn't *like* you. He thinks you're a good intern!" Paula said, and they both laughed.

On the spur of the moment, Raj asked her, "Do you want to have dinner at my place? I'm on call, so I have to stay close. We could watch TV."

"Okay," Paula said. "I just hope you don't get called in too often."

It wouldn't be a real date, but at least he'd spend the evening with a friend. Paula and the other interns also lived in the hospital apartment building. This made it really easy just to hang out together. The thought cheered him.

Chapter Nineteen

Shortly after 4:00 p.m., Dan put his head around the CEO's office door. "Hi, Wendy. You wanted to see me?"

Wendy was sitting on a large couch, and the lighting in her comfortable office was low. "Hello, Danny. Come in."

She beckoned him to join her on the couch, instantly making Dan uncomfortable. He didn't like being called Danny, much preferring Dr. Freedman. Wendy crossed her shapely legs and patted the cushion beside her.

"Sit here, Danny," she said. "I want to talk to you again about your future."

"How's that?" asked Dan, perching himself nervously on the edge of the couch.

"Please, make yourself comfortable," she said and waited until Dan gingerly leaned back before continuing. "Well, as you may know, the provincial government is looking at restructuring some hospitals, and I have every reason to believe that this one is going to be closed."

"Why would they close this hospital when so many people in the community need its services?" asked Dan.

"It's really inefficient."

"Wait a second. Isn't it your job as CEO to make it efficient?"

"As it so happens," Wendy said, "I'm going to be part of the commission, and someone else will take the fall. No one at Queen's Park (Toronto) wants to keep this place open."

"Why do they have to close it? Why not make it more efficient?" Dan was already fond of the place and hated the thought of it closing.

"Dan, this place is too old, and we need a new hospital in Toronto. I'm telling you this so that I can help your career. You know I like you."

Wendy's slick high-heeled shoe touched Dan's leg, and, ever so slightly, she stroked his leg with the tip. Then she leaned into him. Under her low-cut blouse, Dan could see she was wearing a lacy black bra, and he smelled her musky perfume. She put her hand on his shoulder, then ran her fingers through his curly hair. "I'm going to be running a new hospital in Toronto. It will be state of the art. I want you there with me," she purred.

"But I'm just an intern. I still have the rest of this year and another full year of training before I'm fully qualified."

"You can finish your internship at my new hospital. Then I can make you a department head. I'm looking for new, dynamic doctors like you – who also happen to be very hot." Wendy smiled sweetly, then took his hand and pressed it to her breast. "Danny, don't you like me? I like you – a lot."

Dan froze for a moment, then decided to go for it. He slipped his hand slowly down the front of her blouse to her left breast. They moved closer. He could feel her hot breath and was about to kiss her when…. his pager beeped. He snatched his hand back and leaped up. He was needed in the OR right away.

* * *

In the cafeteria, Kelly put down her cell phone. "Did you just page Dan *stat* to the OR?" Paula asked.

"Yes, I did. I felt he was about to become 'Mountain Lion' bait. I don't want that CEO to get her claws in him just yet," said Kelly.

"Don't you mean a cougar bait?" said Paula.

"They're the same thing, except mountain lions are not as good-looking."

"Hey, I'm having dinner with Raj tonight," Paula said.

"That's nice. Is it a real date, or are you two just hanging out?"

"I think he's just being nice."

"What do you think about Sinclair's secretary?" asked Kelly.

"I don't know about her, but her boyfriend is sexy. He can model underwear for me any day of the week!" Paula said.

"Sometimes I think she likes Raj, but why would she when she has that totally hot boyfriend?"

"Maybe she likes a guy who's smart."

"Well, you never know, do you? By the way, my boyfriend is coming to town next week. We should all go out again. It was fun," said Kelly.

"Definitely!" Paula checked the time on her cell phone. "I have to fly now. Talk to you tomorrow."

* * *

Raj had hosted a woman in his apartment only once before – Judy, the Nordic goddess. Surprisingly before she had left, she'd told him that he was really sweet, but he needed – and deserved a real girlfriend – not just a sex partner. Raj hadn't been entirely sure what she was talking about but trusted her wisdom. He still had her number, but he'd not yet summoned the nerve to call her.

Raj's original idea had been to make Paula dinner, but he soon realized that he was too hopeless a cook, and it would have to be pizza. When she arrived, Paula was still wearing OR greens and announced that she wanted to review amyotrophic lateral sclerosis with him. Raj didn't know anything about the disease, but Paula seemed to think he did. Raj gathered that Dr. Froeder had questioned her about ALS and found her knowledge wanting.

He took her through to his little living room, where she sat on the couch and kicked off her shoes. He opened a bottle of Coke and fetched two drinking glasses and a large bag of potato chips. He sat in his one comfortable chair and decided that she looked so serious he should try to brighten her mood.

"Dr. Froeder, are you familiar with the findings of absolute boredom?" he joked.

"He'd ask if that was absolute or reflexive boredom," said Paula.

"Reflexive is when you fall asleep when he starts talking; absolute is when you stay asleep *after* he stops talking."

"The difference is quite subtle because I just get sleepy whenever he gets near me."

"Except when he's touching you!"

"It's his secret weapon!" Paula said and helped herself to a handful of chips. "So, what's new with you? Did you have a good time at Diana's show?"

"Yeah, I did," he said hesitantly.

"You don't sound convincing, Raj."

"I don't know, Paula. The truth is that I need more going on in my social life."

"Me too. But you sound sex-obsessed."

"I am. And I'll accept charity."

"I'm charitable, but not that charitable." Paula laughed.

"I met this girl, an accountant. But she thought I was gay."

"You mean you're *not* gay? I thought you were."

Raj looked at Paula in amazement. How could so many people think he was gay? What the hell was going on?

Paula laughed. "Maybe Froeder thinks you're gay. Has he invited you to the spa?"

"No!"

"It's okay, Raj. No one thinks you're gay."

"Are you just trying to be nice?"

"No, no, no. I saw how interested you were in the nursing students – especially the one with the pink lip gloss."

"Does anyone else think I'm gay?" He was desperate to know.

"Honestly, Raj, I don't know. Maybe you should ask some girl out."

"Maybe."

The buzzer sounded. The Greek pizza Raj had ordered had arrived. Raj let the delivery man up and tipped him generously for finding his way to his little apartment. As they began eating, Raj wondered how he could change the subject. He didn't want to talk about disease or Froeder or his nervousness about asking someone out on a date or even about Dan and the CEO. That left one subject.

"So, how's your boyfriend?" he asked her.

"You know," she said, shaking her head, "I haven't talked to him in over a week."

"Why not?"

"The truth is that I'm sick of him. All we ever do is talk about the same things over and over again: getting married, having kids."

"You don't want that right now?"

"Not with him, anyway. I sometimes think I have a problem." Paula hesitated a moment, then said, "Actually, it's not a problem. It's just that I'm just not terribly attracted to men."

Raj didn't know what to say and was relieved when his pager beeped. He called the inpatient floor, and a nurse told him that Mr. Carter in Room 425 had developed chest pain.

"How are his vitals?" Raj asked.

"They're fine," the nurse said. "He's not tachycardic or anything like that."

"Okay. Let's get cardiac enzymes and an ECG. I'll be right over." Raj turned to Paula and said, "Sorry, I have to go."

"That's okay," Paula said. "I'll come with you."

It took them just a few minutes to get to the hospital, and Raj quickly and carefully examined the patient, Mr. Carter. Paula recognized the patient. She'd seen him when he was admitted earlier and had ordered an ECG but hadn't seen the results. The exam left Raj puzzled, and so Paula examined Mr. Carter also. All they knew was that he had complained of chest pain and felt unwell. He was out of shape, but the two interns couldn't find anything else wrong with him except for a slight fever. Mr. Carter told them he also had some foot pain and a cough, and it hurt him to breathe. That left Raj and Paula none the wiser.

"I'm going to have to phone the staff man on call tonight," Raj said. "It's Froeder, and I hope to God he doesn't come in."

Raj carefully described the man's bizarre collection of symptoms to Dr. Froeder on the phone. At the end of Raj's recital, Froeder was silent for a few moments and then asked Raj the patient's name. Raj could hear an operatic aria being played in the background and the howl of a dog when the singer hit a high note.

"Raj," Froeder said at last, "this man has a pulmonary embolus. I remember seeing the ECG Paula ordered earlier. Get blood gases and a chest X-ray, then arrange a lung scan."

An hour and a half later, Froeder's diagnosis was confirmed, and Raj started Mr. Carter on a blood thinner.

"How the heck did Froeder figure it out without even seeing the patient?" Raj asked as they left Mr. Carter to settle in for the night.

"He's a psychic genius," Paula said.

They were both tired as they headed back to the apartment building. Raj pressed the button for the elevator, and when it arrived, they were surprised to see Diana inside it, dressed in a form-fitting dress and high heels. She was coming up from the parking level.

"Hi, guys." She looked almost embarrassed.

"I didn't know you lived here," Paula said.

"I'm on the third floor."

"You're all dressed up. Were you partying?" asked Paula.

"Actually, I had an audition for a new play."

"Really? What's the play?" Paula asked.

"*Mama Mia*," Diana said, grinning broadly.

Raj and Paula were impressed.

"I'm not the star, but it's going to be fun," Diana said. "I hope you had a nice time the other night. Oh, here's my floor. See you." She stepped out.

Paula noticed the expression on Raj's face as the elevator door closed – a look of longing – and said, "She's really pretty, Raj."

"I know, but she has a boyfriend. The guy you called the Adonis the other night. She's totally out of my league."

"So she has a boyfriend, but you don't know what's really going on between them. And you're an attractive guy."

"Thanks, Paula," he said. "I need a little confidence boost."

"You should ask her out. I think she likes you."

"Maybe," Raj said. "See you tomorrow."

Once inside his apartment, Raj checked his computer to see if anyone had looked at his profile on the dating website he had joined. No one had. Raj rarely ever used his cellphone and never would put any sort of application on it other than medical ones. He felt it looked unprofessional to be always looking at his phone while at work. He finally checked his email and found one from his mother and one from Chandra.

His mother had written: *Aunt Shamila phoned and told me that Roger had scheduled his wedding for the beginning of May. The wedding is to be at a Polo club near London where they ride horses. We are all invited, and they have reserved rooms for us at an expensive hotel. Your father would like us all to go over together. Aunt Shamila says that you can bring a date. The chef catering the event has worked for Madonna and Guy Ritchie. You had better get a new*

186

suit. *We have arranged for two tickets for you. Why don't you take that nice girl Shari that we introduced you to? She keeps calling us just to say hello. I think she likes you. Are you seeing her?*

From Chandra: *Hey loser, how's your dating career? Have you even been on a real date? Remember, girls like it if the guy offers to pay for dinner, something I'm trying to get my boyfriend to learn. Just got off the phone with Mom, and she's in a tizzy. Shamila is outraged. The bride-to-be has her own ideas for the wedding, and her parents – who are paying for everything – have taken over the whole production, leaving Shamila on the sidelines. Her only job is planning a party the day before the wedding. It'll be an English-style wedding, but Shamila was hoping for a traditional Indian wedding. Roger bought a three-carat diamond ring, and it's so big, I think he got it from the Snoop Dog collection! Chan*

Raj closed his computer, thinking about how different his own life was from that of his cousin. No matter how hard he tried, he would never be as glamorous as Roger. It didn't matter; he still loved being a doctor.

Chapter Twenty

"Okay, everyone. That was great! Let's call it a night."

Diana was on stage at the Princess of Wales Theatre in downtown Toronto and had just finished rehearsing a song with the other singers and lead actors. It was one of the first numbers they had to perform, and it had gone well. Diana had landed the part of Lisa, a friend of Sophie, the lead character. Diana was finding the choreography a challenge, but her vocal range ideally suited her part. Sophie was being played by a well-known actress from the UK, Martha Hutchings, and Martha and Diana were getting along fabulously.

Dianna had quickly hired a temp to work at her dad's office in order to get some time off. Her dad wasn't happy and expected her back as soon as she had more time. The past week of heavy rehearsal had been hard, but Diana found that most of the other actors were fun to be around. The director was exacting, but he knew how to put a show together. She still couldn't believe she really was involved in a major theatrical production and sometimes had to pinch herself to make sure that she wasn't dreaming.

She didn't yet have a place of her own in Toronto and had been staying at Star's penthouse on the waterfront. She liked it, especially the lovely views of the harbour and the CN tower. But she didn't want to move in with him. She was now making money – real money – and she had a couple of decisions to make: where to live in Toronto and when to tell her dad that she'd have to cut back on the secretarial job.

"Hey baby, how did rehearsal go?" Star asked when she got back to his place.

"Really well. What are you up to?"

"I'm on a new website called Luminosity. It's for brain training." Star was hunched over his iPad. "Yes!" he exclaimed and pumped his fist. "I just doubled my score!"

"Are you at the genius level yet?" asked Diana. Everything Star did was competitive. One couldn't be a pro hockey player and not be competitive.

"I just passed Laplante," crowed Star as he grabbed his cell phone off the coffee table. "Gotta call him!" Laplante was a teammate who played defense and had a friendly rivalry with Star.

"Hey, Dickhead! I just passed you on Luminosity, and I was drinking beer at the same time. Guess I'll have to send you a box of tampons. Eat that!" They began talking loudly, and Diana inferred from Star's boasting that Laplante didn't believe him.

Diana slipped away to take a shower. When she'd finished, she found Star in the bedroom, changing into faded jeans and a sweater. His hair was pulled back in his signature ponytail, and he was sporting a moustache and goatee for the 'Movember' charity drive. It made him look a lot like the actor who played Thor in the movies. Star had told her that he wanted to do more modeling and that his agent was talking about a job for a watch company that was introducing a retro Czech pilot's watch.

"Hey, babe," he said. "You gotta' get dressed."

"I'm really tired, Star. I thought I'd make dinner, and we'd stay in and watch TV."

"Aw, babe, I want to meet some guys at Bar Moscow. C'mon, it'll be fun." Star had a keyed-up look on his face as if he wanted to get drunk. He had been playing very hard and obviously needed to blow off steam.

"Okay," said Diana reluctantly, "but you'll have to give me fifteen minutes to get ready."

"No problem. We can grab a bite when we get there."

As she dressed, Diana checked the marking on her leg, which had become darker as her tan faded. She put on a lacy top with a low neckline, snug-fitting jeans, and high-heeled boots. She put on large, dangling earrings, did her makeup carefully, and finished the look with her father's old black leather jacket. He had worn it when he travelled across Europe as a student. Diana liked it because it had a large vintage maple leaf flag sewn on the back. The jacket was worn and was a bit too large for her, but she had always loved the retro feel.

When they got to the bar, they found a group of Star's teammates and their girlfriends sitting at a couple of private tables pushed together at the back. A Russian 'business man' owned the establishment and ran the place much like a club he also owned in Moscow. No one bothered to enforce the no smoking rule. The house music was loud, and the team was downing beer and vodka shots like nobody's business. Diana knew she didn't really fit the "puck bunny" role the other girls were working on: she wasn't blonde, she didn't have big fake boobs, and she didn't laugh at everyone's lame jokes. They were nice enough, though, and Diana liked Laplante's girlfriend, Lydia. None of them had believed her when she'd told them that she was an actress. The other girls didn't have jobs other than looking good for their boyfriends.

After her fourth glass of white wine, Diana knew she needed to eat something, but the bar had only pretzels and caviar. Lydia needed to use the bathroom; she nudged her, and the two young women made their way to the back of the bar. There was a lineup at the women's bathroom, so they used the men's instead, careful to touch absolutely nothing.

On their way back, Diana stopped at the bar to buy potato chips and another beer for Star.

"Who's that?" asked Lydia, who was looking down the length of the rather smoky room.

Diana saw Star at the table, but he wasn't alone. Mischa was sitting on his lap and stroking his beard. There she was, smiling and flirting with him. She was wearing a form-fitting miniskirt that was impossibly short, along with her stylish heels. She sat so close to him that it looked as if they were going to start making out. Diana was angry.

Mischa saw Diana approaching the table. She had an insolent look on her face and made no attempt to leave Star's lap. She took a long drag of her cigarette and exhaled the smoke slowly at Dianna. Then she crossed her legs and did a little wiggle – like a lap dance. "So it's the girl next door, and she has returned," she said. "You better go easy on the beer. Star doesn't like his girls fat."

Red with embarrassment, Diana fumed, "I didn't know there was a Russian *slut* convention going on. Why don't you find an old millionaire you can kill off with your smoke breath?"

The others all stopped talking, and a couple of the guys egged the women on. They wanted to see a cat fight. Even Star was laughing!

"Get off my boyfriend, you stupid bitch. I don't want him to get herpes."

Mischa wiggled a little more on Star's lap, and he obviously liked it. Now Diana was as angry with him as she was with Mischa.

"I think you have to make me leave… why don't you go home and make cookies with Mama?" Mischa taunted.

Diana picked up the closest thing to hand – a full glass – and threw beer in Mischa's face. Mischa stared at Diana for a brief moment, not believing what had happened.

"Maybe *you* should go back to *your* momma and learn how to act like a lady! Why don't you get lost – you crazy Russian bitch!" Diana shouted.

Mischa turned feral. She jumped off Star's lap and lunged at Diana, snarling, and slapped her cheek with an open-handed smack, yelling, "Pizda!" (Translation: *you cunt!)*

The fight escalated quickly. The two women grabbed each other and began punching, scratching, and hitting in an uncontrolled frenzy of hatred. Diana was taller but nearly fell over because of her high heels. Mischa grabbed a handful of Diana's hair and pulled it savagely. Enraged, Dianna threw several punches and slaps at Mischa and then managed to grab Mischa's tight silk dress and rip it open. Mischa grabbed a half-full bottle of vodka and tried to clock Diana over the head with it. The girls were finally pulled apart, still punching, scratching, and kicking each other. Two large bouncers descended on the group and pulled the women apart, but not before Diana landed a punch squarely on Mischa's chest and yelled, "Take your fake boobs back to the Kremlin, you bitch!" At that point, the bouncers threw out the entire party.

Chapter Twenty One

"What movie would you like to see, Shari?"

"How about the new one with Matthew McConaughey?"

"Okay, we'll give it a try."

Raj had finally summoned the nerve to call Shari and ask her out. She had suggested they go to an Italian restaurant where a lot of people from her office went. She said they all raved about the food. It sounded good to Raj, who believed that one should never go on a date at an Indian restaurant – it was usually too spicy, and he didn't want to sweat. Now that he'd seen the menu, he realized the words "Italian restaurant" didn't mean what he thought they meant. Shari had ordered mushroom risotto and was eating it delicately. Raj had ordered granchio con rapini, not knowing what it was. It looked like crab and collard greens, and he had just managed to get some on his sleeve and drop a forkful down the front of his new white shirt.

"Damn! I've got food all over me!"

"At least you didn't get any on your tie," said Shari, looking at him disapprovingly. He wasn't wearing a tie, just a new jacket with blue jeans, thinking this was the casual look of a successful, hip guy.

"Actually, when you suggested Italian, I was thinking of a nice plate of spaghetti," said Raj. He had also assumed that the meal would cost a fraction of what this was going to cost.

"Modern Italian restaurants don't serve spaghetti. It's gauche," she sniffed.

"Gauche?" Raj was puzzled. "How is it, gauche?"

A middle-aged man approached their table and said, "Shari, I thought that was you!"

"Henry! How nice to see you," Shari exclaimed. Henry was a man in his forties wearing rimless glasses and an expensive suit. His hair was thinning, and he had a smallish chin. Raj thought he had the look of a man who had money.

"Nice job on the CLB Media merger. It went very smoothly," Henry said.

"Thank you. Raj, this is Henry Pratt. He works with me at Johnson GoodFellow."

Raj said, "Nice to meet you," and shook his hand. Henry's grip was a bit slack, and he wore no wedding ring. He was shorter and smaller than Raj and had an expectant look about him as if he didn't want to get lost. Raj got the impression he had a thing for Shari.

"I'm here with the boss, Old Man Johnson," Henry said. "Do you want to come over and say hello, Shari?"

Shari looked at Raj, clearly excited at the prospect.

Raj said, "Don't worry about me. I'm locked in a life-and-death struggle with this granchio."

"I'll be back in just a minute." Shari got up, and Henry led her away, taking her by the arm as though she were his date.

Raj heard Shari and her colleagues talking and laughing, and he quickly tired of stabbing at the crab, which was still in its shell. At one point, he thought he saw it move by itself. Was it still alive?

The waiter came to the table. Looking at the stain on Raj's shirt, he quipped, "Well, it looks as though the crab got the better of you." Raj hated waiters who tried to be funny.

"I should have ordered spaghetti," said Raj.

"We don't serve spaghetti at this restaurant, sir. This is *new* Italian cuisine. There's absolutely no pasta served here. The head chef, Francesco, was brought in from Tuscany. He's a risotto specialist."

"I didn't know there was a difference. For a *new* Italian restaurant, the bread sticks actually taste kind of *old*."

The waiter rolled his eyes. "They're called *grissini,* and they're supposed to taste like that. We age them in small batch oak barrels imported from Firenze Italy."

Another five minutes went by, and Shari was still not back. She finally arrived after giving Henry a peck on the cheek. "I'm so excited," she gushed. "We're going to be working on a huge project. One of the Big Pharma companies has bought a small Toronto biotech firm called CytoFunction Labs, which makes an arthritis drug. The boss is going to put me in charge of the project."

They finished their meal with a shot of coffee. The bill topped $200, but thankfully, Raj didn't have to tip the waiter a full 20 per cent. Shari calculated the appropriate tip to be $35.67, and Raj generously increased it to $35.70. Still feeling hungry, he stuffed a grissini in his pocket, hoping he wouldn't smell too oaky.

They started walking to the nearby movie theatre, passing some expensive men's clothing shops along the way. Shari stopped to check one window display. "You should get some clothes here, Raj. You'd look really good in something like that," she said, pointing to a dark green suit with an Emanuel Ungaro label. Other clothing bore the Boss Selection label.

"Maybe someday, Shari," said Raj. Most of the doctors he worked with dressed reasonably well, but they weren't debonair. Some of them dressed terribly, perhaps because they didn't need to impress anyone.

When they arrived at the theatre, Shari insisted that Raj get her red licorice. Raj had no interest in the movie, but the theatre was dark and warm. They took off their coats and put them on seats beside them, silently warding off other patrons. As the movie progressed, Raj put his arm around Shari. At first, it was a tentative manoeuver, but he fed her licorice nibs and squeezed her arm a little. She made no move to shrug off his arm, even after she caught him looking down at her blouse.

On the drive over to Shari's apartment after the movie, she said, "You should get a BMW or an Audi, Raj. They've got class. They're not old-man cars like a Mercedes." She had mentioned before that she thought his car was a bit substandard. Raj liked his little Honda because he felt it had a macho edge – something Steve McQueen would drive if he were still alive (and on a limited budget). The friend he'd bought it from had outfitted it with a turbocharger and other racing parts.

"This car is like me – rugged and dependable," Raj said. He revved the four-cylinder engine with the Bosch fuel injector, and the car took off, breaking the speed limit. They arrived at her apartment building a few minutes later. Raj turned off the motor; for a second, they looked at each other, and then Shari looked down. Not sure what to say, Raj, ventured, "I had a nice time, Shari. How about you?"

"I did, too," Shari said with a smile.

"Can I see you again, then?"

"Yes, I'd like that."

Raj got out and opened the passenger door, planning to walk her to her door like a proper gentleman. At the door, they hesitated in the cool November air. Then they kissed – the longed-for kiss. Raj expected it would be magical. It came, it went, but something was missing – that nervous spark that ignites two people.

Raj drove back to his parent's house, wondering whether Shari had felt a spark and if he would too in time if they kissed enough.
198

Maybe only women ever felt it. The women he knew – well, the ones on TV – were always talking about the magical kiss when they decided this man was their one true love. As a rational scientist, Raj theorized the magic was actually some sort of subtle scent or pheromone that attracts two people. He decided he would have to work on his kissing skills.

* * *

Raj could hear the commercial from his bedroom; his father liked the TV quite loud. He had the TV tuned to a South Asian channel, as he usually did on Saturday mornings. Cloying music played in the background as a voice Raj recognized said, "At Mama Gustad's, we use only the finest ingredients and spices. We offer a wide variety of frozen entrées, including biryani, vegetable and chicken curries, and wonderful naan. And try our samosas – just like my mother used to make in Punjab. Simply open the package and microwave for two to three minutes. Come – let me help you experience the flavours of India."

When Raj entered the kitchen, the TV was off, but Radhu was still ranting. "If I hear that fat bastard on the TV again, I shall surely go mad!" he shouted. "Everywhere I turn, there is Gustad hawking his greasy curry. Why does he insist on being in the commercial? His fat head is enough to turn anyone off the food."

"Perhaps his fat head makes people think that he is well fed, and the food is good," Mena said. "How else could he have become so fat?"

"You know that Gustad stole your mother's recipes for that food, don't you?" Radhu said.

Mena said nothing, but when she spotted Raj, she got up and went to the stove to ladle batter into the idli cooker. He poured himself a coffee and sat at the table. His father nodded at him and picked up the newspaper. He looked a bit bleary-eyed to Raj, probably from a shot or two of whiskey last night. Radhu jabbed a finger at the article he was reading. "This damned government, taxing the hell out of us. They tax us and throw away the money on Quebec! How can you make a good living here, Raj?"

As Raj was about to point out that Gustad was making a fortune, Radhu said to Mena, "Thank God our son is a doctor – he can support us, eh?" but Mena didn't respond. Even though Radhu had a reasonable pension, he wasn't rich. He often talked about buying a condo in Bangalore. "A couple of thousand dollars Canadian, and you live like a king," he would say.

Chan came into the kitchen about an hour later, looking disheveled.

"Hey!" Raj. "How are you doing?"

"No food at my house," Chandra groused. She poured a coffee and drank it black, then took a pile of idli and sat at the table, chewing

200

noisily. Raj smiled, thinking of all the years they had sat at this table eating the soft dumplings.

"Raj, do you want to go and see the matinée Bollywood special?" Chan asked.

Raj had some time to kill before going back to St. Jerome, so he took Chan up on her offer, and he drove them both to the Cineplex cinema complex in Scarborough, where two Hindi movies were playing. Chan wanted to expose herself to as much Indian media as she could and was trying to relearn Hindi. When Raj asked why, she said, "Raj, as a Ryerson grad, I'll be qualified to work at Starbucks. What I really want is to go to India and break into the entertainment industry over there. There's a lot more going on in Mumbai than there is here."

"What?" Raj was startled by this news. "You want to move to India?"

Chandra shrugged. "If I can get a good job there, why not?"

Raj couldn't think of a good reason not to and fell silent.

After a minute, Chandra asked, "So, Raj, what's Shari really like?"

"Well, she's really good-looking, and she's an accountant."

"That's good, but accountants tend to be boring. Do you think she's right for you? You've just met her, you know." Chandra was pointing out that Raj's experience in the dating scene was limited – unlike her own vast knowledge.

"What about you and Quentin?" he countered.

"He's just for fooling around with. He's a cheap guy who never pays when we go out. We aren't that serious. I keep him around just to bug Mom and Dad," Chandra said.

"Just to bug Mom and Dad?" Raj laughed. "Chan, where did this evil streak come from? You must have been switched at birth with my real sister."

The movie began with music, which Raj never liked much. He didn't even like the Indian rap music invented in the UK. He understood bits and pieces of the dialogue but couldn't follow the story line. Despite all this, Raj liked Indian movies because the actresses were stunningly beautiful – nice tits, beautiful eyes, and hair.

At one point, Raj glanced at Chan and saw she was mouthing the Hindi words. Their parents had always considered her lazy, which Raj thought was an unfair but easy judgment based only on comparing her to him, who had made it into medical school. The truth was that she had grown into a smart and determined young woman.

On their way home, Chandra brought up the subject of Shari again. "Listen, Raj, just because someone looks right on paper doesn't necessarily mean that she's right for you. You're one of the nicest guys I know – too nice, actually. Be careful. You're a lot like Dad."

"What do you mean – a lot like Dad?"

"Full of pride and easily hurt," Chan said. "You assume that a woman would want to marry you only because she's in love with you."

Once again, Raj had nothing to say in response, and they spoke no more about his love life – or lack thereof. Raj found it weird to get advice from his sister, as he had spent much of their childhood annoying her and implying he was much smarter because he could handle math so easily. But now Raj pondered her comments, wondering if many people stayed in a relationship only because they figured no one else would come along. Probably lots of them did.

Chapter Twenty Two

Diana woke up with a splitting headache, and every muscle in her body hurt. Incredibly, after they were thrown out of the Moscow Bar, Star had brought her home and insisted that he was wildly turned on. It had excited Diana, too.

Star offered her his signature smoothie with cocoa nibs and kale, which she vomited up in the bathroom. She gulped three cups of espresso and three Advils and was feeling almost half human when she heard the television.

Star had tuned his large flat-screen TV to a Toronto station. "The Berry Patch" was on, and he was sprawled on the couch in front of it. Ron Berry, wearing an outrageous tartan jacket, was talking hockey.

"Now, you folks out there in Hockeyland know I'm a fan of the sport. And I'm an even bigger fan of females in hockey. There's an interesting video going viral on social media – an epic showdown of East versus West. Check this out."

Ron narrated as the video played. It showed a dark-haired young woman with a large maple leaf on her jacket confronting another young woman, a blonde who was sitting on the lap of Star Yanofsky, right forward with the Toronto Maple Leafs. The two women had words, and then the maple-leaf woman threw beer in the other one's face. "Cat fight!" Ron said. "See how the blonde goes for the other one's hair and gives her a slap. But it's not over! Maple Leaf punches the blonde right in the tit. That, my friends, is the tit punch heard around the world. Apparently, the blonde gal is a Russian model who has been working here in Toronto. It would appear that the argument was over Star Yanofsky, the Leaf's forward."

"Well, folks, that ain't hockey – but it sure is entertaining. By the way, Star Yanofsky is having a fabulous season. He's in contention for rookie of the year."

Diana wandered into the room, wrapped in a duvet.

"Hey, baby," Star said. "I got a mention on Ron Berry's show."

"What are you talking about?" Diana was still in a muddled haze.

"I got mentioned on the Ron Berry show! Actually, *you* were *on* the show." Star grinned.

"What!" cried Diana.

"Watch this. I recorded it on my PVR. You were really good."

"What are you talking about? I've never been on TV."

"Last night, babe. Someone had a phone and recorded you."

Star pressed Play on the remote, and Diana cringed when she realized she was watching the fight from the night before. The video

quality was poor, but her jacket and dark hair could be seen clearly –
as could the last punch she threw that landed on Mischa's breast. She
could also be heard clearly, yelling, "Take your fake boobs back to
the Kremlin, bitch!" Diana didn't know what to say.

I heard Mischa might need surgery to put her implant back in
place. Looks like she has three boobs now." Star laughed.

Embarrassed and upset, Diana watched the video once more
as Star replayed it in slow motion. How in the world could this have
happened to her? Should she call Mischa and apologize? Scrutinizing
the video, Diana realized there was only a very brief shot of her face,
and a casual observer would not recognize her. She wondered if her
father had watched the show.

She walked slowly back to the bathroom and looked in the
mirror. Her face was red from the slap, she had an early black eye, and
there was a good chunk of hair missing.

* * *

On the Monday after his weekend in Toronto, Raj found that
Paula had been reassigned from the medical ward to the ER. It was
mid-November, and Raj was on the ward by himself, expected to run
the show. When he bumped into her in the cafeteria, Paula said she
was happy with the new assignment, as she had had her fill of Dr.
Froeder.

Over the next few days, Raj managed to get more organized,
and the routine of seeing patients and hunting down lab and x-ray

reports became easier. The nurses seemed to go out of their way to chat with him, and Raj liked the attention. The nurse who had asked him if he was dating anyone continued to question him in a most forward way. Raj thought that it was apt that this buxom piece of eye candy was named "Candy," as if her parents had a premonition about her future. She was the queen bee on the ward.

A few days later, as Raj was eying her shapely legs, Candy asked him, "Dr. Mehta, do you still like working on the Internal Medicine floor?"

"I do," Raj said. "The only problem is that all the patients are sick. I need a job with healthier people."

Candy laughed and asked, "So, have you found yourself a girlfriend?"

Raj stopped for a moment. Had she just asked him about his personal life again?

"Uh, no," he muttered. "Not really. I don't have a girlfriend. I was hoping you'd drop that guy you're engaged to and start going out with me."

"Well, I can't give back the ring," said Candy, "but a few other people might be interested."

"Paging Dr. Mehta. Paging Dr. Mehta." It was influenza season, and Raj had already admitted two patients with pneumonia. "Here we go again," he sighed as he rang the number on the pager.

"Hi, Raj. It's me."

"Shari?"

"Yes, it's me. All I ever get is your answering machine, and I wanted to know how you're doing."

Raj was speechless. He had never expected to get a personal call at work, and he wasn't sure it was a good thing.

Shari said, "I wanted to tell you that our folks are getting together. Isn't that nice? And my parents are going on a Caribbean cruise over the Christmas holiday, and I'm going with them."

"I can't talk right now, Shari," Raj said. Call me at home tonight. We can't take personal calls here."

"Okay, Raj. We'll talk later." Shari sounded a bit miffed, but Raj didn't have time to worry about her reaction.

He reviewed the list of patients on the floor, where beds were in desperately short supply. Mr. Rosenplot's variety of ailments, including chest pain and chronic shortness of breath, kept him on the ward. Since his heart couldn't be tested on an exercise treadmill due to his weak nicotine- and tar-filled lungs, he would have to be treated with radioactive dye and medication injection.

Mr. Rosenplot was not Raj's only worry. His roommate, Royal Finch, had diarrhea, most likely from the chemo he had received at a cancer centre in a nearby city. Royal was a distinguished-looking seventy-two-year-old, and Raj liked him, in part because the old fellow insisted they had the same name, as Raj was the Indian equivalent of Royal. Today, Royal's wife was at his bedside, as she usually was, mopping his brow and feeding him.

"Mrs. Finch, how's your husband?" Raj was keeping a close eye on Royal because his white blood cell levels had been dropping, leaving him vulnerable to infection.

"I think he's holding his own," she said.

Mr. Rosenplot motioned Raj over and whispered, "That guy, he ain't gonna make it."

Before Raj could reply, he was paged to attend another patient who had just been admitted with chest pain after devouring several pounds of Polish sausage at the annual St. Jerome sausage-eating contest.

Raj was starting to feel more like a real doctor. He'd stopped worrying quite so much and now had an idea of what to do regardless of what symptoms the patient was presenting.

Midway through the afternoon, he realized that everything was under control, and he went home to read journals or work out. Instead, he read the Kama Sutra and watched MTV. He had the volume up so high he nearly missed the knock on the door, and when he finally heard it, he considered ignoring it. Perhaps it was just Dan looking for a free dinner. He got up, opened the door, and there was Diana, dressed casually, her hair pulled back in a ponytail. The left side of her face was a bit red, and it looked as if she was developing a shiner. Raj noticed all this with the experienced eye of a doctor but said nothing because he didn't really know what to say.

Diana spoke first. "Hi, Raj. Remember? I live on the third floor." She was wearing an old shirt and jogging pants. There were streaks of something on her shirt – flour? "Could I borrow a cup of brown sugar?" She held up an empty measuring cup.

Raj paused a moment to process what he was seeing and what she was saying, then beckoned her into the sparsely furnished living room, its only decorations a photograph of his parents taken when they were visiting their home village in India and the potted sunflower his mother had given him. In the photo, Radhu and Mena posed in front of a field of sunflowers. The photo had been there for so long now he never really noticed it, but it caught Diana's eye.

"That's interesting. I didn't know sunflowers grew in India," she said.

"They're a major crop in Karnataka state, where my folks are from." He didn't want to say too much. The less he talked, he reckoned, the less chance he had to embarrass himself.

Diana's eyes strayed to the book on the couch, which was open at a picture of a man humping a woman from behind while a few other women looked on, waiting their turn. Raj was mortified. He knew he was a sex-obsessed pervert, but he didn't want her to think the same.

She smiled just for a second and looked about to say something. Raj jumped in to distract her. "Sorry about the messy place. Not much time, you know."

"Your place is cleaner than mine," she said. "I really appreciate your help. I just don't want to go out and be seen in public."

"Are you baking?" asked Raj. "Besides my mom, I don't know anyone who bakes."

"Really?" said Diana. "I like baking when I have to think about things. Actually, I'm baking something for my dad. His birthday's coming up. But I'm out of brown sugar."

Raj hoped he had some, and he used his kitchen only to store beer and warm up frozen meals his mother had made. So he was glad to find a jar of Demerara sugar his mother must have put in the cupboard when he moved in.

"Here you go. Take the jar."

"What about you? Won't you need some for your coffee?"

"Actually, I was thinking of starting a low-carb diet – like Atkins."

Diana gave Raj a funny look. Raj realized that she'd noticed the open package of Oreos lying on the counter, but she took the jar.

"Thanks, Raj. By the way, I hope you had a good time at the play the other night."

"It was a really fun evening. We all had the best time. I'm looking forward to seeing you in *Mama Mia*."

"I'm sorry my boyfriend showed up. He kind of stole the show."

"That's okay."

"Do you watch hockey or any of those hockey shows?"

"Not really. I'm way too busy. Why do you ask?"

"Oh, nothing…" Diana looked momentarily uncomfortable.

"So what are you making anyway?"

"I'm trying to make a pie."

"Pie, I like pie."

"See you, Raj," Diana said sweetly.

Raj didn't know what else to say, and Diana left with a little smile. He closed the door behind her, thinking that he'd completely blown it. There might have been a chance, just a small chance, that she liked him, but she was probably thinking right now that he was a semi-autistic pie-eating pervert.

He put the Kama Sutra back on the bookshelf. It was time to forget the book. Raj was a man of action. Diana had a boyfriend, and he was wasting his time thinking she wanted anything more than just to be his friend.

That night, Raj had his troubled dream once again…

The beautiful woman in the castle was lounging on a bed of cushions. She was veiled and wearing finely spun gold jewelry, and he could make out only her eyes. Then her dress parted, exposing suntanned legs and a swirling pattern of marks on one thigh.

This time she spoke. "It seems we are drawn together once again."

"I can't help myself – it's like you've cast a spell on me."

"Perhaps there are things even more powerful than your science, Doctor."

The woman stood up languidly and stood so close to him that he could feel her breath. Her eyes seemed to pull him in. So hot! She was radiating a feverish sexual energy. Like some feminine magnetic power that made him helpless.

Finally, the dream dissolved into a chaotic mass of swirling bliss…

Chapter Twenty Three

Diana left Raj's apartment, relieved that he had brown sugar. She hadn't wanted to go outside because her face was red and her black eye was getting more obvious. Thank heaven, he seemed not to have noticed.

Upset with herself and Star over the fight with Mischa, she'd hightailed it out of Toronto to lie low for a while. Star had apologized profusely, but not for what he'd done. He said that he wasn't responsible for Mischa's conduct and insisted that "all Russians are like that." He even claimed that the confrontation would be good for her career as it put her on television. She'd nearly punched him in the face after that remark. He then bought her roses, apologized several times more, and said that he would never let it happen again. He did seem truly sorry. She could tell because he looked like a little boy – much like he did back in Grade 8 when they first met. She couldn't resist this.

Star was easy to read, but Raj wasn't. Diana felt there was much more going on in him than she could see. It irked her that she couldn't figure him out. She wasn't even sure that he liked her. He didn't stare at her breasts. Was he gay? She didn't think so. Even his choice of porn was curious. Every other guy she knew watched porn on his computer; Raj was reading an ancient Indian manual.

Dianna returned to her apartment, determined to put all thoughts about both men away. She finally had a great job, and the most important thing was to keep it. She felt that she was on the cusp of finally making it as an actress in Toronto, and no matter what, she wasn't going to let it go.

* * *

The next day, Raj's mind was racing like a computer. Royal Finch was getting weaker and more dehydrated by the hour, and his blood tests showed worsening infection and declining kidney function. Raj had considered numerous possible diagnoses and was in the process of evaluating the umpteen probabilities of what was going on.

Royal's wife asked many questions, and Raj tried to reassure her. It was clear that the chemotherapy had taken a lot out of him, but the negative effect was far greater than anyone could have expected. Raj mentioned this to Dr. Cooper, who saw Royal and had also reviewed his symptoms thoroughly. "I can't explain why he's doing so poorly," he said. "Diarrhea hasn't let up, and I'm worried about his fluid balance."

"Sir, his lactate has climbed, and his renal function is down," Raj pointed out.

"I see that, Raj," Dr. Cooper said. "Repeat his chest x-ray and watch him closely overnight."

The thing that puzzled Raj the most was that Royal hadn't needed chemotherapy. He had been diagnosed with bowel cancer and been given the *option* of chemo, and the dose he'd been given wasn't massive or expected to be life-threatening.

Raj went over Royal's chart yet again, and the only things of note were that his abdominal aorta was a bit enlarged and he'd had a previous stroke. Following Dr. Cooper's assessment, Raj upped Royal's fluid replacement and instructed the nurses to watch carefully for signs of fever. Then he reluctantly left the hospital and returned to his lonely apartment. The uncertainty made him feel terrible, but there was nothing more he could do.

* * *

The call came at 3:00 a.m. Raj had taken to sleeping in his OR greens so that, if he got called, he could spring out of bed, scramble over to the hospital, and get there in minutes.

"Dr. Mehta, it's Joan. Mr. Finch has gone hypotensive, and his O^2 sats are eighty-two percent."

"I'll be right over." A sense of dread overwhelmed Raj. Royal's condition was worsening, but there was nothing Raj could do. It felt like watching a man drown while desperately trying to save him.

When Raj arrived at his bed, Royal had an oxygen mask on, and his breathing was laboured. Candy was monitoring his oxygen level and his pulse rate. Mrs. Finch was nowhere to be seen, and Raj was glad she wasn't there to see how quickly her husband had deteriorated. Raj listened to his chest and checked his pulse, and found his blood pressure desperately low. Royal was dying in front of him. Raj had to do something.

"He's going into cardiac arrest if we don't do something right now," he said to Candy. "Get me an intubation tray, and let's hang some dopamine." The course was set, and there was no turning back.

Candy was as calm and collected as anyone Raj had ever seen. She alerted the other nurses on that floor, and they went into Full Code status. Then she asked, "Dr. Mehta, should I call the ER and get the intern covering to come up and give you a hand?"

Raj remembered that Paula was the intern in ER. "Good idea, Candy. Give them a call."

Royal had lost consciousness and was breathing in loud gasps. Raj moved quickly and asked Candy to hand him the laryngoscope. Looking down Royal's throat, Raj could smell his breath. He cleared out half-eaten food mush with a suction tube, gently pushed the breathing tube down past the vocal cords, then hooked it to a bag that he got Candy to squeeze by hand to inflate Royal's lungs with pure oxygen.

Royal's colour improved a bit, but his blood pressure remained low, and his heart rate stayed around 140 beats per minute, which was far too fast for an older man to sustain for long.

What to do next? Raj was stuck, unable to think, his mind racing from one thing to another, and unable to focus.

Paula arrived, and Raj briefly described the patient and his problems to her. She thought for a second, then said, "Now that he's intubated, why don't we move him to ICU and hook him up to a ventilator?"

Raj quickly agreed. He was flying by the seat of his pants, and he knew it. He had never done anything like what he was doing right now and hoped it wasn't too obvious to the nurses.

Minutes later, the two interns and two nurses pushed Royal's bed, piled with wires, tubes, and machines, down the hall. They all crowded in a tiny elevator and headed for the sixth floor. Raj looked up at the ceiling and prayed that Royal wouldn't die.

Bernadette, the nurse in charge of ICU Room 3, had obviously worked on sick people for most of her professional life. She took one look at Royal and then asked, "Doctor, do you want an arterial line and a central line?" Raj didn't know. He had no real experience with this kind of thing. It was time to call Dr. Cooper, but he didn't relish calling the staff doctor at 3:30 in the morning.

Dr. Cooper sounded tired when he answered his phone. "What's going on?"

Raj went over Royal's story, careful to give all the pertinent information.

Dr. Cooper listened and responded, "So he's in ICU now but you haven't done anything yet."

"Yes, sir," replied Raj.

"I'll be in shortly to supervise while you put in the central line and arterial line. One other thing, Raj – you have to call his wife. Doesn't sound like he's going to make it."

Raj was devastated. In a crass, selfish way, he found himself hoping he wouldn't be blamed if Royal died. Then he banished the thought and suppressed the nausea he was starting to feel. Gritting his teeth, he told himself: *No one forced you into this job. Get the hell back to work, you coward*! Blood cultures, antibiotics, chest X-ray, dopamine, and ceftriaxone: Raj began to do all the things that should be done – except for calling Mrs. Finch. Paula had gone back to the ER, where the staff doctor needed her.

Raj sat for a moment at the nursing station and closed his eyes. Bernadette offered him a cup of burned coffee and asked, "Do you want a private room?"

"For what?" Raj was puzzled.

"For when you call his wife and tell her that her husband is critically ill and might not make it."

Dr. Cooper would be there in minutes, and Raj didn't want him to find he hadn't spoken with the patient's family. He picked up the phone at the nursing station with a shaking hand.

"Mrs. Finch? It's Dr. Mehta. Royal has taken a turn for the worse."

"What's wrong, Doctor? He's supposed to be getting better. I don't understand."

"Royal has reacted to the chemo, and it looks as if he has an overwhelming infection." Raj tried to explain more to Mrs. Finch, but she kept saying, "Oh my God, what am I going to do now?" over and over again. Raj told her to come to the hospital and that Dr. Cooper would be able to tell her more.

It dawned on Raj that it's nice when people trust you, but if things go wrong, their disappointment hurts that much more. He willed himself to stay focused on the job at hand.

Dr. Cooper arrived twenty minutes later, dressed in a shirt and tie and looking ready for the day. "Okay, Raj, what's your differential diagnosis?"

Raj wasn't expecting a question-and-answer session, and he stared blankly at Dr. Cooper. "Maybe he's gone septic?"

"That's the most logical thing to suspect, Raj, but look at his lab results. His BUN is climbing." Raj knew this meant that there was too much urea nitrogen in his blood, and Dr. Cooper showed him the test results that showed Royal's kidneys were failing. They reviewed possible causes of Royal's problems: pneumonia, infection of the bowel, blood clot in his lung – and ruled out each one.

Raj didn't want to do anything more, but Dr. Cooper made him put in a central line, feeding it into the heart through a small incision just below the right collarbone. Thankfully, there were no complications, and they had just finished when a teary-eyed Mrs. Finch arrived.

She looked at Raj, who mumbled, "I'm sorry, Mrs. Finch." Dr. Cooper led her away to what hospital staff called the "quiet room," which Raj thought should be dubbed the "bad news room." Raj went with them.

Dr. Cooper sat down with Mrs. Finch and held her hand. "Mrs. Finch, your husband has taken a turn for the worse. His kidneys are failing, and I believe he has a bad infection. I don't think he's going to live more than twenty-four hours." He didn't sugarcoat anything and looked her straight in the eye. Then he asked whether Royal would want them to keep working on him even with very little hope that he would recover. Fighting back the tears, Mrs. Finch said, "No. Just let me be alone with him for a few minutes".

Royal Finch died at 5:47 a.m. They had been unable to get his blood pressure up, and his heart, struggling to keep blood coursing through his veins, finally succumbed to the workload and the stress. Raj watched the electrocardiogram as it deteriorated from normal electrical impulse to a disorganized mass of electrical activity. He had stayed with Royal while he was dying, and he was upset, feeling that he had not served this man well enough.

Mrs. Finch left, accompanied by her sister, a blank, almost numb expression on her face, but not before telling Raj, "Dr. Mehta, thank you. I know you did everything you could."

Raj left the ICU in a state of numb misery and wandered the halls with his head down, soon finding himself in a seldom-used hallway. He opened a door and found a tiny chapel. It was empty, and he sat down at the front. At least the place was quiet.

Raj fought them, but the tears came anyway. He stayed in the chapel a long time – he didn't know how long – and looked up only when he felt a light touch on his shoulder.

Dr. Cooper was looking at him with a sympathetic expression. "You missed rounds this morning. I surmised you had taken this badly," he said.

"I'm sorry, sir. Just a moment of weakness."

"No, it wasn't," said Cooper. "It was a moment of humanity. We're supposed to care about the work we do. The single most important thing was that you showed Mrs. Finch that you *cared* about her husband."

"But, it's just that we could have…."

"But nothing, Raj. There was nothing anyone could have done. I've been doing this job for thirty years. If there was something that could have been done, we would have done it."

"Thank you," Raj said.

"If it makes you feel better, we'll pray."

"But I'm not Christian."

"Nor am I, Raj, and it doesn't matter. God really doesn't care."

And so Raj, a Hindu, and Cooper, a Jew, knelt and prayed for the soul of a Catholic.

Chapter Twenty Four

"That's a good question, Paula. The new ultra-long-acting insulin has been a great advance in the management of Type 2 diabetics. Many of them I now treat with just one dose of insulin daily, usually at night."

"That's interesting, Dr. Sinclair. Do you use short-acting insulin, too?"

It was Friday afternoon, and the interns were sitting in Dr. Sinclair's basement office. The end of November had arrived, and Raj's time in the Internal Medicine ward was finally over. It had been a long month, but he had learned a great deal. The interns were in the office for an "informal chat," during which the staff doctors probed how well the program was progressing and identified any interns who were nut jobs. There were strict policies about how much work interns could be made to do, and Dr. Sinclair had to make sure that no one complained.

Raj couldn't tell if Paula, with her questions about insulin, was either trying to suck up or she was genuinely interested in amino-acid chains in human insulin. He could never tell with Paula, and that was why he liked her.

They had figured out that having interns was considered a coup for a community with a doctor shortage. They had all encountered local functionaries and politicians who told them, "Remember St. Jerome when you finish your training!"

"Have you been getting lots of experience and good cases?" Sinclair asked the group.

"Yes, Dr. Sinclair," they chimed in unison.

Dr. Sinclair turned to Dan. "It seems the hospital CEO has taken a special interest in you. I saw you the other day up at her office."

"Yes... um..." Dan stammered. "She's very interested in some aspects of our training. She was initially concerned about our lack of experience, but I've reassured her that we're quite experienced and can handle a variety of situations and positions."

"That's good, Dan," said Dr. Sinclair. "Just keep her off our backs while we get the program running smoothly."

"Yes, Dan. What position is the CEO most interested in?" asked Kelly.

Paula continued, "It's good that you have significant experience, Dan, because we all expect you to stay on top of this situation and not have to go down any back channels to satisfy the CEO's curiosity."

Dan growled, "Thank you. Thank you so much for your helpful advice."

Dr. Sinclair turned to Raj. "Well, Raj, at least the CEO hasn't been taking up any of your valuable time."

Raj couldn't resist, "Dan seems to be working very hard on everyone's behalf to ensure that the CEO is satisfied."

Concluding the meeting, Sinclair told them, "I can tell you that you've all passed your performance evaluations. You've all made a real impression on the staff here at St. Jerome. Now, if there's nothing else, we can wrap things up and let you folks get back to work."

The interns left the cramped office. Diana had not been there when they arrived, but she was at her desk when they came out. Perched on the edge of her desk was a man in a leather jacket. They were chatting, but they stopped abruptly, and Diana looked a bit embarrassed.

"Hi, guys. How're y'all doing?" The young man stood up. It was Diana's boyfriend, Star. Paula had called him "Adonis," and it was easy to see why. After an awkward moment, Diana said, "You remember Star, don't you?"

"Star!" Paula and Kelly practically squealed.

Star stood up. He was about Raj's height but had thicker arms. Classically handsome with chiseled, square-jawed features, he had a perfectly proportioned body and longish silvery blond hair. He reminded Raj of the hero on the cover of a Harlequin romance. Star smiled and extended his hand.

Kelly took his hand and gushed, "I think I saw another one of your ads."

Star smiled slyly and said, "Yeah, my agent's got me *everywhere.*" He put on a pair of stylish sunglasses.

"Now I know!" said Kelly. "You're modeling that new line of sunglasses – the ones that let you interface with your computer!"

"How are the underwear sales going?" asked Paula. "I bought some for my boyfriend."

"They're selling really well," Star said. "They're made of seaweed-infused fiber to help with strain injury, you know."

Dr. Sinclair came out of his office, and Star greeted him enthusiastically. "Hey, John! Long time no see. How are you?" He shook the doctor's hand vigorously.

Raj was surprised that Star was on first-name terms with Sinclair. The doc said hello and then straightened his lab coat, mentioning that he was getting together with Star's parents on the weekend. Evidently, Star's charm worked on everyone. Paula and Kelly surrounded Star like a pair of hungry sharks. Raj felt as if he were back in high school, a member of the Geek Squad.

Star boasted, "I really like being involved in new cutting-edge technology. You know, I think I can send emails to your computer with these glasses, Di. I can even turn on your printer."

Diana said drily, "Yes, Star, but will they put the toilet seat down after you're done?" Kelly and Paula cracked up.

Raj realized he and Dan had become invisible, and the two of them left.

The Internal Medicine ward beckoned Raj one last time. Many of the patients he had looked after at the start of his rotation had finally been discharged, with one exception – Charlie Rosenplot – who had been in Room 426 so long that he had made the room his home. He had a photo of his late wife by his bed and some other old photos on the windowsill, including one of Charlie in an army uniform. The Rosenplots had been childless, and many of his family members had died in the Second World War.

"Hey, Doc, how ya doin'?" he called to Raj.

"I'm okay, Charlie. This is my last day here. I'll be moving on next Monday."

"I just get to know you, and they put you in some other part of the hospital," Charlie said.

Raj liked Mr. Rosenplot because he was stoic, which reminded Raj of his dad. He had become a fixture on the ward. The photo of him in uniform was very much like a photo of Radhu taken after he had enlisted in the Royal Navy. Charlie had told Raj that he had lied about his age to enlist at the age of fifteen. He had fought in an infantry battalion and somehow survived. It had been a very personal fight for him, and Raj admired his bravery.

Today, Charlie looked downcast. "I don't know if I'm ever going to get out of this place, Doc."

228

"I think you'll beat the odds and make it out," Raj reassured him. "Is there anything I can do for you?"

"I really miss bourbon. My boy, if I could get some smokes and a bottle of bourbon."

Later that day, Raj bought a large bottle of Jack Daniels and a couple of packs of cigarettes for Charlie. Why he did this was a mystery. Maybe it was a small act of defiance against all the correctness that characterized his life. Raj put his purchases in an unmarked brown paper bag and took them to the nursing station. Thankfully, Candy was there. Raj gave her the bag, and she looked in it. "What's this for, Raj? Are you and I going on a date?"

"Yeah," said Raj. "I'm on a tight budget. They don't pay us much, you know. But this is for Mr. Rosenplot."

Candy closed the bag and tucked it under the counter.

Raj opened Charlie's chart and wrote down the order: "Patient may have 2 oz. Bourbon and 2 cigarettes every Friday night."

"He'll wonder who got the stuff for him. What do I tell him?" Candy asked.

Raj thought a moment. "Tell him it's a gift from the taxpayers of Canada."

* * *

"I wonder how Star got into the modeling business?" Paula said. It was Friday evening, and the interns were at Raj's apartment drinking beer after their usual TGIF dinner. Paula and Kelly were still talking endlessly about Star, which annoyed him. He spoke up. "He's a pro hockey player who sells his body by letting people take seminude pictures of him."

Kelly came to Star's defense. "He does not 'sell his body.' He's a very talented and attractive artist who creates art through modeling. He's very creative, and he's training his brain on that website, Luminosity. They've told him he's a genius. Honestly, why are men always so jealous of other men who are better looking and more successful, talented, and wealthy than they are?"

Kelly obviously had Star on her mind. "What I want to know is if he and that secretary are going out together. Did she introduce him as her boyfriend?"

"No, she didn't, but why else would he come to visit her?" Paula said. "What about your boyfriend Jean Claude, Kelly?"

"You mean Jean Luc? I had to get rid of him. He was too –"

"Stoned?"

"No."

"Stupid?"

"No."

"Dirty?"

"No!"

"French?"

"No!" Kelly exploded. "But it's nice to know what you all thought of him! He was just too jealous. He was always wanting me to come back to Montreal. I think he worried about me seeing other men."

"So naturally, you started looking at other men and dumped him," Dan said.

"Yeah, I guess you're right," Kelly said.

They were getting ready to go out when Raj's phone rang. It was Shari, and she wasted no time getting to the point.

"When are you coming to Toronto, Raj? I miss you. We should go out. I want you to meet some of my friends." Shari frequently called Raj, and if he lived closer, they would probably see each other more often.

Raj's friends were looking at him as he hung up the phone. "A friend of mine," he said vaguely.

Kelly spoke first. "A friend, Raj? Sounds more like a girlfriend."

Raj dodged their queries and tried to change the subject. He asked Dan what was going on with the dietician. It seemed Dan was having problems. He didn't like the way she pestered him to change his eating habits and quoted the calories and grams of fat for everything he ate. Dan had begun to avoid eating when he was with her, sneaking burgers and fries when she was at work.

"But I can't give up on her," Dan groaned. When the others pressed him, he hemmed and hawed but finally admitted the sex was great.

His friends finally took off after midnight, and Raj was glad of it. He wanted to be alone. He kept thinking of Shari wrapped around him like a warm, fleshy blanket scented with perfume. Maybe she would dance for him, swaying her hips ever so slowly and rhythmically. The idea got Raj excited – too excited – and he chastised himself for acting like a horny, slavering left-brain idiot.

He wondered whether to let his parents know that he would be meeting up with Shari this weekend. He decided against it but would tell his sister. He opened his computer and found several emails:

From Chandra:

Hey, screw up! I mentioned to some of my girlfriends that you're a doctor. Even though I told them you're socially inept and were likely adopted, they've expressed a certain desire to meet you. I've tried to garner some sympathy for you. Maybe you can come down on the weekend. Are you coming home for Christmas or New

Year's Eve? We have to go to Uncle Gustad's. By the way, can you get me some free samples of Imodium for his party?

Raj replied:

When you said you were trying to garner sympathy from your friends, do you think they'd work a sympathy hookup? Shari keeps calling me, and we're going out again pretty soon, but I haven't told Mom and Dad just in case it doesn't go well. I'm afraid that if I tell them, they'll start sending out wedding invitations. Did you know that her parents invited Mom and Dad for brunch? Mom and Dad don't even know what "brunch" is!

From Mom:

Hi, son: I hope you are eating well – no greasy food. I just got a call from Aunt Shamila. Your cousin is moving ahead with his wedding plans with Uma. Aunt Shamila has hinted that Uma's family is part of the "billionaire club" in London since her dad runs a bunch of steel mills and hotels. Uma has suggested that her pet dog be the ring bearer. Is this some strange English thing? Why do they love dogs so much? Also, the wedding is supposed to be an English-style affair. Apparently, she went to an English boarding school and didn't want an Indian wedding. Shamila and Gustad are disappointed that they aren't supplying the food for the wedding, but I am sure Roger is relieved – and so are we!

Do you want an extra ticket booked for you? Are you taking anyone to this wedding? Your sister wants to take her boyfriend – the boy who says he is writing a screenplay. She thought that Dad would pay for his ticket! She is stupid, and I think you should have a talk with her.

By the way, Shari's father is feeling much better since starting those exercises for his diabetes. He hasn't been quite able to do them while standing on his head, though. Don't you think this is a bit too vigorous an exercise for a man his age? They invited us over for brunch! Should I take something? Maybe there won't be enough food. What is brunch? Call us soon.

Love, Mom

Chapter Twenty Five

That Friday night, Diana was in bed with Star, who was a bit drunk and being grabby. She had refused to go out, still angry about the fight the last time they went to a bar. She was also afraid they might run into Mischa, who had told everyone she intended to stab Diana in the eye with a fork. As she pretended to sleep, Star's hand crept slowly to her breasts. He snugged up closer, spooning her, and she could feel his erection. She didn't like his smell; it was too musky. Star's agent had asked him if he wanted his own line of cologne and aftershave, which would be called *"Hard Ice – by Star"* and packaged in hockey-puck-shaped bottles. Diana argued that ice doesn't have a musky smell, and Star countered that the cologne was supposed to smell like *him*; and, in fact, it *did* smell – like socks after his workout.

Star kept spooning and grinding until Diana had to give in, although she wasn't in the mood. His favourite way was from behind, but she preferred being on top so that she could take some control. Star had the virility of a stallion, but he didn't have any rhythm or understanding of how to time things for her. Reluctantly, she guided him to the right spot and let him have at it.

As he grunted and sweated, she pondered her life. Did she want Star because she actually loved him? When they first got back together, it felt like old times when they were in high school, and he was a lot of fun. He had come a long way since then, and she was happy for him. Maybe she was just annoyed and competitive and didn't want Mischa to steal him. Was he really worth it? He had put her in a very difficult position by flirting with the Russian model, but he had assured her many times that it would never happen again. She believed him but lately, they seemed to have very little to talk about. In a deep corner of her mind, Diana wondered if she was simply putting in the time.

Then there was the dream, the one in which she was wearing a beautiful sari in a castle, and the intern was about to ravish her…

* * *

Late that afternoon, Dan had been in the CEO's office yet again. After the staff had gone home, Wendy had thrown herself at him, and Dan had given in because Wendy had stroked his 'member', and its response was somehow automatic. Wendy liked his body and caressed his shoulder his muscles. Then she grabbed his buttocks, squeezed several times, and said, "I'm going to ride you like a pony."

Dan lay down on the comfortable couch, and Wendy straddled him and kissed him slowly. He could smell her perfume.

"You're so hot, baby. Do you want me?" Wendy purred.

Of course, he did. He'd had a cougar lover before, and it was exciting.

"I knew we'd be good for each other when I first saw you. Love your sweet body."

"Sure, Wendy… you're such a tiger. I'm afraid you might bite me – and I might like it!" said Dan as he undressed her.

Wendy was so easy to please. She began to ride him hard. Then the phone rang.

"Shit! That's my cell phone." Wendy reached for it and answered. "Hi, honey." She resumed her slow rythm.

"Yes, honey. I'll get Sam his Christmas presents." Wendy held her finger to her lips, signalling to Dan to be quiet. She and her husband spoke a while longer. "Honey, I'm in a meeting right now. Something really big has come up, a really big problem, and I have to deal with it. Can I call you back after I'm done? Okay, sweetie. Love you…"

She hung up the phone, slowly kissed Dan's mouth, and said, "Ride me, you fucking stallion!"

Their love making was long and slow. Finally after an hour, Wendy shivered, held absolutely still for several seconds, and they both finally relaxed.

As they lay on the couch in the afterglow, Dan asked, "Who was that on the phone?"

"That was my husband," Wendy said.

"Really?"

"He's a househusband, kind of small and mousey. I don't know what I ever saw in him."

"Kids?"

"Yes – a thirteen-year-old son."

"Do you... I don't know... ever feel guilty?"

"No. My husband's a loser. I'd like to leave him and get a sweet young doctor, but I have the kid. It would never work out."

Dan changed the touchy subject. "So, what's going on with the hospital?"

"The provincial restructuring commission comes though this area next year," she said.

"What's the restructuring commission?"

"It's a group of bureaucrats, including me, that's coming to close this place. John Sinclair and the hospital board are going to be in for a very nasty surprise," she said.

"That sounds pretty harsh. Don't you like this job and your fancy office?"

"Danny, you're so sweet. This place is a backwater."

"I get it," Dan said. "It's small, and it doesn't really matter to the power people in Toronto."

She didn't argue with him. She just sat up and said, "I have to go now, and that means you have to go."

Dan dressed and left, making sure no one saw him. It had surprised him that Sinclair had noticed the time he was spending in the CEO's office. He smiled to himself – had he just received his grey belt?

He was already tired of Wendy. At first, he had liked her summonses because she was sexy, almost to the point of perversion. However, he had come to realize that she only used people. She was beyond ambitious – she was am*bitch*ous. It surprised Dan that a woman would use him as a sex object, as most women in his life saw him as a future husband. Dan surmised that when people were no longer useful to Wendy, she discarded them, and when they stood in her way, she tried to destroy them.

He made up his mind to tell the other interns what was coming. In order to qualify, they needed two years of internship, and it looked as though they wouldn't be able to complete the full two years at St. Jerome.

* * *

Raj desperately wanted to sleep in on Saturday morning, but his phone rang at 7:30. He tried to ignore it, then reluctantly answered it.

"Hello, Raj. It's Shari."

"Hi, Shari. It's kind of early. I was up late," Raj said.

"Doing what?"

"Working."

"When are you coming to town?"

"I'll be at your place around five, okay?"

"That's great, Raj. And you'd better dress up a bit. We're going out."

After Shari hung up, a lovely sleep washed over Raj, bringing a horny dream involving Shari wearing only Indian jewelry and swaying her hips.

He awoke a while later with an erection as stiff as a board, making a tent under the blankets. Once again, a terribly cold shower beckoned.

Two cups of Starbucks coffee and rounds at the hospital chewed up the entire morning. By late afternoon he was at Shari's new apartment on the fortieth floor of a luxury condo building on Bay Street. Every car in the parking lot was imported and expensive; Raj's little Honda looked out of place. Shari's apartment was scrupulously clean and tidy and featured Pottery Barn decor. Shari gave Raj a tour, smiling as she showed him her brass bed.

"You know, Raj, this place is just temporary. I wanted out of my parents' house. When I get married, my father's going to give me

240

a house. It's a model home in a subdivision he's building near where they live." Shari's father, a successful land developer and homebuilder, had grown rich by tailoring his houses to the ever-expanding Indian community northwest of Toronto. He had built one subdivision around a large Hindu temple.

As Shari got ready, Raj wandered around and looked in the fridge for a beer but found nothing but yogurt and tofu. The freezer was full of boxes of Gustad's frozen food. Raj laughed out loud. Gustad had invaded the yuppie Indian household. Idli, masala dossa, curried vegetables, and the like were all stacked up neatly. A thoroughly modern woman, Shari didn't cook.

Tonight, Raj was to meet Shari's best friend, Gita, who managed a clothing store, and Gita's boyfriend, Krishna, an accountant. She seemed nervous about Raj meeting her friends, but he didn't know if she thought he wouldn't be acceptable or that he would find her friends unacceptable. Gita and Krishna arrived at Shari's apartment around 5:00 p.m., bearing bottles of wine and salty Indian treats.

Once the wine had been poured and they were all seated, Raj asked Gita if she knew Shari from school.

"Yeah, she was the class keener," Gita said.

That didn't surprise Raj at all.

The more he drank, the more he became the life of the party, telling the group about some of his hospital stories. Krishna asked if he had samples of Viagra, and Raj told him that, even if he did, he wouldn't share them.

Krishna and Raj, who were becoming fast friends, wanted to stay in and watch TV. Krishna suggested MTV, which was airing a Katy Perry special, but Raj found an even better show involving Jennifer Garner karate fighting in a leather suit. The girls would have none of this and dragged the reluctant men out the door into the cold December air.

They wound up at a club called Lee's Palace, where a band was playing a cross between reggae and ska. Raj liked it immediately, and they spent the evening dancing and drinking beer. Shari danced close to Raj, occasionally grinding her butt against him. Raj thought she was a graceful dancer.

It was after midnight when they finally left Krish and Gita and walked over to where Raj had parked his Honda. They shivered in the Toronto cold after the heat of the club and the sweaty dancing. Shari held his hand, desperately trying to get warm, and complained about the heater in his car.

Outside her condo building, she said, "Raj, why don't you come up to my place to warm up? A drink or something?"

"Okay," he said, not understanding the implied invitation.

Once inside, Shari turned on the stereo, parked herself close to Raj on the couch, and began to apply her hands and body to him with some vigour. Her eagerness surprised him.

"Come on, baby. You're sooo hot," she breathed in his ear.

Raj felt detached, as if he were watching events from outside himself, and wondered what the hell he was even doing there. Did he really want this girl? Did she want him, or did she just want to move the relationship along? Maybe she just wanted sex, which Raj doubted – but one can always hope.

Minutes later, his body began thinking for itself, and Raj surrendered. Shari was almost too eager. Raj got the impression that she was trying to act like a sex kitten but wasn't very experienced – no more than he was, anyway.

He wanted to look at her body, but she seemed uncomfortable about letting him look and allowed him a peek only after she'd lowered the lights as if she were embarrassed by such an intimate moment. But then she grabbed his shoulders and got on top of him. In the midst of this, Raj thought he'd better not screw this up.

He did not let himself get too excited and tried to think of other things to calm himself and get in sync with Shari. The rhythm of her breathing gradually quickened, and Raj finally relaxed and let things occur as they were meant to. He desperately wanted to take his time and not climax too quickly. It was a matter of pride, and he had to distract himself in order to do this. Finally, after he felt that she was satisfied, he let things go. Spent and sweating, they lay together on the couch afterward. Had she climaxed? Had she faked it? Raj had to ask. "Well, how was that?"

Shari snuggled closer and said, "You were great!"

"Well, you know," he said, "doctors have special training." That made Shari laugh.

"This was my first time," she said. "Was I any good?"

"You were really good – the best."

"Raj, you're the nicest guy I've ever met. I would never have done this if I weren't sure I was serious about you."

Raj pondered this. What did she want him to say? He knew that some profession of love would be in order; he didn't want to say that he loved her. It was just too soon. "I really care about you, Shari," he ventured.

Raj was exhausted by the many days of overwork at the hospital and desperately wanted to sleep. The last thing he heard was Shari talking about her parents, about getting married. Then he was fast asleep.

Chapter Twenty Six

"I'm telling you, in every city where *Mama Mia* plays, somebody in the cast gets married, or someone proposes!" Mary Peters said. She was an experienced actress in her fifties, tall and striking with red hair. She was from the UK and had worked on several overseas productions of the musical. Mary and her friend Lizzy Black were stage actresses playing the mother's friends. Diana loved being in the theatre company with so many old hands.

Lizzy added, "In London, four girls in the cast got married!"

"You have got to be kidding!" Diana said.

"I can't explain it. Maybe seeing women on stage drives men a bit crazy."

"Well, that isn't going to happen to me," said Diana confidently.

The women had gathered in a tiny house they were renting in Cabbagetown just to the east of downtown Toronto.

Lizzy had short dark hair and a butterfly tattoo on her chest. She smoked and drank espresso constantly. "Diana, you're young and pretty. I'm sure that hockey player will pop the question," said Lizzy.

"I don't think so," Diana replied. "Anyway, I'm not sure I want to get married. I want an international career like yours, and that doesn't go with marriage."

The cast had found out that Diana was dating a famous hockey player. Star had been nominated for the Rookie of the Year and was up for the Calder Trophy, and since then, he had been playing hard.

Diana didn't like staying at Star's place when she was in Toronto. When Mary suggested she move in with her and Lizzy, she'd jumped at the chance. The little house suited her fine. A bohemian lot, the women smoked marijuana, drank, and had a good time almost every night. It was almost like being back at university – except that she had more money now. Not much more, but a little more.

She had not quit working for her father. She had been able to schedule her office work carefully around the Toronto rehearsals and borrowed her mother's car to drive back and forth. She was very busy, but she liked having two incomes, which enabled her to afford the ultra-cheap apartment in St. Jerome and the not-so-cheap room in the Cabbagetown house. Star had wanted her to move in permanently and was crestfallen when she said she needed a place closer to the theatre.

Star's publicist, Claire Foster, had set up an interview with *Bro* magazine about his nomination for the Calder Trophy, and the magazine featured Star on the cover. Diana's housemates had picked up a copy because they liked his looks. They knew Diana was dating him and were impressed by his celebrity.

The photos inside the magazine showed Star wearing a fur coat – a bare-chested dude in fur; Star wearing leather pants – a bare-chested dude in leather; Star wearing his signature underwear – a bare-chested, sweating dude; Star sporting a beard and promoting an all-natural beeswax beard product – bare-chested and looking like a Viking. The interview wasn't much more than a 'Bro-Crush-fest'. There were pictures of the interviewer practically man-crushing on Star.

The interview ran:

BRO: Star, when did you realize that hockey was going to be your career?

STAR: I realized it when I got drafted. I was planning to go to college, actually. My dad's a lawyer, and he wanted me to go to law school, but hockey has always been my first love.

BRO: Star, you've become a phenom off the ice as well. People think you're the future of the NHL. There's talk that you're now one of the top menswear models in New York City.

STAR: I need something to do in the off-season. I also plan to join "Models Without Borders" and do some work helping people in the Third World. I was thinking of starting a hockey club in Nigeria.

BRO: So, what are you going to wear to the awards in Las Vegas?

STAR: I think I'll go classic – Hugo Boss, black tie. I'm going to wear this watch – PrimSport makes it in the Czech Republic. You can buy it on my website, StarSport.com.

BRO: We know that hockey is your first love, but is there anyone special?

STAR: Hey man, that's a personal question… but it's all cool 'cause you're a Bro'. Yeah, I do have someone special. You know, I'm a small-town guy who always wanted to make it big in Toronto. There's someone special… let's say she wears a maple leaf on her jacket and comes from my hometown. Some day, I want a wife, kids… you know, the whole Bro'gram…

BRO: So there you have it. Star Yanofsky – red hot on the ice and totally cool off the ice. Dude, you are a total Bro'! I don't want to upset the Bro'tocol, but I'm truly impressed. You are the Bro'thority on cool.

STAR: Thanks, man. I'm going to keep the Bromentum going.

BRO: Honestly, when I see you on the ice, it's like a Brohemian Rhapsody…

STAR: Thanks, Brochacho! Some very extreme Brotality going down…

The article had been well received, and it was obvious to the rest of the cast that Star had meant Diana when he spoke of "someone special." She was flattered and actually flushed when one of the actors read it aloud.

She had called Star, but he was on the road playing in Chicago and New Orleans before the awards ceremony in Las Vegas. He had asked his mother to be his date, and Diana didn't mind, as she was very busy.

Diana had spent the night in Toronto but left for St. Jerome early in the morning. She had to be at work by 9:00 a.m., and she managed it with three minutes to spare. When she arrived, her father was already there, staring at the office clock.

"Hi, Dad," she said.

"That's 'Dr. Sinclair' here, even to you. I was worried you'd be late."

"Well, I'm not," said Diana. "What's up?"

"Christmas is coming Soon, and we have to do the Christmas thing here in the hospital. As chief of staff, I'm responsible for staff morale."

"Shouldn't the CEO be organizing something?" Diana asked.

"The staff can't stand her. So that's not a good idea," he said. "So it's up to me. I mean you. I want you to arrange something for the staff and patients."

"What did you do last year?" asked Diana.

"Marg went around with a trolley of eggnog, Christmas punch, cakes, and chocolates for the various departments."

"Sounds like you didn't do anything. You just let Marg do it all."

"That's pretty much it, Di. I did, however, give her a Christmas bonus."

"That sounds good. How much will I get?"

"You? Nothing, of course!" he said. "But Marg still gets a Christmas bonus even if she's off sick."

"Dad, that's so not fair!"

"Okay, okay! Just make sure you do a good job. Everyone's a bit down about the future of this place. Let's give them a little cheer."

Diana spent the rest of the day being patient with patients, especially those who demanded to see the doctor right away – "I just need a few minutes to get my pills." Even after several months, some of them still viewed her with suspicion and would say, "Marg ran the office better – but you're much prettier than Marg," implying her looks were why she had the job.

Wondering what on earth to wear for Christmas rounds, Diana Googled "Christmas costumes." What she found were either ridiculous or just plain slutty. She finally found a red dress that looked vaguely elf-like. It was on the short side, but she planned to wear green leotards with it. A little Santa hat and her mom's green suede flats would be perfect.

"Dr. Mehta, speed it up! I've probably got another divorce to pay for!" Raj knew that Dr. Williamson wanted to go home.

Raj's hands trembled ever so slightly as he held the needle driver, a pincer that held a wickedly sharp, curved needle with a tiny spot of blood at the tip. It reminded him of a python's venomous fang. The last operation of the day was a hernia, and Raj was closing the rather lengthy incision. He was trying to remember how to tie a proper knot at the end. Dr. Williamson, chief of surgery, was a difficult taskmaster. Just being around him made Raj anxious.

Raj was finding the surgical rotation fun, though in a brutally hectic way. Dr. Williamson was the hardest working man Raj had ever met. He was in his early sixties and was still able to stand for hours at a time without getting tired. He was a tall, heavyset man who was a true general surgeon. Most general surgeons confine their work to the belly area and rely on other surgeons to operate in the chest or other parts of the body – but not Williamson. He had done extra training in cardiovascular and chest surgery, and the only body part Raj hadn't seen him operate on was a brain, though he probably would have if someone allowed it.

Dr. Williamson considered the hospital his personal fiefdom. A large, imposing man with silver hair, when he wasn't in the OR, he cut a conservative sartorial figure in expensive suits and ties. On Raj's first day on the ward, he told him, "The old ladies and men around here want to see a doctor, not some guy who walked out of a GAP

251

catalogue." Since starting on the surgical ward, Raj had begun wearing the grey flannel slacks and the pinstriped, pale blue shirts that his dad had bought.

In a way, Raj was happy to have finally left the confines of Internal Medicine. Surgery had a sense of urgency, and there wasn't time to get involved with people. Patients on this ward were either waiting for or recovering from surgery, and those recovering were discouraged from staying long by the nursing staff and the tasteless food. Dr. Williamson did his part by automatically discharging anyone who was well enough to go outside for a smoke.

Though Raj was becoming more confident as a doctor, he was still nervous about being on call for the surgical service, largely because of Dr. Williamson. The boss made it clear that he expected the intern to do a diagnostic workup on any surgical emergencies and call him only if he was needed. "You can do any minor procedures that don't need anesthesia and send them to my clinic the next day, Raj," he said. Raj had learned a little stitching in the ER, and so he wasn't too worried; however, who knew what sort of problem could come his way?

On his first night on call, he was paged at 11 p.m. and told to come in. The ER was extremely busy, and they had a case they wanted a surgeon to see. Raj could hear a cacophony of noise in the background, with babies crying and people shouting. The snarly nurse he spoke to didn't say what the case was but suggested that he hurry so that he could help clear the department.

Raj walked a hundred steps to the ER in the cold in his hospital scrubs and lab coat. The ER was warm and stuffy from too many people breathing the same air. Raj went to the nursing station, where a nurse handed him a chart for a woman named Sylvie Jacobec.

"You're gonna love this one, Raj," the nurse told him.

An unhappy-looking young woman and a man, whom Raj presumed was her boyfriend, greeted him in the little ER exam room. She was quite attractive despite wearing too much makeup. In an eastern European accent, she said, "Thank God someone's here! I hope you can help me. My stomach is in so much pain, and I just can't take it anymore!"

"Show me where it hurts, Ms. Jacobec." Raj was worried that she might have appendicitis or a hot gallbladder because he didn't relish the thought of calling Dr. Williamson.

Sylvie pulled up the hospital gown to expose her belly. "You see, Doctor, it's killing me."

Her belly was rather thin with a tattoo that looked like an elvish script and a large red jewel embedded in her navel.

"What's the problem?" he asked.

"The jewel – I can't get it out!"

Looking closer, Raj saw that the jewel was wedged deeply in her navel and the surrounding skin was red and swollen. The boyfriend spoke up. "Sylvie's working at the Cabaret. She started her act but couldn't continue because the jewel was hurting so much."

Raj finally realized that Sylvie was a stripper.

"I can't work like this," she complained, her eyes teary. "You have to get it out."

Raj had no idea what he would do to get the jewel out, but he knew he wasn't going to call Williamson, who would probably laugh. He left the room, took the patient's chart, and sat down to think. The swelling around the jewel had pushed it in deeper, and there was probably some suction below it. The trick would be to get underneath the jewel and somehow pry it out. He wouldn't make a skin incision because a bandaged belly would hamper her earning ability - no one liked a bandaged up stripper. His mind made up, he went back to talk to Sylvie and her boyfriend.

After explaining what he was about to do, Raj cleaned her abdomen with slippery iodine soap and froze around the umbilicus with lidocaine. The jewel moved up and down as Sylvie breathed, and she was hyperventilating. It glinted in the bright overhead light, and Raj was momentarily dazzled by its brilliance. He injected sterile water through the border of the belly button under the jewel to create a pocket of fluid that he hoped would pop it out like a champagne cork. It bulged outward and looked ready to pop, but it didn't. He used a small scalpel to pry gently around the glass jewel and slowly pried it out. The skin around the navel was bruised, but Raj had managed not to cut her. There was just a barely detectable puncture site. Raj placed the offending jewel on the table.

"Thank God you came along, Doctor! I am so happy I could kiss you." Before he knew it, Sylvie grabbed Raj's shoulder and planted a wet kiss on his cheek.

"I'll let you get dressed, Ms. Jacobec," said Raj, smiling at his first successful solo surgery.

He stopped her on her way out. "Hey, Sylvie! You forgot your jewel."

"Don't worry about it. Keep it, Doctor. I'm not going to wear it anymore." Raj put the fake jewel in his lab coat pocket and forgot it.

On his way home, his phone rang, but he ignored it. He remembered it while he was watching the news. It was, as he suspected, yet another message from Shari:

Where are you? I didn't get a chance to ask you if you wanted to come on holiday with me and my parents and brother. We're going on a Caribbean cruise. You won't have to pay. Dad is so happy with you and his diabetes that he would just love to have you along. Give me a call, sweetie.

Raj was getting a distinct impression that he was now expected to be around more. Shari had mentioned going away for Christmas, but he couldn't go because he was on call for surgery – which was almost a relief. He called her and explained why he couldn't join her and her family on the cruise.

"Can't someone else do it?" She sounded upset. "We could make a little masala."

"Will you be back before New Year's?"

"Yes, we are. Why?"

"My aunt and uncle hold a big family party on New Year's Eve. Maybe we can get together for that."

"Raj," Shari said. "Do you want our relationship to work?"

"Yes, of course I do. Look, I have to go now if I'm going to be up at six."

"Okay, Raj. Talk to you soon."

What did she mean by "wanting the relationship to work"? It sounded ominous to him.

Chapter Twenty Seven

"Hey, babe. Why don't you come over tonight?"

"What are we going to do, Star?"

"I dunno. Maybe Netflix and chill?

"We did that last night."

"I know, but Big Head Eric is still missing you."

"Big Head Eric has been really busy, and I have lines and songs to rehearse."

"Yeah, but you can study at my place… and chill."

"No, Star. I'm staying here. We're rehearsing lines and dance moves. We're getting really good."

"Babe, I miss you – you know that."

"Is it Star or just Big Head Eric that's missing me?"

"Both of us do… and you can see my new trophy!"

"I've seen the trophy three times already, and you've sent me thirty-four selfies of you and the trophy. I think you should stop kissing it – silver polish isn't good for you."

"You're not seeing anyone else, are you, Di?"

"Where did that come from?"

"I don't know. I just thought you'd come to some games and watch me more."

"You know I've got a job. Actually, I have two jobs. People are counting on me."

"I need you around more, babe."

"I'll see if I can make time later in the week, but it'll have to be a quickie."

"Thanks, babe. I need it. Remember – Netflix and chill, and then we can make smoothie. It's a verb *and* a noun now!"

Diana clicked off her cell phone. Now that Star had won the Calder Trophy, Toronto was officially crazy for him. Rumour had it that he had spawned a fashion trend. His photo shoot in *Bro* magazine had resulted in a run on fur hats, and a furrier had approached him about another fashion shoot. Star had become more possessive of Diana lately, but he thought nothing of appearing in ads surrounded by gorgeous models.

For Diana, Star didn't come first anymore. *Mama Mia* did. The pressure was on her to get her lines and choreography perfect. The director's motto was, "Professionals don't just practice to get it perfect – they practice so that it can't possibly go wrong," and so other cast members were learning Diana's lines, and she theirs. She could now sing all the songs faultlessly.

On top of countless rehearsals, most of them scheduled in the evening, Diana was still holding down her day job at the hospital. Early tomorrow, she would have to drive back. Christmas was coming, and her father kept reminding her that she was responsible for Christmas Rounds.

The multitude of things going on in Diana's life swirled around her as she lay in her bed in the little Cabbagetown house. She knew she couldn't maintain the hospital job and be part of the cast much longer. And then there was Star. She was being pulled in so many different directions.

She fell into a troubled sleep and dreamed.

The air was warm and humid, and it was approaching twilight. She was resting on a reclining couch, inhaling the soft fragrance of jasmine and listening to the soft burble of running water. In the background, music and drums were playing a hypnotic rhythm.

There was a faint movement at the doorway, and a man came forward and stared deeply into her eyes. His scent was like the northern woods. She felt the heat rise in her like a wave of warm ocean water. He touched the swirling pattern on her thigh, making her skin tingle. It was a message: here, he would find what he needed and desired the most. Their lips touched, and their hands explored. She writhed with pleasure .....

"Diana! Wake up!"

"Huh?" Diana was flushed, and the bedcovers were wedged between her legs.

"You told me to wake you up so you can get to your other job," Mary said. "You were moaning."

"Thanks, Mary. I must have been dreaming."

"About Star, no doubt."

"Maybe." Diana grew a little more crimson.

"Just you wait, Di. He's going to propose – guaranteed!"

Diana made it to the hospital in the nick of time. It was early December, and the weather was awful. By 10:30 a.m., Diana needed a break, the combination of the drive from Toronto and no breakfast was wearing on her. She decided to visit the various departments and let them know she'd be coming around for Christmas. Diana wanted to find out if there were any patients that were depressed and lonely.

She wondered vaguely if any of the interns were around. She enjoyed chatting with them during coffee breaks. Paula and Kelly were often around, but Diana hadn't seen Raj or Dan for some time. When she got there, the cafeteria was empty, and Diana bought her usual yogurt, muffin, and tea.

As she was leaving, she saw Raj, looking preoccupied and not at all happy. He was carrying a large plastic jar with a yellow lid and was staring at it.

Diana caught up with him. "How are you, Raj? I was wondering if you were around."

"I am," he said. "Have to keep my day job. How's the acting world treating you?"

"Everything's going well. I hope the show has a good run."

"How's Star? Did I hear he won some award?"

"He won the Calder Trophy. What's in the jar? Your lunch?"

Raj looked sad. "It's not worth knowing, Diana."

"C'mon. Tell me."

"It's a breast tumour, and I think it's a bad one. I'm taking it to Pathology for tumour markers and to get the margins checked."

Diana felt stupid, and there was an awkward silence as they approached an elevator.

"My aunt had breast cancer," Raj said. She used to make my treats when I was a little boy. She died when I was about ten. Such a lovely woman."

"What kind of treats?" Diana couldn't think of what else to say..

"Plantain chips. I had a lot of pressure from my parents growing up, but I think my aunt liked me just for being me. She liked to feed me, anyway."

"I've had plantain chips, Raj. Did you know I've been to India?" asked Diana.

"Really?" said Raj. "You always surprise me."

The elevator arrived at the basement, and as Raj was about to turn towards the Pathology Office, Diana touched his shoulder. It was unlike her, and she wasn't sure why she had. "You know, sometimes I feel – I don't know – that everything you guys do is far more important than anything I could ever do."

"Don't feel that way," said Raj. "Life isn't worth living if you can't smile about something. You've got a real gift."

"And what gift would that be?" said Diana.

"Making people smile!" Raj flashed a genuine smile, showing white teeth. He slipped away, walking a little taller.

* * *

"I'm telling you guys, the CEO wants to close the hospital!"

"No way. Dan. She'd put herself out of a job."

"No, I don't think so," Dan said. "She's got plans to be CEO of a new hospital in the west end of Toronto."

It was Friday night, and, as usual, the interns were at Raj's apartment, drinking beer and eating pizza. Dan was trying to convince the others to do something because the second year of their internships was in question.

"How did you find out about all this?" Kelly asked.

"I've been pumping, Wendy."

"For information?" asked Kelly.

"Just pumping her." Dan smiled.

Paula was incredulous. "She's actually told you all this?"

"Yeah, some restructuring commission will reorganize the hospitals. The plan is to close smaller, local hospitals and replace them with big, regional ones along the highway corridor."

Raj noticed that the other interns were as worried as he was. They had grown fond of St. Jerome. He spoke up. "I can tell you that none of the surgeons knows what's going on, and I've also noticed that no one likes the CEO."

"I get the sense that the feeling is mutual," Kelly said.

"Should we be telling someone? What about Sinclair?" asked Paula.

Raj and Dan didn't think the staff physicians would take the issue seriously, not if it came from them.

"Raj, I've seen you chatting up the Chief of Staff's secretary a few times," Kelly said. "Why don't you tell her?"

"It's not like I really know her," Raj said.

"But you'd *like* to know her!" Kelly was grinning.

Raj turned red. To deflect the teasing, he asked, "Dan, what about you and that dietician? She's a total fox."

"I know," replied Dan. "It's taking a lot out of me to deal with both her and Wendy. I don't think I can do it anymore. Sinclair has noticed I've been spending time in her office. You wouldn't believe the things she makes me do."

Raj's cell phone rang and kept ringing. He wasn't on call, so he guessed that it was Shari. It was. He had to take the call.

"Hey, Raj! I've been thinking about you a lot, sweetie. I don't know why, but I've been so turned on lately. Why can't you come to town more often? I think you work too much."

"Hi, Shari. Listen – I've got a few people here. We're studying for our qualifying exams." Kelly and Paula sniggered at this, and Dan squealed in a high voice, "Oh, Raj! Don't touch me there!"

"Are you actually studying, Raj? My parents want us to have dinner with them this weekend. I was hoping we could get together."

" Maybe Sunday. I'll check my schedule. We're just getting started here, so I'll call you later, okay?" Shari told him to call her that evening and hung up.

"What's going on with you, Raj?" said Paula. She was curious and wondered why he'd seemed so preoccupied this last while.

"I'm seeing a girl – an accountant I met a while ago. She's quite nice."

Paula said nothing, and Kelly quickly changed the subject. "You have to see what I've done – you'll be amazed!"

She grabbed a small shopping bag and went into the bathroom, emerging a few minutes later. She was wearing OR scrubs, but they were different from what they were all used to. These scrubs hugged her shape nicely.

"What do you think?" She turned to the side to show off the top, which was short and had slits on the sides and a deeper neckline. When she lifted her arms slightly, they could see her midriff. She had also inserted spandex panels down the pant legs that made them hug her thighs and flare at the bottom.

Raj spoke first. "Kelly, you look totally hot!"

Paula said that she liked the outfit.

Dan said, "That's awesome, Kelly! When did you get the idea for this?"

Kelly, doing a little ass-wiggle dance, said, "I was on the medical floor, and one of the nurses and I got talking. I think you know her, Raj. Her name's Candy."

Raj nodded. "Right – the totally hot one who's getting married to a cop."

"She thinks we should go into business together," said Kelly. "We're going to call our company Candy - Kelly.'"

"Can you make me a set?" asked Paula.

"I already did!" squealed Kelly, tossing a paper bag to Paula. "Hope you don't mind, but I got your measurements from your clothes in the change room."

Paula dashed into the bathroom and emerged looking like a well-put-together babe – in hospital greens. Both girls danced around the apartment, and Dan put on "Hot Line Bling" way too loud. They goofed around for a bit, but then their mood grew more subdued as they remembered Dan's news.

"I really like it here," Paula said, and the others agreed that the town of St. Jerome had treated them incredibly well.

Raj said, "We have to tell someone. I'm going to speak to Williamson or one of the other surgeons. Meanwhile, we should keep our eyes open and see if anything new develops."

They all looked at Dan. "Hey, why are you looking at me?" he said. "I can't deal with Wendy anymore. She's too demanding. What if my girlfriend finds out?"

266

"I've seen your girlfriend. Don't worry, I'll cover for you, bro'. She won't miss a thing!" Raj chortled.

As they laughed, Raj realized that having this group of friends was one of the best things he had ever had in his life.

Chapter Twenty Eight

"Scalpel."

"Scalpel."

"Suture."

"Suture."

"A little more retraction, Raj. Geez! This surgery would go a lot better with *two* of me and *none* of you."

Raj apologized, trying not to laugh at Dr. Miller's remark. The man was a caricature of himself. The nursing staff had told Raj ahead of time that Miller always claimed things would go better with more of him and fewer of everyone else. Raj had assumed that working with a doctor with a king-sized ego would be detestable, but he was finding the work rather fun. Dr. Miller was a smart, no-nonsense guy who got the job done. He was an orthopedic surgeon in his forties and still looked young and fit. His blond hair and deep tan made him look like a surfer, and he drove around town in a red Corvette with license plates that read "CUTTER #1".

He was arrogant, but Raj figured that a good surgeon could get away with it under the guise of eccentric genius. He could be nice to people, but he could also lose it if things weren't going well in the OR. Raj knew that Miller was vying for the top spot at the hospital and would likely replace Williamson as chief of surgery in the future.

Raj was not supposed to be working with him; however, Williamson had left earlier for the holidays and told Raj to stay on call and work with Miller. Raj realized the two men didn't much like each other. "Yeah, Williamson is old school," was all Dr. Miller would say about his colleague. He had quirks that it took getting used to. He never took the elevator but ran up the stairs two at a time. As his intern, Raj had to do this, too, as Miller liked interns who were in shape.

They were doing a knee replacement on an elderly man. As the work progressed, Miller chatted with the ancsthctist, Frcd Banting, who had worked in the OR for thirty years and was practically an institution. Everyone gossiped in the OR, and behind his back, Miller himself was the subject of much gossip because he had been divorced at least twice and had lived with a few other women. Raj quickly learned that the operating rooms were a zone where 'political correctness' didn't seem to exist.

"So what's with that other intern? I think her name's Kelly," Miller asked Raj

"She's really smart," said Raj. "She's from Montreal."

"From Montreal, eh? That explains why she's so totally hot," Miller said.

"Dave's looking for his next ex-wife," Fred said. "It's part of our Family doc recruitment drive – get you guys married off so you can't leave!" Everyone in the room laughed.

Miller spoke authoritatively, "Women from Montreal are special. I think she's also a competent doctor. I've seen her in the OR a few times lately, along with that other intern – the short one."

"Paula," said Raj.

Raj held the Deever retractor as Miller continued working. He asked Raj casually if Kelly was seeing anyone. Raj told him she had been dating a musician from Montreal, to which Miller responded, "I hate musicians and artsy-farty types."

"I think she dumped him," said Raj.

"Nice," said Miller. "So she's available?"

"Yeah, I guess."

Fred spoke up again. "Whatever happened to Sinclair's daughter? Wasn't she going into music or theatre or something like that?"

"Last I heard," said Miller, "he hired her as his secretary after I fixed Marg's hip a couple of months ago."

Raj had a revelation. "You mean that Sinclair's secretary is his daughter?"

Fred replied, "Yeah, Raj. He hired her because he couldn't find anyone else. No one wanted the job. She goes out with that hockey player, and I think she's working at a dinner theatre."

"She never mentioned she's Sinclair's daughter," Raj said.

"What's she like?" Miller asked.

"She's really nice. She borrowed a cup of brown sugar from me."

"Whoa," exclaimed Miller. "So she cooks. Maybe *I* should date her, Raj – except that Sinclair would kill me."

Fred chimed in. "Sinclair wouldn't want a forty-five-year-old surgeon dating his daughter. Our young intern here should go out with her."

"That won't happen," Raj said. "She's dating a famous hockey player. She's totally out of my league."

The long day finally ended, and the three doctors changed in the locker room. No one bothered to lock the lockers, and Fred opened Williamson's and took out a large jar of clearish liquid with a greenish tinge. In the liquid was a bunch of what looked like pinecones and a few pine needles. He held it out to Raj. "Check this out," he said as he unscrewed the top. Raj took a sniff. The contents smelled strongly of alcohol.

"What is it?" asked Raj.

"Alcohol hand disinfectant,."

"What's the stuff in it?"

"Some botanicals from up north that Williamson puts in it. Smells nice, doesn't it? He uses it as an aftershave and says it keeps his pores small. Really, Raj, he's just too cheap to buy aftershave." Fred poured some on his hands and slapped it on his face. "Want some? Grab one of those urine jars." He poured some more and dabbed it on Raj's face. It stung, but its piney scent was pleasant.

Raj took his little jar home, feeling like a thief. He didn't like the idea of taking something from Williamson's locker, even though the jar of alcohol was a hospital issue.

* * *

Diana surveyed the trolley, which she had decorated with Christmas paraphernalia – even a little Charlie Brown tree trimmed with battery-powered lights. There were small gifts, chocolates, cakes, eggnog, tea, and coffee. She had planned a surprise for the Pediatrics ward. She was going to sing for them and had hidden her guitar on the lower shelf of the cart behind the decorations. It had been a while since she'd played the guitar regularly, but she had been practicing on those nights she was in St. Jerome.

She was wearing the red dress she'd ordered online and green leotards, which matched the green suede flats she'd borrow from her mother. She topped off the ensemble with a Santa hat. Not quite Santa's elf, but not goofy-looking, either. She had sent a selfie to Star, who texted back that she'd look better without the dress or the leotards, leaving just the hat.

Diana was happy. She liked Christmas, and she was doing something fun. Raj was right: if you could make someone smile, it was an accomplishment.

It was the last day of regular work at the hospital before everything except the ER and medical wards shut down for the holidays. Diana wheeled out the trolley and started her rounds.

* * *

Raj was barely awake when his phone rang. It was Shari.

"Hi, Raj. Just getting ready to leave on the cruise. I'm packing two bikinis. They're so cute – I want you to see them."

"Nice, Shari. Sounds like you're going to have fun."

"It won't be half as much fun without you."

"I know," Raj said, "but I have to work."

"Talking about work, my dad's developing a new subdivision in Mississauga, and he wants to put a medical clinic in the centre of it."

"That's nice," said Raj, feigning interest.

"But Raj, there's more. He's giving me a house there."

"Wow!" said Raj, now impressed.

Shari continued, "The medical centre will have all sorts of stuff like a pharmacy and a physiotherapy centre – and he wants you to run it."

"Really? Me?" Raj was amazed. "But Shari, I'm not even qualified yet."

"My parents have met your parents. They really like you. Don't worry, baby. It'll all work out. We'll talk about it when I get back. You'd better make some time for me then!"

"I almost forgot. I have to go to my aunt Shamila's New Year's Eve party. Do you want to go?"

"Of course, Raj. You know I'll do anything for you, anything."

"Thanks, Shari. I'm really looking forward to some time off. See you soon."

As he got ready for work, Raj kept thinking about his situation. Shari had come into his life like a bulldozer, and it seemed that she now had it all planned out for him. Raj liked her a lot, but he felt uneasy. If only he wasn't so keen on having sex with her.

Raj left his apartment and trudged through slushy snow to work, putting his misgivings about Shari behind him as best he could. The hospital was moving towards a holiday shutdown, but Raj had to cover emergencies and the patients in the surgical ward. As most of the patients had been discharged for Christmas, he finished rounds in an hour.

Afterward, he didn't know what to do. None of the other interns were around, and so he made his way down to the lobby, where the women's auxiliary ran a small snack bar offering ham sandwiches and soup at a price interns could afford. The receptionist was there, still nagging everyone to wash their hands, and she now had a whistle she blew if someone tried to sneak in without using the sanitizer. The woman who ran the auxiliary's snack bar seemed to have a soft spot for Raj and always gave him extra; today, they gave him a piece of Christmas cake.

While eating lunch, Raj read the Toronto Sun – mainly Christmas articles, Honest Ed's turkey giveaway, and such. There was a lot of news about the war in Iraq.

Raj thought about the Christmases his family had celebrated so that he and his sister would not feel left out because they were Hindu. This year, for the first time, he wouldn't be home for Christmas Day, as he didn't get off work till December 28th. He resolved to spend the rest of the holiday with them. Shari had agreed to go with him to the annual family party on December 31st at Aunt Shamila's, and his parents would be pleased about that. Chandra would have made plans for New Year's Eve months in advance, likely a party at a downtown nightclub.

Raj finished his lunch and wandered around the hospital until he found himself on the Internal Medicine floor, which had been his home for several months. He knew some of the nurses and was sure they'd give him some of the Christmas treats that patients had brought in for them.

The floor was much busier than the Surgery floor. Surgery can often be postponed until after the holidays, but treating heart attacks or strokes can't. He'd been warned when he worked on the floor that the stress of loneliness and family gatherings around Christmas often proved too much, especially for the elderly. Somewhat gloomily, Raj thought the only difference between him and the patients was that he was a lot younger.

He sat down at the nursing station and chatted with a few of the nurses, most of them young, single, and working over the Christmas holiday, happy for the overtime. Raj, on the other hand, would see no change in his December pay cheque.

Raj scanned the patients' charts to see if anyone he had worked on was still there. A petite Chinese nurse named Glenda asked him if he had looked after Mr. Rosenplot. The poor old guy had been there forever, and Raj was relieved that the bourbon and cigarettes he had prescribed hadn't killed him, though he doubted that Charlie would care. With nothing else to do, he stole a handful of chocolates and meandered down to Room 419, Charlie Rosenplot's address, for well over a year.

From outside the room, he heard happy voices. He was cheered that Charlie actually had some visitors – a long-lost niece or nephew, perhaps. It even occurred to him that Charlie might have got married, as Cooper had suggested. He opened the door and was taken aback to see Charlie talking with a slim young woman dressed in green leotards, a short red dress, and a Santa hat.

"Diana! What the heck are you doing here?

"Hi, Raj. I'm doing my Christmas thing." Diana smiled and turned red as Raj stared at her.

"Hey, Doc! Nice to see you again." Charlie looked better than when Raj had been looking after him.

"I thought I'd come and see if they'd married you off to some poor unsuspecting nurse so they could free up a bed".

"No such luck!" said Charlie, "I don't celebrate Christmas, but who can resist an elf as pretty as this one?"

"It's a present from Santa," said Raj.

"Hey, sweetie," said Charlie to Diana. "How about some more eggnog?"

"Sure, Mr. Rosenplot," said Diana, "but there's no alcohol in it."

"That's okay, honey. I got my own supply." Charlie winked at Raj.

Raj joined Diana at Charlie's bedside, and the old man happily chatted away. It was his second Christmas at the hospital, but he was hopeful of getting out in a few weeks. Charlie had always liked

Christmas because of the pre-Christmas rush – it was good for business. Then he suddenly switched topics.

"Hey, sweetie, you should check out this one here – he ain't Jewish, but he's a good one!"

Diana blushed and sprang up. "Santa's little helper has a few more stops, Mr. Rosenplot, so I'll be going now."

Behind her back, Charlie gestured for Raj to follow her – and he did. They strolled down the corridor together, Diana pushing her squeaky trolley.

"I know that what I'm doing is a bit corny, Raj," Diana said once they were outside the room.

"Not at all," said Raj. "It's a really nice thing to do."

"What plans do you have for the holidays?"

It struck Raj that Diana always had a hopeful face as if something good were just around the bend.

"I'm on call, so I'm having a quiet Christmas at my apartment." He tried to sound nonchalant as if this were cool because he was a doctor.

"That's too bad, Raj. Too bad you won't be having Christmas with your family."

Raj, desperate for company, asked, "Would you like a cup of coffee?"

Diana smiled. "After we visit the maternity ward."

Raj watched her do a round of the ward, cuddling all the babies, putting little elf hats on them, and taking pictures of them for their mothers.

The cafeteria was all but deserted, and they took their coffees to a corner table.

"How did you and Star meet?" Raj asked

Diana looked a little puzzled at the question. "We went to high school together."

"What kind of name is Star anyway?"

"You seem awfully interested in him. Are you gay?" Diana teased.

"No! Really… no!" Raj kicked himself for sounding so stupid.

"He was born with a small star-shaped birthmark on his chin," Diana said, "hence the name. You know, he has a lot of gay fans."

"Well, I'm not one of them," insisted Raj.

Diana thought for a moment, then smiled shyly. "Would you like to have Christmas dinner with me?"

"Where? At your apartment?"

"No, silly." Diana laughed. "I'm inviting you for dinner with me and my mom and dad on Christmas Eve."

Raj doubted that Diana's father would want to see him for Christmas Eve dinner. Though reluctant, he couldn't come up with an excuse and had to say yes.

Diana squeezed his hand and gave him the address. "See you at six, then. Christmas Eve."

Nervously, Raj rambled, "Are you sure it'll be okay with your folks? I really don't want to intrude. Maybe we can do this some other time…."

"You'd better be really hungry when you get there," said Diana.

"I think I'll just be nervous." That made her laugh, and Raj joined in.

"I'd better get back to my rounds," Diana said, and she left with her trolley to offer eggnog and Christmas cake to the few people still around.

What just happened? Raj wondered. At least if he were alone, he wouldn't be stressed. Now he'd have to see Dr. Sinclair and his wife – on Christmas Eve, no less. *Shit! Shit! Shit…!*

Chapter Twenty Nine

After a light lunch on Christmas Eve, Diana went into the kitchen to help her mother, Laura Sinclair, prepare the evening meal.

"Are you going to tell me who this mystery guest is?" Laura asked. She had been pressing Diana to identify him ever since she'd learned she had invited a friend.

"Okay, I'll tell you now. It's one of the interns at the hospital."

"Not Star?"

"He and his folks have gone to St. Martin for Christmas."

"So you met this fellow at work? Is he cute?"

"Mom!" cried Diana. "Why do you always ask me these things?"

"Well, is he?"

"You'll see soon enough. His name's Raj. He's on call Christmas Day, so he can't go home. I felt sorry for him, so I invited him for dinner," Diana said. "Dad knows him."

"Does he know he's coming?"

"No," Diana said. "I didn't tell him."

"Then it'll be a surprise. So, is he cute?"

Exasperated, Diana said, "You know, I'll never understand you! Yes, he's quite attractive – tall, dark, and handsome."

"Nice," Laura said. "I thought the same when I met your dad."

"That he was tall, dark, and handsome?"

"Tall, *white,* and handsome." Mrs. Sinclair laughed at her own joke.

Diana and her mother had always been close, and Diana could never keep a secret from her for long.

"Have you been seeing much of Star?"

"Not that often. Between Dad's job and the new play, I've been too busy. I'm going to have to tell Dad soon that I have to quit."

"Well, hopefully, Marg will be back soon."

"I'm going to miss the job."

"Really? I thought you found it boring."

"It is," Diana said, "but the interns and the other staff are really nice."

Laura changed the topic. "Remember you borrowed your dad's old leather jacket – the one with the maple leaf on the back?"

"Yes. It's too cold to wear it now. Does he need it back?"

"No, but I'm sure I saw it on TV a while ago, on Ron Berry's show. Someone wearing a very similar jacket got in a fight with a girl at a bar, and Star was involved." Laura put down the knife she was using and turned to face her daughter.

Diana's stomach lurched. "Mom! You didn't tell Dad?"

"Don't be silly, Diana. And he didn't see it. But I want to know what happened."

"This awful Russian girl was going crazy on Star. Honestly, Mom, she was such a slut! I couldn't believe it!" Diana was furious with Mischa all over again.

"Maybe you should have walked away," Laura said.

"My pride was hurt!"

"Star has quite a fan club among women, doesn't he?"

"Well, that girl was just awful, and she needed someone to stand up to her."

"I read Star's interview in *Bro*," Laura said. "I saw his picture on the front of the magazine when I was at the pharmacist, so I bought a copy. It sure sounded as though he's thinking of proposing to you."

"I know. Just when my career looks like it's going somewhere, my boyfriend starts hinting at marriage."

"Aren't you just a bit excited, Di?"

"Maybe a bit, but I just don't know. He isn't the same guy he was back in high school. He's just signed a multimillion-dollar deal with the Leafs. It's changed things."

"Maybe he's the same guy, but you aren't the same girl anymore. Give it some time, sweetie. It'll all work out."

* * *

Raj spent the day at home, glad to be off work and that no one on the nursing staff had called him. In the past two days, there had been only a couple of orthopedic cases that he assisted with. Elderly people invariably slip and fall on the snow or ice, often breaking a hip, as these two had. He knew that they would likely never return home, as they were unable to look after themselves now. Like Charlie Rosenplot, the new patients were probably facing a long rehabilitation.

Dinner with the Sinclairs loomed largely. Raj had set aside grey flannel slacks and an expensive sweater to wear for the evening and wondered whether he should wear a jacket and tie. He also had to get some sort of gift for Diana's parents but wasn't sure what. Wine? Some useless Christmassy thing? Raj called his father for advice and wished him Merry Christmas.

"Raj! I thought it was you calling. Do you want us to come up and visit you? Your mother has made some nice mutar paneer, and we can drive up and bring you some chapatis too."

"Not today, Dad. I've been invited for Christmas Eve dinner at a staff doctor's house." Raj mentioned that the doctor's daughter had extended the invitation.

"That is a really nice thing this girl is doing for you. You say her father is a doctor?" Radhu said.

"He's an endocrinologist and head of the intern program at the hospital. What do you think I should take as a gift?" asked Raj.

"Ah, that is a good question, Raj. Take two gifts, one for the doctor and one for his wife." Radhu suggested a bottle of wine – nothing less than $15 – and a tin of shortbread cookies. Raj would have never thought of cookies. "Wear a suit and tie, Raj – something Eugene made for you. And nice leather shoes. These older doctors like people to dress up. And don't forget to compliment the food, no matter how awful it tastes."

Mena took the phone and asked if Raj needed them to come with food, and he had to repeat the entire story. "Are you getting any time off at all?" she asked.

He told her that he would be off a few days after Boxing Day and would come home then, which made his mother happy.

"Will you be staying over for New Year's?" she asked. When he said he would, she said excitedly, "Good. We have been invited to Aunt Shamila's house for New Year's Eve. She has planned her usual big party!"

Raj decided to let her know about Shari. He didn't want his folks too involved with his social life but felt he should at least warn her that he had a date for the party. "Do you remember that girl, Shari?" he said. "She'll be back from her holiday, and she's going to come with me. Actually, Mom, I might not be able to see you until the party, but I'll stay a few days afterwards."

His mother was pleased with the news. She would happily have gone on chatting, but Raj said he had to go out to get gifts for the dinner that night.

Raj hated family parties, and Shamila's were the worst because she always served food from one of her husband's restaurants. Then the old geezers, all sauced up, would sing Indian songs, and the party usually ended with everyone dancing. He hoped that his parents wouldn't embarrass him, even though there was a whole host of other relatives equally adept at looking foolish.

* * *

Hair combed: check. Teeth brushed: check. Nose hair trimmed: check. Matching socks free of holes (brand new from Wal-Mart): check. Breath freshener (double shot): check.

Aftershave: check (from Dr. Williamson's jar; he now smelled like a pinecone). One bottle of Cabernet Sauvignon: check. One tin of Scottish shortbread: check. (His father had said, "If they're not Scottish, they're crap!") For Diana, he'd bought a small box of

Darjeeling tea, pre-wrapped. After one last check, Raj set out, wearing, as Radhu had suggested, a jacket and tie.

The Sinclairs lived a ten-minute drive from the hospital in a large red-brick colonial-style house with a two-car garage and a flagstone walkway. Christmas lights in abundance adorned the shrubbery and the two large trees that dominated the front lawn. Houses bigger and nicer than his parents' made Raj nervous as if he feared being turned away by the wealthy owners because he didn't belong to their set. Now here he was, about to see how the other half lived. He resolved to say very little.

Heart pounding, Raj lifted the door knocker, still unsure why Diana had invited him. Perhaps she thought he was an immigrant who had never done Christmas and that opening this door to him was a charitable, Canadian gesture. He hoped not. He hated pity; he was too proud, as Chandra said.

He let the knocker drop.

Chapter Thirty

The woman who answered the door looked to be in her mid-forties and was clearly Diana's mother. She was elegantly dressed in an expensive-looking cashmere sweater and knee-length skirt. Raj wished her Merry Christmas and shook her hand. She gestured him into the front hall, where Dr. Sinclair was waiting, wearing slippers and a sweater depicting a downhill skier.

Dr. Sinclair formally welcomed him, and Raj thought the old guy almost smiled. As if on cue, the family dog showed up, a large chocolate Lab, also wearing a Christmas sweater. The dog sniffed him and then wandered off.

"It was really nice of Diana to invite me, Mrs. Sinclair. I hope this isn't too much of an intrusion."

"Raj, this is just the thing. The three of us were a bit bored with each other. And call me Laura." Dr. Sinclair didn't offer his first name, so Raj assumed he wanted to be addressed as Doctor or Sir. He wondered where Diana was and hoped she'd rescue him from her parents' scrutiny.

As if she had read his mind, Diana came down the stairs, wearing a beige dress and pearls. Raj thought she looked sublime. "Well, don't you look spiffy, Raj! I see you've met Mom and Dad."

She invited him into the living room, where a wood fire crackled in the fireplace, and the dog was already lying on the hearth rug. The Christmas tree was a designer creation like the ones Raj had seen in department stores, all the ornaments matching perfectly. An upright piano against one wall had been decorated with lit candles and a garland of evergreens.

Dr. Sinclair made small talk about the weather and then offered him a drink. "I have a Scotch. What would you like?"

"Nothing for me, thank you, sir. I'm on call." Raj said

"I remember being on call as an intern. The good old days when we had 8 different types of insulin, including beef and pork insulin".

"That must have been a really interesting time, sir." Raj didn't get the joke as he had always been taught to use human insulin that was synthetically manufactured.

Raj wanted to ask about the changes coming at the hospital, but he wasn't sure if this was the right time. Sinclair stepped into the dining room to top up his Scotch, and Diana came in with a cheese ball on a silver platter. "It's my grandmother's recipe, and we make it every Christmas," she said. "You have to try it." She put the platter down and went back to the kitchen.

The large, pale ball was coated with something. Crackers? Chopped nuts? Around the ball sat crackers, gherkins, and cocktail wieners. Raj wondered how one eats a cheese ball. He spied a small knife and attempted to cut off a piece, but the ball just rolled around on the plate. The stupid thing was a bit hard, and on his next attempt to cut into it, it rolled off the plate onto the floor. The dog came over to investigate. It sniffed the cheese ball and began to lick it. Raj panicked and tried to grab it, but the dog growled and continued licking the cheese ball as it rolled around the floor.

Raj could hear Sinclair on his way back from the dining room, ice tinkling in his glass. He grabbed the cheese ball and planted it firmly back on the plate. Sinclair noticed the dog looking expectantly at it and remarked, "Max really likes cheese, but we never give him any. He's lactose intolerant, and it gives him gas and diarrhea, just like a human." Sinclair took the knife, and when the ball started to move, he steadied it with a fork Raj had not noticed. "Hmm," he said. "It's a bit firm. Maybe Laura over-chilled it. Would you like some, Raj?"

"No thanks, sir. I'm lactose intolerant," Raj said.

They made small talk about the internship program. Sinclair had a lot of questions about the other services, especially surgery. Was Raj getting enough experience? Were they busy enough? What about weekly teaching rounds? Raj had to say that the surgery teaching sessions were somewhat brief (a euphemism for nonexistent), but he made it clear that he was learning a lot.

A few minutes later, Diana announced that dinner was ready, and they sat down at the dining table set with a centerpiece of Christmas ornaments and lit candles. There were several sizes of silver knives and forks on each side of Christmas-themed mats. Silver pinecone napkin holders set on side plates sparkled in the candlelight.

290

Sinclair said grace, then wished them all Merry Christmas. Raj raised his glass of ginger ale to the others' wine glasses. Diana served Raj salmon, green beans, plain white rice, and her family specialty – cabbage rolls. There were white dinner rolls in a basket nestled beside a small pot of butter. Raj waited until the others had started to eat and then tucked in. The food had a pleasant blandness, but nothing had any spice.

"The cabbage rolls are just perfect, Mom," said Diana. Her mom told her that the base of the sauce was Campbell's tomato soup. Diana, who was sitting across from Raj, nudged his leg with her foot and winked at him as Laura went on about there being no trans-fatty acids in the meal.

"The salmon is great, Mrs. Sinclair," said Raj. "It has a very subtle flavor – almost smoky. How did you do it?"

Laura smiled. "Maple syrup and a cedar plank, Raj. A recipe from *Canadian Living*. We used to do a tourtière, but John's cholesterol is now far too high."

"How did you learn to cook? My mom learned from her mother," Raj said.

"I learned from my mother, too. I've been trying to teach Diana some of my recipes, but ever since she came back from India, all she wants to cook is spicy food."

Raj looked at Diana. "You always surprise me!"

"I tried to cook a curry for Dad," she said, "but it was too spicy, and he couldn't eat it. He actually turned red and couldn't breathe for a while. It was scary!"

Dr. Sinclair, carefully eating his salmon, said he'd had to have a shower and a shot of Ventolin after the meal. As the wine flowed, the Sinclairs became more animated. Laura said she was doing a master's at U of T, and Sinclair interjected to say she'd been doing it for about fifteen years now. Laura ignored him and said that her thesis was on Jane Austen and her influence on western culture. She felt that Austen's writings were far more influential than most literary works. "After all, Raj, how many authors have spawned an entire genre of books?"

"What genre is that?" asked Raj politely.

"The romance novel, of course!"

Diana said, "Mom, please don't start on your lecture about the modern feminist movement."

Dr. Sinclair rolled his eyes. "She's going to talk about *The Vagina Monologues* again."

This time, Laura ignored both of them. "You know, Raj, I was in a local production of *The Vagina Monologues*."

"Really? How interesting," said Raj. He had no idea what it was about or if it was even a play. It had its first performance while he was in school, and he'd had neither time nor inclination to see it. Politely, he asked, "What part did you play?"

"Well, there aren't parts as such. It was read to the audience, and I told a story about my mother. We raised $15,000 for a local women's shelter."

Dr. Sinclair remarked, "I'd like to know why there aren't plays for men."

"There is one, Dad. I think it's called *Puppetry of the Penis*." Diana smiled. "I've seen it. It's about two guys, and one of them is really, really big." She was snickering now, and her father glared at her.

Raj tried to keep up the conversation with Laura. "You must be the reason why Diana is into acting." He knew nothing about feminist literature. He had no time to read anything other than textbooks and journals (and the Kama Sutra, but that didn't count).

Laura replied that Diana had always been "a natural artist and actor – a free spirit."

Dr. Sinclair smirked that Diana's "free spirit and acting" had allowed her to pursue her dream of working as his secretary. That annoyed Diana, who said that Marg had likely broken her hip on purpose to get some time away from his office.

The Sinclairs questioned Raj at length about his Christmas experiences. "We don't celebrate Christmas in a true religious sense,"

Raj told them, "but we do the presents and stuff. My parents – particularly my father – have always wanted us to be a Canadian family. Fitting in was a real priority, but he drew the line at hockey because he couldn't stand the cold arenas."

"You must have had a really interesting childhood," Laura said.

"Just the same as most kids in Toronto, I guess. My folks figured that if everyone else got toys and things at Christmas, we'd be upset if we got nothing."

"You mentioned *we*. Do you have siblings?" asked Dr. Sinclair.

"I have a younger sister, Chandra. She's twenty-three – almost the same age as Diana. She's finishing a degree in communications at Ryerson University, but my parents think she's going to wind up as a barista at the Starbucks in Cabbagetown."

"No kidding, Raj?" exclaimed Diana. "I pass that one on my way to rehearsal, but I never go in. I can't afford the lattes."

Diana's parents went on to ask him about his degree and his background. He got the impression that the Sinclairs were impressed by his education, especially by his degree in computer science. After dinner, Diana's parents puttered in the kitchen, giving Raj a moment with her in the living room. She asked him if he was still hungry and offered more of the cheese ball.

"You can take the cheese ball to the hospital. The nurses would probably like something during the night."

Raj said he would, though he planned to throw it out the first chance he got.

"Your parents are really, very nice."

"They are, but it's been a much better Christmas Eve because you're here."

Then Diana's parents came into the living room, Laura with a glass of sherry in her hand and Dr. Sinclair carrying a tray of tea and Christmas cake and the shortbread Raj had brought. Laura had what looked like a picture book and said to Raj, "You asked about Diana's artistic side, and I thought I'd show you some of her pictures."

Diana growled, "Mother, no!" but Laura had already handed Raj the album. There were many photos of Diana growing up, including ones of her when she was eight or nine, wearing a tutu and tiara. To his surprise, in a high school graduation photo, Star was standing beside Diana. Laura explained that Star was Diana's first boyfriend and that they had been Homecoming King and Queen. Star was a quarterback on the football team, and Diana was a cheerleader.

"No kidding! Do you still have pompoms?" Raj was teasing her.

"Diana," Laura asked, "have you seen Star lately? I think I saw him in *Bro* magazine."

Diana looked at her mother coldly. "No, Mother. I haven't seen Star in quite some time."

Dr. Sinclair asked Diana to play a carol or two, and reluctantly, Diana sat at the upright piano. She played Christmas carols and sang while the others warbled along. Raj was thankful he knew most of the words, but he would have enjoyed the evening more if he'd been able to have a few drinks to help him relax. He knew that, if not for Diana's invitation, he would have spent the evening watching TV and eating a frozen dinner, and he was grateful. However, it was late, and he was fading fast. Spending the evening with the boss's family was stressful and to cap it off, he was still hungry.

There was an awkward moment when he said goodbye to Diana.

"Thank you, Diana," he said. "I had a really good time."

"See you, Raj," she said. "Thanks for coming. It was really nice." Then to his surprise, she hugged him – a solid hug, not a fake one.

On the way home, he nibbled crackers, carefully avoiding contact with the cheese ball. He was perplexed. He couldn't decide whether Diana had invited him just to be nice or because she actually liked him. He imagined telling his father about the bland meal, the cheese ball, and the hug from a good-looking girl. He knew his father would say, "You really can't get a much better Christmas than that!" and, of course, he'd be right.

Chapter Thirty One

Diana awoke on Christmas Day after a dreamless sleep. Her parents insisted that they go to church, and afterward, they opened the few presents they had got for each other. Diana received a new iPhone that she would need help setting up, as well as a couple of new sweaters and new boots. The present unwrapping over, they sat down to a late breakfast.

"That boy you invited last night," Laura said, "did you get him a Christmas present?"

"No, Mom, I didn't. I invited him on the spur of the moment. What do you think of him?"

"He seemed nice. Smart, hardworking – a lot like your father."

"I was trying to be nice to him, Mom. I think he's really lonely."

"You know he's madly in love with you, don't you?"

"Mom! You have the wildest imagination!"

"Don't you think it would be hard for any of these young doctors to ask their boss's daughter on a date? In any case, I happen to like men who are a bit shy."

"Well, he's never asked me out. I invited *him* for dinner."

"Well, you'd better not lead him on. Star has already called to wish us Merry Christmas. He wanted to talk to you, but you were in the shower. He'll be back after Boxing Day, and his parents want to get together with us. They're so thrilled about Star winning the Calder Trophy. He says it's all they talk about."

"And it's all Star ever talks about. It's like high school all over again." Diana sighed.

"Star sent us all season tickets to watch the games in the VIP suite. Your dad's really excited about it."

Diana changed the subject. "Did you notice that Raj's aftershave was a bit odd? I could have sworn he smelled like a pinecone."

Laura asked whether Diana might have a little crush on Raj.

"I don't even know what to think anymore. I'm terribly mixed up. All I know for sure is that I want to do really well in *Mama Mia,* so I get offered more good parts."

"Di, these things take time. It'll all work out."

"I hope so," Diana said. "I think I'll go for a walk now, or maybe I'll clean my apartment."

The temperature was just above freezing, and a fine patina of snow covering the trees glittered in the sun – a glorious Christmas Day. As Diana walked through the neighbourhood, she thought about how fortunate she was. She had had a privileged upbringing, and she knew it. The more she thought about it, the more she felt she should be volunteering at a soup kitchen. Perhaps next year…

When she reached the hospital apartment building, she wondered what to do. The urge to do something – anything – overwhelmed her.

* * *

"Raj, do you like this bikini?" It was dark blue with a floral pattern that accented her smooth skin. "It's a little tight. Can you adjust the strap?" Diana appeared. "I can help with that," she said, and Shari giggled as Diana adjusted the strap.

Diana was wearing the same floral bikini in purple. "Does this look good on me, Raj?" She swung around, revealing her heart-shaped bottom, and her cleavage spilled over the bra of the skimpy bikini. She had lovely long legs.

Both women laughed, and then Shari's strap came loose, exposing her breasts. Diana covered them with her hands. Both of them looked at him, smiling, their eyes bright inviting. The contrasting colours of their skin turned him on. Their faces gradually came closer.

"You want us both together, don't you?" They laughed again. "Too bad, Raj. You can have only one of us. Only one. Only one…"

Raj awoke with a tent pole, which dismayed him. Then his phone rang.

"Raj… it's Shari! Merry Christmas! I'm calling you from the ship. I can only talk for three minutes, otherwise, they'll charge me for another 5 minutes."

"It's nice to hear your voice. Are you having a good time?"

"It's absolutely fabulous! The food, the entertainment, the service – unbelievable! But I really miss you. I'm wearing a skimpy little bikini – mainly straps and stuff."

"I hope you're not going to get any grief from your dad," Raj teased.

"No!" Shari was giggling. "But I might get into some trouble with the ship's doctor. He's Italian and really good-looking."

Raj's stomach lurched. "I can't wait till you get home."

"I'll model the bikini just for you when I get back," Shari promised. "Listen, this call is expensive. I'll talk to you when I get home. Bye, sweetie."

There were still two patients on the surgical floor, and Raj did rounds and also saw a patient in the ER. Hospital policy allowed only life- or limb-threatening surgery during the holiday, so he was glad this patient's injury just needed stitches.

Dr. Miller phoned mid-morning, and he seemed disappointed to have no excuse to come to the hospital. Raj could hear children squealing and quarreling in the background. Miller was probably longing for the peace and quiet of the operating room.

Raj finally called his parents, and Radhu surprised him by saying they had gone to church that morning. "Church? You mean a Christian church?" Raj had never met anyone quite so spiritually mixed up as his father. It was as if he believed in every faith and none of them at the same time; he either just wanted to cover all the bases, or he just loved the ceremony.

"Well, son, this is the first Christmas we've spent apart," his father said, adding that Mena had wanted them to drive to St. Jerome, but the roads were icy, and their little car didn't have winter tires. Before he rang off, Raj reminded him that he was coming home after Boxing Day to spend a few days with them.

Somewhat reluctantly, Raj settled down to watch TV and turned the channel to Fashion TV. He had not allowed himself to be so inactive for a long time. In the second hour, Raj saw Star in a commercial for sunglasses. He looked even better on TV than in real life. He was wearing blue-tinted glasses like Bono's, and he was riding a motorcycle with a blonde sitting behind him. It looked as though she was stroking his nipples. Raj wondered how the hell a man could be an NHL hockey star and also a fashion model. He had to admit that Star was far better looking than he was, and he probably made more money in a week than Raj did in a year. The sunglasses he was advertising were probably worth more than Raj's car!

In a mild funk, Raj texted Chandra and asked her what she thought about his being invited to Diana's house. Chan had a way of looking at other people's actions with a clarity that was not obscured by feelings of love or lust.

As Raj sent the text, he was jolted by a knock on the door. He was still wearing greens, and his apartment was a mess. He debated pretending not to be home, but the knocking persisted, and he opened the door. It was Diana.

"How nice to see you, Diana! What brings you here?"

"I was bored at my parents' house and thought you might like some company," she said.

He invited her in, blaming the mess in the apartment on having been busy in the OR. Diana was carrying a bag from which she pulled a tiny artificial tree on a little wooden stand with miniature presents underneath.

"Ta-da! I brought you the Christmas tree! What are you doing for dinner?"

"I thought I'd order Chinese take-out – maybe chow mien and honey garlic ribs,"

"I've got an idea. I can make us something." Diana went to the kitchen and started to rummage around. All there was to find in the cupboard were packets of noodles.

"I thought you were on a low-carb diet!" she said. "But you've got lots of carbohydrates here."

"I lost about twenty on that diet," Raj said.

"Twenty pounds?"

"No – twenty minutes thinking I needed to go on a diet before I forgot the whole thing." That made Diana laugh.

She checked the freezer, noting all the frozen food his mom had stocked it with, and finally checked the fridge. Raj was relieved that there were still several eggs in a carton he'd recently bought. Diana offered to make them each an omelet.

Raj opened a bottle of white wine that had been in the fridge for ages and watched her beat the eggs with a fork. She looked as though she knew what she was doing.

"My parents really like you," Diana said. "They think you're interesting. My dad said Dr. Cooper speaks very highly of you."

Raj was too mesmerized by the way her butt filled out her blue jeans to say anything.

"So what did you get for Christmas? Any new books to read?" she asked, looking over her shoulder. Raj wondered if she had seen the Kama Sutra on his bookshelf.

"I didn't get anything this year as I'm away," he said. "What about you?"

"Dad gave me a new iPhone. Mom gave me new boots and a new dress – the usual stuff. Is there anything you wanted this year, Raj?"

"No," he said, "but I'm sure I could think of something."

The wine was going to his head, and he was about to blurt something when his phone rang. It was Chandra calling to wish him Merry Christmas and sounding as if she were high.

"What are you doing, Chan?" he said. "Sounds like you've been smoking up."

Chan explained that one of her housemates had received a Christmas gift of 'BC bud', and they had all got high – and a bit drunk.

Raj laughed, "You must be feeling that whole joy-and-goodwill-towards-all-mankind thing!"

He explained that he couldn't talk long because he had company and they were about to have dinner, but to watch for his email. The conversation ended with Chandra in a fit of giggles.

"Well, Dr. Mehta, here you go," said Diana, presenting an omelet and chapattis with some salsa she had found in the fridge and another glass of wine. They sat down together at the little table, and Raj put on the radio. Bing Crosby was singing "White Christmas."

Maybe it was just the pleasure of having some unexpected company, but for once, Raj stopped worrying, thinking about neither the future nor the past. Time slowed, and they looked at each other and recognized something familiar. Raj wished he could freeze the moment in time forever.

"This is a cheese omelet!" exclaimed Raj. "Where did you get the cheese?"

Diana explained that she had found the cheese ball he had forgotten to take to the nursing staff and used some of it for the omelet. Raj ate it anyway, reasoning that the cooking would have killed her dog's germs. After dinner, he insisted on doing the dishes while Diana watched TV. He wondered how to entertain her, but he needn't have.

"I've got something I want you to see, Raj," Diana said and pulled out a large photo album. "Are you familiar with fifteenth-century Italy and the Renaissance?"

"No. I was never a student of history."

"When I was sixteen, I spent the summer in Florence as a volunteer for the Catholic church – my mom's Catholic. I led tours of the cathedral, the Duomo. There were lots of other student volunteers, and we had a lot of fun."

Raj opened the book and slowly flipped through photos of paintings and sculptures, each one accompanied by a handwritten note.

"The Duomo was built in the fourteenth century and took over a hundred years to build," Diana explained. "Inside, people tried to capture all the knowledge they had and what they believed in – the essence of their society. Not many people were able to read back then, and books were rare, so they told their stories in pictures."

Raj stared at the vivid photos, some large enough to cover the entire page. "They're really beautiful!" he said.

"Look at this picture and the detailed renderings of the people."

"I don't quite understand the imagery."

"That's just it. Heaven is depicted as a place where time doesn't exist, and so death and decay don't exist either."

Raj said, "That's very sophisticated. It's almost as if they understood the whole theory of space-time relativity. I really believe that some subatomic particles never actually age. Instead, they exist in a dimension where time doesn't exist."

Diana turned the page. "Here's my favourite picture – the Virgin Mary holding her child in heaven."

"What's the significance?"

"Well," she said, "at the end of time, the only thing left is love. And the purest love is the love that exists between a mother and her child. Do you understand?"

"It's a pure love not discoloured by any sort of baser instinct. I don't think I've ever experienced it."

"Oh, but you have," countered Diana when you were born. Your parents felt it, and you were the recipient. And you loved them too. You probably still do."

Raj was acutely aware of her breathing as she showed him the intricate details of her photos, pointing here and there at subtle clues the painters left for others to decipher. Her breasts, encased in a pink sweater, were gently rising and falling as she breathed.

He snapped himself out of his reverie and said, "This album is so profound. Why are you showing it to me?"

"I've shown it to other people, Raj, but you're possibly the only person who might understand it. Anyway, it's Christmas, and I know you like old books, so I thought I'd show you something different from the one I always catch you reading."

Embarrassed, Raj pretended he didn't know what she was talking about, but she had obviously seen the Kama Sutra, and he finally confessed. "It doesn't belong to me, you know. It's my dad's."

Diana smiled. "That's what they all say, but it does look old. Is it an interesting book?"

"Well, it's interesting.....but I'll never be Don Juan."

The low Ikea couch was difficult to get up from, but Raj stood up and held his hand out to pull her up. Their faces were inches apart. For just a moment, as they faced each other, he looked into her eyes and saw *something*. She was so feminine and lovely, and he thought about kissing her.

Then his pager beeped.

Chapter Thirty Two

"Shouldn't you answer your page?" Diana asked.

Raj let go of her hands and unclipped the pager that had been his friend and enemy for the past months. He dialed the number and listened.

"I'll be right over," he said after a minute. "Have some Xylo spray ready." He turned to Diana and said, "I have to go. I feel like the worst host ever."

"Well, Dr. McDreamy – another emergency for the fearless young intern?"

"You won't believe this. A kid has stuck a piece of Lego up his nose, and they can't get it out."

"So what are you going to do?"

"Get it out, I hope, without having to call a real doctor. I might not be too long. Would you like to stay and watch TV till I get back?"

"Thanks, Raj, but I have to go. But I want to take a photo first with my new phone? It'll be the first one." They put their faces together and took a selfie, their smiles wide and genuine, the happy moment captured with digital clarity. Diana added a caption: *Christmas Day with Dr. Raj.*

Diana paused at the door and gave him a kiss on the cheek.

"Am I going to see you again?" Raj asked.

"I'm going to be rehearsing in Toronto a lot over the next while – we have to get the songs perfect. I'll be around a bit to help my dad, but my theatre job will soon be full-time."

As she walked back to the elevator, Diana invited him to opening night.

"That would be awesome!"

Diana smiled and gave a little wave. After Raj's door closed, she took a deep breath and willed herself to relax.

She took out her new cell phone and looked at the only picture on it. On the spur of the moment, she decided to send the picture to Kalpita in Mumbai with the message: "*Merry Christmas, Kal! I'm spending the day with my friend Raj. He's an intern here. Hope all is well. Drop me a line when you get a chance.*"

* * *

The next day Raj caught up with Dan in the cafeteria. He had to tell someone about what had happened to Diana. He was confused and needed expert advice before he saw Shari the next day in Toronto.

"The girlfriend paradox, man," laughed Dan. "That's what's going on. You're totally screwed, you know. No babe wants you when you don't have a girlfriend, but as soon as you do, other women sense it and want you."

"You're kidding, right?" exclaimed Raj. "This is an actual thing?"

"I'm telling you, Raj – women, want you only when you belong to someone else."

"Well, for all I know, I'm in Diana's friendship zone. And Shari's putting the pressure on."

"She wants you to pop the question?" asked Dan.

"I'm getting that impression."

"Well, buddy," said Dan. "You'll have to figure that one out for yourself."

***

A few days after Christmas, Diana and Star were in a loud restaurant in the Distillery District of Toronto. Star, newly enamored of Mexican food, had chosen it.

"Yeah, baby, I've been thinking of you and tacos, but mainly tacos..Ha….ha…!" he joked. The restaurant was called *Emergency Taco – 9 – Juan – Juan.*

Halfway through dinner, Diana put her fork down and said, "Star, I'm going to be working really hard on this play, and I've been thinking –"

Star belched. "Wuzzat, babe?"

"I think we have to take a break, Star. I'm really busy."

Star stopped chewing as he took in what Diana had said.

"But what about me?" he complained, "I need you. I'm launching this new cologne."

Diana ignored this. "You've got the playoffs to get through, and I'll be really busy. *Mama Mia* could be my big break."

"But I thought we were going to get engaged," Star said. "I need you around more. The other guys have their girlfriends and wives around all the time."

"Well, Star, that's not how it's going to be. We *have* to take a break."

"What do I have to do here?" said Star. "My agent wants to get us on 'Puck Bunny Wives' on Fem Network!"

"You think my life's aspiration is to be on 'Puck Bunny Wives'?" Diana said.

"Well, yeah. You're an actress, right? And it's a cool show. Besides, we don't have to get married, just engaged."

"Star, it's just not what I want. I want to be taken seriously as an actor! Someday I want a career like Dame Maggie Smith's."

"Who's Maggie Smith?"

"*Dame* Maggie Smith," said Diana, exasperated.

"Well, I know she must be a woman."

"No, Star. *Dame* means she's been honoured by the Queen of England."

"Babe, you're not making sense... are you on your period? Is that what this is?"

"Star, you are such an asshole!" Diana was really sick of Star's attitude towards her career.

"What does *that* mean? I'm trying to be understanding. My agent says that TV is way better than plays. Besides, *you're* the one calling people dames!"

"Okay, Star, I'm going now. Call me when the season's over, and you're not so high on yourself." Diana threw her napkin on the table and left.

On the streetcar ride to Cabbagetown, she saw not one but two ads featuring him, one for the Toronto Maple Leafs and the other for a sunglasses company. He seemed to be everywhere, staring at her. Her boyfriend was a winner, and so many guys were complete losers.

She didn't know why she wasn't happier, but she did know she had to cool it with Star.

Her phone beeped. It was a text from Kalpita: *"Sorry I didn't get back to you earlier. Nice Christmas? Hellishly busy at work, managing a telecom department. Have my own place and car and driver! Who's the cute guy in the picture? What's going on? Heard you were back with Star."*

Diana texted back: *"Always knew you'd be the boss sooner or later. Don't know about Star anymore. I had to take a break from him. He wants to get married and be on Puck Bunny Wives. I'm in Mama Mia at The Princess of Wales Theatre and loving it! Opening night is coming up."*

"Who's the guy in the picture?"

"He's an intern. We're just friends. There's something about him – kind of the anti-Star. He's quite a dedicated doctor."

Kalpita: *"Your dad likes him?"*

Diana: *"Yes, but Dad's a real fan of Star. Mom thinks the intern's afraid to ask me out because of Dad. I think he's one of those closet super horny guys, maybe a mama's boy. Might even be a virgin."*

Kalpita: *"Sounds like the kind of guy my mother wants to set me up with! Gotta go – meeting with division head. Will try and get to Toronto later this year. Talk soon!"*

As Diana walked the few blocks from the streetcar stop to her house, she passed a small Starbucks, and the young woman at the counter caught her eye. She looked vaguely familiar.

Diana entered the café, and the girl asked what she could get for her. She smiled, showing perfect teeth. Did she look vaguely like ... Raj? Diana suddenly remembered that he had mentioned his younger sister worked at a Starbucks.

"Chai tea, please," she said, then she tentatively asked, "Is your last name Mehta?"

"Yes. How do you know?"

"Do you have an older brother named Raj?"

"Yeah…"

"I know him. He's a friend from St. Jerome. My name is Diana."

"I'm Chandra, his sister," said the young woman.

The two shook hands. There was no one else waiting to be served, so Chandra came around the counter to chat.

"So, how do you know my brother?" she asked.

"He's an intern at the hospital, and I work there for my dad. I met your brother the very first day of his internship," replied Diana.

"It's a small world, isn't it?" Chandra smiled.

"I invited him for Christmas, and he mentioned you. He said you were a student at Ryerson. Here – have a look." Diana held up her phone and showed Chandra the picture of her and Raj.

"That's a nice picture of him!" said Chandra. "Yes, I'm at Ryerson, in my last year in Media and Communications. How about you? Are you a student?"

"No," answered Diana. "I graduated last year. Actually, I'm in *Mama Mia,* and we're in rehearsal."

"That's so cool!" exclaimed Chandra.

"That's exactly what your brother said!"

The two women chatted for several minutes. Diana got the impression that Chandra was hardworking like her brother and that Chandra's parents didn't think much of her career choice. Diana could relate.

After Diana finally arrived at the little Cabbagetown house, she drifted off to sleep with thoughts of warm nights and music, and, again, she could smell the scent of jasmine and pinecones.

Chapter Thirty Three

After Diana left, Star finished his tacos, not too upset by their argument, although he couldn't figure out why she didn't want to be on TV. Maybe she was just jealous of him. Well, a break was just a break, he thought. And he did have a fan club.

He paid the bill, winking at the waitress, who had written her phone number on the bill inside a heart. As he walked to his Porsche parked around the block, his phone rang with the opening bar of "Hockey Night in Canada." He flicked it on. There was no message, just a picture – of tits! They looked familiar. Then a text message arrived.

"Nice, aren't they? Had to get a repair job in Switzerland. Now they're even bigger and better! I miss you, Star."

Star texted back: *"Are you in town?"*

* * *

Shamila's New Year's Eve party was in full swing.

"It's really the most fascinating thing – and the dancers were all topless!" Shamila had been impressed by Las Vegas. She hadn't done any big-time gambling but had spent a lot of time on the slots. She and Gustad had gone to a Céline Dion concert and some sort of "Las Vegas-style Parisian show," as she put it. Raj wasn't sure if that meant topless or just tasteless.

Raj was there with Shari, Chandra, and his parents, and they were all drinking but not eating. The big surprise Shamila had promised was that Roger had brought Uma from the UK for a visit. Clearly, Roger and his fiancée were being fêted like royalty. The house was festooned with decorations, and there was a large buffet of Indian and English food. Not many people were eating – the food looked quite greasy. It was painfully obvious to Raj that Gustad and Shamila were trying hard to impress their future daughter-in-law with their wealth.

After she stopped gushing about Las Vegas, Raj introduced her to Shari, and to his surprise, Aunt Shamila took an immediate shine to Shari. She quickly figured out that Shari might be related to Ranjit Ramsaran, the real estate developer.

"Actually, Ranjit is my father," Shari told her.

Shamila squealed with delight. She told Shari that she herself was a real estate agent and had heard all about her father. She led Shari away to meet Gustad, and Raj and Chandra went into the family room where the old folks had gathered to greet their grandmother. The elderly woman looked at them with rheumy eyes and cradled both their faces in her hands. Then she spoke to Chandra in Hindi, asking if Chandra was getting married. Chandra said no, she wasn't because she hadn't found "anyone half as nice as Grandpa," who had passed away long ago.

Chandra and Raj sat quietly with their grandmother, who kept patting their hands. Chan had not brought Quentin along, and neither

318

she nor Raj felt like socializing. Raj assumed that his family was wondering how a geeky loser had linked up with a good-looking, successful girl like Shari.

Roger and his fiancée wandered into the room, all smiles, and smoochiness, staring into each other's eyes and holding hands. Chandra looked at him, rolled her eyes, and whispered, "It's Elizabeth Hurley and the rich Indian guy she's married to, Arun Nayar!"

"Roger! How are you?" Raj offered his hand. Roger took it and attempted to crush it, but Raj was stronger. Roger had slicked-back hair and was wearing an expensive silk suit and tie. His cologne smelled like money.

Roger introduced Uma, who was polished to bright perfection. Her thin, aristocratic face and lean body reminded Raj of Indian royalty. She was fair-skinned, with dark hair that was coiffed exquisitely. Her earrings were large teardrop pearls. She even had lovely teeth. Uma was wearing an elegant ensemble, perhaps Armani. Noting that Roger and Uma sported matching Rolex watches, Raj stuck his hand in his pocket to hide his Timex.

The golden couple began talking for ages about their polo and their polo ponies, which they had imported from Argentina. Then Roger mentioned to Uma that Raj was a doctor. She asked Raj what he knew about herbal medicine, as she got most of her medical care from a naturopathic doctor because naturopaths "look at the whole person." Raj kept his mouth shut. Neither Roger nor Uma had greeted Grandma, and he was embarrassed that they were ignoring her.

They invited Raj and Chandra to visit them in London so they could spend time at the polo club. "We're members of the Royal Berkshire Club," Uma said.

"You really should try polo. It's the best game in the world," Roger said.

"I always thought hockey was," Raj replied.

"So when's the wedding, and how big will it be?" Chandra asked.

Uma said it would be relatively small – only about 400 people. The chef catered to movie productions and had worked for Guy Ritchie. No meat would be served because Uma was vegan.

Chan laughed as if Uma were joking and then asked whether someone would be filming the wedding.

Roger smirked, "Wedding movies are totally cheeseball Chan. Is this what you've been learning in college?"

"No, Roger," Chandra replied, "but I can video it if you like. Your parents might appreciate it."

After an awkward silence, Shamila and Shari entered the room, a large dog in Shamila's wake. "There you are – all the young people together! Roger, I want you to meet Raj's girlfriend, Shari. She works for Johnson-Goodfellow Consulting." Roger looked surprised.

Uma, Shari, and Chandra introduced themselves – and there they were, the "millennial contingent," as Radhu had said they would be.

"Your mother told me you're working for Goldman Sachs. How long have you been with them?" Shari asked Roger,

"Just a couple of years," he replied, "but it's going very well."

Uma chimed in, "Oh yes, Roger is doing fantastically well."

Roger seemed interested in Shari. "What do you do at Johnson-Goodfellow?"

Shari replied, "I work with mergers and acquisitions, largely finance. Right now, I'm heading up a merger of a Big Pharma company with local biotech. Glaxia is purchasing CytoFunction Labs – it's been in the news already."

"No kidding!" replied Roger, impressed. "Biotech is where it's at. What about China? Do you think many firms are moving into China?"

Roger and Shari carried on talking about money and the stock market until Gustad rounded everyone up for singing and dancing in the living room. Chandra and Raj, reluctant to leave their grandmother alone, offered to get her wheelchair, but she was tired and refused.

In the living room, Gustad declared, "Ladies and gentlemen. As you know, my son is engaged to Uma, who is visiting us from the UK. I would like to welcome her formally to Canada and to our family." Gustad paused for a large gulp of Scotch. "Thank you all for coming. I expect to see you all at their wedding in England."

Raj noticed that Gustad was short of breath and that his collar was too tight around his fat neck.

Everyone clinked glasses, and they began singing a classic Hindi song. The large dog howled along until Shamila silenced him with a sausage roll. The stereo was turned up loud, and Shamila and Gustad led everyone in the Bollywood hands-up-hip-swing all Indians use when dancing. The dog began barking, but Shamila kept giving him sausage rolls to keep him quiet. The younger folks soon retreated to the family room.

"So Raj, have you been a doctor for a while, then?" asked Uma.

"Less than a year," he said. "I'm an intern."

"In England, there are public and private systems," Uma said. "Roger and I go only to a private doctor. The National Health Service ones are terrible."

Raj was about to say that Canada's public system was responsible for Canadians being among the longest-lived people in the world when Shari spoke up.

"Actually, Raj is going to set up a private clinic when he's finished interning. My father has the spot all picked out. It's going to be very exclusive."

Raj was surprised. Shari had mentioned that her dad was interested in setting up a medical facility, but they hadn't discussed it any further.

Roger, as usual, had an opinion: "Raj, go into something private. That's what the smart docs in England are doing."

Uma added, "You should look into naturopathic medicine. I'm sure it will catch on here."

Raj couldn't keep his mouth shut this time. Indicating their grandmother, he said, "You know, Grandma is alive because of doctors like me – not because of naturopaths and their bogus elixirs or some snobbish doctor who deals only with rich people."

During the pregnant pause that followed, Shari eyed Raj carefully. Aunt Shamila came in, hounded by the large dog, which wouldn't leave her alone. Spotting the sausage roll that Shamila was holding in a napkin, she asked, "You aren't feeding him those, are you?"

"Yes," said Shamila. "He likes them, and it's the only way to get him to stop howling."

"Oh my God!" cried Uma. "Harry's part wild, Dingo. You shouldn't feed him meat *ever*! It brings out his wild and ferocious nature! We only feed him soya protein. The natural estrogens in the soy will make him less aggressive. Try this instead." She took a square of tofu from a dish on a nearby table and offered it to the dog, which took one sniff and then started barking at Shamila, who was still holding the sausage roll. Finally, she threw it across the room, saying, "Here, boy! Catch!"

When Raj and Shari left, it was well after 1:00 a.m. Shari insisted that Raj drive her BMW. It drove very nicely, but Raj thought it was no better in the snow than his Honda.

"That was a great party, Raj," said Shari. "Your family is very nice. Shamila is the best hostess I've ever met. She wants to meet my dad to talk about starting up a restaurant in his next subdivision."

"Shari, I never told you I was going to work in the clinic in your dad's building, did I?" Raj asked.

"No, but I thought you were interested."

"Please don't mention it to my family."

"Raj, I was only trying to show your cousin that we have money and are just as successful as they are. You know, we can have everything they have," she said.

Raj didn't say what he was thinking, which was that he didn't want everything Roger had.

They drove on in silence, and as they drove up to her apartment building, she gave his hand a squeeze.

"Are you coming in, Raj?"

Chapter Thirty Four

"Step through, then twirl. That's right. Now, a little louder on the chorus. Excellent, Di. Really good. Once more – and project your voice a little farther."

Diana had been in rehearsal all day every day for the past week. The play was coming together well, and the entire cast felt like one big family. She was having the time of her life. She had become good friends with Stephanie Morton, who played one of the other girlfriends in the production. Stephanie had been in several musicals in Toronto and was an excellent dancer, but Diana was the better singer. After the rehearsal was over, Stephanie and Diana went back to the Cabbagetown house with Lizzie and Mary. The younger members of the cast often congregated there to relax after rehearsal and sometimes stayed till the wee hours, drinking with Diana's housemates.

It was New Year's Eve at last, and the four women got ready for an evening out, starting with dinner at 7:00 p.m. at the Drake, a restaurant and nightclub where young Toronto hipsters gathered. Mary had reserved a table weeks ago. They arrived, and the maître d' guided them to a booth as loud music blared.

A waiter took their coats and announced that the club would open all night, playing music from the sixties and seventies.

Mary said, "I'll dance to anything but ABBA!"

The waiter didn't understand the ABBA reference and smiled vacuously.

Mary explained, "We're in the *Mama Mia* cast. Just make sure there's no ABBA unless you want us to start singing!"

"That's so cool," said the waiter. "I'm an actor, too."

Lizzy spoke up. "A round of Manhattans, and we'll show you how *real* actors party!"

The four women downed their drinks and ordered another round and just enough food to slow their alcohol consumption. They talked about why women who are successful have such a hard time staying in relationships. Both Lizzie and Mary warned the other two that, for women, marriage and acting were almost incompatible and that if they became mothers, they'd probably have to give up their careers. Diana thought about her mother and wondered if she would ever have been born if her mother had pursued the career she wanted. Lizzy seemed to understand it best; several men had proposed to her, but she had turned them all down.

"FOMO. That's what did me in, Di," said Lizzy.

"FOMO?"

"Fear of missing out. It's got to be tough to get married and have kids and then see someone else get a great part or work with someone special. I have worked with many noted Shakespearian actresses. Sometimes their marriages become more like a business arrangement."

The waiter came over with four of the most elaborate cocktails they had ever seen. "Excuse me, ladies. That table over there – they just bought you a round of drinks."

The waiter pointed to a group of men who looked like bankers. The men waved, and they smiled and waved back. Lizzy said, "They're cute, aren't they? They're all younger than we are. Mama wants some man candy!"

One of the men came up and introduced himself as Terrence. "My friends and I couldn't help but notice that you're having a great time," he said. "Would you like to join us in the dance club upstairs?"

Lizzy spoke up before anyone else could decline. "What a great idea!"

The next few hours were more fun than Diana had had in a long time. The men, all in their thirties, said they were senior technology experts, and they proved to be enjoyable company. Everyone loved retro disco music. They had all just sat down to catch their breath when something caught Terrance's attention.

"Whoa! Who's that blonde with all the moves? That's not dancing, that's dirty dancing!" he exclaimed.

What Diana saw made her stomach tighten so hard it constricted her throat. It was Mischa, dancing like a stripper. And there was Star, obviously enjoying it. Mischa was wearing a low-cut minidress and stiletto heels, and her boobs somehow looked even bigger.

"Isn't that your boyfriend, Di?" Mary asked. "Who's that girl trying out for a 'Girls Gone Wild' video? She needs to put her tits away."

"That's Mischa," said Diana through gritted teeth. "She's a Russian model. "

"She's certainly slutting it up, isn't she?" Lizzy said.

"Boy, she doesn't understand the girl code, does she?" Mary said.

"Ergh!! I should have seen this coming," Diana said. " She's been after him for a while now. I got into a fight with her not long ago and punched her in the tit. It wasn't a good scene – got me kicked out of a bar."

"No way!" Diana's friends were impressed.

"Listen, guys, I've lost the mood," said Diana. "I think I'll go home. I've only myself to blame. I told Star I needed a break. I should have stuck it out, I guess."

"Di, just because you said you needed a break doesn't give him the go-ahead to drop his pants for any man-eating whore!" Mary said, and the others agreed.

"I've got an idea – but we'll have to leave quickly, so get ready," Lizzy said to Mary and Stephanie. "Follow me."

They went to the dance floor and danced casually towards Star and Mischa, closer and closer, and then Stephanie, who was taller than the rest, hip-checked Mischa right off her high heels. She landed flat on the dance floor. At the same time, Mary and Lizzy sandwiched Star, and Lizzy opened her silk blouse to flash her breasts at him. "Hey, Star!" called Lizzy. "Have a look at some *real* tits. Whoooooahhh!"

She had unfastened her strapless bra, and now she twirled it in the air and wrapped it around Star's neck like a scarf. He was so taken aback that he didn't realize Mischa was on the floor.

Lizzy squeezed herself up against him, winked, and gave him a quick kiss, leaving lipstick on his cheek.

The three rushed back to the table, grabbed Diana, who was agog at what they had just done, and raced out of the bar into a taxi waiting outside.

* * *

Raj wanted a cigarette. He had never smoked, but it seemed the fitting thing to do after sex. He could feel Shari's heart beating as she lay beside him. He felt comfortable being so close to her. They had made love, and it was better this time. He had been less nervous, though again, he'd had to make himself slow down. Was Shari satisfied with his performance? It *was* a kind of performance. But should it have been?

Raj hid his insecurities from Shari behind a façade of doctorliness. They had shared their bodies, but he was unsure about sharing his dreams and ambitions with her. What he needed to do was to be more honest with Shari and stop thinking about what other people wanted him to do.

He stroked her back. The soft skin of her ass felt so good. He had to stop thinking and just make love again, But his mind wouldn't stop, and as he drifted off, he found himself thinking once again about … Diana Sinclair. It was all too much. He was a master over-thinker. He'd figure it out tomorrow.

* * *

"Do you want tea?"

"Have you got any coffee?"

"Instant. Hope you don't mind."

"That's fine." That was Raj's first fib of the day, and he scolded himself for telling a white lie just to please her.

Shari put the kettle on and then pulled out a box of dosas from the freezer. "They're Mama Gustad's – your uncle's brand. They're vegetarian, and I really like them."

"I like them, too." Second lie of the day.

"Let's go shopping, Raj. There are a lot of good stores around here. We can get you some new clothes, and I want to go to Pier 1 Imports."

"That would be nice." Third lie.

He'd only been awake for half an hour, and he'd already lied three times. He was ashamed, but he couldn't help himself. He resolved to try harder, to be honest.

Their first stop on this shopping spree was a men's clothing store. Raj was overwhelmed by so many garments in one place and couldn't think of anything he needed to buy, but Shari rushed ahead of him, scanning the racks, so he had to follow.

"Raj, I'd just love those slacks on you." Shari was holding up a green pair that tapered to the ankles. She wanted to pair them with a green paisley shirt, worn untucked.

Raj laughed. "Do you have any idea what the staff docs would say if I wore this getup to work? This is for a hairstylist."

"But it would look so good on you, and it's time you started looking successful,"

"Being successful doesn't mean you have to show off. I don't have anything to prove, Shari." Though perhaps he did. Raj wasn't sure.

It was the 1st of January, and it was a sunny day. They wandered in and out of furniture and decor stores. Then Raj spotted a Starbucks, and they went in.

"What do you like to do on weekends?" Raj asked once they were seated.

"Just what we're doing now." She looked at him fondly with her lovely brown eyes.

Hesitantly, he asked, "Am I the first guy... you know... you've ever dated?"

"Pretty much."

"No one ever asked you out? Come on, Shari – you're beautiful! You must have dated in school."

"Not really, Raj. It's hard for an Indian girl to find someone, especially successful girls like me. Though there was one guy...."

"Who was that?"

"You met him at the restaurant, remember? He even asked me to marry him."

"That guy? The metrosexual?" Raj remembered the guy: mid-forties, perhaps older, and looking wealthy. Raj felt a twinge of jealousy.

"Last year, out of the blue, he announced that he wanted to marry me."

"So what did you say?"

"I told him no, of course."

"You weren't interested?"

"He's too old. I want a young man, not some old guy that I'd have to push around in a wheelchair when I'm forty." As she spoke, Shari ran her foot up the inside of his leg.

"Raj, you're one of the sexiest guys I've ever met. That man has nothing on you."

That cheered Raj, and he even started to enjoy window shopping until Shari begged him to go into a jewelry store with her. Raj's misgivings grew by the second as Shari scanned the rings on display. She pointed to one with a teardrop diamond.

"That one's really nice, isn't it?" She asked the clerk what its price was, and Raj flinched when he said it was only $15,995.

Raj couldn't believe what she was thinking. There was no way he could spend that much money on an engagement ring. He steered her out of the store, not wanting to talk about engagement.

"I told my parents I'd see them today," he said. "I haven't seen much of them, and I should visit." This was not an outright lie. He was improving ."I'll call you tomorrow. My mother's not that well. I have to keep an eye on her blood pressure." This was an outright lie, and he had no qualms about it.

"You could stay at my place tonight, you know."

"My parents are expecting me to stay," Raj said. "Don't worry, I'll see you soon."

It was late afternoon and already getting dark. Shari held him with a long kiss. "I hardly ever get to see you," she complained. "Can't you spend the night again? We can make a little masala," she teased, moving her hips slightly.

"I have to show respect to those who put me on this earth," Raj said.

"Okay, Raj. I get it. You're an Indian guy."

"What do you mean?"

"You're a bit of a mama's boy. You understand the way it is... the obligations. I might as well visit my parents, too. My brother's failing out of school, and they're really worried."

Later, Raj pulled into the driveway of his parents' East York home and put thoughts of Shari out of his mind. His mother greeted him at the door, and he gave her a big hug. Raj joined his father at the kitchen table, and Radhu opened a beer for him. "Another year has gone by, Raj. Here's to a good New Year." They clinked bottles and drank while Mena started dinner.

"You had a nice time at your uncle's party? Did Shari? I noticed that Shamila latched onto her for a good part of the evening and introduced her to everyone," Radhu said.

"I wonder why Shamila, of all people, took an interest in her," Raj said.

"She probably sees Shari as a younger version of herself. When you get older, Raj, you see younger people, and you wish you were that person so you could do it all over again."

Raj said nothing.

"So, what are your plans with this girlfriend of yours?" Radhu asked. "She's a nice girl – pretty and obviously successful. Do you know that your mother and I have visited her parents? They seem like good people."

"Yeah, Dad. Shari mentioned that."

"Her father said he wanted to set up a clinic for the Indian community in his new subdivision northwest of Mississauga. He wants you to be the head man. Raj, this guy is a real mover and shaker. There are lots of doctors here from India and the UK, but he wants a guy trained in Canada."

Mena spoke up. "Just think of it! Our son – the head of a big medical centre! All the important people will come and see you, like Dr. Chopra! You will be a millionaire someday, Raj." She was beaming.

It dawned on him that his parents both really liked Shari and that marrying her would make them as happy as they had ever been – second only to having a grandson born ten months later.

"Well, Raj, I must say that I envy you," Radhu said. "This girl is the best thing that has happened to you. So many young people have to accept a marriage they regret, but you won't have to. Not since you were accepted into medical school has your mother been so happy."

Raj didn't have the heart to tell him to slow down a bit – he didn't want to spoil his joy.

Later, while Mena was cleaning up the kitchen, Radhu beckoned Raj into the living room. Clearly, he wanted to have a quiet word about something.

"Raj, I know that you aren't earning much. I can give you money to buy a ring. Just let me know when you need it. It is the least I can do for my son, who has made me so proud. This is why we came to Canada. I had to work so hard and take so much shit from people when we first came. But I knew that someday, *you* would be number one. You will be finished your internship in another year and a half. Why don't you get engaged and plan the wedding for after you have finished at St. Jerome? It would be perfect."

Raj had to stop this train. "Dad," he said, "I'm not absolutely sure about this. I like Shari, but I don't know if she's the right one for me."

"Nonsense, Raj," Radhu said. "Everyone is a bit afraid of change in their lives, but you shouldn't be. I saw the two of you together, and you make a handsome pair. Both of you have made the very best of what Canada gives our people. I came here with nothing, and you have everything. Savour it and enjoy your good fortune." He sat back in his La-Z-Boy and smiled contentedly. Then, his expression changed. "You're not sleeping with her, are you?

Chapter Thirty Five

"Yup, I boobed him!"

"What do you mean – you boobed him?"

"Boobed him! You know, let the girls hang out."

Chandra was amused to see Diana and her friends laugh so uproariously. Lizzy, Mary, Steph, and Diana had walked over to their local Starbucks for a late morning coffee. Chandra recognized each of them, but this was the first time the whole gang had come in. She was fascinated by their stories and eavesdropped as best she could from behind the counter.

"I learned it from a stripper I used to hang out with," Lizzy explained. "You make eye contact, and then you slip off your bra and dance a little closer. You keep him guessing until the last moment – and then you boob him!"

Mary piped up. "I told him they were real. I think he wanted you, Lizzy!"

"He was mesmerized, wasn't he? I think it was the tattoo," said Steph.

"And you, Steph. You body-checked Mischa right out of her high heels! Where did you learn that?" Lizzy asked.

"I was captain of the girls' hockey in high school. That girl didn't know what hit her!"

"You guys are the best, you really are!" Diana laughed again at the memory.

Chandra, still a student, was struck by how much these women were in control of their lives. Diana and Steph impressed her, but Mary and Lizzy *really* impressed her. They were – the whole lot – the most free-spirited, fun people she had ever met.

She thought for a moment, then went over to their table. "Hi guys," she said, "I have to do a project for my last semester, and I'd like to do a documentary on all of you. I'm going to call it 'Women in Theatre – Taking a Bow.' Could I come to your place sometime and videotape an interview?"

Lizzy and Mary burst out laughing. "You want to make a documentary about *us*?" Lizzy asked. "Why on earth?"

"I'd like to show my class what it's like to work in the theatre," Chandra said, ", especially for women. It would be so cool!" Diana's friends were funny and real, and Chandra knew she had found a compelling subject for her project.

Diana said, "I could get you behind the scenes at the theatre if you want?"

"That would be great, Diana! This last project is a big one. We're all making documentaries, and there'll be an award given to the best one."

Chandra and Diana had got to know each other over the few days since Christmas. Chandra found Diana quite friendly, with a "small-town" way about her. She was almost sure that Diana had a thing for her brother, as she had asked about Raj a few times, even asking if he was seeing anyone. Chandra hadn't let on – yet – that Raj had a girlfriend, but she would have to, sooner or later.

* * *

Star woke with a head-splitting hangover. He and Mischa had angry sex. She had slapped him a couple of times and forced him to stay awake despite his having drunk far too much on New Year's Eve.

Mischa's fall on the dance floor at The Drake broke the heel off one of her Jimmy Choo shoes. Enraged, she had insisted on looking for the 'big ape peasant woman', who she claimed, had knocked her over. Star expected her to try and stab the girl with the broken heel. Mischa had become even angrier when she saw the black bra draped around Star's neck. She grabbed it and flung it on the floor. 'That fucking old cow made a pass at you. The stupid woman is old enough to be your mother,' she had raged. Despite Mischa's anger, Star couldn't get the picture of Lizzy's breasts and her butterfly tattoo out of his head. Even before he opened his eyes, he could hear her still ranting about it.

"Hey, babe," he said, trying to pacify her. "Want a smoothie? It's got cacao nibs."

"Fuck your smoothie! Bring me coffee before I slap you again."

"You're still mad."

"Those shoes cost $1,300."

"Tell you what, babe. I'll buy you some new Choos."

"Yes, you will! But I still want revenge." Mischa lit her first smoke of the day. She didn't eat much – just coffee and the occasional salad. "If I ever see that woman again, I keel her."

"You mean kill her?" asked Star.

"Yes, keel her," said Mischa with a feral tone.

"It might have been an accident," Star said. "This kind of thing happens all the time."

"I don't ask you to do it. You are a soft Canadian. Sergei Osakin would understand. *He* is Russian."

Star had noticed that whenever Mischa got angry, she mentioned Sergei Osakin, star forward with the Washington Capitals. Mischa had met him once and obviously liked him, but Star didn't. The guy had a temper and was a sore loser. He and Star were in a scoring race this season. It was well known that, during the last

Olympics, Osakin had carved the Canadian team's Lucky Loonie coin out of centre ice and wore it around his neck on a gold chain when his team won.

Star was getting fed up with Mischa's rages and wished he was with Diana instead. She would be making blueberry pancakes for him. "Hey, Mischa, do you know how to make pancakes?"

"We eat only kasha for breakfast. That way, we don't get fat. Are you getting me coffee, or do I slap you again?"

"Okay, okay," said Star. "Let's go out for breakfast."

"Don't speak anymore until you bring me a cappuccino. And I need soy milk. Other stuff makes me fat."

Star brought the coffee into the bedroom. Mischa lay in bed, the light sheets barely concealing her breasts.

"Maybe you better have a smoothie," she said.

"Why's that, babe?"

"You will need energy." She pulled the sheet away from her breasts slowly and beckoned him closer.

* * *

Chandra was driving downtown with Raj a few days later after he had spoken with his dad. They both wanted to get out of the house. Raj had come to her in a panic when she got home from work, telling her that things were moving way too quickly with Shari but that it was probably his fault.

"How so, Raj?"

He hesitated.

"You've slept with her, haven't you?"

"Yeah. You got to talk to her at the party. What do you think? Is she a good catch?" Raj trusted Chan's opinion more than anyone else's.

"She's pretty good-looking, and she has a really good job. It sounds like you're going to be rich. She wants to set up a fancy office for you and all that."

"I guess so. But there has to be more to life than an endless pursuit of wealth and status."

"What do you mean, Raj?"

"It's like she's trying to make me into somebody different from who I am. I think she likes me, but she'd like a version of me that's a little more … I don't know."

"More like Roger?"

"Yes!" Raj said. "I just don't know if I can fit the profile of what she wants. I keep trying because I want her to like me."

"Raj, it sounds like you're having second thoughts. Sometimes, a person seems perfect in every way except what counts most. You've always been so serious and driven. Maybe you need someone who makes you laugh. What about the other girl you mentioned – the actress?"

"I don't know if she even likes me. We've not gone out on a real date. She already has a boyfriend – you know, the hockey player."

"You mean the one with the Toronto Maple Leafs? What's his name – Star? He's totally hot, isn't he?"

"I'll be lucky if I ever see her again. She's in *Mama Mia* here in Toronto."

Chandra nodded slowly and said, "If she came over and made you dinner on Christmas Day, she likes you. I bet you'll see her again. But you do have to decide about Shari. It won't be long before Shari expects you to propose. Mom and Dad have met her parents. They probably already have your children's names picked out!"

"I just don't know what to do, Chan. I'm terribly mixed up right now."

* * *

"My parents want to meet you again," Shari said.

Raj dodged the issue. "How are your parents? Did they have a nice New Year's Eve?"

Shari wouldn't be deflected. "They want you to come for dinner."

Raj gave up, even though he was sure that as soon as they saw him, they'd know from the guilty look on his face that he was shagging their daughter. "When do they want to see us?" he asked.

"Tonight."

It was Raj's last day in Toronto during his brief Christmas break, and he was looking forward to being back at St. Jerome. He had arrived at Shari's apartment, expecting to go to a restaurant for dinner, which he hoped to follow with the simple pleasure of an evening in front of the television.

"Do we have to go?" Raj asked.

"Mom wants to see you again," said Shari with a finality that brooked no argument, and they left the apartment.

In the parking garage, Raj said, "Let's take my car."

Shari rolled her eyes and got in. "When are you going to get a new car?"

"When I need one," said Raj, flooring it. He turned on the radio loud and bobbed his head to The Bare Naked Ladies.

"Sometimes I think you're still in college." Shari sounded annoyed. "Don't you want to talk?"

Raj turned down the music.

"My parents have prepared a fancy meal for us," Shari said. "They might have some questions for you."

Raj barely spoke again until he pulled into the driveway of the Ramsaran's' home in Mississauga. He suddenly had the urge to pee.

Raj was greeted by Shari's parents with warm smiles. There were hugs and kisses for Shari. They were ushered straight into the dining room, where Shari's brother, Avinder, was already sitting at the table. He was dressed better than the last time Raj had met him, but he still looked sour. Raj tried to disarm him. "Hey, Avinder! Waazzup?"

Avinder smiled and stuck out his hand. "Hey, man."

After they were all served chapattis, curries, rice, and a variety of vegetables, Mr. Ramsaran began the conversation. "Your father agrees with me, Raj. There is too much taxation in this country. All these politicians do is take our money and squander it!"

Raj swallowed a lump of cauliflower and considered his response. He had hoped the conversation would be light. "Dad must've forgotten that taxes pay for our health care," he said, hoping he'd cause no offense. To Shari's mother, he said, "Mrs. Ramsaran, this is one of the finest meals I've ever had. "My mother does cauliflower like this. I often wonder if the art of Indian cooking will be lost in Canada."

Mrs. Ramsaran looked hard at Shari, who was picking at her food.

Raj continued, "My sister doesn't eat much Indian food, and she doesn't know how to make it, either. Mom believes she's a lost cause."

Raj expected Mrs. Ramsaran to agree, but what she said was, "Well, Raj, it seems that modern women in Canada don't think they need to learn to cook at all."

She eyed Shari as she spoke and Raj, realizing he was again in dangerous territory, said nothing. After dinner, the two men went to the den, and the old man poured them both a Scotch. Shari and her mother were cleaning up, and Raj wondered if Shari was getting a lecture about learning to cook.

Old Man Ramsaran sat in his leather swivel chair. He was pudgy, sleepy-looking, and slow, but this was obviously a façade. Raj thought that as a wealthy land developer, he was shrewd as hell. "Raj," he said, "You and Shari have been going out for quite some time."

"We've gone out a few times, sir," Raj said.

"You and my daughter are both adults, educated and all that. This is a modern world we live in – and a strange one at that. What are your intentions toward my daughter?"

Raj took his time answering. He still didn't know what his intentions were. Finally, he ventured, "Mr. Ramsaran, we are still getting to know each other. I respect your daughter a great deal, and I hope that I can earn her admiration."

Mr. Ramsaran frowned. "You are not gay, are you? I don't want my daughter marrying some guy who does not know what side of the fence he is supposed to be on!"

Raj was stunned. "There might have been a misunderstanding, but Shari and I have cleared that up."

"How?" demanded Ramsaran.

"Maybe... maybe Shari can reassure you," stammered Raj.

"Listen, Raj," declared Ramsaran. "I like you, but if you are not serious about my daughter, then I want you to fuck off!"

There was a long pause as Raj stared at the old man. "Okay," he agreed.

They spent the rest of the evening watching a Bollywood movie on the giant TV screen in the living room. The movie featured several big stars, one of them his favourite, Katrina Kaif. Ramsaran noticed Raj eyeing her appreciatively and smiled.

"Nice looking, eh?" he laughed and handed Raj another Scotch.

On the way back to her apartment, Shari said, "I think my folks were reassured, Raj. You were nice to my brother, and they appreciated that." Then she added calmly, "My mother asked me if we were sleeping together."

Raj kept driving, his pulse pounding. He said nothing.

Chapter Thirty Six

"Aren't you going to ask me what I told her?" Shari sounded miffed at his apparent lack of concern.

"You'd better tell me so we can get our stories straight," said Raj.

"I told her we weren't having sex."

"Okay," said Raj, exhaling with relief.

"She didn't question me about it. I almost think she was disappointed. My mother's a bit strange. She said I'm going to have to spend next weekend with her, learning how to cook."

Raj could tell that the visit had rattled Shari. She seemed on edge as if she wanted to say something to him but couldn't get it out. Raj decided not to spend the night with Shari, and, as it turned out, she didn't want him to stay, saying she had a ton of work to do.

Raj promised he'd see her soon but didn't set a firm date. He just wanted to get back to the hospital and what he understood.

As he drove back to St. Jerome, he wondered what to do. His parents liked her, and it seemed that her family wanted him to propose. He and Shari didn't talk much; it was almost as though if they did, they'd find out they had less in common than either realized.

Raj parked outside the St. Jerome Hospital apartments, feeling like an old friend being welcomed back. He had been away for over a week and was ready to get back to work. The next couple of months in family practice would be important since he was considering becoming a family doctor and emergency specialist.

* * *

"Doc, I really like this stuff." Raj's patient, a short bald guy, pulled out a package of Ginseng tea. "I get so much power from it, Doc! Look at me! I feel as strong as two men!" Raj took the package. On the back of it was a direct translation from Chinese: "Tea makes you strong like a horny old goat." His patient stood all four and a half feet tall and, with his large ears, looked like a hobbit. He suffered from chronic headaches and had not had a job for more than ten years. He was now trying to get his ginseng through the provincial drug plan for the disabled.

"Mr. Hormel," Raj said, "this isn't a pharmaceutical product. In fact, several studies have shown that it doesn't do anything at all."

"What do you mean? Look at me, man! I'm doin' just great!" Hormel slurred his words, and his glasses were crooked.

"There's no way the plan will cover that product – and for that matter, I don't think it's helping you much," said Raj.

Hormel had talked his ear off for five minutes about ginseng, but Raj didn't mind at all. He had begun to realize that "going to the doctor" was not just going to the doctor. Some patients came to access all manner of services and drugs, which a doctor has to approve.

The hospital had set up the Family Medicine Clinic to handle "orphan" patients like Hormel. The office was separate from the ER so that the emergency didn't get overwhelmed. Raj had assumed that they would be poor people, but he was quite wrong. They were from all walks of life, but their family doctors had either retired or moved away and had not been replaced.

Raj was quickly involved with the Family Practice service. It was less stressful because the staff doctors didn't quiz him as much. He was getting along well with the four staff doctors in the Family Practice group. He'd quickly learned that when he couldn't make up his mind what to do, he could get the patient to come back in a week or two so that he could take another crack at it.

Shari had called a couple of times. Sounding miffed, she kept reminding Raj that *she* called him, but he never called *her*. Raj used the excuse of having to work long hours when he last spoke to Shari, apologizing profusely and then telling her about his many sick and dying patients, real and imagined. Yet again, Shari mentioned that her parents had been discussing *his* future, which made Raj laugh. Why would they be discussing his future when he didn't even know it himself?

During their last conversations, Shari said, "By the way, I'm going to Texas on business – a pipeline company merger."

Impressed, Raj said, "That sounds pretty big time!"

"It is, Raj. I think I'll be made a partner very soon." She added teasingly, "You know about those Texas guys – tall and rugged."

"So I hear," said Raj. "Are you taking your bikini with you?"

"No – but will you miss me?" asked Shari.

"Very much. I'll talk to you soon."

"Bye, Raj."

His final case of the day was an elderly couple, Edna and Red Wells. Raj had them in to go over the results of Red's blood work. He told Red that he was getting early diabetes and high cholesterol, but it was Edna who did most of the talking. They were both hard of hearing.

"You mean Red's getting diabetes? How could that be? We've always eaten the same food, and there's no diabetes in the family," she said.

Raj noted that both were overweight. "Mrs. Wells, it may be your diet. Maybe Red is taking in too many calories and too much food that's high in cholesterol and starch. Certain foods promote the problem, like high-fat dairy food and baked goods."

"Well, Red just loves his Velveeta cheese."

"He should cut back a bit. " Raj said.

"I don't know, Doc, he loves that cheese. What'll diabetes do to him?" she asked.

"It will affect his heart and kidneys. It will also increase his risk of stroke and affect the circulation in his feet."

"Red has the nicest looking feet." She turned to Red, who adjusted his hearing aide. "You have the nicest feet, Red. Show the doctor your feet."

Hurriedly, Raj said, "That's okay, Edna. I don't need to see his feet yet."

Later that evening, Paula, Dan, and Kelly were at Raj's apartment watching TV and eating potato chips. Raj needed to unload.

"Diana invited me to her play. I think she was just being nice, though. It's not a date."

"Why don't you just ask her out on a date and get it over with?" Kelly said. "She probably likes you. And if she likes you, then Star will be a free agent! I swear, all Toronto seems to be in love with the guy. Did you know the Leafs are in the playoffs?"

"Since when did you become a hockey fan?" Paula asked.

"It's always more interesting when you've met one of the players," Kelly said. "Star's become the poster boy for all that's cool in Toronto."

Raj sighed. "I think I'm in the friendship zone."

"But, Raj, you're a friendship zone *virgin!*" said Kelly and Paula simultaneously. They burst into laughter.

"Anyway, she's only around a day or two a week helping out the new temp secretary. I probably won't see her much." Raj shrugged.

"I'd like to see *Mama Mia*," said Paula, sounding glum. "I haven't done anything for the longest time. Christmas in Penford, Alberta, has to be the most boring thing on earth. Can I come with you?"

"Wait for a second," Kelly said. "If Paula's going, I'm going too!"

"Me too, man!" Dan chimed in.

Raj felt he had to tell them about Shari. "So, I've met this girl. It's kind of a setup. My parents know hers." He showed them the pictures of Shari he had on his phone.

"She's really pretty," Dan said. "I wouldn't mind if my parents set me up with a babe like her. She has nice... uh... eyes," he said, outlining imaginary breasts with his hands.

"Let me get this straight, Raj," Paula said. "Your parents know some people, and they've found someone nice for you?"

Raj replied, "That's right. We've met a few times."

"Is she right for you?" asked Paula.

"I'm not sure. She's an accountant and has a fantastic job."

"Is this a kind of deal where you check each other out and make sure you have the right résumés?"

"Whatever do you mean, Paula?" Raj asked.

"Lots of people just want to marry a résumé. You know – the right religion, the right job. It's really tiresome."

"That's right," Dan said. "My folks want me to marry a nice Jewish girl. That's why I'm dating this hot Catholic chick from the Philippines."

"What happened to the dietician?" Raj asked.

"She wanted to do an intervention," Dan said, reaching for more chips. "A cleansing thing. A yoga retreat – no sex, no meat, no alcohol. I had to break it off, man just had to!"

Paula, who genuinely liked the dietician, said, "Dan, she wanted to make you a better version of yourself."

Dan snorted. "My version of me eats burgers and shags chicks from the Pacific Rim. Hey, Raj – I guess I've got my yellow belt now, eh?"

Raj sighed, "Dan…you really are my inspiration."

Paula said, "Maybe you just don't want to fuck things up by thinking only with your little head and not the big one."

Raj learned that his friends' personal lives were complicated, too. Kelly had finally stopped seeing Dr. Miller, the "surfer surgeon," because she couldn't handle being around his whiny kids. Paula had spent Christmas at home in Alberta and had seen her old boyfriend, but she had no desire to go home once her residency was finished.

"He expects me to help on the ranch – and work as a doctor in my spare time. I don't think so."

"I hear you," Raj said. "Shari wants me to start working at a clinic her father is building as soon as I'm done, but I want to do an extra year of ER training. Think Sinclair would recommend me if I asked him?"

"Sure he would, Raj," said Paula, then she added, "I just love Psychiatry. It's more interesting than anything else I've done so far. I hear you're coming to Psych in a couple of months. I'll still be there. But tell me, how serious are you about Shari?"

"I just don't know. There's family pressure," he said.

Dan spoke up. "Talk about pressure, I still get a summon from the hospital CEO."

"What's Wendy up to now, Dan?" Kelly asked.

"She wants me to follow her on Twitter. She says she needs more followers. Can you believe it? I don't follow people on Twitter."

"Dan, you need to keep pumping her," Raj said.

Dan seized the opportunity to be serious. "People here are oblivious to what's going on, even the docs. She just closed a hospital up north. Raj, you should tell Diana so she can tell her dad."

That sobered them all up, and the others soon left. Before he went to bed, Raj emailed his mom:

Thought I'd drop you a line. I'm back at work and enjoying it. Working with a group of family doctors and it's going well. I'm thinking about becoming a family doctor with extra training in Emergency Medicine. Have you been in touch with dad's cousin in the movie business?

In the morning, he read Mena's response:

It was nice to have you home. I must tell you the news. Shamila has a very expensive Bukhara carpet, a thing of great beauty and worth many thousands of dollars. She likes to walk on it in her bare feet. She noticed a spot on it that looked like dog pee, and the only dog that had ever been in the house was Uma's. No one saw the dog pee on the carpet, so the stain might be spilled champagne or something. In any case, Shamila is angry about this whole thing but refuses to speak to Uma about it, or even Roger. As for your sister, we will get in touch with Dad's cousin. She really should find a job close to home. I think she will just wind up getting sick in India. I don't know why she can't be more like you. We are all getting excited about Roger's wedding. Are you taking Shari? Call me soon.

Chandra had told her parents she wanted to go to India and look for a job in Bollywood. Afterward, she'd phoned Raj to report that Radhu was not totally against it, but Mena was distraught with her being so far away. Raj admired Chandra for going out on a limb. Somehow he knew things were going to work out for her.

Chapter Thirty Seven

The screen in the conference room beside Dr. Sinclair's office was showing an electrocardiogram with a bunch of squiggly lines that had to be interpreted. He was teaching and testing the interns on the interpretation of electrocardiograms.

"Very interesting, Dr. Mehta. You've identified heart block. What type of heart block is it?" asked Sinclair.

"Mobitz type II… I think." Raj said.

"Treatment options?" Sinclair asked.

"Um… Take a pertinent history and keep him on telemetry. There isn't any medication that'll help. He needs Cardiology to put in a pacemaker."

"Now, what if he's on a beta blocker and diltiazem?"

"We could withdraw the medication and simply observe, but we'd have to be pretty confident not to ask ICU or a cardiologist to take over."

Sinclair clicked on the next slide. This one showed an ECG with a chaotic scribble of lines. No one could make out what was happening, but nor did anyone want to screw up on Sinclair's quiz. Raj always volunteered to go first, as he'd realized that the first question was usually the easiest.

Sinclair fixed his steady gaze on Paula. "Paula, what do you make of this ECG?"

Paula shifted uncomfortably in her seat. "I think it's a sinus rhythm, but there seem to be artifacts and what looks like a run of premature ventricular contractions."

"That's a good start, Paula. What else do you see?"

"A wandering baseline?"

"Yes, and what else?"

The questions and answers went on for a long ten minutes. Sinclair was patient. Nonetheless, it was Friday afternoon, and rounds were dragging on.

* * *

Chandra was sitting quietly in the wings at the Princess of Whales Theatre, videotaping as the director made minor adjustments to the dance routine. She was struck by how much stage production differed from making TV and movies. She had spent the previous evening interviewing Lizzy and Mary, who'd had a lot to say about the industry and about their lives as actors.

Chandra: Elizabeth, what are your thoughts about roles for older female actresses?

Lizzy (*long drag on a cigarette*): Well, honey, it's like this. You have to be really old and butt ugly to play an old crone or Lady

Macbeth, or you have to be young and good-looking for all the other roles.

Chandra: What about Maggie Smith?

Lizzy: As I said, you've got to be really old, and then you can play the Queen. I'm really glad Toronto is putting this show on. You know, before this, I'd never been to Toronto. It's a lovely city – very young. You feel the energy.

Chandra: Do you like your current role?

Lizzy: You bet! It's fun, and there's some drama. The thing with acting is that it's about women's right to work.

Chandra: What do you mean?

Lizzy: Originally, all women's roles on stage were performed by men. Acting was one of the first jobs that women had to fight for. Mary and I are just continuing the fight for stronger women who came before us.

Chandra: So you see your role as helping younger actresses?

Lizzy: Absolutely!

When Diana's turn came, she spoke first about her background and education, and then Chandra asked her what the worst job she'd ever had was.

Diana: Working as a medical secretary in a hospital basement.

Chandra: A role in *Mama Mia* is a big change from working as a medical secretary.

Diana: I know! It's really exciting.

Chandra: What are the challenges starting out as an actor?

Diana: The biggest is landing the first job and keeping yourself employed. I've been really lucky. Lots of really good actors are waiting tables, hoping for the big break.

Chandra: How do you see your future unfolding?

Diana: I don't really know. I'm hoping *Mama Mia* leads me to other parts, but we'll see. I think it's going to be hard finding a balance between a career and a personal life, especially at the beginning. I've found you need support.

Chandra: Is there anyone who's supported you?

Diana: There's an intern at the hospital who's been very supportive, and I want to give a shout-out to him – and to the other interns. Thank you, Raj.

The cast and staff had warmed to Chandra and saw that the documentary could be a good promotional tool. Her life had suddenly become extraordinarily busy. A mediocre student at college, she had finally found something she was passionate about – filmmaking. Diana had smoothed over the producer's and director's concerns to allow Chandra backstage access, and filming had gone so well that

Chandra was starting to think that her documentary would be one of the best in her class. Time was moving quickly towards her submission deadline and the opening of *Mama Mia*. If it impressed her instructors, Chandra's film might even be featured at the Toronto DocNow film festival.

* * *

"Doc, ya gotta understand. When I said he had a big crap, I'm talking *enormous* – we can't even flush it!" Raj was trying hard not to laugh. The woman went on to tell him that she'd had to pick her eight-year-old son's poop out of the toilet at his grandmother's house and take it home to flush.

Raj had a look at the boy, who had a stunned look and said very little. He had rings on several fingers and a ring in one ear. What eight-year-old boy has an earring? He had a little belly that hung over his track pants. Raj had begun to notice that even some of the young children in St. Jerome were overweight and out of shape. After a thorough physical exam, Raj found nothing wrong except that he wore a significant amount of bling for a kid his age. He quizzed the boy about if he were afraid the toilet would swallow him, which made him laugh. Raj told him to eat prunes and raw vegetables daily and to avoid popcorn, and other dry foods, then sent him home.

Shari was due back from her business trip later that day. He had to tell her that he'd decided to do an extra year of training, and this probably would not be in Toronto. The boy was the last of his office patients, and so he hung up his lab coat and walked home with a purpose – he was hungry. Mr. Noodle had found its way back into his diet, but he had taken to putting sliced radish on top for a vegetable. He realized that his diet wasn't much better than the boy's. He had the stereo blaring so loud while he boiled water for the noodles that he almost missed the knock on the door. It was Shari.

"Shari! What brings you here?" Raj was shocked to see her. Shari had never been to his apartment. He didn't think she even knew how to get here.

"I'm back from Texas, and I thought you needed company. I had the limo driver bring me here – business expense, you know." Happily, she went on. "I just helped put together a three-billion-dollar merger of gas companies planning a huge pipeline from Alberta to the Gulf of Mexico. "The boss is making a big announcement next week. They're calling me the Wunderkitten!"

"Wow, Shari. That's impressive."

Embarrassed that he was about to eat a thirty-three-cent Mr. Noodle with sliced radish, he suggested they go out to celebrate.

"Why don't we have a bite in Toronto?" Shari suggested. "And you can spend the night at my place."

Raj went to his bedroom to change and came out to find Shari looking at the photo of his parents in front of a field of sunflowers. Raj loved the picture because it showed his parents – their smiles so genuine, in their element – where they seemed most at home.

Shari remarked, "Your family's from South India."

"That's right. Sunflowers grow everywhere there."

"Your family's beginnings were quite humble, weren't they?"

"Yes. Still can't believe how far they've come."

Raj had changed into a sweater and blue jeans. This wasn't what Shari had in mind, and she told him that his regular wardrobe was too casual.

"Why aren't you wearing that new outfit we bought last week?" she asked.

"The pants need hemming," said Raj, choosing a quick lie over the truth that he hated the outfit.

"What do you want to eat?" he asked, hoping she'd say Chinese.

"Let's eat Italian," she said.

Neither of them said a word as they started on the drive to Toronto. It wasn't until they were on the highway that Shari broke her silence. "Raj, I was away for a whole week. I didn't call because I wanted to see if you would call me, and you didn't."

"Sorry, Shari. I was really busy at work. I had to deal with all the admissions, and there was a steady stream of sick people.

"It doesn't take that long to make a phone call. I always call you," she said.

"You're right. I should have called. I'm sorry. Did you have a nice time?"

"It was okay. Do you ever think about me when I'm not around?"

"All the time, Shari, but my job's taking a lot out of me."

"Sometimes I think you don't want to spend any time with me."

"That's not true," Raj insisted. "It's just that I don't get much free time."

They drove on in silence. Shari seemed not angry so much as sullen and perhaps irritated or upset. Raj didn't know what to say, so he clammed up, reckoning the less he said, the better. He felt that if he said anything, she would jump all over it.

As they came into Toronto, Shari took a deep breath. "How come you never want to make love to me? It's always me who starts it."

"Well…" stammered Raj. "I always thought I should act like a gentleman."

"That's fine, Raj, but I always get the feeling that you have either somewhere to go or something you have to do." She went on. "I just don't feel that we're connecting."

Raj had no idea what he was supposed to say. Why did women always want to talk so much? He took a deep breath.

"Maybe we're moving just a bit too fast. Why don't we slow it down a little?" It wasn't the best time, but under the circumstances, he thought he'd best tell her what he was planning. "I was thinking of doing an extra year of training in Emergency Medicine."

"Why are you mentioning this now, Raj? I thought we were talking about us." Shari sounded annoyed.

"You said we're not connecting, so I thought I should tell you."

Shari turned away from him and folded her arms over her chest. She was getting angrier. "What about *me*, Raj? What about *our* plans? I thought you were going to be done in one more year. Now what?"

"Well, I think the more training I have, the easier it will be to get a good job."

"My dad will set you up with your own clinic, Raj. What more do you need?"

"I'm not sure I want to work in a private clinic, Shari. It's a nice offer, but I'd like to work somewhere where I'm really needed, and if I have extra training, I can do more. I thought I could go to the far north or even overseas."

They finally arrived at Shari's place, their conversation so animated they had forgotten to stop and eat. Shari's face showed confusion, anger, and pain – Raj could see them all. It was the first time Raj had looked at Shari's face and tried to understand her – what *she* wanted, what *she* needed.

"Raj," she said, starting to tear up. "Do you want to marry me, or have I imagined this whole thing?"

Desperately, Raj replied, "Shari, of course, I do! It's just that we've been moving really fast, and I need time to think about things. I've been working so hard that I never have enough time to think, not even about us."

"Raj, you don't love me, do you? If you did, you wouldn't be able to live without me," said Shari, and the bitterness in her voice cut his heart like a scalpel. She was really crying now. "I don't fucking believe this. How could I have fooled myself into thinking that you were in love with me? I'm such a fool."

Raj offered her one of the tissues he always had on hand for his allergies.

"Fuck you!" she shouted. "You screw up my life and give me a Kleenex. You're such a bastard! Raj, I'm the best thing that ever happened to you. I'm going to make more money than you ever will. My father was going to set you up in a million-dollar clinic. You should be thanking my family and me for helping you and your low-class family move up. I deserve someone who actually loves me!"

Raj was shocked. He didn't want to fight and had no idea what he'd done. Then it dawned on him that the problem wasn't what he'd done, it was what he hadn't done. He hadn't fallen in love with her. She was right. He had wasted her time.

Raj tried to apologize. "I'm sorry, Shari. I'm really sorry. You deserve someone better. It's not you – it's me." As he said it, he knew it sounded lame, but he couldn't think of anything else to say.

"*It's not you, it's me?*" she mimicked. "You are *such* a bastard! I can't believe I fell for you. The only person you'll ever love is *yourself*."

Shari got out and slammed the door shut so hard that the whole car shook. She turned back to Raj and yelled, "And I hate this low-class, immigrant piece-of-shit car. You should have a pizza delivery sign on it. You loser!"

Raj could not believe what had just happened. There was a rushing sound in his ears, and then he finally remembered to breathe.

Chapter Thirty Eight

"Dad, have you got anything to drink?"

"Raj, a member of the Royal Navy, always has something to drink. Would you like grog or whiskey?"

Raj, with nowhere to go after the breakup with Shari, had come to his parents' house. His head was spinning, and he needed someone to talk to. Strangely, he felt a bit lighter, as if he could breathe more easily. Still, Shari's criticism had stung, especially her remark about his family.

Raj sat down with Radhu and unloaded as they sipped Scotch on the rocks. It was the first real conversation he'd had with his father in a long time. It was rare for Raj to come to his father with a problem.

"Dad, Shari just broke up with me. There were just too many things that weren't working out."

His father looked surprised. "What happened, Raj? I thought you really liked this girl."

"Dad, I couldn't do it. She wanted to get married, but too many things just weren't right. I think she finally realized I don't share her goals, so she dumped me."

Dad took a long sip of Scotch and rolled it around in his mouth while swirling the ice in his glass. "Well, perhaps it's best you broke up. An unhappy marriage does no one any good."

"Dad, I tried," Raj said. "I just couldn't be who she wants me to be. I tried, and I'm so sorry about it now."

"Would she take you back? Maybe it was just a lovers' quarrel."

Raj took a large gulp of his Scotch; it burned all the way down. "I thought about that, but I don't think so. We just want different things. It would never work out."

Radhu poured them another drink.

The first drink had already loosened Raj's tongue, and he started to unload more. "In any case, I'm not going back to her. It was too hurtful."

"She hurt your pride, then?" asked Dad.

"Yes. But it's over, and I'm relieved."

"Well, you're back to square one. Your mother really liked Shari, and she's the one who will be most upset."

"Aunt Shamila liked her, too, didn't she?"

"Yes, Raj, but you're the one who had to marry her, and if it wasn't going to work out, then let everyone else be unhappy. They'll get over it." Radhu swirled the ice in his glass for a moment, then said. "I want to tell you that I'm sorry."

"Sorry for what?" asked Raj.

"Sorry for pushing you so hard when you were growing up. I was tough on you – much tougher than I was on Chandra."

"It's okay, Dad. I know you were trying to make me into something better."

"I never was much of a father. I was a taskmaster, even though I never wanted to be that sort of father. My own father was a good man. He did all sorts of things like playing soccer and cricket with us. I never did anything like that with you."

"I don't remember. We didn't miss out on much," Raj said.

"I just felt that I had to make you tougher than everyone else. I should have told you how proud I was when you graduated from high school. Instead, I think I told you that it was going to be much more demanding in university."

"But Dad, you were right. It was."

"So many times, I forgot to tell you how much I wished for your happiness but was negative instead, warning you to work hard and keep studying. I don't think you even smiled when you graduated from medical school. Your mother and I never saw you laugh for the longest time."

"Really?" asked Raj. "Was I that unhappy?"

"I wondered if you were going to crack under pressure, but you are made of stronger stuff than I am. I was a lazy guy in my twenties – not half as good as you. My own father, if he were alive, would tell you the truth of it."

Radhu put more ice in their glasses and refilled them with Scotch yet again.

"It's good to talk to you. We never do that anymore, not enough," Radhu said. After a moment, he added, "You know, your mother is going to be upset. Let me tell her – it'll be easier."

"It seems to me that Mom wants me to marry because she wants another daughter," Raj said.

"She does, Raj. It's because Chan is always flitting about, doing this and that. She drives her mother mad, I tell you."

They clinked glasses and took another drink. The combination of liquor and no dinner was making Raj feel tipsy. From the recesses of his memory, something came back.

"Dad, who was the girl?"

"What girl, Raj?"

"The girl in the photograph I found inside your Kama Sutra."

"Ah," Radhu sighed. "You would have to mention her tonight. It was so long ago, but I will never forget her."

Raj waited while his father took a slow sip of his drink. "The young woman in that picture was named Sangita, and I met her when

I was a teenager. I have never really told anyone, but I was in love with that girl. She was the most beautiful woman I had ever laid my eyes on. She had everything – looks, money, everything. Her family owned the movie theatre and the supermarket in our little town, and, back then, they were the only ones with electricity."

"How did you meet her?"

"We met at senior high school. She liked me because I was a cricket champion."

"You two looked like quite an item, Dad."

"That we were, and she was the first girl I ever kissed. I still remember her smile, her skin, and how she smelled." Dad's face took on a faraway look, and he smiled as he remembered her through the fog of alcohol.

"Obviously, it didn't work out," commented Raj.

"No, Raj, it didn't. And when it didn't, my family was angry."

"Why was that?"

"Sangita's family had money, and we were poor. Not dirt poor, but we didn't have much."

"So what happened?"

"Marriage to Sangita offered me everything except what I wanted most, which was to get out of India and start my life fresh. If

I had married her, I would never have left India. I would have been living *her* life. I would have had her family's wealth and would have had to spend the rest of my life proving to her parents that I was worthy of it. I wanted my own life, not someone else's. Most of all, I wanted to leave India."

"Did she want to leave India, too, Dad?"

"You know, Raj, I think she did, but her family wouldn't allow it. Why would she go so far away when they were doing so well? Her mother and father wanted her close. It was understandable."

"So it ended?"

"Yes, Raj. It came to an end when I told her I was leaving to join the navy."

"That must have been tough."

"It was, Raj. She cried and cried, and I never saw her after that."

"The picture was taken before you broke up, wasn't it?"

"Yes. We were deeply in love."

"Any regrets, Dad?"

Dad smiled, took a slow sip of his drink, and looked at Raj for a long moment. "Any regrets I had were washed away the day you were born under the Maple Leaf. That is the truth."

"There's a note on the back of the photo. It's not your writing. It's in Hindi, and I couldn't read it. Was it important?"

Dad smiled, but his eyes were sad. "It is a quote from Abdul Kalam, a famous Indian statesman who would become President of India. What it says is, 'You have to dream before your dreams can come true.' He spoke about many things like self-sacrifice and peace."

"Wow, Dad. That's profound."

"Sangita understood it, that's why she wrote it. She understood that she wouldn't be part of my dream, yet she wanted me to be happy."

"That's quite a story. Do you ever think about her?"

"Raj, I'm married, and the past is the past."

They were both sleepy. Dad yawned, then said, "Do me a favour, Raj."

"What's that?" Raj yawned too.

"For God's sake, make yourself happy. Don't go through life unhappy trying to prove something. I didn't come all the way to Canada to see my children unhappy. It's your life – live it." Radhu leaned on Raj's shoulder, and they stood up. The old man embraced Raj tightly and kissed his cheek.

***

After an hour of hearing his father downstairs complaining about Gustad's TV advertisements, Raj finally got out of bed. Radhu always had the TV on too loud nowadays. He probably needed hearing aids.

He went into the kitchen, where Mena had already started making breakfast.

"The big doctor has returned to visit me!" she said. "Come give your mama a hug, Raj." Mena could be strong when she needed to be, and she squeezed him tightly. When he was younger, he wouldn't hug her back, but now he did.

They settled into their comfortable Saturday morning ritual. Radhu drank coffee, read the newspaper, and complained. Mena made idli and served them with chutney and cilantro on top.

"So, what's new with you?" she said. Raj wondered whether his mother knew he'd broken up with Shari or if his father had forgotten to tell her.

"Shari and I broke up, Mom."

"You did! What happened?"

"I wasn't able to give the relationship enough time, and she wasn't happy about that. I also want to take another year of training, and she wanted to get married."

Mena nodded. "These young women, they need everything – money, career, a doting husband. They will never be happy."

"Maybe," said Raj, "but I think it's for the best. Better to break up than to be unhappily married."

"Raj, when you are married, you have to sacrifice. Don't worry – someone else will come along."

"I hope so, but I'm going to concentrate on my career for the next while." Wanting to change the subject, Raj asked, "What's new with you, Mom?"

"Raj, my dear, my blood sugar is up, and my knees are hurting me. The doctor says that I might have to take more pills for diabetes, and I don't want to." There was an implied request in this. Raj suspected that she wanted him to say it was okay to let her sugar run a bit high, so she could tell her own doctor that "my son, the doctor, said it's okay," but Raj wasn't about to be trapped.

"Mom, it's very important to get the sugar level under control. You'll have to exercise more and eat less rich food if you don't want to take more pills." He felt sorry for her; the weight she had gained in recent years had led to diabetes.

Mena filled him in on the family gossip, which was mostly about Roger and Uma. "The wedding is to be an English ceremony." This didn't surprise Raj, as Gustad and Shamila so loved English things.

"Aunt Shamila is now frantically trying to help make the arrangements. The wedding is to take place at Roger and Uma's country club, the Royal Berkshire near Windsor Castle. Isn't that exciting, Raj? They're getting married near Windsor Castle!" Uncle Gustad and Shamila are flying several waiters and staff from his restaurant over to London to help serve the meal for everyone the day before the wedding."

"What about the caterer? You know, the fellow who worked for Madonna and Guy Ritchie?" Raj asked.

"Apparently, he suffered a groin injury from doing Pilates – rolled off a giant ball incorrectly. Shamila claims he must be an idiot, as normal men don't roll around on a giant ball like cats or dogs. Shamila and Gustad really don't like the fellow. He wants to make food that is pseudo-Indian."

"Pseudo-Indian?"

"You know, all these fancy chefs take some sort of crappy English food like fish and chips and dress it up with curry sauce and chutney and act like it's good! Gustad is so angry he intends to take frozen entreés with him on the plane."

Raj mentioned that Chan was going to film the wedding. Roger had "hired" her, though he hadn't offered to pay her anything. They both laughed, knowing that Roger was cheap only with his own family.

Raj noticed that Mena's sunflowers had turned towards the sun and thought to ask her something he'd never asked before. "Mom, why do you like sunflowers so much?"

Mena glanced at Radhu and smiled. "They are all that I have left of India. You see, I first met your father on a dirt road outside our village near Bangalore, where the fields were full of sunflowers. Canada is so cold, and the sunflower is a bit of sunshine that I keep in my heart."

Mid-morning, Raj left his parents' house for St. Jerome, his car loaded with frozen chapattis and vegetables in plastic containers once again. As he drove, he wondered if he would see Diana again.

Chapter Thirty Nine

Toronto had enjoyed a mild winter that slipped into early spring. After several grueling weeks post-season, the Toronto Maple Leafs were finally eliminated from the playoffs. Star suddenly found himself with nothing to do. This particular Sunday night, instead of playing, he was alone at home, staring at his huge television screen. Mischa was in New York for a photo shoot. It was almost time for the hockey game to start, and Ron Berry's pregame show was on.

"Well, folks, you all know about the very interesting scoring race between Leafs' forward Star Yanofsky and Sergei Osakin of the Washington Capitals. You guessed it – Osakin clobbered Yanofsky. It certainly didn't help that the Leafs are once again out of the playoffs. I tell you, I feel for those Toronto fans. They just can't catch a break. Some people honestly believe they blow it in the playoffs just so they can start their holidays earlier. Anyway, despite some excellent ice time, Yanofsky trailed Osakin in goals and assists." Berry put on a serious face and spoke in an almost reverential tone. "It's no wonder, really. Osakin has won the Rocket Richard Trophy five times. He's also won the Art Ross Trophy, the Hart Memorial Trophy, and the Lester B. Pearson Award as the league's MVP. Was it ever a race? I just don't think so. Osakin is a proven winner, and Yanofsky is a young rookie. And let's face it – he'll be lucky to have any kind of career like Sergei Osakin's."

Star turned down the volume, rolled his eyes, and then closed them, replaying the final game in his mind. He had done everything he could to ensure that Toronto made it through the conference playoffs, but the other teams were simply better. He had worked so hard himself and driven everyone on the team so hard that the loss was crushing. Some of his teammates were still pissed at him because he had accused them of not giving one hundred percent. It sounded to Star like Ron Berry had a 'man crush' on that fucker, Osakin. At least Star had all his own teeth – pictures of Osakin frequently showed him missing a front tooth.

Star opened his eyes and turned up the volume, paused the screen, and rewound the last twenty seconds. Ron Berry was replaying the winning goal in the final game of the Washington Capitals playoff series. Osakin neatly stickhandled the puck into the net, making it look effortless. Then he whipped off his helmet and high-fived his teammates as the timer hit zero, and the fans went crazy. Osakin turned to the stands, and so did the camera. It focused on a woman with blonde hair, a Washington Capitals jersey hugging big boobs, who was waving and blowing Osakin a kiss. What the fuck! **It was Mishcha!**

Star was livid. The camera followed Osakin as he skated up to her, and they embraced. Mischa had told Star she had to go to New York City, but there she was in Washington! The game had played last night. Star grabbed his phone and pulled up Mischa's number. He called.

"Da?" answered a deep, heavily accented voice.

"Hey, is Mischa there? Who's this?"

"It's Osakin. I see your name on the phone, so I answer. Ha! I steal your girlfriend! So easy for me to win – and for you to lose!"

"Fuck you, Osakin."

"Yes, yes, Yanofsky. She's fucking me already. So hot, so sexy, like a she-wolf. Anyway, she is Russian; you steal her, and I take her back."

"What are you fucking talking about?" Star yelled.

"No one steals Russian women! I make you pay. She's mine now. She tells me to tell you to fuck off because of you pretty-boy loser."

Star's chest heaved with tense rage as he gripped the phone. Osakin went on, enjoying the whole thing. "And she say you have small cock – all Canadian men have small cocks like dog or goat or something. She says you drink smoothies. Maybe you want me to send you breast milk to make a smoothie? Ha! When you lose next World Cup, you can go back to the junior league - where you would be in Russia."

Star was angry, but he recognized he was being baited. The prick did this sort of thing for a living – he wasn't a real sportsman.

Star spoke with quiet venom in his voice. "You tell Mischa that I'm calling only because I've got a message for her. Tell her she's got herpes! And you probably do, too, you fucking hack! Maybe you can mug a gorilla and get new teeth while you're at the zoo getting your herpes checked out. Bet your ass I'll see you at the World Cup – and I'm taking back the Lucky Loonie, you dumb fuck!"

Star flung the phone at the wall, denting it and cracking the cover. He was angry – really angry at Mischa but even angrier with himself. A large unopened

bottle of vodka beckoned from the kitchen. He would have a drink and figure things out…

* * *

At 9:00 Tuesday morning, Diana walked through the hospital entrance. Today would be her last day there, and she was glad the job was coming to a close. *Mama Mia* had, quite literally, become her life. She spotted her father walking through the lobby.

"Hey, Dad! How's it going?" she said, greeting him with a wide grin.

"Aren't you chipper!" he said.

"I am! It's my last day."

Dr. Sinclair smiled and said, "I guess I'll miss you a little bit, although Janice is doing well as your replacement. But as long as you're here, can you deliver these notices to the right departments, please? And also, will you be around for dinner? Your mother wants to see you."

"I think so, Dad."

"Thanks, Di. Come by the office after you deliver these, and I'll get you to do some typing for me –Janice is a bit behind – then you can go."

Diana made most of the deliveries, then realized she hadn't had any breakfast and went to the cafeteria. She bought a muffin and coffee and, spying Paula's short bob and Kelly's red curls joined them at their table.

"Hi there, you two!"

"Hey, stranger. You're back?"

"Just for the day. It's my last day."

"How's Mama Mia going?" Kelly asked. "When's opening night?"

"We open in a couple of weeks. But there's a preview of the show for VIPs in a week. The premier of Ontario, the mayor, and lots of local celebs have been invited."

"That must be so exciting! And we're coming to see the show."

Cautiously, Diana asked, "So… where's Raj these days?"

"He's in the Family Practice office," Paula said. "I think he likes it there. They don't really give him much of a break, though."

"That's right," Kelly said. "I hear it's really busy."

"So why are you asking about Raj?"

"I just have to deliver this letter to him." Diana tapped one of the undelivered notices

Paula wasn't going to let it go. "How is Star these days, Diana?"

"I really don't know. We broke up a while ago. It wasn't working out."

The girls' manner changed abruptly. "I'm sorry to hear that," said Kelly.

"Don't be. It just didn't work out," said Diana.

A few minutes later, she went down to the Family Practice unit, located in a ground-floor addition to the hospital, and spoke to the receptionist, who led her into the staff room. Raj was sitting by a Dictaphone, deep in thought.

"Hi, Raj," she greeted him.

"Diana!" exclaimed Raj, his face registering his surprise. "This is great! How are you?" The disapproving eye of the receptionist hinted they should take a break elsewhere, and so they walked slowly to Sinclair's office. Raj was waiting for the right moment to ask her out.

"Are you liking Toronto, Diana? It must be nice to be where all the action is. Lots of clubs, so much to see," he said.

"So," said Diana, "are you going to come and see me in the show?"

"Of course," he exclaimed. "We're *all* coming. Is it okay if we hold up signs?"

"No, Raj," smiled Diana. "This is a *musical,* not a hockey game!"

"So there won't be any guys with their faces painted?" he asked.

"No," she laughed, " but sometimes old people do get up and dance. *Mama Mia* is known for that. In London alone, the show was responsible for several broken hips and a groin injury."

Raj laughed and then said hesitantly, "Diana, would you like to go out with me sometime?" He looked at her with a hopeful smile.

Diana smiled. "Yeah, yeah – I'd like that. Give me a call."

As they approached Sinclair's office, Diana's phone rang. She fished it out of her back pocket and saw Star's name. She couldn't think why he would be calling. The number disconnected, and at that very moment, they heard a loud crunching noise, and then a car horn blared.

* * *

When Tuesday morning dawned, Star had only an hour's sleep. He had been up most of the night, drinking vodka and ruminating. The Vodka bottle was half empty. In his relatively short life, he had never had to deal with losing. He had always been a winner – the guy that everyone wanted to be.

He was angry that Toronto had not made the playoffs, and now Osakin had upset him so much that he was seeing everything through a red, angry veil. Mischa's conniving was unforgivable, and it was obvious that she didn't care about him at all. In his vodka-soaked haze, the one thing he kept coming back to was Diana. He realized that she was the best thing that had ever happened to him, and he had let her go!

He had to find her, apologize and beg her to take him back. Why had he let her walk out of his life? Feverishly, he formulated a plan, which consisted of drinking a smoothie to give him the energy to think clearly. Then he drove to Tiffany's and bought a four-carat diamond ring. He held the blue velvet box carefully, looking at it before he put it in his pocket. He drove to Diana's house in Cabbagetown, only to find she'd left earlier that morning. He jumped back into his Porsche and sped off, trying to compose himself during the drive out of Toronto. He would talk to Diana, and she would see that they were meant to be together. Then he'd go down on one knee, whip out the ring, and propose.

Just outside St. Jerome, Star picked up speed. His phone rang, and he answered it, still sipping his smoothie and trying to stay calm, although he was sweating profusely. It was tricky juggling the phone, his smoothie, and the steering wheel all at the same time.

"Hi, sweetie. It's Claire." Star's agent had been working on a deal with a major beverage company to produce his smoothie. "Starbucks isn't interested, but the Better Cup is willing to try it. They want you to be in all the advertising, and they're thinking of something like *Be a Star with Star's Energy Smoothie*."

"Sounds good, but you have to mention the cacao nibs," said Star.

"But there's a problem, Star," said Claire. "They want to replace the cocoa nibs with acai berry nibs."

"What the hell?"

"The cacao nibs are really expensive, and there's a world shortage. And there's another problem. It seems they're hard to drink."

As Star turned into the street where the hospital was located, he took the last sip of his smoothie, but the cocoa nibs were stuck in the straw.

He heard Claire say, "Something about the nibs getting stuck in the straw," but between sucking hard on the straw, trying to steer the car with one hand, and talking on the phone while also trying to text Diana, he realized – too late – that he had taken the last turn too quickly. The tires squealed, and in the blink of an eye, Star's magnificent sports car crashed into a fire hydrant.

The Porsche 911 hit the hydrant solidly, and the impact triggered the airbag, which inflated so fast it smashed his drink into his face. Star choked on cacao nips as he lost consciousness while attempting to text, talk, drive and drink a smoothie. The car was ruined, and so were his $400 sunglasses that were smashed against his face. Somehow the blue velvet Tiffany box was undamaged and remained safely in his pocket.

Chapter Forty

Diana, Raj, and about a dozen other people ran out the front door and found the car with its front end smashed in. The hydrant was spouting water around the steaming $200,000 mass of metal. Raj looked in the cracked window but could only see that someone was slumped over the steering wheel.

Dan and Kelly came running out. "What happened, Raj?"

"This car just crashed," said Diana. "It's Star's car. You've got to get him out!"

The driver's door was jammed, but Raj and Dan managed to pry it open and lift Star off the seat. The airbag had deployed. A large straw was stuck between his teeth, and his sunglasses had smashed against his face; he was gurgling as he tried to breathe. Raj dragged him out, turned him on his side in the rescue position, and pounded his back. A small plug of congealed cocoa nibs came out. Star seemed to breathe a little better, but one leg was broken and was lying at a funny angle.

"This guy's in trouble, man," Raj said.

One of the orderlies had raced back inside to fetch a stretcher. The interns hoisted Star onto the stretcher and wheeled him into the ER.

Dr. Marley was all business. "Okay, guys, what have we got?"

"A twenty-four-year-old hockey player crashed his car into a hydrant right outside the hospital."

"He's unconscious," said Rick, "so we have to tube him and get him straight to the OR. This leg looks like a compound femur fracture."

In the space of just a few minutes, Star had had an ECG and blood taken for routine tests, a tube had been inserted down his windpipe, and he was sedated through an intravenous line. X-rays had been ordered, and the orthopedic surgeon had been called. In less than five minutes, Dr. Josh Brevin appeared in the ER. A large man in his fifties reviewed the X-ray, examined Star's leg, and said, "Okay, we're looking at inserting an intramedullary nail, and we have to clean up the wound. We need consent if there's anyone around who can give it." He looked at Dan and Raj. "I don't have an assistant on call, so which one of you is going give me a hand?"

"Sir, I'm on call right now for Medicine," Dan said.

"Then you're off the hook," Brevin said. Pointing a beefy index finger at Raj, he said, "That means you, Mehta. Go out and talk to the next of kin and get me the go-ahead. I don't want this open fracture to get infected. Let's give him 2000 mg of Ancef stat. And deal with this, will you?" Brevin tossed the blue velvet box to Raj. The nurses had found it after they removed Star's clothing in preparation for surgery.

Raj walked out to the waiting room where Diana, upset and crying, was talking on her phone. She looked up at Raj. "Thank God you're here, Raj. Is he going to be okay?"

"He needs surgery right away. You've got to get his parents or someone to give us consent. We can do the surgery anyway, but it's important that we make every effort to get consent."

Holding out the little blue Tiffany box, Raj asked, "Do you know what this is?"

Diana took the box and sat down. "I haven't a clue."

"Look, Diana, I've got to go. I'll be in surgery with Dr. Brevin, and I think it's going to be a while. Tell his parents we have to do emergency surgery, so he doesn't lose his leg."

* * *

"Raj, make sure we get the C-arm."

Raj looked around the operating room and spotted the large portable X-ray machine in a corner. He marvelled at how quickly Brevin moved for a big man. Donning OR greens and his Spider-Man OR cap and 'scrubbing in' took Brevin less than five minutes. Raj hurriedly got ready to assist.

"Good to see you, Raj. How are you?" Fred Banting was the anesthetist on call.

The team got down to business and explored the large open wound on Star's leg. The underlying bone had a large break, and Brevin had elected to insert a long metal rod through the marrow cavity, but the broken end of the bone had cut some of the deep structures within the leg. As they explored the wound, something let go, and bright red blood began shooting out of the wound. It was arterial – bright red and squirting with every beat of Star's heart.

"Shit, this guy's blood pressure is dropping. What are you doing down there?" Fred, normally unflappable, sounded worried. He called for a couple of units of blood.

Brevin muttered, "More traction, Raj – and get that suction in and suck out some of this fucking blood."

Raj did so, but the blood filled the cavity more quickly than he could suction it out. It spilled out and over the operating table, and the floor rapidly became sticky

Brevin swore. "Shit. He's going to bleed to death right here on this fucking table!"

Raj was tense with worry, and his heart was racing. "Should I put some pressure on the femoral artery?" he asked. Brevin nodded, and Raj put pressure on Star's groin over the femoral artery. The blood flow seemed to slow down.

"Keep up that pressure for a second so I can find the torn artery," said Brevin. He hunted around, then clamped a mass of tissue. "There! I think it's stopped for the moment".

"His blood pressure's coming up a bit." Fred was pumping blood into Star's intravenous line. Brevin stepped away for a moment to catch his breath. Raj had no idea things could get so dire so fast. The surgeon and the anaesthetist were both sweating under their waterproof surgical gowns, and the nurses were scared.

Fred gave Star an additional paralyzing agent and continued to pump blood into him. "I hope you're not going to be too long. I don't want him to get too cold. Good thing he's really healthy and has lots of reserves."

"What are we going to do about that artery?" Raj knew there was the risk that it would start bleeding again if not repaired or at least tied off.

"Let me call Williamson. He's not on call, but he might come in," Fred said, already calling up the Chief of Surgery's number on his phone. He surprised Raj by telling the chief he had to get his ass in quickly.

Williamson was scrubbed and in the OR within thirteen minutes, a personal record. "What have you got, Josh?"

"Fracture mid-shaft femur, and I'm going to nail it," Brevin said. "The problem is I'm getting too much bleeding around here." He poked the wound.

Williamson released the femoral artery clamp. There was a slow trickle at first and then a torrent of blood. "It's one of the perforating arteries," he said and got straight to work. Raj watched as
396

he teased through the tissues and finally found where the artery had been shredded. He painstakingly tied off everything, removed the damaged section, and rejoined the artery. To finish, he neatly reorganized the wound and tacked everything down.

"Will he have nerve damage?" Brevin asked.

Williamson shook his head. "He'll be okay because it's a lower motor neuron, and it'll grow back, but he'll need lots of therapy."

Two hours into the surgery, Raj's mind was numb, and his feet hurt. He didn't know how the two older men kept going. Mostly he was just watching as Williamson and Brevin put Star's leg back together. After giving Star two units of blood, Banting had settled down with a crossword puzzle, and seeing that he had relaxed somehow relaxed the rest of the team.

"So who is this guy?" asked Williamson.

Surgeons were so action-oriented that they would often do all sorts of things to people without knowing much about them. He said, "Dr. Williamson, the patient's name is Star Yanofsky. He's a forward with the Toronto Maple Leafs. Dan, Kelly, and I found him in his smashed-up car just outside the hospital. Looks like he ran into a fire hydrant."

"Was he drinking?" Williamson asked.

"Not in the usual sense, sir," Raj said. "It looked like he choked on a smoothie."

"Smoothie? What the fuck's a smoothie?"

"One of those health drinks, sir. When we got him out of the car, it looked like he was choking on it."

"Anyone knows why he crashed?"

"Sir, he might have been using his phone while he was driving."

"Perfect," said Williamson. "The fucker just ruined my golf day, talking on the phone and drinking a fucking smoothie."

Banting looked at Raj. "Wait for a second, isn't this the guy who was going out with Sinclair's daughter? Did you ever get to ask her out, Raj?"

"I think he was coming to see her when the accident happened," Raj said, ignoring Banting's second question.

Brevin stopped stitching and looked over at Raj. "Let me get this straight, Raj. You're keen on this girl, Sinclair's daughter, and this Star guy shows up and smashes up his car, and you and Dan find him and save his life." Brevin summed things up in a way that only a surgeon could. "Seems to me you got screwed on this deal. Well, the only thing he'll be playing with for the next six weeks - *is himself.*"

Back to business again, he said, "Raj, we'll have to watch for fat embolism, so put him on low-dose heparin."

Raj and the two surgeons left the OR a few pounds lighter from sweat loss, their OR greens spattered with blood. Banting was keeping Star intubated as he had lost so much blood and would keep him sedated in the Intensive Care Unit, at least for the night.

As they walked into the lounge, they were met by a large crowd. Diana was talking with a well-dressed couple in their fifties, whom Raj assumed were Star's parents. Raj nodded at her, but she didn't smile. Mrs. Yanofsky was hyperventilating, and Diana was patting her back.

"Doctor, can you tell me what's happened to my son?" Star's mother, upset and tearful, stood beside her husband.

"Your son is going to be okay," Brevin said. "We repaired the fracture, but it will take many weeks of therapy before he has the strength to walk again." Brevin introduced Williamson as the hospital's Chief of Surgery, who had assisted him in the very difficult operation. "And this is Dr. Mehta, one of our interns. He saved your son's life by getting him into the hospital before he died of blood loss and choking."

Mr. and Mrs. Yanofsky thanked Raj, pumping his hand vigorously, then asked if they could see Star. Brevin said they could as soon as he was moved upstairs to ICU. He warned them he was still unconscious but would be awake soon. Then he asked Raj to take the family to the ICU. The Yanofsky clan, along with Diana, followed him to the fourth floor, where he escorted them to the ICU waiting lounge. After Star was cleaned up, he was finally moved to an ICU room, where his family finally got to see him. His parents and Diana crowded into the little ICU room.

"Oh my God, what happened to his eye?"

Raj feared that Mrs. Yanofsky would start crying again as he explained, "That's a reaction from his drink that got into his eye. There was some sort of particulate material in the liquid."

"Was he drinking vodka?" Star's mother asked.

"It was his smoothie," Diana said. "It has cocoa nibs in it, and they must have got into his eye and irritated it." She added, "Mr. Yanofsky, Star had this in his pocket when we found him. I should give it to you – I don't know what to do with it." Diana placed the little velvet box in his hand. He opened the box, and a flawless, star-cut, four-carat diamond in a white-gold band winked in the light.

"My son has always had strong feelings for you, Diana," Mr. Yanofsky said. "I think he was coming to propose to you."

Chapter Forty One

Diana and the Yanofskys stayed in the little ICU room for most of the night and the next morning. Star looked as if he had returned from the war, rather than a car accident while texting and drinking a smoothie. Several of his aunts and cousins kept a protective vigil just outside the ICU in the waiting room.

The next day the ICU waiting room was full; however, one person in the crowd was causing more noise and confusion than everyone else. It was Claire, Star's publicist, and agent, who had driven immediately to St. Jerome when she learned of the accident on the news. She demanded to see Star right away and would not be satisfied until she was allowed into the small ICU room with Diana and Star's parents. In front of Star's family, Claire grilled Diana about the accident like a prosecutor in a courtroom.

"So it was you Star was trying to contact, was it?" She sounded haughty.

"Maybe, but Star and I haven't seen each other for quite a while," Diana said.

"I hear he bought a huge diamond ring. Was it for you?"

"I really don't know. As I said, we haven't talked in a couple of months."

Claire continued her interrogation. "Did you get a call or a text from him?"

"I think he tried to text me, but I didn't get a chance to answer. We heard the crash and went outside to see what it was."

"You've gone out with him before, haven't you? It sounds to me like Star was in some sort of lovelorn state and wanted you back."

"Perhaps, but things hadn't worked out. I've got a job now, and I've –."

Claire cut her off. "Did you know Star is currently the highest-paid rookie hockey player in Canada? He's also the Toronto Maple Leafs' assistant captain. Did you know that?"

"No," replied Diana. "I didn't know that."

"Star is also the new face of F-Motosport Eyewear and has a deal on the go for his energy smoothie."

"We saw he was drinking a smoothie when the accident happened," Diana said.

"Don't blame the smoothie!" Claire shouted. "Star is the guiding light and hope for millions of Toronto hockey fans that someday Toronto will win the Stanley Cup. Star loves his smoothies – and they're healthy."

"I'm not blaming the smoothie," Diana said, "but every once in a while, the cocoa nibs get stuck in the straw."

Claire shook her head. "Listen, honey, I know an accident caused by a broken heart. Star was desperately trying to get in touch with you."

Diana was flabbergasted. Why was Star's agent trying to blame her for the accident? She had simply shown up for her last day of work at the hospital. She didn't want to tell Claire that the last time she saw Star, he was dancing and making face time with Mischa – who was, Diana, assumed, now Star's girlfriend. Star's parents were in the small room, and Diana wouldn't speak ill of Star in front of them.

"I was *not* on the phone with him when he crashed. I was working," she said

Claire was relentless. "Star spoke to me about you. He wanted both of you to be on Puck Bunny Wives."

"He mentioned it," Diana said, "but I told him I wasn't interested."

"Well, this is just the sort of story they're after. Romance in a life-and-death situation. It's got the makings of a fabulous new season." Claire eyed Diana like a hawk after its prey.

Just at that moment, a nurse came into the ICU room and noticed that Star was slowly waking up. She said that she was going to get the doctor to lend a hand. Diana thought about leaving, but she needed to see how Star was. While waiting for the doctor, the group saw him slowly squirm in the bed and then heard him mumble, "Oh, my head! Where am I? Why does my cock hurt?"

Kelly, who was doing her ICU rotation, rushed into the room, closely followed by the nurse. Kelly pushed everyone aside and told them all to leave for a moment while she examined Star.

"Hi, Star, I'm Dr. Davis. I'll be looking after you."

Star stared at Kelly and whispered, "You're beautiful. Are you an angel? I'm in heaven, right?"

"No, Star. You're in the hospital. You had an accident. Don't you remember?" Kelly said.

"Remember what?"

"You had an accident just outside St. Jerome Hospital. Can you remember it?" said Kelly.

"A bit. What kind of accident was it? Was I playing hockey?"

"No. You crashed your Porsche. Do you remember anything about it?"

"I sort of remember drinking something."

"That's okay, Star. This happens to lots of people after a head injury. It'll get better soon," Kelly assured him. As Star fully regained consciousness, Star's parents and Diana were let back into the ICU room. Star ignored everyone but Kelly. He complained about his dick, and Kelly obliged by decompressing and removing the catheter in his bladder.

Diana, seeing an opportunity to escape, slipped away unnoticed as everyone's attention was focused on Star. She was desperately tired after staying up most of the night and had to get back to Toronto as she had a rehearsal that day.

As she drove out of the hospital parking lot, she wondered if the enormous diamond was meant for her. What was she supposed to do now? Seeing Star had reminded her that she did like him, but liking someone just wasn't enough. On top of that, their relationship always seemed to be about him, never her. She was tired of it all.

When she arrived at the Cabbagetown house, Mary said, "Hey sweetie, your hunky hockey player came around yesterday looking for you."

"I know, Mary. I know."

"He was slurring his words a bit. I'm sure he'd been drinking – a lot."

Lizzy said, "I could smell the booze on him, too. I'd venture to say he'd been drinking all night."

"Well," said Diana, "he had an accident outside the hospital."

"Not surprised," said Mary. "Is he okay? I wouldn't want an accident to spoil that lovely face."

"I think he'll be okay, but he broke his leg and had to have surgery."

"Why was he looking for you?" asked Lizzy. "He took off like a shot when we said you weren't in town."

"I just don't know," sighed Diana. "He had an engagement ring with him. His dad thinks he was going to propose to me, but now he has amnesia." The past twenty-four hours had been the worst she'd ever been through, and she burst into tears. "Honestly, I thought he was going to die. If it wasn't for Raj and the other doctors …"

Lizzy and Mary sat beside her and comforted her. "It's okay, Di. You were scared. It'll pass."

"I know, I know, but it took me totally by surprise – and then they showed me the ring."

"So what are you going to do?" asked Lizzy. "Marriage proposals from millionaire hockey players don't come along every day."

"Well, he doesn't remember why he came to St. Jerome, and I sure didn't want him to ask me in front of his parents."

"Why not?" asked Mary.

"Because I'd have said no."

"No?" Lizzy sounded amazed. "But he's probably the wealthiest, best-looking guy in this town."

406

"I just can't," replied Diana. "My life would be total chaos. I was actually hoping to see another guy at the hospital – this doctor I know. And as crazy as it sounds, he's the one that saved Star's life."

"You like this doc?" asked Lizzy.

"I do, but he'll probably avoid me like the plague now. And my dad's his boss."

"Diana," Mary said, giving her a hug. "You're young and beautiful and talented. Things will work out."

Lizzy looked at the clock and realized they had to get to the rehearsal, and two cups of strong coffee later, the three were on their way.

* * *

A few days later, Raj ran into Kelly in the hospital cafeteria. She was letting her coffee cool while she admired her French manicure, which complimented the blue and pink scrubs she was wearing under her lab coat. A few minutes later, Paula entered the cafeteria and sat down with them. She wasn't wearing a lab coat because Psychiatry discouraged it, because lab coats frightened some patients.

"Nice manicure," said Paula.

"Thanks. Just got it done."

"What's the occasion?" Paula was smiling. "And how's your 'Star patient'?"

"Kelly, you've been looking extra nice these past few days. What's with that?" Raj said. He was pretty sure it was because she had been put in charge of looking after Star.

"He's really improving, but he's developed retrograde amnesia. I think I'm going to hang on to him a little longer, maybe repeat his CT scan. I had a very long talk with him yesterday about what happened."

"Details! Details!" Paula said.

"He remembers watching TV when he saw his girlfriend, a Russian model and apparently a total tramp, cozying up to another hockey player, and it really upset him. He admitted to drinking half a bottle of vodka and deciding he still had feelings for Diana Sinclair."

"And what about the ring?" Paula asked.

"He doesn't remember buying it. You know, he's such a sweet guy, driving down here to make a romantic gesture. I think that, underneath the tough guy act, he's really sensitive." She winked at Paula and added, "The other day, his back hurt so much from being in bed that I tried a little therapeutic massage on him."

"So is he as big and as muscly as he looks?"

"He sure is. And he shaves every part of his body – *every* part. You have to see him, Paula. He's an Adonis – *so beautiful*."

Raj had to ask, "Kelly, are you developing a crush on Star? Not that I blame you."

"He calls me his little angel doctor." Kelly was glowing. "His agent is arranging a photo shoot for the local paper, and I'm going to be in it. For some unknown reason, his agent can't get enough of me. She keeps talking about a show called 'Puck Bunny Wives'. Have you heard of it?"

Paula and Raj both said they hadn't.

Kelly stood up and said, "Gotta run, guys. Raj, when you can, you should drop by the ICU. Star wants to talk to you."

* * *

Later that week, Raj sat at his tiny kitchen table, mechanically chewing warmed-up Mr. Noodle and vegetables. He wanted to call Diana, but what about Star and his engagement ring? Would he look like a jerk asking her out while Star was recovering from his near-death experience?

He wanted to phone her but couldn't think of what to say that didn't sound lame. In a funk, he turned on his computer and checked his emails. There was one from his mother and a couple from Chandra.

His mother wrote:

Hello Raj: As you know, Roger's wedding is in a few weeks. Shamila has arranged tickets for all of us at Multi-Globe Travel. When she made the arrangements, Dad told her that you would need two tickets because you were going with Shari. So now we have a spare ticket. Dad and I can't cancel it because it isn't in our names. Gustad and Shamila are on the same flight but in First class. Shamila insists that we each take an extra suitcase to fill with food. She's unhappy with the meal arrangements and they want to take some of their own food. Drop us a line. We saw Deepak Chopra. He said we are all evolving.

Chandra wrote:

Thought I'd let you know I just won the top prize for my documentary,

Women and Theatre: Taking a Bow at the Ryerson Documentary Film Festival. Bet you never thought I'd ever win top prize in anything!

Party tonight!!!!

Text me later, alligator! I may be drunk – and stoned. If you see Diana, thank her for all her help.

Raj reread his sister's email and put two and two together. Chandra's winning documentary was about the theatre, plus Diana was in a play. She must have helped Chan somehow. How did they ever meet?

His sister had sent another email only a few minutes after the first. It had a large attachment, and the message was simple: *Check this out. Gorgeous, isn't she?*

Raj opened the video Chandra had attached and found himself staring at a close-up of Diana looking at him. She looked beautiful. He was so stunned he missed the question Chandra asked her, but he did hear her reply.

> *There's an intern at the hospital who's been very supportive, and I want to give a shout-out to him – and to the other interns. Thanks Raj – hope to see you soon!*

The video came to an end.

Chapter Forty Two

Raj enlarged the video to full screen and replayed it a dozen times. Then realizing how obsessive he was being, he buried the file in a folder on his hard drive. He was debating whether to go to work or jump in the car and drive to Toronto when his phone rang.

"Hello, Dr. Mehta. Are you planning to come to the ICU today?" It was the head nurse, but it didn't sound urgent.

"Why would I be needed in the ICU? Isn't Kelly Davis on?"

"Yes, and Dr. Davis said to tell you that you should drop by today."

"Okay. I'll be over later this morning."

Raj called the Family Practice office and said he was needed in the ICU. He took his time getting dressed, then strolled over to the hospital. The weather had warmed up, and it was turning into a lovely spring. Outside the ICU, there was a television crew in the waiting room, and a tall, overweight woman was talking loudly. "Cory, get me an Americano."

"They don't have a Starbucks here, Claire," said a young man who sported a Bluetooth earpiece and gelled hair.

"Get me a coffee before I strangle you!" Claire shouted.

"How about Tim Horton's?" Cory's voice was quivering.

"Just get moving, Cory, before I stomp you."

Cory moved quickly, a man on a mission. Claire seemed to be guarding the entrance to the ICU. When Raj approached, she demanded to know who he was.

"I'm Dr. Mehta," he said.

"Right. Star wants to talk to you. Come along, doctor." She led the way to Star's ICU room, then blocked the door.

"I spoke to the hospital board about reinforcing security around here," said Claire.

"Security?" He was incredulous.

"There might be a lot of crazy fans. Better to keep it tight, keep it right." She opened the door.

"Hey, dude, so you're the guy who saved my life, eh?" Star, reclining in bed, looked as if he ought to be in a TV commercial. Several pairs of ultramodern sunglasses lay on his bedside table alongside magazines and a laptop, and there was a set of small weights on the floor.

"I really didn't save your life. I just dragged you out of your car, and you coughed up something that was stuck in your throat. Anyway, it was Dr. Brevin and Dr. Williamson who really saved your life."

"Yeah, I know, man, but you rock!" Star asked Raj if he wanted a smoothie. "I've got an extra one Claire made for me this morning."

Raj picked up the large plastic cup and took a sip. The drink was thick and bland. "What's the gritty stuff?" he asked.

"It's cacao nips," Star replied, then added, "So my car's totaled."

"Too bad, man. It was a really nice car."

Star beckoned Raj closer and lowered his voice. "When I was in ER, did they check me out?"

"What do you mean?"

"Did anyone check my blood alcohol? It's kind of important for my insurance and my job and everything." Star looked genuinely worried. There was no trace of bravado.

Raj was surprised. "Star," he said. "I remember exactly what we ordered – the standard blood tests for anyone with acute illness."

"Fuck," muttered Star.

"We did a standard blood count, electrolytes, and kidney functions. I think we typed and cross-matched you for blood. We didn't check your blood alcohol level."

"Thank God… and praise the Lord! Doc, you have no idea how relieved I am. Phew, that was close. So, so close."

"So what happened, man? Explain it to me," said Raj.

"I got loaded the night before. This skank was screwing around on me, and I caught her at it and told her off. Anyway, Doc, I was drinking and got to thinking that I really want to get married. Went a little crazy and bought a ring! Di's the one, the total package. I asked her to marry me."

His heart sinking, Raj said, "When did you ask her?"

"I called her just this morning. You know, I had to nearly die to realize she's the one."

"So what did she say?"

"She said she'd think about it. She knew I was still really doped up and still a bit spaced out from the head injury. I think she thought I was joking, but she did see the ring – it's a star shape, you know. She asked me if the proposal was because of my head injury, but I told her the ring was for her."

"She said she'd think about it?"

"She said I had to work on getting well first. Then when I'm back to myself, she would think about it."

"So she didn't say yes?"

"She'll come around. She always does. We're meant to be together."

"Star, maybe – " Raj began.

Star ignored him. "I'm thinking of getting one of those Mercedes four-wheel-drive trucks. I think the crash stats are better."

"So –" Raj tried again, but Star interrupted him again.

"Diana said you dragged me out of the car. I thought I should write a book or movie about this whole deal – you know, to just give back something to the world. So other people who have the same thing happen can read the book and feel better."

Raj finally got his question out. "So you're not going out with her now?"

"Not right now. We've been on and off for a while, but Di's always known she's number one. She knows what a chick magnet I am. It takes a really strong woman to be with a guy like me, you know."

Raj felt he had to say something. "I know exactly how you feel."

"You probably know the scoop around here. Dr. Kelly – is she seeing anyone? She's totally hot."

"I don't think so," said Raj. "Man, you're incredible."

"I know, Doc. I can't help how hot I am. Hey – you're not gay, are you?"

"No, Star. Totally straight," said Raj.

* * *

Diana had been working long days leading up to the command performance. On top of rehearsals, the cast was trying on their costumes again, and many alterations had to be made. There was a lot of standing around and waiting, but nervous energy was building among the cast that felt good. The director was confident that the show was going to be a smash hit yet again.

In the dressing room afterward, some of the girls were talking about their boyfriends, and Diana felt a pang of loneliness. Mary and Lizzy had dates with the guys they had met at the Drake Hotel on New Year's Eve; they had become "friends with benefits." An early spring heat wave had settled on Toronto, and everyone wanted to shower, rest and get out of the humidity.

That night, Diana went to bed thinking that the job and her life were turning out to be just what she had imagined and what she wanted. She drifted off as she lay in the little cabbage town house.

The night was clear and the moon hung low over the garden wall of the castle. The air was humid, the foliage was lush and she breathed in the faint scent of hibiscus and jasmine as she walked along a stone path lined with sconces, the flames flickering in the light breeze.

"The stars shine brightly on you," said an unexpected voice.

She turned. "You! Why are you here?"

It was the old woman she had met in India – the one who had drawn the markings on her leg. She rested her arthritic hand gently on Diana's shoulder. "Yes, child, the stars burn brightly for you. You will bring joy and happiness, and people will love you."

"But Auntie," pleaded Diana. "Will I ever be really happy?"

"You will never be alone again, child," smiled the old woman. She pointed to the star-chipped sky. "Each one of them is a soul waiting to be born on this earth and, someday, they will blink for you. For if you don't dream of things to come, how will you ever make your dream come true?"

The dream faded in a swirl of colour.

While she was eating breakfast the next morning, she received a text message from Raj:

So excited for you. I know you're busy, but I want to congratulate you and wish you luck. Chandra got the top prize for her documentary! You helped her so much! Wish I were there to see you. Talk to you soon.

Diana wondered if the dream had been some sort of premonition. She texted him back:

So happy Chan got the medal. That sister of yours is talented. We met at Starbucks. I got her backstage access and she did the rest. Today is going to be crazy. The premier of Ontario and the mayor and a bunch of VIPs are coming. We've got to get together soon!

Diana smiled as she sent the message.

* * *

Raj leafed through the entertainment section of the Toronto Sun. There were ads for *Mama Mia*, and he scanned the columns for a mention of Diana, even though he knew it was too early for any reviews. Then he had a moment of madness. He so wanted to see Diana perform that he decided he would sneak into the theatre. He would have to be in disguise to get in without a ticket. As a doctor? No, that wouldn't work. A security guard? Maybe, but he didn't have a uniform. Then it came to him. He could wear a paramedic's uniform and pretend to be on hand in case of emergency. That was it! But there was a problem – paramedics always show up in pairs and with equipment. What to do? He reached for his phone.

"Hey, Dan! What are you up to tonight?"

"Not much, Raj. Want to do something?"

"I was thinking we should see *Mama Mia*."

"I didn't know it had opened. Where did you get tickets?"

"That's just it. There aren't any."

"How do we get in, then?"

"I thought we'd sneak in dressed as paramedics."

"What! Are you bloody crazy, Raj? Is this a chick thing?"

"Dan, I've got a plan."

* * *

Raj was in the ER trying to get a line on a paramedic's uniform – two, actually. "Tom, when do you and George get off shift?"

"Five o'clock," said Tom. "Why do you ask?"

"I need a favour, a really big favour."

His plan was to get two uniforms and medical kits. He and Dan would drive to Toronto and get into the theatre, saying they were there in case one of the VIPs had a heart attack. Tom made it clear they couldn't have the ambulance, so they planned just to get dressed ahead of time and walk into the theatre, hoping that security wouldn't get suspicious.

Raj had to promise Tom a free sample of Viagra in return for borrowing his uniform. Tom drew the line at lending Raj his ID badge, but Raj's intern ID badge looked similar enough. Raj's uniform fit reasonably well, but Dan's was a bit large. They clipped on their ID badges, donned stethoscopes and glasses, and, their disguise completed, they smiled at each other. They had a large red medical box filled with medical equipment and a search and rescue backpack with portable oxygen. As Raj stuffed a dozen red roses in the medical box, Dan rolled his eyes.

On the little card, Raj had written: *Diana: I just saw your show and it blew me away! Dan and I sneaked in as ambulance attendants. We're up in the balcony. Hope to see you soon. Raj*

Raj explained that he planned to talk their way in by claiming they were there at the mayor's request.

"That doesn't sound convincing," Dan said. "If you do strike out, we'll go cruising for chicks, okay?"

"Right, Dan. I go to Toronto to see Diana and go cruising if it doesn't work out. What are you thinking? Listen, if things go south, just run like hell and meet me back at the car."

"If you pull this off, Raj, you owe me big time. I'm thinking of an extra weekend on call."

"Deal, my friend."

* * *

In front of the theatre, the paparazzi snapped photos as a line of limousines disgorged people dressed in gowns or tuxedos. Raj found a parking spot a few blocks away from the hubbub, and he and Dan walked to the theatre carrying their paramedic gear, including two-way radios. They approached the ticket kiosk, and Raj was glad to notice that the attendant looked like an immigrant. Maybe her English wouldn't be that good, and they would pull off their bluff.

"Hello. We're with St. John's Ambulance. The mayor sent for us."

"Is someone sick?" the attendant said with a perfect Oxford accent.

"No, we were ordered to stand by. We're from Toronto, EMS. We parked the ambulance around the back so we won't disrupt traffic. We got orders from the mayor's office. He's here, isn't he? There'll be a big problem if we were called to stand by and he isn't here."

"Who did you say called you, sir?"

Raj was alarmed to see her pick up the phone. "I think it was some guy with the mayor's office. Yeah, he's paying us to stand by in case of any medical problems. You know about the mayor's problem, don't you?"

"No, sir. I am unaware of any problem the mayor may have."

"The mayor suffers from … "

"A supernumerary mammary gland." Dan came up with this on the spot.

"Right … and sometimes he needs oxygen." Raj held up the backpack and showed her the canister of oxygen.

422

Behind them, a large group was trying to get through the entrance doors. Raj and Dan were blocking their way. The woman put down the phone and waved them into the theatre. They ran up the stairs to the unoccupied balcony.

* * *

The curtain rose after thirty minutes of speeches by various dignitaries, and, as the play began, Raj slipped downstairs to deliver the roses, which he'd tucked into the medical box.

He didn't know anything about who gave flowers after a show, but in the movies, they always appeared when the actors took their bows. He picked up a copy of the program, found a tiny photo of Diana, and approached one of the ushers. He took him aside and pulled out the flowers. "These are for her," he said, pointing to Diana's picture in the program.

"No problem, guy," said the usher, holding out his hand for a tip. Raj had anticipated this and handed him five dollars. The usher sneered a bit when he saw the fiver and then held up his hand again, and Raj had to fish for his wallet. He only had a twenty, which the usher snatched.

Diana's songs were the highlight of the show for Raj. Her voice was clear and sweet like a bell. It was a magical two hours, and in no time, the rousing ending brought deafening applause, and the cast took their bows.

When Diana came out, an usher handed her a bouquet of roses, and she looked surprised and happy. But with the next bow, the card Raj had written to her fell out of the bouquet, and Diana, still smiling and waving, didn't notice it fall.

After most of the audience had left the balcony, Raj went downstairs to see if he could get backstage. The lobby was still filled with people, and Raj spotted several security people watching the crowd. Outside the door, reporters and cameras rushed forward as one large group exited. Raj asked a security guard what was going on.

"It's the mayor's entourage. He's hosting a party for the cast at the Lieutenant Governor's office at Queens Park. The theatre owner, Mr. Mirvish, is being presented an award from the City of Toronto."

Just at that moment, the mayor came into the lobby, accompanied by several cast members. Beautiful young women surrounded the mayor. Raj spotted Diana among them, but she didn't notice him. Paparazzi surrounded the group and took pictures. His heart sank. This had been his only chance to connect with her before he left for England.

"Raj, what's going on?" Dan had sneaked up behind him.

"I just struck out."

They walked back to the car and threw their gear inside.

"So she didn't get the card, Raj," sympathized Dan. "Don't worry, man, you're going to get this girl. Want to get some Chinese? The least you can do is take me out for dinner since we're not going cruising."

They drove to Chinatown and went to a place with barbecued squid and pork carcasses hanging from hooks in the front window. They sat down near a counter where a chef was hacking up meat with impressive speed. Raj tried to set his failure aside.

"Are you sure Diana is worth all this effort?" Dan asked

"I just have this feeling, Dan." But Raj was keen to change the subject and asked after Dan's latest girlfriend.

"Haven't seen as much of her lately," Dan said.

"Why's that?"

"She wanted me to meet her parents."

Raj knew that Dan was opposed in principle to meeting the family too early – if ever. There didn't seem to be anything else to say on the subject of girlfriends, so during the meal, they talked about work, both of them concerned about the hospital closing. Raj had put off talking to any of the staff doctors, and he knew he had to soon.

It was a long ride home.

Chapter Forty Three

"Congratulations on the big win!" Raj said. "I always knew you had it in you. I'm going to get my friends to come down for a screening."

"Thanks, Raj. I still can't believe they liked it that much. The secret was that the women I interviewed were incredibly good. By the way, I want to thank you. Without you, I never would have met Diana Sinclair."

"How *did* you meet her?"

"She came into the Starbucks one day after Christmas. She asked me my name and told me she knew you."

"Yeah," said Raj. "We spent Christmas Day together."

"She introduced me to some of the other actors, and, next thing I knew, she'd arranged for me to go backstage to film and interview people."

"That was really nice of her," said Raj, wistfully.

"It would never have happened without her. Did you get the file I sent you? She likes you, you know."

"Chan, you won't believe this, but I actually got in to see the preview performance last evening."

"You got in? Wait a sec… You've got a thing for her, don't you?"

"Well, the whole thing went down in flames. But she's really, really good! The show was fantastic. Mom and Dad would love it."

"Speaking of Mom and Dad," said Chandra, "you'll be on the plane just with them; I have to go a day later. Shamila's arranged to have us take extra bags for their frozen crap – as if we need to be embarrassed any further."

"Why can't you come with us? I can't deal with Mom and Dad by myself."

"That's my other big news! I've landed an interview with none other than Mark Daniel!"

"Who's Mark Daniel?".

"He's with *The Toronto Sun*. My film is going to be at the DocNow festival, and he's going to cover it."

"Wow, Chan! This is the dream, isn't it?"

"Yeah, it is. I figured it would be best not to make him wait till I'm back from London."

"So I'm stuck with Mom and Dad by myself?" moaned Raj.

"Not for long. I'll be home tomorrow to help you guys pack, and I'll be in London the next day. I won't miss much more than the pre-wedding party. Mom and Dad said they don't mind because this is the first time I've ever won anything!"

After Raj hung up, he started to think about what he had to do before leaving. He wanted to warn Dr. Sinclair or Dr. Williamson that the hospital was in danger of closing. He also had to go to the local MultiGlobe Travel office to finalize his flight.

At first, Raj had thought it was very generous of Shamila to buy their tickets, but now he wondered whether paying for their flights and having them each carry an extra suitcase full of Gustad's frozen food was cheaper than sending it by air freight. Raj took the day off from the clinic and hurried down to the local Multi-Globe Travel office in a small storefront three blocks from the hospital.

Raj had almost five thousand in his bank account, a pittance compared with the millions of pounds Roger told him he had accumulated. Raj had been shocked at the time. What guy in his twenties makes that kind of money? Only a banker – or a hockey player.

The travel agent, a middle-aged Greek woman, greeted Raj.

Raj explained that his aunt had reserved tickets for his family from Toronto to London.

She brought up the booking on her computer. "There are five tickets, all paid for and held in reserve," she said. "These are flex tickets. You just have to book your departure twenty-four hours in advance. We're still waiting to hear about the departure date and time for three of the tickets."

Raj said, "One of them is for me. My sister is coming a day later. The third ticket was for someone who isn't now going."

"Because the tickets are already paid for, all the third person has to do is call and let us know who's travelling, and we'll assign them the tickets." She pecked away at her computer and smiled. "Yes, sir. You're booked to travel with Mr. and Mrs. Mehta."

"By the way, my aunt, Shamila Gupta, bought the tickets. Are she and her husband booked on the same flight?"

The woman pecked away again. "Yes, but they're in first class. Very nice."

"Are there any more first-class seats available? Perhaps two together?"

The agent checked. "Yes, sir. There are seats still available."

"How much would it cost to bump my parents up to first class?" Raj asked, and when he was told "$1,154 each," he took out his credit card and said, "Do it." This significantly depleted his life savings, but he had a stable job. Interns were never laid off – unless the hospital was closing. It was time he did something for his parents.

They would arrive Thursday night for the Saturday wedding. Shamila and Gustad's party was happening on Friday evening at a club near their hotel in St. John's Wood. The pre-wedding party was a longstanding Indian tradition.

After the wedding, Raj and Chandra and their parents would stay for a while in London to visit with the rest of the family and do some sightseeing. Raj would have preferred to spend his holiday pursuing Diana Sinclair, but it wasn't meant to be.

* * *

Raj hurried back to the hospital to check on his patients before leaving on holiday. He rushed into the lobby, summoned the elevator, and was delighted to see an old guy in a wheelchair exit through its door – Charlie Rosenplot!

Charlie wore a stylish hat and a suit a few sizes too big for him. He was freshly shaved and looked quite spruce; he no longer had the grey look of a man with not enough oxygen in his system. The middle-aged woman pushing his wheelchair smiled at Raj.

"Doc! I was hoping I'd see you again." Charlie offered a bony hand, and Raj shook it. "Can you believe it? I'm actually getting out of this joint. I'm going home – with Elaine here."

"Yes, we're engaged." Elaine showed Raj her engagement ring, which held a large diamond.

"Things are looking up for you, aren't they?" said Raj.

Charlie smiled. "The love of a good woman is all I need. What about you, Doc? Any luck?"

"Well, Charlie, my luck might change."

Charlie left the elevator with his fiancée. "Your luck is gonna change, Doc. I can feel it. See you, Doc... and look after yourself!"

Charlie Rosenplot had been in hospital for some seventeen months, all told, and yet he had managed to get engaged and be discharged. Raj recognized his fiancée as one of the nursing assistants. Thinking about Charlie's good fortune gave him some relief from the worry about what he had to do next – talk to Dr. Sinclair.

In his basement office, Sinclair was eating a healthy lunch of bottled water and a sandwich made with twelve-grain bread. He had probably not ingested saturated fat in years, and a buttery croissant would send him into coronary arterial spasm. He looked tired.

Raj told him the bad news.

Sinclair frowned. "This sounds serious. How do you know we may be on the hit list for closure?"

"I did some checking on line. This hospital is old, and the commission seems to be targeting the smaller, older ones. Maybe you should check into it. It might also have something to do with the hospital's efficiency. These days, it's not just how good your outcomes are. You also have to be able to do it cheaply."

"Cheaply?" snorted Sinclair. "Cheap usually means crappy, you know. I'll have to look into it. Maybe I'll have a talk with the chairman."

"And I thought I should remind you I'm going on holiday for a week."

"Okay," said Sinclair. "You deserve a break. I see you were in the ICU."

"I was, but it's Kelly's turf now."

"And she's making the most of it." Sinclair pointed to the front page of the local newspaper, which had a photo of Kelly and Star. "Okay, Raj, get out of here and enjoy your break. I've got things to do."

Raj left the office quickly without saying a word, not wanting to mention Diana's name accidentally. Why did Sinclair have to be her dad?

* * *

Raj found his father sitting on the couch with one bare foot up, his big toe quite bruised and swollen.

"I tell you, woman, the bag is cursed!"

"Dad! What's this? Have you got gout?" asked Raj.

"That stupid frozen excuse for Indian food that your mother's sister has asked us to bring – the bag fell on my foot! One of its wheels got stuck. It's full of ice packs and wretched food."

Raj found Mena and Chan in the kitchen, where they were keeping a low profile lest Radhu started shouting at them. They were to leave for the airport in an hour. Shamila, Gustad, and Grandma were supposed to meet them there.

"Raj, check this out," said Chandra, holding out her iPhone, and Raj watched a short video of her receiving her award for the film. "I didn't invite any of you because I didn't think I'd win. I'm so glad someone filmed it."

"This is so cool!" Raj said.

"You can see I'm actually speechless."

"For once."

Chan punched him.

Radhu had plastered Canadian flags all over their bags and coats. When Raj asked Chandra why, she said, "Are you kidding? He doesn't want them to think we're American!" Radhu had stuck a Canada pin in the lapel of his coat and even one on his hat. Raj reckoned that if there were a button that said, "Don't shoot me, I'm not an American or a terrorist!" Radhu would wear it.

A ramshackle old limo arrived, and its elderly Sikh driver grumbled when he saw how many bags there were. He and Raj started to load the trunk of the ancient vehicle.

The final bag was the old maroon one that had fallen on Radhu's foot. The driver had a struggle lifting it into the trunk. Just as it tipped in, Mena said, "Be careful. There's food in that bag!" and the driver twisted around to see who was talking. He let out a yelp as he twisted while still holding the heavy suitcase.

"Oh God, I have put my back out!" he said through gritted teeth.

"You see? The bag is cursed, I tell you!" Radhu said.

Raj rushed over to the driver and asked him if he was all right. The driver mumbled something in Punjabi and laboriously got into the cab. Chan waved goodbye and promised to be on the flight tomorrow.

The driver stared at them venomously in the rear view mirror as he drove to the airport. When they arrived at the airport, rather than asking him to handle the suitcases, Raj and Radhu together got the heavy maroon bag out of the car. Radhu's mood was especially foul because he felt obliged to tip the cabby an extra five dollars for the back injury. He and Raj slowly dragged the bag past the new self-serve machines to the check-in desk. Raj was hoping the maroon bag would be disallowed.

"Let me guess – you guys are Canadian." said the counter guy, seeing their multiple Canada flag stickers.

Mom and Dad handed him their bags, which went through without any problem. Then Raj put his own bag and the extra one packed with food on the scale. His bag snagged on the conveyor belt, and the clerk ran after the bag to straighten it out. Annoyed, he checked Raj's bag in but forgot to note the weight of the maroon suitcase. He twisted to lift it onto the conveyor – and he wrenched his back! He bent over in a painful spasm, and it was now too late to weigh it; the bag trundled its way into the luggage-sorting hall.

"You see? I told you that bag is cursed," Radhu said to Mena. "I am afraid to go on this flight. Maybe the bag will make the plane too heavy. Between that bag and Gustad's extra fifty pounds of fat, we are all doomed."

"Oh, shut up." Mena was unusually irritable.

Raj smiled ingratiatingly as the clerk gave them their boarding passes while bent over, massaging his sore lumbar region. The family slunk away with their small carry-on bags.

"Geez, Mom," said Raj. "He's the third person who's hurt himself with that bag – first Dad, then the cab driver, and now that guy."

"Don't worry, son," she replied. "That fellow is probably a temporary worker. Did you not see his hairstyle and his earring? He is probably gelling his hair right now." Mom walked through the entry gates as if her statement explained it all and said she hoped Shamila and Grandma wouldn't have any trouble with Customs.

Raj was happy to be rid of the old suitcase, but his mother had also packed a small carry-on bag for him. In it were Raj's phone, a few books, and several small jars of her mango chutney, brought at Shamila's request. Mom couldn't fit the jars in her own bag and had packed them in his carry-on. Raj wondered why Chandra couldn't have brought them with her tomorrow.

They still had to get through airport security before boarding the plane, and Raj worried that his jar-filled bag might be too heavy for a carry-on. It had been so long since the family had travelled they were unfamiliar with the rules for carry-on luggage. Airport security officers, most of whom looked to be from the West Indies, milled about the security door waiting for passengers, wands in hand to check for concealed weapons. At the doorway stood a short guy with a Michael Jackson hairdo and a visible gold tooth. His nametag read "Henry" but bore no surname. He appeared to be moving to a dance rhythm that he alone could hear, waving his metal detector wand about as he worked.

"Place yo' bags on de conveyor, please," said a lady whose nametag identified her as "Cerise", who was monitoring the x-ray machine. Everyone else went through without much difficulty, but when Raj heaved his carry-on bag onto the belt, Cerise asked him to stop. "Sir, can you open de bag, please?" she requested – but it wasn't a question, and the look on her face was not very pleasant. Cerise fished around inside the open bag and found the un-labeled jars of homemade chutney. With suspicion, she asked, "What dis, sir?"

"Would you believe it's my Mom's chutney?" Raj replied.

Cerise looked hard at Raj, her face reflecting her disbelief. "You better open de jar, sir."

"What?" exclaimed Raj. He didn't want to have to tell her that the chutney would stink up the entire security area. Mom made it really spicy, and the aroma was terribly strong – so strong that the smell alone would make people sweat, and he had even seen white people become slightly nauseated when exposed.

Cerise looked angry. Henry stopped his jiving and ambled over, and other agents observing the exchange slowly edged closer. Cerise got out her walkie-talkie and warned Raj, "Listen, sir, don' make me call Security. Open de jar… NOW!"

By this time, a little West Indian lady named Sissy had arrived. "Wha' wrong heah, Cerise?" she asked her colleague, looking at Raj with a challenging expression. Slowly, as if she thought Raj didn't understand English, she said, "You gotta open de *jar,* mon."

Raj realized that everyone was apprehensive, if not in a state of total fear. For all they knew, it could be a biological weapon. He took the jar and struggled to open it. "It's a bit stuck," he said. He twisted the lid, and, with a loud pop, the jar opened. In the silence that followed, Raj thought they were expecting a silent cloud of death to rise from the jar and kill everyone in the vicinity. Mom and Dad looked stricken. Everyone in line stood immobile, staring at Raj and the jar. Cerise took the jar and examined it closely, inside and out, as

Raj's heart pounded like a jackhammer. Cerise sniffed the open jar and exclaimed, "Oh, man... dis baad!" She passed the jar to Sissy, who took a sniff, waved her hand in front of her nose, and exclaimed, "Rass! Dat's de bomb, a'right!"

The pungent smell wafted slowly through the airport security area. Henry spoke up. "Hey, lemme check dis out." He took the jar and sniffed deeply. "Oh yeah... dis good wit' some jerk pork an' black-eyed peas an' rice!" he smiled. Everyone relaxed.

Cerise said to Raj, "You lucky I'm just gonna confiscate dis – to have wit' me curry an' rice tonight! An' you can join me, ya sexy little mon! Maybe I need to have you strip down... maybe a little strip search..." Cerise winked at Raj and waved him along.

Worried that he had drawn too much attention, Raj moved on quickly as the group of security agents laughed. Carrying his much lighter bag, Raj joined his parents, and they walked quickly to the boarding lounge, eager to leave the confrontation behind.

Mom asked Raj, "What did you do to make them so nervous?"

"It was the stupid chutney," Raj replied.

Mom said indignantly, "I am so angry. You know, I made that chutney, especially for this occasion."

Dad spoke up. "Do you want our son in jail, woman – all for a jar of chutney?"

At last, a clerk announced that the aircraft was ready for boarding and that passengers travelling in first and business classes should now board. They saw Shamila, Gustad, and grandma board ahead of them. They had been waiting in the first class lounge.

Raj nudged his dad. "That means you and Mom. You're in first class."

Radhu didn't believe him until Raj showed him where on their boarding passes, in small letters, it said *First Class*. Radhu was thunderstruck, no doubt worried that this would cost him extra.

Raj explained that he had upgraded their tickets, and somewhat reluctantly, they boarded the plane and were escorted to the first-class cabin. It was their very first time travelling first class.

Ten minutes later, Raj settled into his cramped economy seat for the long flight.

Chapter Forty Four

Hi, Diana, how's it going?" asked Chandra.

"Good. We had a fantastic performance. I was up till three this morning meeting the local big wheels."

"Hey, do you have plans for this afternoon?"

"Laundry, maybe."

"I'm meeting Mark Daniel, the entertainment editor from the *Sun*. He wants to do an interview, and I thought we could do it at the theatre."

"Sounds cool. What do you need me to do?"

"Just moral support, and maybe clear it with the theatre, if that's not asking too much. It would be great if he could meet one of the cast. He might even want some pictures."

A bit reluctantly, Diana agreed. "Give me an hour so I can look presentable. It's so damn hot all of a sudden. I'll meet you at Starbucks."

The early and warm spring had transformed Toronto into a sweltering, muggy city wholly dependent on air conditioning. When the two young women arrived at the theatre, they waved at the security guard. He knew Diana well, having seen her come and go over the past months. Mark Daniel was waiting for them in the lobby. He looked like an entertainment editor – a hipster in glasses and Lulu Lemon wear.

The interview was going well, and Mark had a great deal of insight into filmmaking. About 30 minutes into the interview, the lobby lighting flickered and went out briefly, only to restart at a dimmer level. They could hear the sound of a motor churning somewhere, then it stopped, and the lights came back to normal.

As the three were wondering what had just happened, two men – a man in a maintenance uniform and a distinguished older man in a dark suit came into the lobby.

"You're sure there's no other way, Harv?" the older man asked.

"If the air-con unit breaks down in the middle of the show, with that many people, it'll be a catastrophe," Harv said. "We have to replace the whole unit, and it will have to be ordered from the States."

"How long will that take?"

"A week minimum, maybe two. Then I'd like to test it by running it a couple of days and, in this heat, it'll take a couple of days just to cool the building down."

"But the opening night is this Saturday!"

"It's up to you, sir."

"It would be far better to postpone than have everyone sweating buckets in here and then be forced to cancel shows anyway." The theatre owner thought for a moment. "We'll postpone the opening for two weeks. Let's get moving. We'll put out a press release. I'll contact our insurers – they should cover this." Then he spotted the little group and walked over, offering a hand and a smile.

"Hi! I'm David Mirvish."

"Mark Daniel, from the *Sun*. This is Chandra Mehta, who just won Ryerson's top prize for her documentary about the cast of your show. And this is Diana Sinclair, a member of the cast."

"I haven't seen your documentary," said Mirvish to Chandra, "but I would like to." To Diana, he said, "I saw you perform at the dress rehearsal. You were very good. Well done!"

Diana blushed. "Thank you, sir. And congratulations on your award from the Mayor."

"Thank you," replied Mr. Mirvish. "It was really an honour. I wish my father were here to see it. Lovely meeting you, but I have to run. The ventilation and cooling system just broke down. Diana, I'd appreciate your letting the cast know we're postponing the opening for two weeks and that they've got some time off. We hope the place will be cool enough to open in a couple of weeks. These older buildings are really tough to maintain."

The trio left the theatre to finish the interview at the nearby coffee shop. Mark asked Chandra many questions about women in
442

film and asked if she was related to the Toronto filmmaker Deepa Mehta. Chandra said that Deepa was her role model, but not a relative, not as far as she knew.

Turning his attention to Diana, Mark asked her, "What about you, Diana? Sounds like you just got a paid week off. What will you do?"

"I don't know! This is a big surprise." Diana said.

After Mark left, a plan suddenly came to Chandra – a most unlikely plan, but a plan nonetheless.

"Hey, Diana, how do you feel about crashing a wedding?"

* * *

An hour into the flight, Radhu wandered to the back of the plane looking for Raj and found him in an aisle seat. "Well, Raj, you really surprised us."

"Dad, I'm glad to do it. It isn't a big deal."

"Raj, it *is* a big deal. Right now, your mother has had a glass of champagne and is in the process of telling Shamila off. Their seats are next to each other."

"What? Mom drinking? She *never* drinks! Oh, no…"

"It's all coming out!" Radhu chuckled. "She's been boasting about Chandra and her top prize and that you are an inch taller than your cousin Roger. It's been going back and forth for the past hour. I came back here to get away from them."

Raj shook his head. "I had no idea that the agent had given you seats next to Gustad and Aunt Shamila's. She probably assumed you'd want to sit together."

"Never mind, Raj. It's just that the wedding has brought up old rivalries between the two sisters. Did you know that Shamila always wanted to name her son Raj? She's never forgiven your mother for having you first and naming you Raj."

"Really? I thought they wanted to give him an Anglo name."

"Yes, Raj, but 'Roger'? Shamila has always tried to be your mother's boss, being the elder sister and all."

"Are you happy you're going to see the rest of the family?"

"Sure, I am. It is going to be a fun time, but I'm glad we will be in the background. Time enough for me to worry when you and Chan get married."

"Well, Dad, don't worry about that anytime soon," Raj said, adding that he didn't have a girlfriend, let alone a date for the wedding.

Radhu changed the subject. "I had Eugene make a suit for you."

"Thanks, Dad. But what if I've got fatter since he took measurements?"

"Don't you worry. By the way, perhaps you should consider making a speech at the wedding."

Raj was astonished. "Me? Make a speech? I barely know Roger."

"People would expect it because you and Chan are his only cousins in Canada. Would they not assume the two of you grew up the best of friends?"

"But, Dad," protested Raj. "It's not like India."

"Well, Raj, that is too bad. In India, the two of you would have been best friends. Many times, I think we have lost as much as we have gained in coming to Canada."

To mollify his father, Raj said, "Maybe Chan and I can come up with something. But I hope so many old folks will be making 'big talk' that I won't have a chance to speak."

"Well, Gustad will be doing a lot of talking. This much we know." Dad laughed.

"Remember the time Roger washed and ironed his five-dollar bills? He thought that's what money laundering was."

"That would be a good story for your speech, Raj. Didn't you and he do fun things together when you were younger?"

"Well, once he tried to charge me twenty-five cents to use the bathroom. I refused and peed in their back yard."

"Perhaps you should come up with something more appropriate than that," Radhu said. He told Raj to get some sleep and return to business class.

Raj thought about what his father had said. Their relatives in India did seem close as if they still lived in a village where everyone knew everyone else and looked out for each other. In the big Toronto mosaic, it didn't work that way. Roger and Raj should have been the best of friends, but they had never got along. The one thing they did have in common was that both of them wanted to be successful Canadians, and that hadn't left much room for family, friendships, or even for thinking about who they really were.

Raj knew almost nothing about his cousin except his proclivity for expensive luxury items and a burning desire for wealth and recognition. He should be happy that Roger had found true love. Now that he thought about it, Raj realized he was a bit jealous. He felt that Roger would never believe he could metamorphose from being the 'nerdy science club guy' even though Raj had spent the last several months dealing with all sorts of medical emergencies and was now a doctor. Deep down, Raj knew there was more to come than just work – it had to. He finally fell into a fitful sleep.

He was in the ancient palace garden, small fruit trees and lush foliage and the fragrance of hibiscus and sandalwood surrounding him. Water burbled along a tiny creek. It was approaching dusk, the sky darkening. As he strolled down the stone path he heard music and occasional laughter. Then he noticed a shadowy form in a dark blue silk sari flitting among the shrubs, and he caught a glimpse of dark hair. It was her! She seemed to be leading him on, never quite allowing him to catch her.

He felt a hand on his shoulder. He turned and faced an old woman in a threadbare shawl. Her rheumy eyes were smiling and she reached up and caressed his face. He stared at her, trying to plumb the secrets locked within her.

"Peace be with you, son."

"And with you, Grandma."

"You heart is troubled and I see you are in a hurry."

"Yes. Grandma. I was following someone I thought I knew."

The old woman took his hand in a surprisingly strong grip and led him to a stone seat under a flowering Ashoka tree. "Please, son, sit down and rest a moment. I will show you a secret."

She gestured at the tree, where he saw two tiny birds with red and blue plumage perched on a low branch. The birds eyed them with curiosity, ruffled their feathers and appeared to fall into a relaxed slumber.

"Those two there? See how contented they are. They found each other after flying thousands of miles to this place. They had to work for their happiness – just like you and everyone else."

"How did they find each other, Grandma?"

"Just by being themselves."

There was a message, but he couldn't grasp it. As clever as he was, there was no formula, no algorithm or piece of knowledge that he could use……

Raj surfaced from his slumber with a sore neck and back and a dry mouth. He shifted uncomfortably in his seat.

"You're having quite a hard time, aren't you?" the older woman seated beside him said. "I can't sleep on a plane. It's too nerve-racking, don't you think?"

"I guess I nodded off. Just the exhaustion of the last few days," said Raj.

"So you're Canadian, then?" she asked.

"Yes. I was born in Canada, but my family came from India by way of England. How about you?"

"I'm from England originally," she replied. "I'm going back to visit family." The woman introduced herself as Eloise Hawfinch.

"When did you come to Canada?" Raj asked.

"Before you were born," Eloise said. "My husband was with the Canadian army, and we met in England shortly after the war. I was only eighteen at the time. He dragged me back to Canada, and we've lived there ever since. And I've enjoyed living in Canada very much."

"Where's your husband then?"

"He passed away seven years ago."

"I'm sorry to hear that," said Raj.

Eloise looked at Raj with a bemused expression. "You know, it really isn't too bad. He lived a good life – the life he wanted to live. In the end, he had no regrets, least of all marrying me."

"I've been thinking about that," Raj said.

"Thinking about what?"

"Living a life with no regrets." Raj was surprised at how easy it was to confide in a stranger. Perhaps the anonymity made it easier – or it was her age and experience. He began talking.

"My problem is that I met this girl, and we became friends, and then I realized I liked her more and more…" He told Eloise the whole story, concluding with his attempt to see her on stage and then having to go to London for the wedding. Then he asked, "Do you think I screwed up?" he asked. "Maybe I should have come on stronger."

"I see. You think this girl might see you as just a friend and that the other young man is the one she really loves?"

"Yes," Raj said. "Like I'm in the friendship zone and not someone she'd be interested in romantically."

"Maybe she's just waiting for you to make a move."

"Could be. I hope so. I just can't tell. And the problem is that I'm in London for a week, and she's in Toronto."

"If she really likes you, then you shouldn't worry about it. A week is not long, and things have a way of sorting themselves out. One time, I told my husband that I didn't want anything for my birthday, and he didn't get me anything!" Eloise laughed.

Raj didn't understand her comment. Eloise responded to his confused look. "My husband was the kind of man who could screw things up, but you know, he was persistent. If he screwed up, he would try to fix it, and he'd eventually get it right."

Still puzzled, Raj said, "I don't really get your point."

"My dear young man, there's nothing nicer than a man who shows persistence. If she likes you, then she'll like your persistence. She'll realize that you are the 'Rock of Gibraltar', and that never goes out of style. Persistence and patience, my dear young man. Besides, you never know what lies around the corner."

Chapter Forty Five

The pilot landed the plane at Heathrow so smoothly it was met with applause. Once the plane had taxied to the gate, Raj said goodbye to Eloise and slowly made his way off. Inside the terminal, there was no sign of his family, but he spotted them well ahead of him in the lineup for Customs. Once they were all through, he joined them in the luggage hall. "Looks like you all had a restful flight," he said just to be pleasant because his grandmother and father were the only ones who looked as if they'd slept.

"Yes, son, the flight was most excellent," Radhu said. Mena and Shamila said nothing, and Raj noticed they would not look at each other. Gustad, too, was uncharacteristically silent. Grandma was her usual quiet, serene self.

As they waited for their bags, Radhu took Raj aside and said, "Apparently, your mother told Shamila that it was a waste of time and energy for us to bring all that frozen food with us, just so she and Gustad could show off at the wedding." Mena had accused Shamila of trying to make the pre-wedding party about their food business and had said that Shamila would only embarrass herself and the rest of the family.

"Wow! Mom really let loose, didn't she?"

"I think it was the champagne," said Radhu. "Your mother and Shamila have never had much to drink. There is a saying: *The drunken mind reveals what the sober mind conceals.*"

The maroon suitcase was the first to appear on the baggage carousel. Two people attempted to pick up the bag, and both strained their backs. This was how Raj and Radhu recognized the bag, and together they heaved it onto a cart. Once outside the terminal, Shamila and Gustad were whisked away in a fancy Mercedes taxi. Because the group and the luggage were too much for a regular taxi, they had to wait for a "people mover" – a Chrysler minivan – driven by a young man named Ibrahim who looked African or West Indian. Raj expected a thick accent, but he spoke pure Cockney.

They got in the minivan as Ibrahim loaded the bags, and just as he tried to lift the maroon suitcase, Mena warned him, "Be careful with that." The bag seemed to stop in mid-lift.

"Oh, bollocks!" Ibrahim, clutching his wrist, doubled over in pain.

Raj ran to the back of the van and heaved the suitcase in as Radhu roared, "That bag is cursed. Even in England, it is cursed! Let's leave it here at the airport!"

"No!" retorted Mena, surprisingly angry. "We are going to take that stupid bag of food for Shamila so that she can embarrass our whole family at her son's wedding."

Ibrahim climbed into the van, clutching his wrist, looking quite uncomfortable. Ibrahim drove slowly through heavy traffic on the M4 toward London. Raj, Radhu, and Raj's grandmother sat in numb silence while Mena ranted on about her sister.

"All Shamila did all night long was go on and on about her son Roger. I didn't get a wink of sleep. She thinks that her son is some sort of genius. Genius at what? Bilking poor retirees out of their retirement savings so that millionaires can add another million to their bank accounts?"

Mena accused them of fancying themselves aristocracy: the Duke and Duchess of Mississauga. "They'll have to adopt a native animal for their coat of arms – the Mississauga raccoon! Their stupid little empire has been built on the backs of new immigrants who toil at their factory making greasy food. They'll only embarrass themselves in front of their daughter-in-law and her family. This is not like India or Canada. The English claim to hate people who are stuffy and pompous, but they invented it!"

When they got to their hotel, Radhu tipped the cab driver for hurting himself by lifting the maroon bag, and this annoyed him. "You know, that cost me an extra ten dollars! It costs more than two Canadian dollars to buy an English pound, so everything costs twice as much!"

Raj thought it best not to ask his dad how much the room cost. He went up to his room and lay on the double bed, glad to be out of the cramped plane seat. He thought about texting Diana, but he

453

couldn't think of what to say or what time it would be in Toronto. He dozed off before he could figure it out.

* * *

Diana called home from the airport lounge in Toronto. She was about to board a flight bound for London. She had packed a carry-on bag with clothes and was there with Chandra, who had somehow talked her into going with her.

Her mom said, "Your father is staying late at the hospital – something about a secret meeting with the chairman of the board. He said one of the interns – that young man you invited for Christmas Eve – warned him that the hospital was in danger of being closed."

Diana was too excited to take this in and said, "Mom, opening night has been postponed until they can get the air conditioning fixed. You won't believe it, but I'm going to London for a wedding."

"You're not eloping, are you? Whose wedding are you going to?"

"A cousin of a friend. I just got a week's holiday because the show's opening has been pushed back."

"How did you get a ticket?"

"They had an extra one. I'm staying with my friend Chandra, so it won't cost me anything."

"I wish I were coming with you, Di. It sounds exciting. Make sure you text me when you land, and also text me the name of the hotel. Have fun."

"Okay, they just announced boarding for our flight. Talk to you soon, Mom. Love you."

Chandra had made it clear to her that she didn't want to attend Roger's wedding, she didn't want to fly alone, and she didn't want to spend a week in London with her family. She had given Diana the hard sell. Diana had mentioned that she'd been to London before, and Chan had begged her to come to show her around.

Diana hoped to see the London production of *Mama Mia* to compare it with the Toronto show, make some notes and discuss it with her director. She didn't want to go to the wedding, either, and would feel awkward showing up out of the blue. She was going to be a wedding crasher. Idly she hoped there would be so many people no one would notice.

Then there was Raj. Chandra had glossed over the fact that Raj would be there, almost as if she didn't want to mention him. Diana wasn't satisfied with that, and after they'd found their seats and settled in, she asked if Raj would be taking a date to the wedding.

Chandra laughed. "You know my brother, right? I mean, you've actually talked to him, haven't you?"

"Yes."

"Then you know he's not much of a player, Di. What about you? What's been going on with you?"

"I guess it's going to be a long flight, Chan, so I might as well tell you."

"Okay, let's get some wine."

When it arrived, Chandra raised her plastic glass and said, "Cheers! Thank you, Aunt Shamila. So, Diana, what's been happening with you?"

"I told you I split up with Star a while ago," Diana said. "Things weren't going anywhere good."

"That interview in *Bro* magazine made him sound serious about you."

"I guess it did," said Diana. "He always sounds serious, but it's really all about him – *his* career, *his* needs, and what's best for *him*. He kept bugging me about going on this show called 'Puck Bunny Wives.' His agent kept telling him he should be on the show, but you're expected to be engaged or married."

"Is the show any good?" asked Chandra.

"All the wives are pretty and blonde and have big boobs," said Diana. "And they just manufacture petty conflicts to create a story line. It's all so boring."

"But you'd really stand out, Di. Star knows that I'm sure," said Chandra.

"I thought about it, but my résumé would take a hit if I was on that show. I'm trying to build up some serious acting cred', and one bad move would haunt me forever. Star got mad when I refused to be on the show, and we had an argument. I told him to call me once he'd grown up."

"Star isn't the sort of guy that takes no for an answer, is he?"

"That's for sure. And next thing I know, he's dating this sleazebag Russian model. I saw them when I was out with friends. Do you remember my friend Steph? She body-checked her and broke her heel. Anyway, Chan, I was quite happy to put the whole thing behind me. Then, on my last day at the hospital, I was talking with your brother when I got this blank text from Star. We heard a loud bang and ran outside. Star had crashed his car. Your brother saved his life. If he hadn't been there, Star might have died."

Chandra was amazed, "Raj didn't tell me about that, Di! He never talks about these things to anyone."

"Star had to have emergency surgery, and when he finally woke up, the first thing he did was propose to me. He even had the ring."

"No way, Di! Omigod – your life is like soap opera! That's so romantic. What did you tell him?"

"I just couldn't bring myself to say no. I didn't want to be mean, so I told him he had to get better first."

"That *Bro* article made it sound like he wanted to marry his high school sweetheart," said Chandra.

"But that's just it, isn't it? I'm not his high school sweetheart anymore. I'm an actor trying to make a career performing on the stage. There's a lot of pressure. I can't let go of my job and career, I've worked too hard. Anyway, the whole thing was probably because he'd broken up with that skanky Russian model. I don't want to be his rebound."

"The rebound proposal," said Chandra. "I think Oprah did a show on that. It's just the sort of thing guys will do."

"And I also found out he'd been drinking," added Diana.

"Really?" Chandra laughed.

"Lizzy and Mary said he smelled of booze."

"So you actually got the *drunken,* rebound proposal?"

"I guess I did – but don't depress me. I'm trying to have fun."

For the first few hours of the long flight, the two drank a lot more wine and talked nonstop. The thinner atmosphere inside the plane and the alcohol had made them talkative, and the wine was starting to slur their speech.

"You know, Chan," said Diana. "I just want to go out with a man who isn't a full-time job."

"And I just want to go out with a guy who isn't a total loser! My ex-boyfriend worked at a video store and was also writing a screenplay. It took me a while to realize I had a bad case of LBS."

"What in the world is LBS?" asked Diana.

"Loser Boyfriend Syndrome. I dumped him a week ago," said Chan. "Now that I think about it, you're the only one I know who's been proposed to – and by a guy who isn't a total loser. Actually, you're the only girl I know who's been proposed to under *any* circumstances."

"It's a bit ironic that I didn't say yes, isn't it?" said Diana, looking downcast. She wanted to talk about something else. "Chan, there's something I want to ask you about your brother. Shortly after he started at the hospital, everyone was talking about how he saved a young boy's life. When he came to the office for something, I asked him about it, but he didn't say anything. Most guys would have bragged about it, but Raj didn't."

"That's my brother, Di," said Chandra.

"I don't get it, Chan."

"There's a level to my brother that I'll never figure out," Chandra said. "He's very proud, but he's always worried – worried he'll appear too clever but eventually look stupid. "

"Well, he's not like any guy I've ever met."

"He had a girlfriend for a while, but they broke up. She was pretty and smart, but she just wasn't the right one."

"When did they break up?"

"A couple of months ago, and I'm glad. It was one of those cases where both people have the right résumé, but they're all wrong for each other."

The cramped confines of the airplane, combined with the alcohol and low lighting, were making them both sleepy. Chan yawned, which made Diana yawn too.

"Di," Chan asked drowsily, "do you like my brother?"

"Yeah, I do."

Chapter Forty Six

Uma Khan had grown up in the United Kingdom and wanted an English church wedding – just like her Cambridge friends. There would be an Indian ceremony for family members the next day, and the whole thing was to be a week-long extravaganza paid for by her parents.

The Friday evening party was supposed to be an informal affair, where both families could meet and get to know each other, but Gustad had rented a private club at enormous expense. The meal was Gustad and Shamila's only chance to show off their wealth. The club was festooned with flowers, and Gustad had taken some of the decorations from his restaurant near Toronto and brought them to London. It made the surroundings more familiar to him, and he drew strength from this. A large assortment of English and Indian food was served buffet style.

Raj wasn't surprised to see that Shamila was decked out in a purple, sequined gown and masses of gold jewelry. Gustad wore an expensive suit, which seemed to have trimmed a few pounds off his belly, and his thick neck was cinched by a starched white shirt and colourful tie. The contrast with Uma's parents was striking. The Khans were dressed in just as conservative and equally expensive attire, but Raj thought that Mr. and Mrs. Khan had nailed the look of understated elegance.

A long train of people lined up outside the entrance to the room to meet the bridal party. Behind them was a table for guests to leave their gifts for the happy couple. The whole affair was like meeting royalty. Raj thought that if he ever got married, it would be on a beach somewhere far away.

The Mehta family finally reached the head of the line and greeted Shamila, who said, "Raj, it's good to see you. Are you all by yourself? Where is Shari? You know, we arranged a ticket for her."

"Hi, Aunt Shamila," Raj said. "Congratulations on Roger's success. I always knew he'd find someone as great as Uma." Raj didn't want to talk about his ex-girlfriend, but Shamila persisted.

"So what happened to Shari?"

"She's not in the picture anymore," Raj said.

"Poor Raj. I'm going to get you fixed up as soon as I get back." Shamila patted his cheek, and all the gold bangles on her arm jingled.

"Thank you, Aunt Shamila, but I don't need fixing up."

Shamila had already focused her attention on the next person in the line – Raj's mother. "It's good to see you, sister. Is Raj all by himself? Don't worry, I'm going to get him fixed up as soon as I get back."

Mom thanked Shamila and walked forward with her arm through Raj's. "Oh… she drives me insane!" she said in a whisper under her breath. She was clenching her teeth but managed to smile at Gustad, who was the next person to greet them.

As they proceeded along the line, followed by Radhu, Raj spied an attractive young woman whom Mena said was his cousin Sabina. He had two cousins in England – Sabina and Ravinder. They were both a few years younger than Raj, closer to Chandra's age, and were very English.

Raj and Mena next met Uma's parents, and Raj introduced himself and his parents. Mr. Khan offered a firm handshake, and his wife smiled and said, "We've heard all about you from your aunt Shamila. She tells us Roger is a role model for you."

"Yes," Raj said. "In fact, I became a doctor largely because Roger became a banker."

At the end of the queue stood the bride and groom. Roger and Uma were dazzling, he in a black tuxedo and she in a pearl-accented white sheath dress and Manolo Blahniks. Raj thought they looked like polished gemstones, and they reminded him of Brad Pitt and Angelina Jolie. They air kissed Raj and his parents, a European custom that Raj hated.

Roger asked Raj where Chandra was and if she was still in school. Raj explained that she was finishing up her degree in Communications and just had won an award for her documentary. "She'll be here for the wedding tomorrow. She had to do an interview today, and that's why she's not here tonight."

"A documentary, you say," Roger said. "That's great. Better than learning how to communicate coffee orders to the late-night insomniac crowd!" Roger let out a haughty laugh that Raj assumed he had cultivated since moving to London.

Uma looked uncomfortable, but she smiled and said, "Raj, I want you to meet my bridesmaids tonight – they're so much fun!" She winked at Raj as he moved on and finally made it into the room.

He went over to his English cousins and introduced himself.

"So you're Raj, then. How are you?" Sabina's voice was cool, even though they hadn't seen each other for years.

Raj said, "It's nice to meet you again. I guess the last time we met was when I was eight and you were four or five. So what are you up to these days?"

"I work for an Internet company," Sabina said much more warmly.

"That sounds cool. What do you do there?"

Sabina grinned. "I keep the chat rooms moving along. The company is an Internet dating service, and they need people to help break the ice."

"You must meet some unusual people," Raj said.

"Oh, yes," replied Sabina. "England is full of pervs. A lot of people over here are into '50 Shades'. English men are strange, and

464

too many of them don't look after themselves – out of shape and pasty. What do you do, Raj?"

"I'm a doctor."

"You're another rich one like Roger, then."

"Sadly, no, Sabina. My annual salary is probably what Roger makes in a month."

Sabina introduced him to her brother, Ravinder, who had joined them. Ravinder was a software engineer. They tracked down a waiter for drinks, which seemed of prime importance to the English cousins. Together they found a table, left their jackets there to claim their seats and started to help themselves at the buffet. Raj decided he liked his English relatives. They were much more down-to-earth than he had expected. He told them about Chandra, and they seemed keen to meet her the next day.

The three cousins drank, but none of them ate much, as they all found Gustad's food too greasy. Raj told them the story about his near arrest in Canada over the chutney. They joked that he had a suspicious-looking face and that England really didn't want Canadian chutney.

Roger and Uma were moving from table to table and asking if everyone was having a good time. Raj was enjoying himself, or was until Roger approached, trailed by Uma and the two sets of parents.

"We've arrived at the rowdy table! How is everyone doing?" Roger asked

"We're fine, Roger, but we're running up quite a bar tab."

"Not a problem," Roger replied. "We bought extra wine coolers and less champagne since we knew you were coming." Roger let out his hearty laugh again.

There was a moment of silence at the table, and Raj got the impression that his English cousins found Roger a bit of a snob.

Raj broke the awkward silence. "So, Roger, where are you going for your honeymoon?"

"Spain, my dear boy, and then we're going to tour around Italy and rent a boat in Portofino."

Uma said, "Actually, Roger is renting a yacht, and we're going to sail the Italian Riviera – just the two of us and my dog."

Shamila couldn't resist adding her two cents. "I just love Italy! We went there last winter. It's just lovely. Have you ever been?" she asked Uma's parents. She then listed off all the places in Europe she had visited. It looked – at last – as though the Khans were finding her tiresome as Mr. Khan said politely, "Yes, we like Italy. We go there quite often and stay at a small house in Tuscany."

Shamila remarked, "We stayed at a rather exclusive resort on Capri."

"I don't like resorts too much," said Mrs. Khan. "Anil must have a very low cholesterol diet since his heart attack, and we find hotel food a bit greasy."

"Greasy!" cried Shamila. "Oh, yes! The food is *terribly* greasy. Just awful!"

When Roger, Uma, and their parents moved on, the cousins had trouble controlling themselves. Ravinder began a passable impression of Shamila: "This is *very* greasy, dear. Those Italians don't know how to make proper sausages. They have to be fried up, just the way Jamie Oliver does them!" Sabina apologized for having been so cool when Raj had introduced himself, explaining that she had assumed that he – and all their Canadian relations, for that matter – were as snobbish as Roger and his parents. Raj laughed and assured her that only Roger's family had pretensions of grandeur.

The older guests had taken over the back of the room, drinking Scotch and smoking cigars. Raj noticed that Mr. Khan and his father seemed to be hitting it off. Shamila and Gustad were, indeed, trying hard to impress Uma's parents and were plying them with food and drink. After consuming a spicy samosa and some curry, Mr. Khan looked as if he were about to have a heart attack. His condition didn't get any better when the DJ began playing Bollywood rap music. Several glasses of ice water, a Zantac that Raj had in his pocket, and, finally, a small bowl of ice cream calmed Mr. Khan's stomach. Grandma had offered him a clove, claiming it was a stomach remedy, but it only made him feel worse until he had the pill and ice cream.

Raj sipped at his Pimm's. He was having fun getting to know Sabina and Ravinder, but he wished Chandra was there. His loneliness caught him off guard. It felt strange to be around so many people and still feel a bit lonely.

"Cheer up, old boy! You look like you just swallowed a urine sample!"

"Uncle Dinesh! How are you?"

Raj's uncle, the doctor, had arrived. At sixty-six, he was the picture of staid English professional charm in his navy blue blazer and grey flannels. "Well, my boy, congratulations on your MD. You know, in England, we get a Bachelor of Medicine, not a Doctor of Medicine. I think the MD is better."

"Why's that, Uncle Dinesh?" asked Raj, to which his uncle replied, "Better pay!" and they laughed.

Uncle Dinesh told Raj that his heart failure was improving with medication. Raj knew he was a very well-trained and astute physician, the equal of anyone Raj worked with, who was now enjoying his retirement. "Why are you looking so down, Raj?" he asked.

"Girl troubles," Raj said.

Patting Raj's shoulder, Uncle Dinesh sat down and confided in his nephew. "Raj, I never married. It was because the girl I fell in love with – an ICU nurse at the hospital where I did my training – ran off with an accountant."

"That's too bad, Uncle," Raj commiserated.

"An accountant! Imagine how boring her life has been!

Raj had to ask, "But couldn't you have found someone else?"

Dinesh was silent for a moment and then said, "Raj, if she was willing, I would marry her today. She was just that special. I couldn't find anyone else that came close to her."

"I guess that can happen." Raj sighed deeply, aware that he was thinking about his own situation.

Dinesh laughed. "Well, it won't happen for lucky Roger, so let's drink to him – especially since he's paying. Hear, hear! A toast to Roger!" The cousins and Uncle Dinesh proceeded to down two drinks each, one for Roger and one for Uma.

Raj thought that Dinesh didn't look unhappy. Maybe unhappiness was like a vacuum, and something always filled the void. He saw a worrisome similarity between himself and his uncle, but he realized he was too lazy to let work dominate his whole life. Something was bound to happen to change things. He just didn't know what it would be.

The party got steadily louder. Many photos were taken, and there was lots of dancing. The DJ had stopped playing just rap music, and a lot of the older folks were now dancing. Much to Raj's surprise, the old folks – his parents included – were quite good dancers. Less concerned with how they looked and focusing only on enjoying themselves, they had nothing to prove. That was how Raj wanted to feel.

As the night continued, his cousin Ravi got so drunk that he had to throw up, and he did – in one of Gustad's potted plant decorations. It was a dazzling display of nastiness, and the cousins moved quickly to hide the plant. Ravi was sure Gustad would find it and know who had done it.

"Don't worry, Ravi, I've been to Gustad's restaurant. People throw up on the plants all the time," Raj joked.

As the party finally drew to a close, Raj's father took him aside. He didn't like the idea of Ravi having to find his own way home and suggested he stay with Raj in his hotel room just down the street.

"Do I have to?" Raj complained.

"Yes, Raj, he's your cousin. That's what families do – they look out for each other."

Reluctantly, Raj propped Ravi against his shoulder for the two-block walk to the hotel. He threw some spare blankets he found on the floor for his cousin, who seemed to have finished throwing up. His cousin kept apologizing for the trouble he was causing. Ravi tumbled onto the makeshift bed and fell asleep immediately, but Raj lay awake, listening to Ravi snore. The wishful, childish fantasy of having a beautiful girl accompany him to the wedding hadn't worked out for him. Perhaps, he thought, that kind of luck only happens to handsome men from wealthy families who know how to make all the right moves.

Melancholy from all the alcohol, Raj decided the world was full of married people who didn't love each other but who had got together to stave off the loneliness. He resigned himself to the idea that, in the end, he would marry someone just to stop himself from going crazy.

Raj fell asleep wondering how many married people he knew secretly harboured an unrequited love for someone else, people whose lives were filled not with happiness but with quiet desperation. He couldn't see why he should be any different.

Chapter Forty Seven

Diana and Chandra arrived at the hotel at 11 p.m., tired, hungry, and in need of sleep. They wheeled their suitcases into a small room, one of four reserved for the Mehta family. They ordered chicken salad wraps from the late-night menu and changed into their nightclothes.

Chandra stood in the window, taking in what little view it offered of the busy street below. "Isn't it just great to be in London?" she said.

Diana joined her. "It sure is. But Chan, do I *have* to go to the wedding? Maybe I can just hang out here and order a movie."

"Diana! Yes, you do have to go!"

"Won't people think we're a lesbian couple?"

Chandra laughed. "But that's what I want! To keep everyone guessing!"

Diana asked, "Will my dress be okay, or is this a traditional wedding where everyone wears a sari?"

"You want to wear a sari? Look what I brought." Chan opened her suitcase and pulled out the three silk saris her mother had packed for her. They were beautiful, and each had intricate embroidery in metallic thread. Diana held them carefully so that they didn't wrinkle. She admired the green and the purple ones, but the blue one surprised her –she recognized its elaborate embroidery, a pattern of stars in a deep blue sky. She tried to think where she had seen it before. Was it in the dream?

"Are you okay?" Chandra's question brought her back to the present. "Do you like that one? My cousin Sabina is coming by tomorrow morning so we can help each other put our saris on. The wedding's at one o'clock, so we've got to be ready by eleven."

Chandra hung the saris in the wardrobe and then said, "I couldn't help but notice that beautiful pattern on your leg. Where did you get it?"

"In India, when I stayed with my friend Kalpita," replied Diana. "I'm not sure what it says, and I've always wondered about it. The old woman who painted it said it wasn't for me but for someone else. I still don't get what she meant."

"I know who could tell you – my grandma. She can read Hindi and even some Sanskrit."

"That would be great. I've had it about a year, and it's still a mystery."

Their food arrived, and they washed the meal down with beer from the minibar. Diana started to relax and stopped worrying about the wedding. Perhaps it wouldn't be so bad, after all, and might even be fun. The series of events – the dream, the play being postponed, the extra ticket – made her wonder if something had brought her here. She felt like an actor in a play, but she didn't know the script. She got into bed, full and tired, more confident now that everything would work out. What was the worst that could happen anyway?

* * *

Raj awoke at 9 a.m. with a hangover. He'd been too drunk to remember the golden rule about drinking a lot of alcohol: take two aspirins and drink a litre of water before going to bed. His internal clock was completely screwed up. Ravi, it seemed, had no internal clock. He was still sleeping, snoring quietly under the blankets on the floor.

Raj walked into the bathroom and almost stepped into a stream of vomit that led to the toilet. Ravi – that idiot! Why hadn't he cleaned it up? The sight of the vomit made Raj queasy – especially as he recognized some of Uncle Gustad's food in it. This was just the sort of thing he was expecting – and it had happened. He was on his own in London in a bathroom filled with vomit, and he had to urinate badly, which he couldn't do unless he stood in the vomit. He couldn't even get to the sink. It was like some sort of vomit bomb went off!

He decided to use his parents' bathroom instead. He dressed quickly and knocked on their door, but there was no answer to his knock. His bladder was ready to explode. Chan's room was next to his. Had she arrived? Should he wake her up? He knocked gently on her door.

* * *

Diana had showered but was still wet and wearing only a towel when she heard a faint knock. She assumed it was the maid wanting to collect the dinner trays from the night before, She ignored it. She would put the trays outside the door later when they were both up and ready to get dressed. Chan was awake but still lying in bed.

Diana said, "I've showered already, so the bathroom is all yours. You know, I'm a little nervous about meeting your family."

Chandra reassured her. "Mom and Dad are great, and you know Raj already."

"And I'm really nervous about him, too."

* * *

Raj reasoned that there would be a bathroom down in the lobby and pressed the button for the elevator. He was self-conscious about not being properly dressed, which wasn't helped when the elevator door opened and the elderly couple inside glared at him. Raj stared back as he imagined them reporting him to MI6 as a potential terrorist. At long last, he found relief in a toilet in the hotel lobby. Now it was time to kick Ravi out and get someone to clean up.

Raj rode the elevator back up, thinking only about how to get rid of Ravi and have the bathroom cleaned. He had to get dressed soon. The wedding was starting at 1 p.m., and it was getting late. As he approached his room, a young woman wrapped in a towel was crouching down to leave trays in the hallway. Her towel briefly parted over her leg and ....wait, he recognized its inked decoration!

475

"Diana, is that you?"

Diana looked up and turned a deep shade of red as she recognized him.

"Yes – in the flesh. How are you, Raj?" Diana pulled her towel tight.

"Is this a total coincidence, or did my sister somehow talk you into coming?"

"Raj, it's a long story. Can I talk to you later – like when I'm wearing clothes?"

Raj couldn't help staring at her beautiful legs just a moment too long, then abruptly snapped out of it. "Of course!" he said.

Diana put her hand on the doorknob and pushed, but the door wouldn't open.

"Oh my god, Raj, I've locked myself out!"

Raj knocked on the door, then put his ear to it. It sounded as though Chandra was in the shower and couldn't hear.

"You can wait in my room till she's out of the shower, but I have something to tell you."

"Thanks," said Diana. "I can't believe how embarrassing this is."

Raj held his key card, nervous to the point of feeling sick. "You're going to see something in there, just remember it isn't what you think!"

"Raj," Diana hissed, "just let me in before someone sees me!"

Raj let her go in first, then saw that the scene was worse than he thought. Ravi was now sprawled across the messy bed. He must have woken up, seen the empty bed, and climbed in. He had passed out again and was snoring. Now he stirred, opened his eyes briefly, farted, rolled over, and went back to sleep.

"What the hell, Raj?" exclaimed Diana.

"It's not what you think, Diana. He's my cousin. He had too much to drink last night, and we couldn't let him go home."

"Did you guys sleep in the same bed?"

"No!" cried, Raj. "Are you kidding? He slept on the floor and must have woken up while I was out of the room."

"Raj, could I use your bathroom and get dried off?" asked Diana.

"Um…sure. Just have a seat while I clean up in there." Raj slipped past her, furious with Ravi for spoiling everything. The bathroom was indescribably disgusting. He balled up toilet paper and tried to clean up the mess while trying to keep himself from retching and still make small talk through the closed door. "So, Diana... Did you have a pleasant flight?"

"It was pretty good. Raj, are you okay in there? It sounds like you're being sick?"

The bathroom was looking better and Raj, now in sweat, spread some towels on the floor. He quickly washed his face and hands and left the bathroom, taking a hotel bathrobe with him.

"Please, allow me." Raj slipped the bathrobe around Diana, and she snugged it tight around herself. He caught the faint scent of her and was again enchanted.

Diana sat down on the only chair in the room and unwrapped the towel around her head, releasing her hair in loose waves over her shoulders. Her face, freshly scrubbed and free of makeup, glowing with health and vitality. She was, Raj thought, sublime. She smiled, revealing her perfect white teeth. Beside them, Ravinder snored on.

Raj took a deep breath. *It was his one chance, and he was determined to take it. This time he wouldn't fuck it up, not if he could help it.*

"Diana," he ventured. "Would you be my date for this wedding?"

Diana paused for a moment, looked a bit coy, and then put her small bare feet together and smiled. "Umm, yes, Raj, I'd like that."

Raj grinned with happiness. "Uhh.....go ahead and use the bathroom. I can't vouch for the smell. I'll see if Chandra's available."

Raj stepped out of the room, afraid he had imagined the whole thing. He knocked at his sister's door. "Chandra! Are you in there?"

Chan opened the door. "Hey, bro'. Why so loud?" She was brushing her wet hair.

"What the hell, Chan! You brought Diana?"

Chandra laughed. "Sure did! Pretty cool, huh?"

"Chan! She's in my room now, with just a towel on!"

"Well, you should thank me for that."

"Listen, our cousin Ravinder is also in there, sleeping off a hangover. He's in my bed!" exclaimed Raj.

"What the hell have you been up to? What happened to Di? I had a shower, and she was gone!"

"I practically ran into her in the hallway," said Raj. "I asked her if she'd go to the wedding with me. She has to come back to your room and get ready." He thought for a moment, then asked, "Have you told Mom and Dad?" She hadn't.

"Leave it to me. I'll talk to them."

"Thanks, Raj. By the way, was the suitcase a problem?"

"Don't ask!" huffed Raj. "Some of it's lying half digested on the floor of my bathroom!"

Chapter Forty Eight

"Sabina called," Chandra said. "She's on her way to help us with our saris. She says you should wake Ravi up and send him home to get ready."

Raj had escorted Diana, wearing the bathrobe, to his sister's room. He liked her in just the towel, but he was also keen to see her in a sari. Chandra pushed him gently out of the room, and from behind the closed door, he heard her say, "This is so exciting! Just like a Bollywood movie!"

Raj went back to his room and yelled, "Ravi, ya fucker! Get the hell up! We've got to get ready for the wedding." Ravi was finally stirring, and Raj heaved him out of bed and pushed him out the door. Then he went to his parent's room to get his new suit.

"Raj, did you sleep okay? There was a lot of drinking," Radhu said.

"Sure, Dad. No problem. The suit?"

"I took the liberty of getting you a new shirt and tie, too. It's time you started looking like a successful man." He looked closely at Raj and said, "You seem happier and more yourself today, Raj. This is good. Get dressed now and meet your mother and me downstairs. We'll eat before we go so we're not too hungry. I want an old English breakfast."

Mena spoke from the bathroom. "Remember what Dr. Chopra says about your diet!"

"Screw it! I don't care," Radhu said. "We are in England, and we will do as the English do."

Raj was about to tell his father about his date but then decided he'd just surprise his parents; he didn't want to deal with a lot of questions, not now. He grabbed the garment bag, dashed back to his room, shaved, and primped. He opened up the bag and was genuinely surprised. The suit was made of fine black silk that shimmered when the light glanced off it. The swirling blue and silver tie was designed by Jerry Garcia of the Grateful Dead. The shirt, of the finest cotton he had ever encountered, was made by a company in Montreal. Even the socks matched. Raj was impressed. He hadn't realized that his father's taste could be so stylish. The suit, tailored in a slim European style, fit him well.

The morning passed in a blur, and at 11:30, Raj was ready. He joined his parents and his grandmother in the hotel restaurant for an English breakfast of eggs, bacon, sausage, and fried bread, a contrast to Radhu's usual breakfast of whole wheat roti and yogurt.

"Raj, are you having an okay time?" Radhu asked. "I just want to tell you that your mother and I are really proud of you, and don't get yourself so worried."

"Worried about what, Dad?"

"About getting married. Just because Roger is getting hitched doesn't mean you have to. You should just take your time. You'll find someone."

"Well, there's something you should know …" He couldn't finish his sentence because three young women all dressed in magnificent saris had just entered the restaurant. It took him a moment to recognize Chan, Sabina, and Diana. They all wore long gold earrings and necklaces of gold and pearls. Diana caught his eye, and he looked her up and down, his mouth slack. She was wearing a dark blue sari over a light blue camisole, a necklace of spun gold and pearls, and gold sandals. Her slim body moved with sensual grace. The effect was stunning. Raj was speechless.

"What is this?" Radhu looked surprised to see the three young women, but he did know how to greet them. He stood up and bowed to them. "I feel I am in the presence of three movie stars!"

Raj introduced Diana to his parents and grandmother. He mentioned that he had met her at St Jerome hospital.

Diana said, "I was invited to come…" She was blushing, not sure whom she should say had invited her.

Chandra was about to say that *she* had invited Diana, but Raj shushed her. "I invited Diana to be my date tonight," he said.

Mena and her mother shook hands with Diana, but neither woman said a word.

Diana tried to break the ice. "It's Raj's cousin who's getting married?"

To Raj's relief, his father came to the rescue. The old man seemed quite happy – even excited. He somehow guessed that this was the girl who had invited him over for Christmas. He looked squarely at Diana and, smiling, took her hand. "Yes, my dear. Raj has told me all about you. I would like to thank you and your family for inviting my son for dinner over Christmas. That was a most generous thing you did. I am so happy to make your acquaintance. Tonight you shall be the guest of my family and me."

Mena, who hated surprises, finally managed a smile. Her mother whispered something to her, and Mena said, "Diana, you look lovely in that sari. You know, it is over thirty years old and has never been worn. My mother thinks it might be one of her old ones. It's as if it was made for you."

"Chandra loaned it to me," Diana said. "I hope you don't mind."

"There's nothing better than being young and beautiful and wearing a sari," Mena said.

The three women joined the Mehtas at the table, and while they waited for coffee and toast – none of them wanted the English breakfast – they chatted about the challenge of putting on a sari and about the pin that holds the whole thing together, which, if it lets go, means the whole thing unravels and you're naked. Raj logged this tidbit away for future use. Raj's parents asked Diana about her parents and her job. She mentioned that her father was a doctor at the same hospital as Raj – but not that he was Raj's boss.

When they stood up to go, Raj slipped next to Diana. His parents saw her take his hand but said nothing. They would save their questions for later. For now, they were happy to see their son smiling.

* * *

Radhu had rented a minivan to ferry the family to the church west of London, and it was waiting outside their hotel. To save money, Radhu had not hired a driver. He was going to drive it himself.

Raj was impressed that his father remembered to drive on the wrong side of the road. The wide Chrysler minivan was ill-suited to the narrow London roads that were always packed with parked cars. No one else seemed to notice Radhu's erratic driving; they were too busy looking out the windows at the sights. They passed Baker Street, home of Sherlock Holmes, and after many turns, finally got to the motorway heading west out of London. Pastoral scenes of little farmhouses and grazing cows and flower gardens flitted by as they drove. Raj found out just how easy it is to see the charm of England. After half an hour, they left the motorway and were driving into Windsor when the minivan drifted too close to the left and knocked the side mirror off an expensive Mercedes.

"Nice move, Dad," said Raj as his father sped away from the scene of the crime.

"That's what insurance is for," Radhu muttered.

They easily found the chapel, which looked to be hundreds of years old, probably older than Canada itself. It was a beautiful building of cut stone and had spacious grounds to the side that accommodated the many cars that were arriving. The crowded cemetery in the back was a reminder that "matching, hatching, and dispatching" was an important part of any church's work. The wedding invitation had specified no children so that squalling babies would not spoil the day. Chan took out her video camera and began filming.

At the chapel entrance, Shamila and Gustad were shaking everyone's hands. Uma's dog, which was tied up outside, dressed in a bowtie and doggy tuxedo, was growling at the women's extravagant hats, especially Shamila's, which was as large as a sombrero and sported several feathers that jiggled with every move of her head.

Inside, the old chapel was awash with colour as the sun streamed through the stained glass windows.

Raj's parents and grandmother were ushered to a pew near the front, where Roger was already standing and staring down the aisle. Diana, Raj, Chan, and Sabina sat down well back from the action. Soon, everyone was seated. The organ thundered, and the hushed crowd turned to watch the bride enter. Three bridesmaids, elegant in blue and violet gowns with matching bouquets, led the procession, followed by Uma in a billowing, low-cut white gown and veil. She walked slowly up the aisle on her father's arm towards Roger and his groomsmen, who stood in front of the altar, all wearing stylish black tuxedos.

The ceremony began with a reading and a blessing by the minister, an elderly, dignified Englishman who had likely performed this ritual a thousand times. He spoke of the importance of marriage and the ups and downs of married life, joking about how often he had to say sorry to his own wife. Diana squeezed Raj's hand as she listened. The place was getting stuffy from the body heat of so many people, but they hung on him every word. The minister blessed the two gold rings that would bind Uma and Roger's lives together, and everyone strained to hear the couple repeat their wedding vows.

Raj glanced at Diana, seeing her smile, and her face lit up when she realized he was looking at her. The ceremony concluded with the familiar phrase, "You may kiss the bride." The guests cheered loudly, and the organist began to play. Roger and Uma – the shiniest couple Raj had ever seen – left the chapel to cheers. A modern couple from vastly different parts of the world had connected through common interests – horses, money, and allergic rhinitis.

Once everyone was outside, the photographer took command, ordering various groups of people to stand next to the happy couple and say cheese. Friends and family chatted and took their own pictures, the mood was light and fun. Diana introduced herself and chatted with complete strangers, and Raj watched as she made her way through the crowd, admiring her easy confidence and the way she smiled as she went out of her way to meet people. Then she went into a huddle with Chandra and Sabina, and it looked to Raj that they were making a plan. A few minutes later, Diana rejoined Raj.

"Raj, that was a beautiful wedding," she said. "You didn't tell me your family was so good-looking."

"Some of us are – me and a couple of others – but some look like hobbits, and we try to hide them." Turning serious, he asked, "Diana, what did Chandra say that made you come to London? Did she tell you I was feeling like a total loser and desperately needed a date?"

"No, she didn't! I unexpectedly got the week off, and she offered me the extra ticket."

"So she didn't handcuff you and kidnaped you, then?"

"No, Raj. It was free will, maybe friendship. Maybe wanting to see if there was something more…"

Diana looked at him with deep brown eyes that sparkled and seemed to laugh at him. Her face, her hair, her lips, the way she held her hands – It was all becoming too much for him, and he murmured, "You know Di', I'm falling for you."

Diana and Raj had their first kiss in the garden of the old English chapel. The moment, so soft and tender, was a mere flicker in time. But for Raj and Diana, it wasn't just a moment – it was the beginning.

Chapter Forty Nine

"You English have such a sense of style. Everything is so elegant and formal here. I must say, I've really enjoyed being in the UK." Shamila was impressed by the church.

"Thank you, Shamila. Your party last night was very nice," Mr. Khan said.

"Why, thank you. It was quite difficult to organize everything from Canada. My husband actually made the food and brought it from home."

"The food was interesting – rather spicy, but your nephew was able to help me," said Mr. Khan.

"My husband is always looking to expand his food empire. In fact, he wants to start a new business in the UK producing frozen entrées," Shamila said, hoping that Kahn would be interested.

"I don't eat much-frozen food myself," said Mr. Khan, "but I'm sure the foreigners will enjoy it."

Raj noticed Shamila had become quite the oily sycophant since learning that Mr. Khan was a member of the billionaire's club. Her blandishments were becoming tiresome, and Gustad's food had almost killed the old bugger. Raj didn't understand what it is about money that makes people behave differently. Raj couldn't see the dollar signs that his aunt saw when he looked at Mr. Kahn. He saw only another old man like his father, coping with the illnesses that age brings on.

The wedding party had moved to the Royal Berkshire Polo and Country Club, a bastion of old English money. It was quite the poshest place Raj had ever seen. Through a huge window, he could see people riding their horses around the beautiful grounds. At the far end of the property, a group of men sat smoking around a wood fire, grilling meat, and Raj surmised they were the Argentinians. Roger had mentioned that he and Uma had their "own" Argentinians, and Raj presumed they looked after their horses.

Raj wandered over to the bar to get drinks for everyone, intending to achieve a pleasant stupor. He wanted Diana all to himself, but she had disappeared with Chan and Sabina, who were speaking to Uma. A long line slowly formed to congratulate Roger and Uma and their families. This time, it was more fun with Diana and his cousins along. Finally, Diana rejoined him as they came up to the happy couple.

"Hullo," said Roger. "Do I know you?"

"Roger, Uma, this is Diana." Though she hadn't yet agreed to be his girlfriend, Raj was emboldened by her smile.

Roger seemed surprised, and Raj expected him to say something like, 'However, did you meet Raj?' But Roger, for once, was speechless. To cover the awkward moment, Uma said, "Roger, dear, your cousin was such a help to my father. It was very good that he was here." Roger ignored his new wife and just stared at Diana as she shook his hand. Uma interjected, "I'm pleased to meet you, Diana. I'm so glad you could come to the wedding."

"Me too, Uma!" Diana replied.

Raj had a hunch that something was going on among the young women, but they weren't sharing the secret. Chan, who was filming the proceedings, hissed at Roger from behind, "More smiles – like Brangelina."

When it was finally time to sit down, Raj found their table at the back of the room, well away from the head table. The Guy-Ritchie chef apparently healed from his Pilates injury, served up an Indian-themed vegan supper. The speeches flowed along with copious amounts of champagne.

Uma's father was, mercifully, a man of few words. He thanked everyone for coming and bid the newlyweds a long and prosperous life together. He couldn't resist calling Uma 'Daddy's little girl.' He said Uma had gone to a private boarding school because he wanted her to have the best education, but he had missed her a great deal. He called Uma his "greatest gift" and, next to his wife, the person he trusted and loved the most. The speech was touching and poignant.

Gustad had his own take on what to say at a wedding. "Friends, family, thank you for coming to London to share this most joyous occasion. My son Roger, having been raised in Canada, has been our greatest hope for the future. When I came to Canada, I had not ten dollars in my pocket – not ten dollars, I tell you! With hard work and my mother's recipes from India (Radhu coughed loudly at this remark), I was able to build a new national brand in the food industry. Now, Mama Gustad's frozen food is going international. It will be imported in England and will be available at your neighbourhood grocery soon. Through hard work and diligence, Roger has reached the zenith of his career, and I am so very proud of him." Gustad was rambling, possibly already drunk. "We welcome Uma wholeheartedly into our family, and we know that Roger and Uma's union will be fruitful – yes, very fruitful." Gustad took a long drink and shouted, "Please raise your glasses in a toast to the bride and groom. Hear, hear!"

After the toast, to the relief of everyone in the room, Gustad sat down, looking overcome by emotion. The rest of the guests then sat down to dinner. The food looked and smelled surprisingly delicious. It was some sort of fusion cuisine, beginning with vegetable samosas and a green salad with a hint of cumin in the dressing.

As dinner was being served and the musicians were setting up beside the large central dance floor, the guests started to relax. Raj was surprised at how comfortable Diana was with people she didn't know. She talked to Mena and Radhu about her acting career and how she had met Raj. She and Chandra explained how they had met and how it had led to Chandra's award-winning documentary. Diana even told them about how Raj had saved Star after the accident. Raj hadn't told any of his family about his little adventure, but Diana described it as if it were a big deal. Raj didn't think it was, but as he heard her talk, it occurred to him that she really respected his work.

As the wine flowed, the main course was served – pilaf rice with curried vegetables in a cream sauce. Chandra was flitting about, filming the wedding party, and she occasionally adjusted Roger's hair. When Raj asked why she kept doing that, she said, "Aunt Shamila requested a more *Colin Firth* look."

Soon, Roger's English buddies were telling stories about him for the amusement of the guests. Their stories involved Roger drinking, chasing girls, and making money on the currency-exchange market.

As dinner went on, the room grew overheated. Raj stepped out for some air and found Gustad outside with Shamila. His uncle was breathing hard, and Raj helped loosen his tie so that he could take in the cool English air. The Argentinians were nearby, one of them playing the guitar. The meat was roasting on a big spit, and they cut off slabs of it to eat. They waved at him, smiling and drinking beer. They were a scruffy lot from living with the horses, Raj assumed, but they looked content. For once, Raj could relate. At that moment, he was content to be just who he was. It was a new feeling, and he liked it.

He didn't know what the future held, but he thought that being with Diana would bring balance to his life. He had worked so hard, never thinking about anything other than being a good doctor. His spirits lifted when she was around. She was a gift – *a gift just for him!*

When Raj returned to the hall, to his surprise, Diana had left the table. He saw her with the musicians, along with Sabina and his sister. Uma and her bridesmaids had come onto the dance floor as the band warmed up. Uma had changed from her wedding dress into a slim black evening gown.

Diana took the microphone and spoke to the audience. "Ladies and gentlemen, Uma has asked us to give her something special on her wedding day. Here she is... the beautiful bride with a wonderful song just for her husband! Folks, it's their song – the one they fell in love over."

There was a huge cheer as she took the microphone, waving and smiling. The band started a slow, steady beat with the drums and bass guitar and the young women began clapping and swaying their hips. Raj recognized the song. The band's intro rose to a smooth crescendo, and the opening chords of "Take a Chance on Me" began. Uma began, and then Diana and the rest of the girls sang along behind her in harmony.

Roger, unable to resist, ran onto the dance floor and swept his bride off her feet as the song concluded. The couple kissed deeply as their friends and family cheered. It was one of the most romantic, glorious moments Raj had ever seen.

Raj and Diana spent the rest of the evening together, dancing and chatting with other guests. Raj was a little surprised to find that he was having fun. He had spent much of his adult life constantly worried about the future, but being with Diana allowed him to just live in the moment.

It was Roger and Uma's night, but he was happy to bask in the shadow of their limelight. He had finally realized that all the great things about being an adult were there for him and that all he needed was someone to share it with.

Around midnight, Diana and Raj sat down with Chandra, exhausted. The reception was still going strong, but they needed to catch their collective breath. Chandra brought over her elderly grandmother to sit beside Diana. "Grandma," said Chandra in Hindi, "this is my friend, Diana. She wants to show you something." Chandra had Diana pull the sari up to reveal the markings on her left thigh. The old woman looked at them closely, touching them with her arthritic hands. Then she smiled at Diana and cupped her cheek softly. She spoke to Chan in Hindi.

"Diana, my Gran, can tell you what this means," said Chandra.

Diana, with a worried expression, said, "I hope it isn't anything weird or stupid!"

Chandra replied, "Not at all, Di. It says *You have to dream before your dream can come true.*"

Diana heard Chandra, but it didn't quite register. "What did you say, Chan?"

"You must have had a dream or something. It tells you that if you don't dream about something, then it can't ever come true," said Chandra.

Diana realized that she was holding Raj's hand and squeezing it. Her palm was sweaty, but Raj held her hand tightly.

Later, Raj and Diana went up to his hotel room. The bathroom had been cleaned, and the large, comfortable bed looked inviting.

Raj helped Diana take the sari off, but as she unhooked the pin, she pricked her thumb and yelped.

"It's okay. Let me have a look at it."

Diana held up her thumb, but the bleeding had already stopped. She smiled a slightly tipsy smile. "Okay, Mr. Kama Sutra," she ventured. "What are you going to do now? Maybe you should... kiss me better?" Raj kissed her, and they tumbled onto the bed. It was a wonderfully romantic moment. They were in London together, in love and ....totally exhausted from jet lag. Moments later, they fell asleep in each other's arms.

They dreamed of walking hand in hand through a palace garden beside a burbling stream, a soft breeze carrying the scent of jasmine, hibiscus, and pinecones.

Diana looked up at the stars in the night sky and wondered if some of them were twinkling - just for her...

THE END

Made in the USA
Columbia, SC
17 August 2023

21664312R10305